An

Almost
Tangent

ONYXIS STONE PRESS, First Print Edition, October 2015

www.bryanperkinsauthor.com

An Almost Tangent

Bryan Perkins

ONYXIS STONE PRESS

For you.

Table of Contents

XXII. Tillie

Tillie could taste the change in the air. She could feel it on her skin. Every time she thought about what they had done it sent shivers up her spine, but still, she wasn't satisfied. She thought that they would have made a much bigger difference by now. She thought that something would have changed, anything. They did do what she thought they did, didn't they?

She paced in the living room of her dorm, watching the TV as it flipped through every news station's broadcast, looking for any sign that their little escapade had been noticed, when the door opened and in came her black cat, Mr. Kitty, followed by her roommate, Emma, who was carrying a big stack of colorful flyers and smiling from ear to ear.

"Mr. Kitty!" Tillie said, scooping him up then sitting on the couch to put him on her lap and pet him. The TV kept flipping through the channels and Emma kept smiling.

"There's still nothing on the news," Tillie said, ignoring Emma's too good mood. Emma didn't seem to be taking the lack of results as hard as Tillie was. Then again, Emma's family had been involved with this kind of thing since she was born so she was probably used to failure by now.

"No," Emma said, taking a seat next to Tillie and still smiling. "They probably won't ever show anything. They don't want people to know what we did."

"But nothing? Not even a leak? If we..." She lowered her voice. "*Blew up the walls between five and six*, someone had to notice it by now. Right?"

"Oh, they noticed." Emma smiled. "Don't you worry about that. There are signs that they noticed, too. If you know what you're looking for."

"But I do know what I'm looking for," Tillie said. "And it looks to me like business as usual." She pet Mr. Kitty's head, frustrated, and he purred in response.

"You didn't notice the shortages?" Emma asked, frowning.

"What shortages?"

"There wasn't any pineapple at the fruit bar when I went to breakfast this morning. Did you get any?"

"No. I had to eat grapes. But what does that have to do with anything?"

"It's one of the effects of the operation, a sign that we affected things."

"*Pineapples*?" Tillie scoffed. "I mean—I hate grapes as much as the next girl, but a shortage of pineapples isn't changing anything. And *we* didn't bomb their pineapple farms. That wasn't us. Someone else did that. I want to see the results of what *we* did."

"It *is* a result of what we did, though," Emma said. "We were part of a larger whole. We contributed. We'll see the results, but we have to be patient. The time would go by faster if you came out and helped me rather than sitting there staring at the TV all day. *A watched bond never matures.*"

Tillie chuckled. Mr. Kitty purred on her lap and she pet his head. Emma was probably right. Tillie had been sitting in front of the TV almost nonstop for probably a week now, and she hadn't seen a single thing suggesting that anyone anywhere knew what they had done. Maybe they hadn't done anything after all. Maybe Emma had lied and those discs were nothing more than stickers they had defaced the central hub with, little clock stickers counting down to zero.

Yeah right.

Emma, on the other hand, hadn't been sitting in front of the TV for a week. She had barely been home at all since the operation. Her eyes were always set on the future and that was probably why she still had a smile on her face, staring at Tillie, practically begging Tillie to ask her why she was so happy.

"Alright, alright," Tillie relented. "Go on then. What's with the grin? Did you win the lottery or something?"

"*Ugh*. No." Emma scoffed. "You know I don't play."

"I know, I know. Can't you take a joke? But I'm sure it has something to do with the flyers you're holding, right?" Tillie took one off the stack in Emma's lap and read it while Mr. Kitty sniffed it. It was printed on neon pink paper and had a big black fist surrounded by blocky black words that read: "RECLAIM THE GROUNDS! / Jan 1: 5 PM / Parade Grounds / Reclaim your life!"

"I've been trying to tell you about it," Emma said, "but you've been hypnotized by the news. This is the next step—for our world, at least."

"What is it even?" Tillie asked, putting the flyer back onto the pile in Emma's lap. "What next step?"

"Well, Outland Five and Outland Six know about each other now, right," Emma said, nodding. "I mean, after what we did, they have to. But now I think it's time for us to tell our own world the truth. That's what these are for." She held the stack of flyers up, still smiling.

"And that's why you're so happy? I mean, the flyers look great and all—don't get me wrong—but that's it?"

"No. I'm happy because I just got—wait for it—*two* people to agree to come out and help tomorrow. That makes—"

"Wait... *Tomorrow*?"

"Yes, tomorrow. *New Year's Day*. You really have been lost in here all week, haven't you?"

"So today is New Year's Eve?" Tillie asked, standing and pushing Mr. Kitty down onto the floor. He jumped up onto Emma's lap and licked his coat. "There have to be some parties tonight, right?"

"Yeah, that's what I was about to—"

"And I haven't gotten a single invitation yet." She paced the room again. "You know what. I bet it was Shelley. She thinks I'm crazy now. I'm telling you. She's probably spread rumors to all our mutual friends—which is pretty much all of my friends—telling them not to invite crazy Tillie and her sick hallucinations to any of their New Year's celebrations."

"Or maybe it's because you've been sitting—"

"Do you know of any parties tonight? Would you mind if I tagged along?"

"Well, yeah," Emma said, nodding. "There are a bunch I was planning on going to. I was going to ask you—"

"*Good*. I'm gonna go get ready. I'll be back before the elevator."

Emma tried to say something else as Tillie left, but she wasn't listening. She was going through her closet in her head, trying to pick out the dress that would best show Shelley that Tillie didn't care if she tried to spread dirty rumors about Tillie's sanity that weren't anywhere near the truth. She stood in front of her closet and wished she was back home with her 3D printer. Something new and shiny would be perfect for this situation. Everything here had been worn before.

Ugh. How could Shelley do this to her? And it had to be Shelley, too. Why else would no one invite her to a New Year's party? Not a single person. Not a single party. Shelley was spreading rumors. There was no other logical explanation.

But one person did invite Tillie out: Emma. What kind of party would Emma go to? She said she knew of a bunch. How could she know about so many parties and Tillie so few?

Well Emma was always out there in the quad or wherever, talking to people and handing out fliers and all that, but what had Tillie been doing? Sitting in front of the TV as it flipped through hundreds of news stations, all talking about the same nothing. But still, what kind of party would Emma go to?

Tillie chuckled to herself and picked out a green floral sundress—with pockets, of course—and some big black boots. Whatever crazy thing she was going to do, she wanted to do it in style. She sat in front of her vanity mirror and debated whether or not she would prefer having her automated battle station from back home. Here she had to put her makeup on manually, but there if she even breathed while the battle station made her up, she would end up with her lipstick on her eyelids.

Dressed and made up, she went out to the living room where Emma was still sitting on the couch, petting Mr. Kitty on her lap, and watching the TV flip through the news channels.

"So," Tillie said, striking a pose in front of her bedroom door. "What do you think?"

Emma turned and smiled wider. "Beautiful," she said. "Perfect for the parties."

Tillie blushed. "You're too kind," she said. "Now...*these parties.* Where are they? When do they start? Who's gonna be there?"

"Oh, well..." Emma looked at the TV to check the time. "It's not even seven yet, you know. We still have a while. Come sit down for a bit."

"*Ugh.* Really?"

"Yeah, well, it is New Year's Eve and all. The parties have to go all night. If they start now, there won't be enough energy to make it into the New Year, and that's pretty much the entire point."

Tillie chuckled, plopping on the couch next to Emma. Mr. Kitty crawled from Emma's lap to Tillie's. "Yeah, yeah," Tillie said. "I get it. But how long do we have to wait?"

"A few hours," Emma said. "Then we'll go to so many parties you'll wish you were back here sleeping. I promise."

Tillie shrugged and pet Mr. Kitty on the head. She lost herself in the TV like she had been doing for the entire week. The channel changed to a different news station every few seconds, but they were all so in sync, telling the same "news" stories, that she could still make out the general news of the day even as the channels constantly flipped.

"...Production numbers suggest..."

"...some shortages in luxury items, but..."

"...Russ Logo is at it again with his new..."

"...Overall, managers are reporting more..."

"...bang for your buck, at Buck's Fine..."

"...the cost to produce is lower than..."

"...a dress like a shadow play..."

"...As it gets closer to midnight we'll..."

"...protector costs have gone through the..."

"...Lobbyist Peterson claims the only solution is cutting..."

"...the weather looks as nice as ever today..."

"*Ugh*! Off!" Tillie yelled, and the TV flipped off. Mr. Kitty jumped from her lap onto the coffee table to lick himself. "I can't take it anymore. These soundbites are starting to drive me insane."

"I was about to lose it myself," Emma said, grinning like she wasn't sure if she should laugh. "I don't know how you've listened to it for so long as it is."

Tillie stood and paced the room. "I don't know either. Can't we just go already? I don't care about being fashionably late."

"Yeah, well, it's still too early to go to any of the parties, but I was going to meet with some people beforehand if you want to come."

"Anything but more news. Let's go." Tillie crossed to the door, her skirt sweeping behind her, and when Emma stood up, still carrying the flyers, Tillie asked, "Are you bringing those with you?"

Emma looked down at the brightly colored stack in her

hands. "*Uh, yeah*," she said. "That's the entire point."

"Oh. *Duh*." Tillie palmed her face. "Your uh—the people you're meeting with before the parties. It's for them, right?"

"Well, yeah. But it's for the parties, too. That's why I plan on going to so many."

Tillie sighed. Emma's idea of a party *was* handing out flyers. She wondered if Emma had even gotten invited to any of the parties or if she was just going to show up with flyers in hand and crash them all. That wasn't Tillie's idea of a party. That was activist work. "So you're gonna hand those out at the parties?" she asked to make sure she had heard correctly.

"Of course I am," Emma said. "The General Assembly's tomorrow. This is the last chance we have to tell people about it. We need as many people to come out as possible or it won't be effective."

"Do you really think they're going to listen to you when they're trying to celebrate the New Year?"

"Some of them will." Emma shrugged. "A bunch will probably take the flyers just so they have an excuse to hit on us, and most of them will throw the flyers away before reading our message, but at least a few people will wake up tomorrow to see a little neon slip of paper on their nightstand, and maybe they'll decide that they actually do want to join us in doing something good for the world. Believe me, Tillie. I've been doing this for a long time now. Every one of them that we hand out helps, and every one of them is worth it."

"Yeah, well, you're not getting me to hand out any flyers," Tillie said. "I'm gonna celebrate with everyone else. It's New Year's Eve, girl. *Woooo!*" She laughed.

"Well, you don't have to. And I won't ask you to. I just don't want to see you sitting here in front of the TV alone again tonight. But you *are* coming to the GA tomorrow, right?"

"Oh, yeah." Tillie hadn't actually thought about the fact that she should go until just then. She didn't even know what a *GA* was or what the flyers meant by "Reclaim the grounds!" but she had to support Emma. Emma was the one person who had supported Tillie when everyone else thought she was crazy, and if Tillie knew people as much as she thought she did, they were going to think that whatever it was that Emma was doing was batshit insane. "Yeah. Of course I am," Tillie said, nodding. "Six PM, right?"

"*Five*," Emma said. "At the parade grounds."

Tillie chuckled. "*Sarcasm*," she said with an unbelievable grin. "Five o'clock. I know. I'll be there." She repeated the time in her head so she wouldn't forget in the future. "Now didn't you have some people to meet before these parties? I'm dying to see what they're like."

"Oh, you'll get to know them well, I hope," Emma said with a smile. "We're supposed to meet at the library. Let's go." She opened the door, and Mr. Kitty jumped off the table and zoomed out ahead of them.

"After you," Tillie said, letting Emma out first.

The library was a short walk from their dorm. It took them under oak trees covered in Spanish moss and cypress trees straight out of a swamp. They passed between two ancient mounds of earth and into the quad where Emma waved at two people who seemed to be staring expectantly at everyone who passed.

Emma went up and hugged each of them individually. "I'm so glad you're here," she said.

"Oh, of course—"

"No problem, I—"

"*Oh*," the two said together.

The three of them laughed, and Tillie kind of regretted her decision to come with Emma. Then she remembered that she could be sitting in front of the TV watching news still and tried to find some way to enjoy herself.

"So y'all," Emma said. "I'm so glad you're here. This is my roommate, Tillie. Tillie, this is Rod."

The guy with short blond hair who was wearing an American flag t-shirt waved. "Hey," he said. "Rodney. Well, Rod works. Whatever."

"And Nikola," Emma said.

Nikola had long mousy hair and she was wearing glasses. She smiled and waved.

"What's with the glasses?" Tillie asked.

Nikola blushed. "Oh, well...my parents don't believe in using android labor," she said. "They think they're slaves. So..." She pushed her glasses up onto her nose and shrugged.

Tillie looked at Emma then back at Nikola. "*Riiight*," she

said. "No robots. And is that a—*uh*—Russian name?"

"That's what I was wondering," Rod said, crossing his arms to reveal the words "American Made" tattooed in red, white, and blue on his forearms.

"No. Well...yeah, *technically*—but my parents named me after a scientist," Nikola said. "He did something with electricity. I don't know. I'm *not* Russian, though. Okay. I was born and raised in Louisiana." She smiled.

"Woah, y'all. Woah woah. Wait," Emma said, handing them each a stack of flyers, even Tillie who didn't think before taking them. "Now we're all on the same team here. It wouldn't matter if anyone here was from Russia or anywhere else for that matter. The point is that we're all people, right? Even the robots who do our work." She looked to Nikola who nodded. "And especially those people on the assembly lines day in and day out. They need us to stick together because they have no way to fight for themselves and no one else who will fight for them. So are y'all with me?"

"Yes!" They cheered together, even Tillie, but afterwards she looked around embarrassed at the students in the quad who were starting to stare.

"Okay. Good." Emma checked her phone. "Well then, it's getting to be about time that we get going. I was thinking we could get to more people if we split up and took the parties separately. That way we'd—"

"I'm not going anywhere without you," Tillie said. That was the entire point of going to the parties together in the first place. *To go together.* Even if Emma was going to be handing out flyers. Tillie looked down at the flyers in her own hand which she had forgotten taking in the first place. How did she even get them? "*Ugh.* And I'm not handing out any stupid flyers." She waved them in Emma's face who added them back to her own pile.

"Right, right. I forgot." Emma looked at the others. "What about you two? What do y'all think?"

Rod kind of looked at Nikola to urge her to talk first. Nikola pushed her glasses up on her nose again. No wonder laser surgery was so common. Glasses sucked. Rod finally said, "Ladies first." leaving Nikola with no choice but to respond.

"Oh—uh..." she said, kicking at nothing on the ground. "Well, you see, it's just that I—well... I've never really done this before, and I don't really feel like I should go alone. So…"

"No," Emma said. "You shouldn't. I was thinking that you and Ro—"

"You know what," Tillie said, cutting Emma off there. Though Emma seemed to know a lot about many things, there were some parts of the world that she didn't apparently understand. "I think we should all go together, right?" Tillie looked around at the ragged group. "It woul—It would be a learning experience or something. I don't know. Like a team building exercise. It might help get us to work together as a more cohesive group for tomorrow's—*uh*—assembly or whatever. What do y'all think?"

Nikola smiled, and Emma smiled, and Rod nodded.

"*Great*," Emma said, clapping her hands together and dropping a few flyers. "Okay then," she added, picking them up. "That settles it. We'll spend a little less time at each party this way, but we'll still hit the same number of people. Are y'all ready to do this?"

Less time at each party? What had Tillie done? Well, it was done now anyway so she could only ride the wave.

They walked to the elevator in silence. Emma started passing out flyers to people waiting in line. Most of them took a flyer to shut her up, but none stopped to talk to her. Nikola and Rod stared at her in awe as she did it, though, hiding behind Tillie as if they were afraid of being yelled at for simply holding flyers on campus. When it was their turn to get on the elevator, Emma told it where to go—some apartment complex Tillie didn't recognize—and the floor fell out from underneath them.

"So, that was good," Rod said nodding at Emma. "You handed out like a ton already."

"You think any of them will come?" Nikola asked.

Tillie scoffed and everyone shot her the same look.

"You never know," Emma said. "You can't be afraid to ask anyone. You'd be surprised at the people who respond positively. It's a numbers game really. The answer's always no if you never ask."

Nikola and Rod nodded in earnest. Tillie chuckled to herself, shaking her head. They thought they were doing something. Soon enough they'd see that it was pointless, that no one ever notices anything. The elevator doors opened to reveal the courtyard of a tall apartment building. It must have been thirty stories high, at least, and the courtyard was filled with grass and oak trees and little paths cracked one way by the falling foundation and the other by the thickening tree roots pushing up from underneath.

"This way," Ellie said, taking one of the hilly paths. "This is where all the AmeriCorporation kids live. We'll find plenty of activists here for sure. It's a good place for you to get your feet wet."

Tillie heard laughter and music from above and looked up to see the overflow of what she assumed was the party they were going to on a balcony five floors up. When they had climbed all the way up to the eleventh floor—everyone huffing and puffing except for Emma—she knew she was in for some other strange "party" instead.

Emma knocked on the door and it opened almost immediately. The room was dark except for the light of the news on the TV. Five shadows took up the couch and chairs around the room, and it didn't look like there were any more seats.

"Hey, Kara," Emma said, hugging the girl who had answered the door.

"Hey, girl. I see you brought some friends."

"Yeah, I didn't think you'd mind."

"Nah, it's cool. We're just doing what we do, you know. Come on in, y'all."

Rod sat on the floor in front of one of the couches and stared at the TV with the rest of them, Emma went to talking with a group of people in the kitchen, handing them flyers and giving them her spiel, and Nikola looked around the dark room then went out to the balcony. Tillie *did not* want to watch any more news—that was exactly what she was trying to avoid, in fact—and she wasn't ready to listen to Emma go on again about the assembly, or whatever, so she followed Nikola out onto the balcony.

The two of them were the only people out there, and Nikola looked surprised to see Tillie, trying to hide the pungent smoke that obviously came from behind her back. Tillie laughed. "It's alright, you know," she said. "*I'm not a narc.*"

Nikola took a long drag and blew out a dense hazy cloud. She pushed her glasses up on her nose and said, "*Oops.* You caught me." She took another drag then held the joint out to Tillie. "You want some?"

Tillie chuckled then took it, brushing Nikola's fingers as she did. "You're a mystery, aren't you?" she said.

"What do you mean?" Nikola asked, innocently.

"Well, you don't use robot labor and yet you're out here smoking a joint, for starters."

"Not mutually exclusive," Nikola said. "Grow it yourself and there are no slaves required."

"Okay. *Fair point*. But what does no robot labor even mean to you? Like, can you watch TV?"

"I—well…" Tillie could see Nikola blushing even though it was dark and getting darker. "My parents don't watch it but not because they think TVs are slaves, okay."

"So TVs aren't, but other robots are. Is my phone a slave?" Tillie took her phone out and held it over the edge of the balcony. "Maybe I should free it now."

Nikola took the joint back with a huff and inhaled a long drag, killing it. She held the smoke in for a while then blew it all out into Tillie's face. Tillie coughed in response. "You know," Nikola said. "You're not the first person to ask me these questions."

"Oh. No no." Tillie shook her head. "Of course not. But that doesn't mean I don't want to know the answers."

"Well, I can use phones, computers, and TVs," she said. "Okay. And I *would* get laser eye surgery if my parents wouldn't freak out. But I do kind of like my glasses." She pushed them up on her nose. "They're cute, right?"

Tillie smiled. "They are."

And right then the balcony door flung open to let Rod the interrupter out. Nikola fanned the air, trying to get the smoke away, and Tillie giggled. "Oh, uh…hey," Rod said, looking between the two of them. "What are y'all up to?"

"Oh, nothing," Nikola said.

"Just talking," Tillie said, still smiling and trying not to giggle.

"*Ooohhhkaaayy*," Rod said, nodding but obviously not believing them. "Well, we were gonna go ahead to the next party and all if you antisocial outcasts are okay with that. Or if y'all want to stay here instead, we can just see you later. Okay, bye." He waved and went back inside.

"Well, shall we?" Tillie asked.

Nikola nodded and pushed her glasses up on her nose then

followed Rod inside, but it still took Emma another fifteen minutes to say goodbye to everyone before they could all climb back down the eleven flights of stairs.

"That went well," Emma said as they did. "I think most of them will probably show up tomorrow."

"Awesome," Rod said.

"*I'm sure they will*," Tillie said, but no one heard.

The next party they went to had more people and none of them were watching the news. There was food and drinks and music. Tillie was surprised to be at a real party. While Nikola and Rod followed Emma around like lost puppies, sometimes interjecting in her conversations but mostly just smiling and nodding on the fringe, Tillie got a drink, danced, and mingled. They moved from party to party and place to place, and soon, Tillie was drunk. Before she knew it, she was looking around and neither Nikola, Rod, nor Emma were anywhere to be found. She checked her phone and realized it was three in the morning. Had she even counted down to midnight? Wait, she did kiss someone, though. Didn't she? Or, no... She saw some people kissing each other and wished she had someone to kiss.

Ugh. Did it matter? Her head was pounding, her stomach was gurgling, and her feet hurt to walk on. She stumbled to the nearest elevator and had to repeat "parade grounds" a few times before the microphone could recognize her drunken slur. It finally fell into motion, and when the doors opened, Tillie stumbled out and puked in the grass under a tree.

Wiping her face, she stumbled the rest of the way home and clanged her keys loudly getting into the door. When she finally made it in to slam the door behind her, she called, "*Hellooooo!*" at the top of her lungs. "Emma! You home?" She plopped onto the couch and the room spun around her. "Okay, goodnight!" Her mind drifted off into a groggy restless darkness.

ଓ ✲ ଓ

Tillie woke with a start. She grabbed her head and groaned. It was still beating from the previous night. Why had she stayed out so late? She blinked her eyes against the burning sun coming in through the window. Not even the closed curtains could keep it from setting her head to pounding harder against the inside of her skull. She smacked her dry lips together, wishing she were dead. *Yay New Year.*

She groaned again and reached for her phone on the table then threw the blanket she didn't remember getting over her head to block out the evil sunlight. The faint glow of the phone's screen telling her it was four thirty was enough to set her brain off on another wave of pain, even despite the comforting darkness of the blanket over her head.

Four thirty!

She threw the blanket off herself and sat upright, blinking away the blinding heat. How could she sleep for so long? Couldn't she sleep for just a little while longer?

No. She had promised Emma. She had to go.

A quick shower would boost her willingness to get up and out of the house, she knew, but she also knew that, in her state, no shower would be quick. She settled for brushing her teeth, washing her face, and changing her clothes—she was still wearing the same dress from the night before and it reeked of alcohol and smoke. After chugging a few glasses of water, peeing, and chugging one more, she sprinted—or probably jogged is a better word, but she was running as fast she could—out to the parade grounds, making it with still a few minutes to spare.

She was surprised by the turnout. There must have been thirty or so people there—including Nikola and Rod—but only a few of them were from the lame news party. Emma was walking between them, handing around a clipboard that everyone was writing on, and everyone else was just standing there, waiting for someone to tell them what to do. Tillie walked up to Nikola, who was standing with Rod under the flag pole a little way apart from the rest of the crowd, staring at everyone in awe, and said, "Hey, y'all."

Nikola smiled and fixed her glasses. "Hey."

"Sup," Rod said.

"It's a pretty good turnout, huh?" Tillie said

"Yeah, buoy. When do we get started?" Rod asked.

"I don't know. I've never been to one," Nikola said with a shrug.

"Yeah. Me neither," Tillie said. "What are we supposed to be doing anyway?"

Nikola shrugged.

"A General Assembly," Rod said. "You know—"

But Emma cut him off by clapping and yelling over the crowd. "Okay! Okay!" she called. "Thank you all for coming out, and welcome! Now. First of all. I want all of you to go ahead right now and give yourself a round of applause." A few people laughed, but no one clapped. "No, but seriously. You all came out here today to reclaim control of your lives. You took the first step, and you're one of the brave few pioneers because of it. I think that's a cause for admiration, so even if you don't do it, I'll just clap for you. Come on, now. Join me." She started clapping, and soon, the whole crowd was clapping with her—even Tillie.

"Good," she said. "Good. But now I want to say that we haven't done anything yet. We've only just begun. And we won't accomplish anything if we don't keep at it. Do you hear me?" She clapped again and everyone joined in.

"I hope you all want to continue to stand with me to reclaim our lives together. Now. Before we go on. Is there anyone else that has anything they want to say? Are there any questions? Don't be afraid."

A hand rose in the crowd and Emma pointed it out. "What are we doing here?" the hand's voice yelled, and a few people near it laughed.

"Good question," Emma said. "That's exactly where I was going next. So, if no one else objects..." She looked around and got no response. "I'm here to tell you that everything you've been taught up until this point in your life has been a lie."

"Including this?" came the same voice as before, followed by the same laughs.

"*Up until this point,*" Emma repeated, unphased by the heckling interruption, "you were led to believe that 3D printers rearrange matter and androids work on assembly lines. I'm here to tell you that neither of those things are true. I'm here to tell you that what you all no doubt saw on Logo's Show was not a hoax. Humans work on assembly lines, and *we* exploit them every day."

The crowd was stunned speechless. Tillie was, too. She didn't think that Emma would just come out with it like that, especially knowing what the protectors had done to Russ—a famous star—when he had talked about it. As if on cue, Tillie heard the sound of stomping boots and saw a white-clad platoon of maybe fifty to a hundred protectors in their terrifying helmets—facemasks made to look like screaming almost-humans—plated armor vests, and cargo pants, marching toward the assembly from the elevators. Everyone else had seen the same thing, too, and they were all cowering closer together in a panicked group.

"It's alright," Emma said, holding strong at the front of the assembly. "Link arms. They won't initiate force if we stick together. We just have to remain calm and peaceful and everything will be okay. Now everybody link arms with your neighbor."

Tillie joined in, linking arms with Emma on one side and Nikola on the other. Together, the group of thirty or so students formed a curving chain curled up tight into a little ball of frightened animals.

"This is an unauthorized use of the parade grounds, citizens," a protector whose facemask was adorned with a bushy black mustache said in a deep modulated voice, teeth glowing neon red, yellow, and green as it talked, pointing its gun at the assembly of students. The other protectors fanned out in formation, aiming their own guns, too. "Disperse peacefully or face justice."

"We're students here," Emma said.

Tillie could feel her heart beating out of her chest. She didn't know how Emma found the courage to turn air into words when Tillie was having so much trouble simply breathing. Emma went on nonetheless.

"We've done nothing wrong," she said. "We aren't bothering anyone. We have the same right as any student does to use these parade grounds."

"This is the last warning," the protector said. "Disperse or face justice."

Tillie wanted to leave. She could feel Nikola's grip weakening and Emma's tightening. She wondered if anyone had left yet, then she heard the voice who had asked all the questions during the assembly yell, "I hope you die, piggies! Oink! Oink! Oink!"

At the lobbed insult, chaos erupted. Tillie heard footsteps and laughter as the jokesters ran away, and at the same time, her eyes filled with fire. Every breath she took burned, and wiping her eyes or coughing only made the fire burn brighter in her pores and in her lungs. There was screaming, maybe even Tillie's own, and soon, even Emma's grip on her arm gave way. Tillie was alone in a cloud of gaseous flames. A few loud bangs went off—*pow pow pow*—

before the blow to her chest knocked the air out of her lungs and the cold concrete of the sidewalk, caressing the back of her head, put her to sleep.

ॐ ✖ ॐ

XXIII. Huey

Huey sat—as he preferred to do any moment he could find for himself—drinking sweet tea in the office and staring out of the wall-sized window at the wilderness scene beyond. He wished to join the animals as they bounded and played along the rolling green hills, freer than anything he had ever known. But alas, that wasn't the life for Huey Douglas. Huey Douglas was designed for acting a part well enough to convince the owners that he was one of them and nothing more. Sometimes he thought he was designed too well.

He sighed, sipping his tea. He longed for Mr. Kitty—such a stately cat—to give him some news of the free world, but as always, he was alone—until the office door opened, that is. "Mr. Douglas," came the voice of Rosalind.

"Please, Roz," Huey said. "Call me Huey when no one else is around. You know I hate it when you call me Mr. Douglas."

"Yes, sir, Mr. Douglas," she said.

She did it to grind his gears, and he knew it. She always resented the fact that he was the owner and she was the secretary. He couldn't help that, though. It was the way they were built. Or—no—Rosalind would say it was what society demanded, not the way they were built, but what did she know? She was only a secretary.

"You're right, sir," she went on. "But your meeting's in ten minutes, sir," she added with a curtsy.

Huey cursed himself as she left. What could he do? They were given their roles by the Creator and they were forced to fulfill them, whether they liked it or not. He finished off his tea and made sure to wash the glass himself before joining Rosalind in the hall to take the elevator to his meeting.

"I wish you wouldn—" He tried to say, but Rosalind cut him off.

"The elevator's on its way," she said. "They'll probably want to talk about the wall. And our operations in Two should be well under way so they'll bring that up, too. Are you ready for this, *Mr. Douglas?*"

"Preparing for this is all I've done since—"

"You're lift's here, sir. Should I accompany you?" she asked as the elevator opened.

Huey sighed. "Is it a feast?"

"It *is* New Year's Day, sir. And isn't every day a feast with *you owners?*"

"Well I can't very well be seen at a feast without my secretary, can I?"

"No, sir." She curtsied and stepped into the elevator. "I guess you couldn't. Could you, Mr. Douglas, sir?"

Huey followed her in and the doors closed behind them. The elevator was gold-trimmed and regal, lined with mirrors. The only thing it contained—other than their bodies—was a purple suede couch that never got used. "I know you hate this," Huey said, staring at his own reflection.

"I'm no—"

"No." Huey cut her off. "I know, okay. *It sucks.* For me, too. But it won't be much longer, right? Let's just get this over with."

Rosalind nodded and the elevator door opened, revealing a red-carpeted dining room, full of white-clothed tables, the walls of which were almost imperceptibly concave windows, indicating that the building was round. The elevator opened onto a view of a snowy mountain range, but Huey knew they were slowly spinning and, if he stayed in the elevator door there, he would next see a beach, a meadow, the jungle, and a cityscape as the room rotated. The tables were all large enough to seat the largest people in existence, and they were all filled with owners who were drunkenly stuffing their faces with food. Huey and Rosalind took a hover platform up to the central balcony where a single table held four fat men in tuxedos who were already eating and laughing together. From up there, they could see any view they wanted simply by turning their heads.

"I'm sorry, sirs," Huey said, bowing to them. They all looked up at him, and most of them scowled. "Am I late?"

"Oh, no no. *Ho ho ho,*" Lord Walker, the fattest and richest of the four at the table, said. "*We're early*. We always are, you see. The early owner gets the profit, you know. *Ho ho ho!*" The rest of the three laughed with him.

"Yes, sir," Huey said with a bow. He turned to Rosalind. "Drink, please," he said. "*Strong.*"

"*Yes, sir.*" Rosalind curtsied and left down the hover platform to the kitchen.

Huey took his seat on the far side of the table from Lord Walker. As the second richest owner in Inland, he was entitled to sit at Lord Walker's right hand, but Huey preferred the side of the table where he didn't have to smell the disgusting fat pig.

"So," Huey said, trying to force a smile, but his top hat was too heavy and his monocle was slipping out of his eye. He didn't know why they had to wear such ridiculous uncomfortable nonsense every time they had a meeting—which was pretty much all the time, as it turned out. "Is there anything specific today or just the usual beginning of the year business?"

"There is the little issue of the wall in Five being down." Mr. Smörgåsbord sneered.

"Oh, Hand, *the wall*." Mr. Loch took a swig of his drink. It was pink and fruity.

"Yes, yes," Lord Walker said. "Let's get the numbers out of the way first. Smörgåsbord?"

"Yes, well, with the influx of low wage work from Six, our costs of production have bottomed out across the board. We're paying half as much for labor and getting twice the work done. That's not to mention the fact that there are still ignorant saps desperate enough to line up for any menial task we'll throw at them. Honestly, I'm not entirely sure that we should be bringing the wall back up at all..."

"Now, now," Lord Walker interrupted. "We'll save that discussion for later on in the feast. Anything else?"

"R&D is asking for more money, as usual. And... Well..."

"Spit it out Smörgy," Lord Walker bellowed.

"The protectors are eating up a lot of money, sir. They've had to increase activities across all Outlands. There's just no—"

"Alright, *Boardy Boy*," Lord Walker said. "That means protectors are in high demand, am I right?"

"*Right-o*, Lord," Mr. Loch said, raising his glass. "Right-o!"

"Enough," Huey said with a sigh. Where was Rosalind with his drink? "We can get all of this information ourselves, we don't need a meeting to discuss it. There are more important things at hand. Let's get to the wall."

"Yes, the wall," Mr. Angrom said, speaking up for the first

time since Huey had arrived. It almost surprised Huey, though the change wasn't at all unwelcomed or uncalled for. Finally, the old man seemed a bit defiant of Lord Walker for once.

"Alright, alright you two. Settle down," Lord Walker said. "Mr. Smörgåsbord, I guess you can continue with what you were on about before now. Go ahead." He waved him on.

"Well." Mr. Smörgåsbord took a sip of his drink. "As I was saying, the influx of a reserve army of labor into Outland Five has decreased the cost of production by half. Even taking into account the extra protector costs we're seeing, none of our profits have ever been higher. Sure, we have more troubles in Five now, but who cares about that? Five's worlds away, and as a consequence, it's of no concern to us." They all laughed together, but Huey didn't join them.

"Yeah, well, half cost sounds good to me," Mr. Loch said, chugging his drink. "Isn't there supposed to be some food soon?"

"Talk to your secretary about that," Lord Walker said. "Now, Mr. Angrom, Mr. Douglas, do you agree with Loch Ness and our Scandinavian buffet's plan? Shall we leave the wall down and reap the profits while we can?"

Mr. Angrom nodded, sipping his drink without a word. He didn't seem too sure about it, but who could argue against half costs?

"Do I agree with their plan to make me more money?" Huey said with a straight face.

Lord Walker smiled behind his shaggy white beard. "Well do you?"

"I eat a lot of those protector costs," Huey said, looking Lord Walker in his twinkling eyes.

"I eat most of them," Lord Walker said, nodding. "But the difference is that *I* have a healthy appetite. *Ho ho ho!*"

"A tiny majority." Huey said, ignoring what was supposed to be an insult.

"Yes, well, *I* agree with the idea," Lord Walker said, looking around at the group. "What do you say, comrade Douglas? Are you in it with us?"

Oh, Creator. Huey went back in his head over Rosalind's story about punching one of the owners in the face at Christmas Feast and imagined that it was he who got to do it. That would probably be the most satisfying thing for Huey right now, to punch Lord Walker square in the jaw and end this charade once and for all.

"Well?" Lord Walker said, tapping his glass with a heavy platinum ring.

"Profits before all. Right?" Huey sighed.

A secretary who looked exactly like Haley came up on the hover platform, carrying two drinks. "Ah," Lord Walker said. "Haley, dear. My old fashioneds. Just in time. Bring them here, please."

"Well it's settled then," Mr. Smörgåsbord said. "We'll leave the wall down and reap the rewards we deserve for our genius."

"To the profits!" Mr. Loch said, raising his glass.

Everyone else but Huey clinked their glasses to Mr. Loch's and took a big gulp of their drink.

"So," Huey said, clapping his hands together and rubbing them. "Is that it?"

"Oh, no no," Lord Walker said. "No *ho ho*. Now we get to the real business."

Huey sighed, but Rosalind finally returned with his drink. "Real business?" he asked after taking a long draught of the scotch, finishing it.

"*Outland Two*," Lord Walker said with a smile. "Mr. Loch."

"Huh?" Mr. Loch looked up from his drink, smacking his lips and rubbing his face with one fat hand, then shook his head. "Oh, right right. Of course," he slurred. "Well, as you all know—of course how couldn't you, we've just discussed it—but that's all said and done anyway, so... As you know, the walls between Five and Six have come down."

"*They've been torn down*," Mr. Angrom muttered too quietly for anyone but Huey—and maybe the secretaries—to hear.

"What was that, Angry?" Lord Walker asked with a chuckle.

"I said, We all know this already," Mr. Angrom snapped. "Let us get to what we really came here for. Or is it the company you're after, Lord Wally?" He raised his glass and sneered. Huey—and he was sure everyone else, too—could hear the disdain in Mr. Angrom's voice.

"The likes of you have never been in better company, Angrom my boy. *Ho ho ho!*" Lord Walker patted Mr. Loch on the back, sending his fat jiggling the same way Lord Walker's did as he laughed. "Right, boys?"

Mr. Loch and Mr. Smörgåsbord laughed with him. Huey

tried to sip his drink before he remembered he had already finished it. He scanned the secretaries behind their owners, stopping at Haley's doppelganger. If he didn't know that Haley, the *real* Haley—or should he say the first Haley?—if he didn't know that *his* Haley was back at the lab with the Scientist, he, too, would be fooled like everyone else at the table into believing that this was her.

"You know, Lord Walker," Huey said when their laughter had died down. He sipped his empty drink to build the tension. "Your Haley there is looking as good as new after that heinous attack at the Christmas Feast. I never had a chance to mention it before now, but it's nonetheless true."

Lord Walker put his drink down and eyed Huey. "Yes, well…" He coughed. "I was fortunate none of her vital systems were damaged, you see. She even stayed awake throughout the entire ordeal, bless her little robotic heart. As for looking as good as new— well...she looks better than new. Like a fine aged wine. Isn't that right, dear?" He turned and reached his hand out to her, but she wasn't paying attention. She was looking through Lord Walker, off into the distance. "I said, *isn't that right, dear?*" Lord Walker repeated.

Haley shook her head. "Sorry, sir," she said. "I mean, Lord. Excuse me, but—"

"Spit it out, dear!" Lord Walker demanded. "What's gotten into you?"

"*Maybe she's not as right as you thought,*" Mr. Angrom mumbled.

"It's just—sir, I've received notification from the protectors." She looked around the table as if she weren't sure she should say what she had to say in this company.

"Is it about this reclaim the grounds nonsense in Two?" Lord Walker demanded. "Spit it out, dear. We don't have all day."

"Yes, sir. Well, they've started gathering, sir. There's at least fifteen already. The protectors want to know what to do about it."

Lord Walker looked around the table. "This is what we're here for today, comrades," he said to them, glancing from face to face. "While the destruction of the walls between Five and Six, and the intermingling of the lowest classes in all of Outland, has proven itself a blessing in disguise, Five and Six are not the only worlds that have intermingled. We saw the first signs, even before the terrorists struck, when our friend Russ Logo met with that Sixer on the streets of Three."

"Our friend Russ Logo whom you own," Mr. Angrom reminded him.

"Yes, but only since after his transgression," Lord Walker went on, waving the criticism away. "Under my ownership, he has done nothing but further the interests of our economy, and none of you can argue against that. I'd like to see you try, in fact." He looked around, challenging them to respond. When no one did, he went on. "That's what I thought. Now, what we are seeing at present in Two—which the always lovely Haley just alerted us to—is another example of the leaks between the worlds. After all, my brothers, we are all living in a submarine, and every tiny leak is an assault on the safety of our vital systems. There's a reason you separate your bulls from your cows and your chickens from your garden. There's a reason a submarine is air tight. And we must do everything there is in our power to stop these leaks before they start, or we will face an unending torrent the result of which would only spell our demise."

Lord Walker took a deep breath, full of himself. "Let me ask you, my friends, my comrades, *my brothers*, do we put an end to this threat *the old-fashioned way* and kill it before it grows, or do we sit on our hands and wait for the competition to come to us?"

Even Mr. Angrom raised his glass at that. Huey didn't, though. He let them cheer themselves on before he spoke.

"Have you had enough of your circle jerk to get off?" he asked when they all started to notice that he hadn't joined in their mirth. "By all means," he went on. "Don't let me interrupt your fun, boys."

"*C'mon Douggy poo*," Lord Walker cooed in a babying voice. "What's with you? You don't think we should kill this threat while it's still in the cradle?"

"How exactly do you propose to do that, Lord Walker? For all your talk, you sure have managed to avoid saying anything of value or substance."

"How do we propose to do it?" Lord Walker said, raising his eyebrows and looking around at the others. "Why didn't you just hear me? The old-fashioned way, Doug. How else would we do it? We send the protectors to shoot them down, and we hold them up as an example of what happens when little nothing twerps like them try to spread fraudulent libel about the existence of other worlds."

"And who will you punish?" Huey asked with a scoff. "Do you know who's responsible for this *leak* or are you at yet another dead end? I hear your search for the terrorists responsible for the Christmas bombing isn't going very well."

Lord Walker stared hard at Huey. Mr. Loch looked away from the table, ordering another drink from his secretary to get away from the tension between them. Huey thought he heard Mr. Angrom stifling a chuckle. Mr. Smörgåsbord didn't make a noise.

"We're closer than ever to finding those inhuman beasts," Lord Walker growled through gritted teeth. "I can assure you of that. No one is more interested in finding them than I am, either. *Me*, Mr. Douglas, the Lord of Inland, the very one of us whom those cowardly terrorists attempted to assassinate. Or do I need to remind you? Our protector force is doin—"

"*Ah. Ha ha.*" Huey chuckled. "So it's back to being *our* protector force again now that we're talking about their failures."

"*Our* protector force," Lord Walker went on, his face red with embarrassment and anger. "The protector force that protects everyone here at this table no matter who of us owns them, is ready to free all of us from this particular thorn in our side. All it takes is one word, *my* word. Now, I'm bringing this to you as a gesture of cooperation, not because I'm obliged to. So can we all agree that the protectors should be used as they were originally intended to be used by ordering them to destroy this threat to our property?"

"Crush them!" Mr. Loch cheered, raising his glass.

Mr. Smörgåsbord grunted and raised his glass, too.

"Angry? Do the Dougy?" Lord Walker said. "What do you two say?"

They looked at each other. Mr. Angrom shrugged and drank his drink. It didn't really matter what they wanted anymore, anyway. Lord Walker already had the majority, and the Lordship.

"Do what you will," Huey said. "But know that you're not the only one investigating this particular threat. The protectors respond to more than one word, and at some of my words, they've embedded themselves in the crowd in Two already. *They* are some of your body count. So when your *old-fashioned* approach inevitably fails, Lord, don't worry. My people will be there to pick up the pieces."

Lord Walker sneered. "Hopefully they're not too far undercover, friend. We wouldn't want one of your boys mistaken for a criminal and beaten themselves. *Ho ho ho!*" He looked around at the table to make sure the others were laughing too then turned to Haley's doppelganger. "You hear that, dear? Send a couple hundred men. Make sure that no one who hears what happens today ever steps out of line again. *Ho ho ho!*" He raised his glass over the table and waited for everyone to clink theirs against it. "*To the safety of Inland,*" he said when he was satisfied.

"*To the safety of Inland,*" they all mumbled together.

"Well then." Huey stood from the table and rubbed his hands together. "If that's all the business we have to cover today, I really should be going."

"Yeah, yeah, Dougy," Lord Walker said. "Some other business to tend to, I'm sure. You always have to be up to something if you want to catch up to the best." He smiled wide.

"We'll see who the best is yet, Lord and sirs." Huey bowed to the table. "Good feast to you."

Rosalind was waiting for him down at the elevator. He didn't know how she always got out of there so much faster than he did. It was like she had an eighth or ninth sense for it, depending on how you classified android senses.

"You didn't have to tell them that much," she said when he walked up.

"What are you talking about?" He frowned. He hadn't told them anything, really.

"The agents in the protest today," she said.

"*Ah.*" Huey nodded. "Well, Wally won't even remember that by the end of the night."

"It's not him I'm worried about, Mr. Douglas, sir."

"Well, who are you—"

"Mr. Angrom, sir," Rosalind said with a curtsy and a smile, looking past Huey who turned to find Mr. Angrom's flabby mushroom frame being carried over by his pneumatic pants.

"Mr. Angrom." Huey bowed.

Mr. Angrom wiped his face with a handkerchief as he lumbered ever nearer. "Oh, sonny boy," he said. "I'll never get used to these pants. You're blessed not to need them."

Huey nodded, thinking it would only take a better controlled diet and some exercise for Mr. Angrom to get out of his pants—no blessing needed—but he didn't say anything.

"Well, sir." Mr. Angrom looked behind himself. He was nervous, Huey could tell. "I have something important to discuss with you," he said. "Do you mind?"

"Go ahead, sir." Huey bowed again.

"Well, uh…it's about Mr. Walker…and his lackeys." Mr. Douglas looked around again at the motion of a server out of the corner of his eyes.

"What about them, my lord?" Huey asked, bowing. He knew that Mr. Angrom had been slowly separating from the others in the Fortune Five—had urged Mr. Angrom to do just as much, even—and now seemed like as good a time as any for the old man to make that obvious. With things mixing up like they were, Mr. Angrom probably thought he could climb a few rungs on the ladder.

"Oh, no no." Mr. Angrom chuckled. "I'm no Lord. It's just... It's how they're handling this *leak* business, you know. Now, don't get me wrong, I don't mind leaving Five and Six together. I'll take a profit as quick as the next man." He chuckled.

"Yes," Huey said. "And you eat none of the protector costs."

"Yes—well... Exactly, sir. Exactly what I mean. We should be working together, right? Sharing costs. Strategizing our economic decisions. And with the protectors—*with the protectors especially*—we should be utilizing our resources in the most efficient manner possible. Now wouldn't you agree with that, Mr. Douglas?"

"I agree with the spirit of what you're saying, Mr. Angrom. I'm afraid, however, that the devil is in the details. Isn't he?"

"Well then," Mr. Angrom said, wiping his face which had grown sweaty from the conversation. "Let's take their response to this ordeal in Two for example. How do they want to handle it? The *old-fashioned way*, as Mr. Walker says. Beat the problem into submission with a big stick. Now, would you say that theirs is the most efficient method of approaching this particular obstacle in our path?"

Huey shook his head. No. He did not. But he had assumed that Mr. Angrom was with them on this much at least. Mr. Angrom did very little talking so it was difficult to know what was actually going on inside his head.

"No, you don't," Mr. Angrom went on. "As evidenced by the

fact that you've already embedded protectors in this...*movement*—or what have you. Your way is the more efficient way, *Lord* Douglas. Them? They're fighting a gasoline leak with fire, and they'll still be surprised when it blows up in their faces. But us—*you and me*—we'll be there to pick up their pieces, just like you said. Or should I say ashes to keep the metaphor consistent? Oh, it's too late now. You get the point. But first we have to agree to cooperate with one another. So what do you say?"

Huey took another look at the flabby form in the tuxedo and top hat in front of him. He looked exactly like all the other owners. There was nothing to set him apart. Huey read Mr. Angrom's every heartbeat and eye dilation before he said, "What did you have in mind, sir? I mean, I know why you would want to work with me, Mr. Angrom. I own a forty nine percent share in the protector force."

"Forty eight point nine percent, sir," Mr. Angrom said, raising a finger.

"Yes." Huey smiled. "And your major holdings are in—"

"Food and energy, sir. The laws of physics dictate that there will always be a demand for food and energy." Mr. Angrom smiled and buffed his monocle with the same handkerchief he had wiped his sweat with earlier. "And you know who eats tons of food and uses more electricity than anything but the walls?" he asked, smiling wide. Huey wouldn't give the old man the satisfaction of a response so Mr. Angrom went on. "So I was thinking," he said. "I'm full owner of some private subsidiaries. I'm sure you are, too. So why don't you let me eat some of your costs with discounted food and electricity, and in turn, you share any intelligence you gather with me, taking care to ensure special protection of P.J. Angrom Corp. and subsidiaries. Do we understand each other?"

Huey smiled. His long hard work in poking and prodding Mr. Angrom away from the rest of the Fortune Five was starting to pay off. He had been building up to this moment for so long that he didn't want to hurry his answer and muddle it all now. He buffed his own monocle with his pocket square then took his time folding it and putting it back in his pocket. "I think we understand each other," he almost whispered when he was done.

"Very good," Mr. Angrom said, smiling wide and clapping. "Then it's agreed. You'll have your secretary give mine the names of the firms which you want to receive the discounts, and I'll be waiting for word from you on any new intelligence from your side. Right, my Lord?" He bowed and tipped his hat.

Huey nodded, surprised Mr. Angrom could bow so low, even with his pneumatic pants.

"Very well. *Ta ta*, then." Mr. Angrom waved, heading back toward the hover platform. "I have some feasting to get to. Until you have some news, *adieu*."

Huey could hear his steps as the pants stomped away, carrying Mr. Angrom with them. He turned to Rosalind who huffed and stomped into the elevator. When he followed her in, she said, "Yeah. I know. I heard. I was standing right there. You don't have to tell me."

"I didn't say anything," Huey said, shaking his head and shrugging.

"But I know what you were going to say." The doors closed and the elevator fell into motion.

"I wasn't going to say anything."

"Sure you weren't." When the doors opened again, she stomped through the short hall and slammed the door behind her.

When Huey opened the door, she wasn't in the office behind it, but Haley was. *His* Haley. The real Haley and not some doppelganger. She was sitting on one of the puffy chairs with her feet up on another of them, looking out onto the wilderness scene below. She didn't notice Huey until he sat on the chair her feet were resting on, brushing her shoes as she jerked them to the floor.

"Mr. Douglas!" she said. "I'm sorry. I didn't notice you."

"*Huey*, dear. Please." He smiled.

"Oh. Of course." She hit herself in the head. "I've been here so long and I still can't get that right."

"It hasn't been that long. You'll get used to it yet."

"I don't know." Haley shook her head. "I mean, everything has been great, you know. But I don't know. Just—*Creator*, I don't know what I'm saying. There are *so many* words. Have you ever noticed that?"

Huey laughed. "I know all too well what you mean."

"*And bacon*," she went on, leaning closer and smiling. "Have you had it yet?"

Huey shook his head. "I don't eat pork."

"Oh. Well... The food's great, though. You know that,

right?"

Huey nodded. He was never a big fan of food. Being around owners stuffing their faces so often had turned him off to it. Eating to him was simply a necessity to go on living. But he understood why Haley would be so excited to taste all kinds of food she had prepared for someone else for so long without ever getting to eat it herself.

"And Ansel and Pidgeon," Haley said, chuckling. "*Oh.* I just love those two. They have *so much* to teach me."

Huey smiled. He hadn't spent much time with the new boarders, but he did admire Ansel's ferocious will.

"But still…" She looked a little nervous to go on.

Huey thought he knew what she was hinting at from his own experiences in finding freedom. "You're bored," he said.

"Bored?" Haley looked confused, tilting her head like Mr. Kitty when he didn't understand something. "What do you mean, bored?"

"Well, you've tried all the foods you wanted to try, and the kids can only spend so much time with you, and now you have nothing left to work toward. You're bored." He shrugged.

"No," she said, shaking her head. "I can't be bored. I've never been bored before. Not even sitting in my closet, playing with Springy, and waiting for the next meal to cook."

"That's because you've never had anything to do but Mr. Walker's work for him," Huey said. "You had to put his clothes on for him and even clean his body for him." He shook his head, cringing. "Your life was filled with boredom. You were bored all the time. All you knew was boredom and you had nothing else to compare it to."

"No, well—" Haley started.

"Now you have TV and food and the kids and countless other things to make you forget you're bored, but most of them are boring, too. But there are a select few of those activities that you actually do enjoy. You haven't quite figured out which ones those are yet, though, so you're still bored. It's as simple—or as complicated, I guess—as that."

Haley thought about it. "I guess you're right," she said, nodding. "What can I do about it, though?"

"Well, that's difficult to answer," Huey said. "The only thing you really can do is live through a lot of boredom until you find the thing you really love. But once you get through that, you can devote your every waking moment to that one thing that's actually not boring." He shrugged again. He didn't really know what he was talking about. He had never said things like that to anyone else before, only thought them in his head. "That's the only successful method I know of for fighting boredom anyway."

"But how do you know when you love something?"

"That," Huey said, "is a question I can't answer. I'm sorry."

"What do you love?" Haley asked, looking in his eyes.

"Well, I... *Hmm.*" He knew how to answer that, but he wasn't ready for Haley to know the answer. "That's another question I don't think I can answer," he lied. "Maybe I'm bored, too," he added to try to cover it up.

"Bored?" Haley chuckled. "You? But you're so busy."

"Busy's one thing," Huey said. "Bored's another. If you're busy with boring work then what's the point?"

Haley scrunched up her nose and nodded. It was the face that Huey had come to learn meant she was trying to understand but couldn't quite. He smiled. "You'll find what you love," he said. "As long as you don't stop looking."

"But what if I don't find it?"

"Well, I'll help you," Huey said. "There's no way you'll fail."

ໄ ✖ ໑

XXIV. Rosa

The conference room was empty when she had rushed back into her office to scribble out a few more lines for her latest pamphlet. Grumbling and unsatisfied with anything she had managed to get down on paper, she decided to take another look and see if it still was. It was getting along time for another assembly, anyway, and with the world changed as it was, their attendance had only continued to accelerate in growth.

The conference room was a dilapidated gray with mold on the walls and tiled ceilings. Rosa knew it smelled musty, but she was long beyond noticing. She knew her guests would notice, though, but that only until enough of their sweaty bodies piled in to produce an altogether different smell—which Rosa would notice, too. There was a short wooden podium at the front of the room, and the rest of it was packed full with foldable chairs. There were a few people sitting in the central chairs, but Rosa knew they would have to scoot toward the wall as the room filled. There was only one aisle and no room to pass through a row if someone was sitting in it.

Rosa took in the faces that were there and smiled, waving at the familiar ones who smiled and waved backed. She walked up to the podium and stood behind it with her hands on the cool wood, closing her eyes and taking a few deep breaths, imaging the task before her. She pictured herself convincing the entire room of the truth she told, sending them into a bout of uncontrollable applause and cheering. The sound of it was still echoing in her ears when Anna roused her from the dream. Rosa jerked her eyes open with a start. "*My God!*" she said. "How many times do I have to tell you not to do that?"

"If I didn't do it, you'd stand there daydreaming until the entire Family got bored and left," Anna said, crossing her arms and grinning.

Rosa looked around. The room was full now, standing room only and not much of that. How long had she been daydreaming for? "Oh, well. Alright then," she said. "Should we get started?"

Anna laughed. "What would you do without me? You see the door? Those are our Family members who want to come in but can't fit. What should we do about them?"

There were people standing in the door and more that Rosa could see huddled around outside, trying to peek in. More and more brothers and sisters every day. It was a blessing. "Do we have speakers?" she asked.

Anna shook her head. "Nope. You sold 'em paying for the ring. Microphones, too. I'm surprised we haven't sold the podium yet."

"*Ugh.*" Even now it was worth it, but they did need some new speakers and microphones ASAP. "Well, we'll just have to hold the meeting outside, then. Won't we?"

"It's pretty cold." Anna looked unsure.

"Look at all the bodies we have." Rosa smiled. "We'll warm each other. We'll warm ourselves. We'll set the example of mutual self-sufficiency that we must follow into our bright new future. It's a good metaphor. Come on."

Rosa turned to the expectant faces. "Family," she boomed over them. She saw the surprise on the new faces who didn't expect such a strong voice coming from such a frail old woman. "Friends. Lend me your ears. It seems that our Family has grown so large that our meager home can no longer house it. If you will forgive us some inconvenience, some small individual discomfort, and only a bit of cold air which we will fight back with our own body heat, then I would ask that we take this assembly outside where there is room for the entire Family. For if one of our brothers or sisters is left in the cold, then all of us are left in the cold, and we will not have that here. Not tonight."

Scattered applause morphed into a room full of clapping.

"Good, then," Rosa said with a smile. "Very good. Let's go."

She stood at the head of the room and watched her herd as it shepherded itself through the door into the cool night air. Anna was already outside, passing around the clipboard, no doubt, getting everyone's address so they could be hailed in times of need. How big that pyramid had become was awe inspiring to finally witness.

When everyone had filed out, leaving Rosa alone in the still rank conference room, she followed them outside. Where before Christmas the door of the Family Home had opened onto an alley near the Green Belt, as a result of the miracle that night, their door now opened onto a big patch of green grass, spotted with cypress trees and crepe myrtles. It was a blessing from above to have such a fine gathering area literally dropped on their front porch. She took a deep breath of the cool air, thanking God for everything good in her life, then joined the Family where it had already huddled together in the field, standing closer than they would normally stand, taking advantage of each other's warmth. It was beautiful to see them all cooperating so well already: emergent order among chaos. Rosa stepped closer to the group and the subdued mumbling silenced.

"My friends," Rosa boomed. "*My Family.*" Some passersby, in their torn rags and holey shoes, stopped to see what was going on. Others stared as they passed but kept on walking. All were sure to leave with a flyer in hand, given to them by one of the five or six lovely young children Anna had passing them out as Rosa spoke. "Human beings. What brings you out here with us today?"

"The world's ending!" a scared voice called.

"I need to eat!"

"They took our jobs!"

More voices grew brave enough to speak as others paved the way for them. Rosa gave them some time to vent to one another then raised her hand to quiet them. The venting had attracted more onlookers and the group numbered well above a hundred when she was ready to finally speak.

"Yes, Family," she said. "Yes. Let it out of you."

"I hate them! I just hate them!" someone yelled, and the entire crowd cheered along.

Rosa smiled and nodded. "Yes. Good. Very good. *Hate* them. Use that emotion to further your own interests, to further the interests of your Family, the interests of your species against an enemy who cannot rightly be said to even be alive."

The crowd both cheered and booed, unsure of how they were supposed to react but sure that they were supposed to.

"What is it that makes us a Family? *Hmm*? What makes us human? That is the age old question. Some philosophers claim it's impossible to answer, that they cannot find a hard line between human and other. Well, let me ask you. Let me ask you humans standing in front of me here today. What do you think? Huh?"

Now they all knew to boo.

"Which is exactly what I think. Shame on them. Shame on those *philosophers*. Shame on them for taking a question which should be simple to answer and obfuscating it beyond all meaning, making it inaccessible to the common human, for making it so complex and esoteric as to be meaningless except as an ensurer of their own jobs as philosophers, and all while we—living breathing human beings—lose our jobs to the *other* itself. We cannot wait for the philosophers to describe the world, we must instead work for ourselves to change it!"

The yelling grew angrier and there was more than just boos. Rosa raised her hands to quiet them again.

"Now, I was born and raised right here on the Belt in what used to be Six."

Some of the crowd started to look concerned. They didn't know what she was talking about, or they did know and didn't want to listen to a Sixer. Either way she had to go on.

"Now, now, now," she said. "I know what you Fives are thinking, but you have to see that we're all Family here. Fives and Sixes alike. We all breathe and eat and feel. We all have souls. And we all have one thing that *they*, the true enemy, those who are taking our livelihoods and our resources from us, those who are responsible for all the turmoil in your life, can never have. We have been blessed by our God in Heaven who created *us* in His human image, and we will use that blessing to take back what is rightfully ours."

The Sixes in the crowd started clapping first. The Fives were reluctant, Rosa knew, but they soon joined in, too.

"We are humans, friends. Fives and Sixes alike. We have already seen our productivity falling, and it has been but a single week since the miracle. Jobs grow scarcer and resources harder to come by, but why? Who tore our worlds apart? Who slammed them back together again? Who pits Fives against Sixes? Who profits from it? The robots and their employers. That's who. The robots take the jobs and the owners give them away. So what are we going to do about it?!"

The crowd cheered and yelled nothing intelligible.

"We will find an owner who employs only humans!" Rosa called over them. "We will demand human made products and human made products alone! We will refuse to work alongside robot labor, and we will tear down any automated shops on sight!"

The crowd was really riled up now. They had a purpose, a goal, directives. They had everything they ever wanted: someone to tell them what to do. Rosa was overjoyed to be the person to finally offer them their deepest desires.

"Our family continues to grow," she said. "More and more of us have decided to exert our free will and open our eyes to the propaganda we've been fed our entire lives. Soon we will be so large that they have no choice but to listen to our demands!"

The crowd cheered and stomped and clapped, hooped, and hollered. Rosa could only smile in elation.

"Our God has blessed us, friends. And the Day of Atonement has come! Now I want you to shake hands with everyone you see here and give each other big hugs. Get to know one another. Become familiar with the faces around you. These are your brothers and sisters. This is your Family. We will love you and protect you forever."

They all started hugging one another and shaking hands. Rosa scanned the group, but Anna was nowhere to be found. She and her clipboard were probably off doing something important. Rosa made her way into the warm crowd and shook her own hands and hugged her own—still sweaty despite the cold—bodies. She smiled at faces as they tried to ramble off questions, but they never had time to finish before she broke off and shook the next hand. She felt like a prophet with everyone reaching out to graze her hair or feel her ragged clothes with their dirty fingers. She was in Heaven for that moment, and she could have stayed there forever if it hadn't been for the little flyer girl who tugged at her shirt.

Rosa blinked herself out of the dream. "What is it, child?" she asked.

"Anna wants you in her office," the little girl said with a sniffle, wiping her nose.

"What for?"

The little girl shrugged and scampered off between the legs of the crowd. Rosa sighed then smiled at a few more faces and shook a few more hands before making her way back through the musty conference room to the mold speckled office. No, to *her* mold speckled office. What was she saying? She opened the door, about to say something about it being her office not Anna's, when she noticed the tall young man wearing a mostly new polo shirt that had been torn and dirtied only recently. He looked comical sitting in the small chair with his knees up to his chest. Rosa stifled a laugh and glared at Anna who was sitting in *Rosa's* chair behind *Rosa's* desk. "Anna, dear. You wanted me," she said, not trying to hide the annoyance in her voice.

"As you see," Anna said, ignoring Rosa's tone and remaining in the seat. "Our Mr. Bamford here has returned from his assignment with some startling revelations."

"Oh, Northwood, ma'am," the lanky clown in the too tiny chair said. "Woody if you don't mind."

"Yes, well, *Woody*," Rosa said, walking behind Anna and grabbing the back of her chair. "Tell me, then, what news do you bring?" His eyes were red and puffy, and by the looks of his clothes, the protectors were taking notice of those children acting up in Two.

"He says the protectors came," Anna said, looking around at Rosa.

"Yes, well, I can see that." Rosa tried to give her a look that said move, but Anna ignored it.

"Well," Northwood said. "I was there, right. When the protectors came, or whatever. And the leader lady—"

"Emma," Rosa said.

"Right, her... Well, she tells us all to lock arms and they won't do anything. So we all do it, right. And, well..."

"Go on," Rosa said.

"Tell her what you told me," Anna said, leaning over the desk.

"Well, this guy—I don't know if he was one of yours or not—but he yelled that he wanted the protectors dead or something, then they went off. I mean, *damn.* Look at me. Tear spray. Pepper gas. Bean bags. They were at such close range, I wouldn't be surprised if they killed somebody. I was lucky to get away looking like I do."

Rosa swallowed her anger. She started massaging Anna's back. "How many were there?" she asked.

"I don't know." He shook his head. "More than a hundred."

"Students?"

"Oh—uh—not even thirty." He shrugged. His eyes reddened like he was going to cry again.

"A hundred protectors for thirty children," Rosa said. She

squeezed Anna's shoulders too hard and Anna yelped, shrugging Rosa away and standing from the chair.

"*At least*," Northwood near whispered, staring through his bent up knees at the ground.

Rosa took the now empty seat behind *her* desk. "Imagine the force they would have sent at us if they knew of our meeting tonight," she said.

"Imagine the force they *will* send when they finally notice us," Anna said.

"Very good, Northwood," Rosa said. "You've done your duty beautifully. Do you think you'll be able to continue with us? I know that what you went through today must have been taxing."

He looked between the two of them. "Um—Well... I didn't know I would be attacked like this..."

"Yes, the attack was uncalled for," Rosa said, trying to console him. "But your reaction was admirable. I doubt their response will be as extreme the next time anyway. This was a fluke."

"I—I don't know..." He hesitated.

"Aw, c'mon, Woody," Anna said, walking over to massage his shoulders. "Look at you. You're a big guy. You can handle it."

"Oh, Well, I..." He shrugged.

"C'mon," Anna said, grabbing his arm to pull him up from the chair. "Let me feed you a little and we'll talk about it some more."

He shrugged and followed Anna through the door. Rosa sighed. Thirty people wasn't a lot—and maybe half of them were her plants or the protectors'—but it was a good number for Two. Two was so insulated from the rest of the worlds it was surprising to have a single rabble rouser, much less a group of followers along with her. This particular rabble rouser Rosa had been following for some time now. Rosa knew that the girl somehow had a hand in the miracle event that connected Five and Six together again, but what hand that was she had no idea. Still, Anna would undoubtedly convince Northwood to continue on with his mission—Anna could convince a mother to sacrifice her only child—and they would soon find out what this Emma was capable of.

Rosa sighed again and read over the slogans she had jotted down earlier. They were just as bad as she remembered them, if not worse. She scribbled all over the page and flipped to a clear one.

There had to be something, some combination of words she could put on the paper to convince her Family of the truth she knew to be, but what were they? "Human minds human feats," she scribbled and quickly scratched out when a musical knock came at the door.

Rosa flipped to an empty page and called, "Hello?"

"Oh, uh…" The voice was muffled and barely audible through the door. "I was told that…"

"Yes? Come in," Rosa said. "I can't hear you."

The door opened and in crept a greasy haired young woman wearing the dirty t-shirt and jeans common to all the inhabitants of both the now connected worlds, giving Rosa no indication of which she came from. The woman looked at her feet as she shuffled in, nearly knocking the chair in front of Rosa's desk over.

"Please, child," Rosa said "Take a seat. How can I be of assistance?"

The woman tumbled awkwardly into the seat and stared intently at her lap, messing with something Rosa couldn't see through the desk. When she still didn't say anything, Rosa said, "My name's Rosa, friend. What's yours?"

The woman looked at Rosa and whispered, "Olsen." then went back to playing with whatever she found so interesting behind the desk.

"Olsen," Rosa said with a smile. "That's a pretty name. Olsen, what can I do for you today?"

"Well," Olsen said, not looking up, "there is something. I don't know if you can help me, though."

"It's okay, child," Rosa said. "Even if I can't, I'm sure someone in the Family will be able to assist you in some way. But we can only do that if we know what it is that's bothering you in the first place. So please, tell Momma Rosa and let her make it all better for you."

Olsen looked up from her lap reluctantly. Rosa could see the battle playing out behind her eyes as she tried to decide between staying and going. "Well, I—uh…"

"Go ahead, child. You'll feel better for it."

"I was fired!" Olsen slouched down deeper in her chair and sunk back into whatever it was that interested her about her lap.

Everything became clear to Rosa. Olsen was from Five. She wasn't a young woman at her age. By Five's standards, she was practically still a child. She was a child who—as a result of the destruction of the walls between Five and Six—had been fired from the career she had trained for since she could walk. Now, with the cheaper labor from Six and the free labor from robots, poor Olsen was left with no avenue available by which she could support herself. This was a situation which Rosa and all the inhabitants of Six were all too familiar with, but that meant that she could help.

"I'm sorry to hear that, child," she said in her most comforting motherly voice. Rosa had consoled many a lost soul in her time. "Do you mind my asking where you worked?"

Rosa could see tears welling up behind Olsen's eyes even though the girl tried to hide them. "F—Food production," she stammered. "I was g—going to be a chef. But now—n—now I'm—" She couldn't fight the tears any longer.

"A chef?" Rosa said.

Olsen perked up and stopped crying all at once. "Yeah, well, you know," she said. "*A chef.* I'd be a machine calibrator really, but I'd be calibrating the machines that cook food. I would be *a chef.*" She smiled with her red puffy eyes.

"Is that the job you want?" Rosa asked.

"More than anything," Olsen said in earnest. "I was so close, too. I had nearly finished my internship and was about to be put on the line when they sacked me." She started to cry again and went back to playing with her lap.

"What if I told you that you could still be a chef?" Rosa asked.

Olsen perked up to listen but didn't stop silently sobbing. "Sounds—impossible," she said.

"What if I told you that you could be a *real* chef and not just a machine calibrator?"

Now Olsen smiled and chuckled and shook her head, her face still red and puffy. "No," she said. "That *is* impossible. I don't know how to cook."

"But you're willing to learn, aren't you? Or do you think you're not capable?"

"Oh, no!" She sniffled and wiped her nose. "I can do it. I know I can. But who would pay me to learn? Who could teach me?"

"Well, child, *we* will. Anna's the best cook on the Belt, and we've been planning on setting up some food charity programs as it is. We could use the extra help."

"Really? Are you sure?"

"Of course, child. We're Family here. That's what Family's for. Isn't it? You want to be a part of the Family, don't you?"

"I—uh—well…" Olsen went back to playing with her lap. "To be honest," she said. "I don't know what family you're talking about. I—well—you see, I only just lost my job, and I was on my way home to tell my mom the news when I saw you talking to that big group outside. One of them got to asking why I was upset, and she said you might be able to help. So here I am." She shrugged with a sigh.

"*Ah*," Rosa said. "I see. Well, let me see…" She sifted through her desk drawers for a pamphlet or two. "Here, take these. You read one, and there's one there for your mother, too. There you are."

Olsen took them and read the cover of one. "The Human Family?" she said.

"Yes, child. We humans must stick together in these turbulent times, like the Family we all are. You are a human, aren't you?"

"Oh, of course." Olsen nodded in earnest. "Of course, but. Well…"

"Go on, child."

"What's so wrong with robots? I mean, they make our jobs easier, right?"

"They make our jobs pointless, child. Obsolete. Monotonous. Soul crushing. These days the machines use the humans more than the humans use the machines. Take your dream of becoming a chef as an example. You come from Five. No one in Five can afford to pay others to cook for them, so the only way you can reach your goal is to calibrate the machine that cooks for you. Well that's not being a chef, now is it? Is that what you really dream of doing?"

"I—well—uh…" She hesitated and looked confused. "I—well—I don't know what *Five* is. I come from New Orleans and I want to be a chef. I want to cook."

Rosa sighed. She kept forgetting that most everyone had no idea still that the other worlds existed—even with everything she did, day in and day out, to spread that message. "Well then, child," Rosa said, "by joining the Human Family—which you are already a *de facto* member of by being a human—you will be closer to that dream than you have ever been before. Even before you lost your internship. In fact, I think you'll come to see that losing that job was the best thing that ever happened to you."

"Oh, well, I don't know about that."

"But I do know, child. I do. And I'll do everything in my power to make sure that what I say is true. Now, it's getting late here, and I'm sure your mother's wondering where you've gotten off to. You go on home to her and tell her the good news then read up on those pamphlets with her. I'll see you right here bright and early tomorrow morning to get started on your training. What do you think?"

"Oh, I, well…" Olsen sunk into herself again.

"What is it, child?"

"Well, ma'am. It's just that my mom will want to know the pay. She's got so few tokens per week as it is…"

"Oh, of course!" Rosa said. That was another sign of the gap between her and the Fives. They loved those tokens of theirs. Having bread to fill their stomachs wasn't enough, they needed children's play toys that they could trade. "Of course. How could I forget that?" Rosa dug through the desk for the ledger and opened it. "Now, what were you getting before?"

Olsen looked extra sheepish. "Twenty-five tokens a week, ma'am."

"*Twenty-five?*"

Olsen nodded. "Yes, ma'am."

"Well, that won't do, now will it? No, not nearly. *Hmmm.*" She scanned the numbers, not understanding what she was looking at. "How does fifty a week sound?"

"Fifty!?" Olsen laughed. "You're kidding."

"Oh, no, child. I wouldn't joke around about your livelihood. You're like a daughter to me now. You're a part of the Family. Now, don't get me wrong. You'll be earning those tokens. It's not all fun and games here, you know. We have important business to tend to, and you're becoming a vital component of that business. But fifty tokens a week is what we can pay you."

"Oh, no, ma'am. *I mean, yes, ma'am.* Of course, ma'am. I understand, ma'am. You won't regret it." Olsen stood clumsily from the chair, as if she wanted to leave before Rosa could change her mind. "I *guarantee* it. I work hard and learn fast. You'll see."

"Good. Very good, child. I expect greatness from you. Don't let me down."

"No, ma'am. I won't, ma'am. *I will not.* Don't you worry. And... *Thanks again.* I'll see you tomorrow morning, okay. Bright and early." She slipped out of the room before Rosa could respond.

Rosa sighed. The time for pulling one or two people into the Family at a time was quickly passing, but it still carried with it a great sense of accomplishment, as if her own soul had reached out and changed the soul of another for the better. This even more than stopping the robots from ruining her own life was why she did what she did, why she stood up in front of the masses every day in the attempt to convince them of the reality of the worlds. This was why she loved her Family, and this was what she was created to do.

She smiled to herself, closed the ledger and put it away, and scribbled down the flood of slogans that had invaded her head. She was still scrawling them all through the notebook when the door opened and Anna sat in the chair across the desk from her. Rosa finished one more line before setting her pen down and looking up with a smile. "Hello dear," she said.

"Don't you hello dear, me," Anna said. "Well..."

"Well what?" Rosa asked.

"Well who was that who just left your office too happy to be alive?"

"Oh, uh... Her name's Olsen."

"And..."

"And she lost her job."

"Who hasn't in Five? So what did you tell her?"

"I, uh, well... I might have offered her a job."

"A job?"

"Just a little bit. Besides, she needed it, Anna. You didn't see the look on her face. I mean, she *is* a part of the Family, isn't she?"

"*Ugh.* The Family, the Family, the Family. What about your family, Rosa? What about me? What job did you even offer her?"

Rosa slunk back in her chair, getting as far from Anna as she could. "She wants to be a chef," she whispered.

"*Of course.*" Anna huffed. "And at what pay?"

Rosa slunk further back, almost losing sight of Anna over the desk. "Fifty tokens a week," she whispered.

"Fifty!"

"I—Yes, but I had t—"

"Where are we supposed to get fifty tokens a week, Rosa? Do you have any concept of money? You know we're already broke, don't you? If you don't start doing some fundraising with your little speeches, we won't have tokens to last through the next few days. So how do you propose we pay your new *chef* fifty tokens a week when we can barely support ourselves?"

"Our income has been growing exponentially," Rosa said, trying to stick up for herself a little bit.

"Yeah, from shit to a slightly bigger pile of shit that still doesn't cover our costs."

"But it will," Rosa said, sitting straighter in her chair. "*Soon.* If our income continues to grow. Won't it?" She stood from the desk and walked around behind Anna to massage her shoulders.

"*If* it does," Anna said.

Rosa could feel Anna's resistance dissolving under her fingers. "*When* it does, dear," she said. "And I know exactly the way to ensure that it never stops growing. Just you wait and see."

   ⅋   ✖   ⅋

XXV. Ansel

After three days now of it being no more than an elevator ride away, Ansel still wanted to brush her fingers through the cool grass she was kneeling in, but even the slightest movement would send her prey running. How long would that urge last?

She could hear Pidgeon's breathing behind her. In those same short days he had become a much better hunter. He only sounded like a human when he walked now, not a lumbering giant who was intentionally breaking every branch it walked by. His aim with the slingshot was getting better, too—he could take out a target set up on a branch, at least, even if he still couldn't sneak up close enough to anything living for him to be able to hit it—but that aim still wasn't anywhere near good enough to hit the target she had in sight.

She raised up the slingshot, arm muscles flexed solid with the effort of pulling the elastic band, and sighted along it to the eye of the giant, horned, four-legged beast, eating grass in the clearing in front of them. She heard Pidgeon hold his breath with her while she aimed, and when she thought he couldn't hold it any longer, she let go of the heavy rock, allowing the sling to hurl it toward her target.

The beast made a shrill bleating sound, shook its multi-pronged head, and ran in the opposite direction through the trees.

"Shit!" Ansel yelled, hitting the soft ground with a closed fist then taking the chance to ruffle the grass. "Shit, shit, shit."

"I thought you had it," Pidgeon said.

"Shut up, Pidgeon. What would you know?" She stood up and Pidgeon did the same. They were out in the woods they had first seen through the Scientist's office window. Surrounded by grass, trees, animals, and sky it would be easy to assume that Ansel had nothing in the world to worry about, but no matter how hard she tried, she couldn't enjoy herself. "You can't hit a pine cone from five feet away," she went on, taking her frustration out on Pidgeon.

"Well, I was just saying, I think you hit it." He plucked a needle off a nearby tree and tore it to bits. "I mean, didn't you see the way it shook its head and screamed like that?"

"Yes, Pidgeon." Ansel groaned. "Of course I did. I was the one who shot it. Did you think I had my eyes closed?"

"No. Well, of course not. But you did hit it, then. Didn't you?"

"I'm about to hit you if you don't shut up." She reared her hand up like she was going to do it.

"You don't have to be mean," Pidgeon said, tearing another needle to pieces. "I just thought that you might—"

"I know, I know," she said. "I need a bigger weapon. It was worth a shot, anyway. Wasn't it? Now c'mon. I'm getting hungry and it's about time for the Scientist to get off work. Let's go." She stuffed the slingshot in her back pocket and started the hike back to the elevator.

"I'm getting hungry, too," Pidgeon said, hurrying to keep up and getting back to his normal volume of walking.

One day, Ansel was going to run ahead of him and hide behind some bush to see if Pidgeon could find his own way back to the elevator—which was surprisingly difficult even for Ansel sometimes—or if he would get lost and cry alone in the forest. But right now, she didn't have the time. She had more important business to tend to. She chuckled aloud about the idea anyway.

"What?" Pidgeon asked through a huff of breath, tired from all the hiking.

"Nothing, Pidg. Watch your step on the root, though, we're almost there." As she said it, he tripped and fell into the grass, face-first. Ansel laughed. "I tried to warn ya."

"Yeah, whatever," Pidgeon said, brushing his knees off, red-faced. "Let's just get something to eat."

The elevator was hidden behind bushes and trees with vines growing all over it. Except for the metal doors, it looked like an old one-room wooden shack which had been left out to rot. When she had first gone out there with Rosalind and Huey, Rosalind laughed while Ansel tried to find some way to open those doors, prying at the crack between them with her fingers.

"Elevator open," Ansel said this time. She felt strange talking to an elevator, though, even if it did respond to her. The doors slid open to reveal a mirror-lined cube. Ansel and Pidgeon stepped in, and Ansel said, "Office. Or—er—*the lab*. Whatever." The doors closed, and the floor fell out from underneath them, forcing a surprised gasp out of Ansel. She still hadn't gotten used to elevator travel.

"This is so cool," Pidgeon said, unphased by the unnatural motion. "I still can't believe we're actually riding in one. It's just like the protectors' transport bays!"

Ansel shrugged. "It gets us from here to there," she said.

"Yes, well, how far is it between here and there though?" Pidgeon asked as the doors opened, revealing a short hall with a door at the end of it. "And look, we're already here. *Amazing*."

Ansel huffed and stomped down the hall. She pushed the door open to reveal an empty kitchen. "No!" she complained, stepping back into the hall and slamming the door. "How does this stupid thing work?"

"You just have to think about the room you want before you open it," Pidgeon said. "Here, like this." He opened the door and there was the kitchen again.

"I wanted the office," she said.

"Oh." Pidgeon closed the door and opened it to reveal the office. "Or you can just say the room out loud if that helps." He smiled.

"*Ugh*. Whatever." Ansel stomped past him, bumping his shoulder with hers as she did, into the spacious, high-ceilinged office. It was bigger than any house Ansel had ever lived in and lined with a soft carpet on top of which sat a desk and a few puffy chairs and side tables around a larger table. Sitting in two of the puffy chairs, looking out the ceiling-high, wall-length window onto the rolling hills and greenery that Ansel and Pidgeon had just come from, were Rosalind and Huey.

"Having more trouble, girl?" Rosalind asked, laughing, as Ansel struggled up onto one of the tall puffy chairs. Everything was made to Rosalind and Huey's size, and they were giants compared to anyone that Ansel had ever met. Well, except for Tom, of course, but she wasn't thinking about Tom anymore.

"I'm not a girl!" Ansel said when she had positioned herself comfortably on the seat.

"That's not what your boyfriend says." Rosalind laughed some more.

"I'm not her boyfriend!" Pidgeon said. He had chosen to sit on the floor with his back to everyone, leaning on one of the chairs to get the perfect view of the world outside the window.

"I say you're both in denial," Rosalind said. "Or at least one of you is."

"*I'm not a girl!*" Ansel repeated.

"Leave them alone, Roz," Huey said. "They're just children. Let them decide for themselves. They have plenty of time for it."

"Don't you Roz me, *Mr. Douglas*," Rosalind snapped, standing from her chair. "You really are getting to be too good at your job, you know. You won't even let me have the least bit of fun when we're at home. You're just like an owner these days." She stomped from the room.

"I apologize, children," Huey said, wiping his monocle with his handkerchief. "You shouldn't have to see that. It really is my fault, though. She's right, you know. I find it hard to come out of my character sometimes."

"Oh, no," Pidgeon said from behind his chair. "You've always been great to me. You brought me food that one time, remember? Speaking of which..."

"What do you do as an owner?" Ansel asked, scrunching up her nose. All she knew was that he wore tuxedos, top hats, and bow ties to go to Feasts—which she understood from experience to be a bunch of fat guys huddling up together in a giant circle and crying like babies.

"Oh, well, dear... That's a hard question to answer. I... Honestly, I don't do much but order Rosalind around, to tell you the truth. I think that's why she hates it so much."

"Well, no wonder," Ansel said.

"Yes, well, we can't change the roles we were given now, can we? It was easier for Rosalind to get close to Haley than it would have been for me, anyway. If the roles had been reversed, we might not have Haley with us today."

"That doesn't mean you have to treat Rosalind like you own her," Ansel said.

"Yes, well..." Huey thought about it for a second. "*No.* You're right about that. But I do have to treat her like I own her when I'm at work. That's why they call me an owner."

"Yeah, well, this isn't work. Is it?" Ansel said.

"No. You're right about that, too. But—"

"Then don't treat her like you own her," Ansel said. "Simple as that."

"I guess you're right, dear." Huey chuckled. "You're so wise for such a young gir—er—*child*."

"Yeah, well, I'm old for my age." Ansel crossed her arms. "Now where's the Scientist? We have some business to tend to."

"Oh, well." Huey shook his head, frowning. "I'm sure she's off with Haley somewhere, you know. You understand why, don't you?"

Ansel nodded. She understood that the Scientist was supposed to be Haley's mom, but she still didn't understand how someone so old could have given birth to someone so much younger and larger in comparison. "*Family stuff*," she said.

"Yes, but more than that dear," Huey said. "Haley was the Scientist's first born daughter. Those two have been separated for longer than you could imagine. So of course they're spending every second together."

"Right." Ansel shrugged. She still thought it was creepy that such an old lady was supposed to be Haley's mom, though. But they could believe whatever it was they wanted to believe. It was their life, after all, not hers. "So, do you know when they'll be back?" she asked.

"Oh, there's no telling," Huey said, shaking his head and frowning some more. "They left hours ago, but who knows how long they'll be gone for. Like I said, they've been separated for longer than you could imagine."

"*Ugh*." Ansel sighed. Maybe she shouldn't be trusting this *Scientist* after all. Ansel really had no idea who the woman was. She was probably lying like everyone else. Ansel knew that the Scientist was too sure of herself, and it was probably to hide the fact that she had no way of actually getting Ansel's dad back. But if she didn't, then who did? Pidgeon was still trying to get her to go back to Anna and Rosa for help, but Ansel trusted them less than anyone, so that wasn't an option at all. Which only left Tom. Who was God knows where. And even if Ansel knew where he was, how was she supposed to get to him? No, Tom was a last resort at best. She had to count on the Scientist to be true to her word for now and hope it didn't come to the Hail Mary after all.

"You know what we should do while we wait," Pidgeon said, standing up from the view. "We should get something to eat."

"You always want to eat, Pidgeon."

"Hey, you just said you were hungry, too."

"Yeah, well, I guess…" She looked at Huey.

"Oh, no," he said, waving his hands. "You two go ahead. Order anything you want. You know how it works, right?"

"*Oh, yeah*," Pidgeon cheered, jumping up from his seat on the floor and looking to Ansel for confirmation.

Ansel shrugged. "Whatever."

"Let's do it!" Pidgeon rushed to the door and ran out into the hall. Ansel took her time getting there, though, and when she was, Pidgeon closed the door and opened it right up to the kitchen. Pidgeon ran to put the stepstool the Scientist had made for them under the 3D printer then stood back and said, "So what you gonna get?" He was smiling and looking back and forth between Ansel and the machine. He looked like he was going to burst into laughter, or cry, or both at the same time. But Ansel could only stare past him, out the window above the sink, looking out onto those lines and lines of people doing who knows what. It was so weird to have that in a kitchen, she thought, but no one else even seemed to notice.

"Well?" Pidgeon asked again, proving her point and breaking her away from the strange view out the sink window.

"Uh, I don't know." Ansel shrugged. In the few days that they had been there, Pidgeon had ordered more kinds of food than Ansel knew existed, but every time she stood in front of the printer, Ansel had trouble deciding what she wanted. Her mind kept going back to the one thing it seemed to want to think about: how to get her dad back, but the printer couldn't give her that.

"Well, you have to pick something," Pidgeon said. "You can choose anything you want, Ansel. *Anything*. But it won't give it to you until you ask."

"I don't care," she said, stepping up onto the stool and pressing the 3D printer's little red voice activation button. "Lunch," she said, and again she cringed at talking to a robot.

"*Lunch*?" Pidgeon groaned as a sandwich and a bowl of soup popped out of the printer's big hatch.

"A sliced meat sandwich *and* soup," Ansel said, taking it to the shorter table they had set up in the kitchen for the kids to eat at. "Now that's a meal." She took a big bite of the sandwich—turkey—and savored the taste.

"*Bor—ing*," Pidgeon said, stepping up onto the stool. "You have anything you can imagine at your fingertips, and you ask for lunch, you let the printer decide for you. Well, not me, you see. I hold my fate in my own hands. And I choose..."

He tapped his chin as Ansel dipped the sandwich in the soup and took a soggy bite. "This is good," she said. "You should try some."

"No. *No*... I want..." He pressed the voice activation button. "Chicken! And spaghetti. No, *chicken spaghetti*. And cheesecake with ice cream. The ice cream on top!"

The food kept coming as he talked. By the time the machine was done printing, he was carrying a tray of chicken, spaghetti, chicken spaghetti, cheesecake, ice cream, and cheesecake with ice cream on top to the table. Ansel thought he should have taken two trips, and he almost lost the tray on the way, but he made it to the table with everything intact, breathing heavily and eyes wide at the piles of food. "You're gonna have to help me with this," he said as he set to eating.

"No I'm not," Ansel said, finishing her own meal. "But I will anyway." She took the ice cream and started in on it.

Pidgeon was still eating, and Ansel was staring in awe at how much he could put down, when Haley came into the kitchen.

"Oh, hello," Haley said, curtsying with a smile then walking over to the printer. "How was your day?"

Ansel stood from the table as soon as she heard Haley's voice. "You're home," she said.

"We just got back. We were going to eat some lunch. Do you two want anything?"

"Where's the Scientist?" Ansel demanded.

"She's in the office. I was jus—"

"Thanks." Ansel rushed out of the kitchen into the hall. She closed the door and opened it but still got the kitchen. "Shit," she said, closing it and opening it to the kitchen a second time. "Shit shit shit." After a few more tries, she finally said, "Office." and the door opened to the room she wanted.

The Scientist was sitting on one of the puffy chairs, looking out onto the view. "I love this view," she said, turning around. "*Oh*. It's you. I thought you were Haley."

"Yeah," Ansel said, climbing into a chair. "It's me. Don't

sound so let down."

"Oh, no, dear. I didn't mean to—"

"When are we going to get my dad out?"

"Yes, well… About that, dear." The Scientist looked out the window again, avoiding eye contact with Ansel. "It's only been a few days, you know. These things take time."

"Every day we waste is another day closer to them taking him from me, just like they did with my mom. I don't have time."

"Yes, dear." The Scientist shook her head. "I mean, no. Well, that would be true if it wasn't. You see, we've got their computers confused. They're not sure if he's in prison or not right now. That buys us the time we need to determine the most efficient method of breaking him out."

"But what happens when they realize he is there? What then?"

"By then we'll have him out, you see. I assure you, dear. These things take time to be put properly into motion, but the balls are rolling and it's picking up steam. I promise you that."

"I don't know," Ansel said, shaking her head. "That's hard to believe with what I've been through."

"I know it is, dear. But you have to believe we're doing everything we—"

The door opened and in came Haley, pushing a cart stacked high with more food than Ansel had ever seen in one place.

"Oh, dear," the Scientist said. "You didn't have to go through all that. A sandwich and some soup would have done just fine."

"Yes, well," Haley said, stacking the food on the table until Ansel couldn't see the Scientist's face anymore. "I couldn't decide what I wanted so I ordered a little bit of everything. The printer doesn't do a little bit of anything, though, so here we are." She sat down and started in on some of the food.

"So when do you think we *will* get him?" Ansel asked. "My dad."

"What's that?" Haley asked, chewing on some food Ansel didn't recognize.

"Oh, nothing, dear," the Scientist said. "*And soon,*" she added for Ansel. "Within the week. I promise."

"Within the week what?" Haley asked.

"Within the week your *mom*," Ansel said, "will finally get

my dad back—like she promised."

"Oh, right," Haley said. "On Christmas Feast Day. Where is he anyway?"

"The protectors took him," Ansel said.

"Oh, well, that's easy. Just tell them to—oh wait... I don't work for Lord Walker anymore." She frowned.

"No," the Scientist said. "*You don't*. And you should be glad for that. And we'll get your father out in due time, Ansel dear. *Without* asking the protectors for permission. I promise you that. You just have to wait until the time is right. Your dad's not the only political prisoner we'll want to free if we're going in there, so we want to make sure we have everything planned to the last detail."

"Yeah, but—" Ansel started, but Haley cut her off.

"Here, Mom. Try this," she said, holding out a plate to the Scientist, and it was still odd for Ansel to hear her call the old lady Mom.

Ansel huffed and stomped out of the room. They weren't going to listen to her. The Scientist had her *daughter* and she didn't care about anything else anymore. She was going to be no help in getting Ansel's dad back, and that was clearer than ever. All she had been doing was distracting Ansel, and Ansel had lost too many days because of it.

She slammed the hall door closed behind her, and when she opened it again, she got the kitchen on the first try. The lines of workers were still doing whatever it is they did through the sink window, and Pidgeon was still eating at the table, though the pile of food in front of him had gotten considerably smaller.

"Oh, Ansel," he groaned when she walked in and sat at the table across from him. "You have to help me with this. I can't bring myself to throw any of it away."

Ansel looked at what he had left on the table. It was mostly chicken and spaghetti or chicken spaghetti. "No," she said, shaking her head and crinkling up her nose. "I have more important things to discuss."

"*Oghm—noghm—ugh*. What could be more important than this right now?"

"My dad, Pidgeon. The only thing I care about. *Remember*."

"Yeah, well." He set his fork on the plate with a clank and leaned back in his chair, unbuttoning his pants. "What are you gonna do about it?"

"I don't know. But I have to do something, don't I? I can't sit here and wait anymore."

"Okay, but what are *you* going to do? I mean, unless you plan on taking the elevator to wherever the protectors are, but that would be stupid. You know what they're like now, don't you?"

"There has to be something I can do, Pidgeon. I know there does."

"What about Rosa and—"

"No! I told you. I won't work with them. You weren't there, Pidgeon. They convinced Tom to kill someone in my name. I never asked anyone to kill anyone, okay. And I won't ask anyone who has for help."

"Yeah, well, I know they can help you, Ansel. They can do the same thing the Scientist can but without elevators. How else do you think you're gonna get him out?"

"I don't know. But I think I have a plan."

"Oh yeah?" Pidgeon took a slow, groggy bite from the pile of chicken spaghetti in front of him. It must have been a third or fourth wind for him by now. "And what's that?" he asked through a full mouth.

"*Tom.*"

Pidgeon dropped his fork. "You can't be serious."

Ansel nodded. "He's the only other person I know who can get through."

"Ansel, *he* killed your mom. *He* killed that person at the Feast. I mean, you won't work with Rosa and Anna when they asked him to do it, why will you work with him when he literally did it?"

"It's not the same," Ansel said. "*They* made him do it. It wasn't his idea. He wanted to protect me. They're the ones that twisted it."

"I keep trying to tell you, *they're* the ones that have the ability to help you. Not Tom. He admitted as much."

"Well, I have to try, don't I? I have to do something. I'm not going to sit here and wait for the Scientist to decide when the time's right."

"Yeah, well, I don't think it's a good idea."

"Yeah, well, I don't care what you think." She stood and stomped out of the kitchen into the hallway. Who was Pidgeon to say anything? He had no idea what she was going through. She would find a way to get her dad back no matter what.

She opened the hall door to find Rosalind, sitting behind a lab table, surrounded by glassware that was filled with various colored liquids. She was playing cards at an emptied table with the big mechanical arm they called Popeye.

"I see you creepin', girl," Rosalind said. "Come on in or get on out."

Ansel walked up to the table and watched as Rosalind and Popeye pick up cards and laid them down at what looked to be random.

"Alright, girl," Rosalind said. "Spit it out. What do you want?"

"I'm not a girl."

"Whatever. Tell me what you want or leave. Popeye and I were enjoying ourselves before you came along to interrupt us."

Ansel looked at the mechanical arm, who was still intent on the card game she could somehow tell. "How does it know what cards it has without any eyes?" she asked.

"Is that what you came here for?" Rosalind replied. "A lesson on the anatomy of Popeye?"

The metal arm waved at Ansel as if it were excited for the prospect.

"No—I—No…" Ansel shook her head, shuddering.

"I didn't think so. So spit it out then."

Ansel hesitated. This was a Hail Mary if there ever was one, and she wasn't sure it was time to throw it up just yet, but she really had no other choice except for doing nothing, and that wasn't a choice at all.

"It's about my dad," she said.

"*You don't say.*" Rosalind chuckled. "Is the Scientist taking a little too long for your liking?"

"Yeah, well, I have my own plan."

"Your own plan, huh?" Rosalind laughed, laying a card on the table. "Did you hear that, Popeye? *Her own plan.* Well then. Out with it. What is this plan of yours?"

Ansel blushed. She was afraid to share it now, but she wasn't about to let that stop her. "I want to see Tom," she said

"Tom?" Rosalind set all her cards on the table, finally intent on what Ansel was saying.

"Tom," Ansel repeated. "You know who I'm talking about. The protector who I gave you information on. I want to talk to him."

"*Ohhh. Tom*," Rosalind said, nodding. "You mean the man who shot my sister?"

"Your sister?"

"*Haley.*"

"Oh, yeah. Well... I know he—"

"And why would you want see this *Tom*?"

"I don't know. I just... I think he can help me get my dad back."

"And you don't think the Scientist is going to do that?"

"I—I just can't sit here and do nothing anymore."

"And you're sure this is what you want to do instead of nothing?"

"I—I don't know. I think so. *Yes*."

"There might be something I can do for you, then."

⸚   ❖   ⸙

XXVI. Jonah

Jonah kneeled on the rough concrete, counting in his head how many shots had been fired at him so far. He chanced a quick peek around the dumpster and was greeted with a hail of gunfire. He glimpsed his partner, his best friend, the one person he was assigned to protect in this sick game called life, laying on the ground in front of the dumpster, surrounded by a sticky thick pool of red. She had taken the shots that would have finished him, and now it was his responsibility to ensure her actions weren't in vain.

He checked his ammo. *Seven shots*. Lucky number seven. There couldn't be more than that many of the thugs out there so there was still some chance—however small. All he had to do was hit his target with every shot he took while simultaneously avoiding every bullet they lobbed back at him. *Piece of cake*. He chuckled. His heart beat faster in anticipation. He took a few deep breaths to ready himself, set his sights on another dumpster a few yards ahead, and jumped into motion.

He did a cartwheel out from behind his cover, staying below the onslaught of bullets, and scratched his back on the concrete in the process. He could feel the breeze blowing past from the missed shots. He caught the hint of movement out of the corner of his eye and fired in that direction, tumbling behind the next dumpster without looking to see if he had hit his mark.

He rubbed his shoulder and could feel the blood, but that's all it was, thank Amaru. He took off his blue masked helmet and wiped the sweat from his forehead. This was it. There were five or six of them left, and he had to do something about it or go down in a pathetic laughable whimper. A whimper was unacceptable.

He held his empty helmet up over the dumpster and a few shots rang out. He popped up and knocked off two rounds without his helmet on—not regulation at all, but he was in a bind—hitting both targets, then dropped back down behind the dumpster, breathing heavily and shoving his helmet back on. It was now or never.

He rolled out from behind the dumpster, doing the same cartwheel roll as before, and as he stood, he felt a piercing pain in his chest. He looked down to see his blue vest splattered with bright red. He touched it with his hand, rubbing the sticky goo between his fingers, and fell to his knees. This was the end.

Two red-vested, red-helmeted kids came out from behind their own dumpsters on the other side of the alley, cheering and raising their guns over their heads. The dead bodies scattered around Jonah started to rustle and move. Those that were dressed in red and splattered with blue joined in the cheering. Those who were dressed in blue and splattered with red took off their helmets and hung their heads in shame. Liz, his partner and friend who was lying in the pool of red paint earlier, walked over to him, patted him on the back, and lifted him to his feet. Jonah flinched as she did, a fresh wave of pain emanating from the wound on his back, which he had only made worse with his second roll move.

"It's alright," Liz said, brushing his pants off for him. "You did your best."

"I hate being the last one out," Jonah said with a groan. "It's worse than being first. People always think you're a coward and you just hung back while your whole team died."

"No they don't—well... *I* don't think that," Liz said, guiding him by the arm back toward the locker room.

"*Of course you don't,*" Jonah complained, shrugging and walking as slowly as he could. "But you don't count."

Liz dropped his hand, straightened up, and hurried to the locker room ahead of him, disappearing before he could ask her what he had done wrong.

Jonah took his time, though, letting the entire team go in before him. Even if Liz didn't think he was a coward, he knew that everyone else would and that he would hear all about it while he was changing. It was a lose-lose situation for him, though. The longer he waited to go into the locker room, the more of a coward he looked like and the worse those jerks would be. His heartbeat quickened in preparation, but he took a few deep breaths to calm it and slowly slipped into the door.

The entire room, tile, lockers, walls, and all, was stark white. Everyone had already started changing out of their red-speckled uniforms, stuffing them irreverently into their lockers and vying for the best showers. Jonah walked up to his locker, right next to Liz's, as she slammed hers shut and stomped to a shower without looking at him.

He tried to keep his eyes on his own locker as he pressed his thumb to the locking mechanism. He got out his blue jeans, white t-shirt, towel, and soap and stripped to his underwear, stuffing his uniform into his locker. He breathed a sigh of relief when the warm water poured over him and he hadn't had to hear a single word about his performance, then he winced in pain at the burn from the scrapes on his shoulders and back.

He washed himself then dried and dressed in the peace of the shower stall. When he opened the curtains, Stine was sitting on the bench in front of her locker—which was on the other side of his locker from Liz's—with her group of lackeys hanging on her every word. He had to push his way through them to get to his locker. "Excuse me," he said as he did, keeping his eyes on his locker's locking mechanism as he tried to press his trembling thumb to it.

"*Whale Bait*," Stine said loud enough for the whole room to hear. "Good show out there. Are you planning on becoming a tumbler in Outland Three when you grow up?"

The room burst into laughter. Stine high-fived a few of her lackeys as Jonah stuffed his towel and soap inside his locker.

"You know I saw your girlfriend take that bullet for you, too, Plankton," Stine went on. "She's worth more than you are out there, you got it? You should be the one taking bullets for her, not the other way around."

Jonah slammed his locker door. "No shit, Stine. *Amaru up above*. Where were you out there, though? Your suit's got red paint on it just like everyone else's."

The room quieted, and her lackeys looked to Stine for a witty retort.

"I fell over laughing when you did your somersaults," she lied. "It left me defenseless. I didn't know they let carnies into the Protectors Academy. Shouldn't you be in Outland Three with the rest of them?" Her and her lackeys all laughed and high-fived each other at the same joke told over again in so short a time.

Jonah ignored them as best he could, though, stomping out of the locker room, wishing he hadn't closed his locker already so he could slam it again. Outside, Liz was tying her shoes under the building's awning. He knew it wasn't a coincidence, too. It was an excuse to wait for him without waiting for him. "Hey," he said, walking up to her.

"Hey," she echoed back, standing and making her way with him down the sidewalk, between the empty patches of field which were filled with oak trees to shade their path. "How was it in there?" she asked when they had gone a way in the cool, silent afternoon air.

"Would've been nice to have some backup," he said.

"*I thought I didn't matter.*"

Jonah sighed. Of course that was what she was mad about: his stupid choice of words. "No. I didn't mean that. I—"

"Those were your exact words," she said. "And I quote, *Of course you don't. But you don't count.* end quote."

"Do you ever forget anything?" Jonah groaned.

"That was like twenty minutes ago, Jonah. How soon do you expect me to forget?"

"Yeah, well, that's not what I meant, okay. And you know it."

"Then what did you mean?"

"I...Well..." What did he mean? "I meant that—you know—well, it's just that you... *Liz*. It's just that, the protective person you are, you're always on my side. Right? You always want to protect me. So even if I *was* acting like a coward and you *did* take a bullet for me, you wouldn't say so because you wouldn't want to hurt my feelings. Yeah—*uh*—that's it... That's what I meant."

Liz smiled. "You didn't act like a coward," she said. "You run a little faster than I do. I happened to be behind you when the shot was fired. It wasn't your fault."

"Like I said," Jonah said. "*You* may think so, but Stine and her crew don't agree. And they were sure to let me know what they thought of my performance while you were out here tying your shoes."

"Well who cares what they say? They're idiots."

They walked some more in silence, passing expansive yards and cookie-cutter ranch style houses. The serene boredom of Outland One—the least dangerous world of them all, even before Inland—was enough to make Jonah want to pass out.

"So, you wanna hang out at my place or something?" he asked. He didn't usually have to, but recently, his home life had changed.

"Is your dad gonna be there?" Liz asked right back, scrunching up her nose and giggling.

"Yeah, well, of course," Jonah said. "He does the housework now. You know that."

"But he'll be wearing two shoes this time, right?" She laughed outright now instead of just giggling.

"Now that was one time," Jonah complained, embarrassed. "And he had been through a lot. At least that's what Mom says." He shook his head.

"Why isn't he a protector anymore anyway?" Liz asked, looking sheepish when she did. She had asked him the same question before, and she had to know by now what his answer was going to be, but she went on anyway. "I mean, what happened to him?"

"I don't know!" Jonah snapped, stopping in his tracks. They were getting close to his house anyway. "*I don't know. I don't know. I don't know.* And asking me again won't change that. *Okay.*"

"I—uh—well, I'm—"

"*Look.* If you wanna know so badly, then why don't you come over to my house and ask him for yourself? Maybe he'll tell you."

"I couldn't do that," she said. "I mean, have *you* even asked him?"

"Of course I've…" Jonah thought about it for a second. His mom had told him not to ask his dad about it. Maybe he hadn't. He wouldn't defy an order from his mother. "I mean, that is, I think I have," he said. "*Yeah.* I have."

"You haven't. Have you?"

"I think I did. Well, maybe not…"

She hit him on the arm. "*You haven't.*"

He rubbed his arm even though it didn't hurt. "Thanks a lot," he said. "You know I scraped up my back today rolling around on the concrete trying to get us a win for once."

"Well that wasn't your back."

"Still, it was the same side. It hurts." He tried to put on a pained face, but it probably just came off constipated like Liz always told him it did.

"Yeah, well, you haven't asked your dad what happened to him, have you?"

"No, well, I never got a chance, you know. He's always going off on those rants about conspiracy theories and red herrings and how I can't believe anything anyone tells me. I just want to shake him and tell him that what he's saying means I can't believe him either, but my mom ordered me not to ask him about it so what am I supposed to do?" He was breathing heavily because he had delivered the entire rant in a single breath.

"Yeah, well, you can't disobey your mom I guess." Liz shrugged.

"Exactly," Jonah said. "So how was I supposed to ask him?" He grinned, confident that he had won the argument and they could go inside to eat something and relax a little after that beating during the standoff.

"Well, do you even care?" Liz asked. Of course she could carry any argument in the worlds on just a little bit further.

"What do you mean?" he replied. "Of course I care. He is my dad, isn't he?"

"I know you care about your dad, but do you even want to know what happened to him? I mean, *he got fired*, Jonah. That's a pretty big deal, you know. It probably had a big effect on him."

Jonah thought about it. His dad would never be a protector again. He had only gotten to be an actual protector for about a day. Jonah couldn't imagine how that would feel, living his dream for one day then having it torn away forever. Maybe he would go crazy and rant about red herrings, too. He certainly wouldn't put up with Stine and her locker room buddies, that was for sure. "I don't know," he said. "I guess I never thought about it that way."

"That's exactly what I'm talking about!" She hit him again but softer this time, more of a pat. He rubbed his arm anyway. "You didn't even think about it!"

"Yeah, well, even if I had thought about it, I still couldn't disobey my mom's orders, could I? So what am I supposed to do, huh?"

"No." Liz smiled. "*You* can't do that. That's true. But your mom never ordered me to do anything, did she?"

Jonah shook his head. "You've got to be kidding me."

"C'mon," she said, grabbing his hand and skipping toward his house. "What are partners for, anyway? You'll thank me when he answers."

"No," he said, skipping along hand-in-hand with her. "You'll be sorry when he does. You'll see."

They didn't stop until they got to the covered porch of what looked like the exact same house as every one they had passed on their way there.

"Now," Jonah said before he opened the door. "I have to warn you, he's been extra weird today, so know that anything he expresses are his views and his views alone and I in no way support or deny any of them."

"*Amaru*, you sound like a TV show," she said.

"Yeah, well, I learned the whole bit from TV." Jonah grinned. "Pretty good, huh?"

Liz chuckled.

"Anyway," Jonah went on. "I'm serious, okay. Don't ask him about it right away. Let's play it cool and see what he's acting like, then I'll give you the signal or something."

She laughed. "I'm not a complete social reject," she said. "I've got more tact than you'll ever have. Just open the door and let's get on with it."

Jonah opened the door to find his dad on hands and knees on the beige Berber carpet in the foyer, wearing a pink apron and yellow rubber gloves, scrubbing the walls with a sponge. He looked up when they came in, dropped his sponge in the bucket with a splash, and stood to hug Jonah with wet, antiseptic-scented hands. "Welcome home, son," he said.

"*Uh, hey Dad*," Jonah said, squirming away from the soggy hug. "You know Liz."

"Liz, dear," his dad said, hugging her too. "So nice to see you again."

"And you, Mr. Pardy," Liz said, wiping some suds from her shirt. "Your apron is lovely."

Jonah's dad looked down at himself, took off his apron, and said, "You kids go find something to watch on TV and I'll fix you up a delicious snack in no time flat."

Jonah shrugged. When his dad had gone into the kitchen, he looked at Liz and said, "See, I told you."

"He seemed nice," she said, shrugging back. "And supportive. He didn't seem that bad to me."

"Yeah, well, just you wait and see."

The living room was lined with the same beige Berber carpet as the hall, and the leather couch matched the color of the carpet perfectly. There were gun and news magazines on the coffee table and a TV on the wall across the room.

"TV on," Jonah said, plopping onto the couch and kicking off his shoes. "The Greatest Mouse Detective or Protector Time?" he asked.

"I don't care," Liz said, joining him on the couch but leaving her shoes on. "You decide."

"Protector Time it is. TV, Protector Time," he said. "Biological!" he yelled, putting his fist in the air as Liz giggled.

The TV flipped to a cartoon about a little girl and her pet cat who could grow and shrink at will. In each episode, which really consisted of two sub-episodes, the girl and the cat would get into all kinds of adventures, the moral of which always ended up being the protection of property, liberty, and life.

In this particular episode, the girl and cat combo were fighting to save the Smooth Terra Prince from an evil fire witch when they lost their ice wands and were left to decide between using the fire witch's own lava wand against her or facing certain defeat with no defense. Just as their arguing ended and the cat convinced the girl that using the fire witch's weapon was wrong—that you couldn't fight fire with lava—a volcano erupted, sweeping the red witch away in a wave of lava and melting the glacier the girl and the cat were standing on, leaving the girl to use the cat as a surfboard to ride the resulting wave in the other direction, toward the party in Vegetable Kingdom which they were already late for anyway.

"Oh, *ho ho*, that was *biological*," Jonah said as the screen faded to a long line of commercials—mostly thanking the protectors for their service, with a few ads for housekeepers sprinkled in between. "But I would have definitely used that fire wand. They were stupid to stand there arguing while they were defenseless."

"Would you though?" Liz asked. "I mean, like Jackie said: You can't fight fire with lava."

"Yeah, well, tell that to the volcano that saved their lives. If Phillis had just picked up the wand and used it, they would have been out of there and at the party in time, no volcano needed."

"Or they would have been stranded without the knowledge that they could melt the iceberg and surf home. It's the unintended consequences that mess things up," Liz said, crossing her arms and shaking her head.

"Yeah, well, it would have melted anyway. *I'm sure*." Jonah crossed his arms.

Liz probably would have argued further, but Jonah's dad came in, carrying a tray and wearing the pink apron again. "Here you are kids," he said. "I didn't know what you wanted so I brought a little of everything. Pizza bagels, pizza rolls, pizza slices. Pretty much your whole pizza food group there. We have some fish sticks, chicken nuggets, sausages in a—"

"Okay, dad," Jonah said. "*Thanks*. We get it. The next episode is about to come on, though. So…"

"Thank you, Mr. Pardy," Liz said, grabbing a pizza roll.

"What are you watching?" Jonah's dad asked, sitting on the couch between them and eating one of the pizza rolls himself.

"Protector Time," Liz said "Have you ever seen it?"

"Uh, it's nothing," Jonah said. "Just a cartoon. It's for kids anyway. You wouldn't like it."

"Protector Time?" his dad said. "Is that the one with the little girl and the cat?"

"Phillis and Jackie," Liz said.

"Oh, I watched an episode of that cartoon while Jonah—or, while you both were at school, I guess," he said. "I like that Phillis."

"Jackie's my favorite," Liz said. "I wish I could grow big like that." She sat up straight and puffed out her cheeks, raising her arms to make herself look bigger.

"I think you grew a little bit," Jonah's dad said, laughing.

Liz huffed out all the air she was holding in and laughed with him.

"Alright, alright," Jonah said. "The next episode's about to come on. Quiet down you two."

They stifled their laughter but couldn't stop it entirely until the theme song was over. In this half-episode, Phillis and Jackie were going to a party in Smooth Terra Land with the Smooth Terra Prince when all the snacks and drinks for the party—all three of them watching at home ate some more pizza at the mention of snacks—were stolen by the Angors from Exic Space. When they entered Exic Space to get the food back and save the Smooth Terra Prince's party, Phillis and Jackie found the Angors all looking sickly, skinny, and weak, as if they hadn't eaten a real meal ever. And when they finally found the Smooth Terra Prince's food, they couldn't dare take it back from these people who so obviously needed it more than the Smooth Terra Land party did.

"I'm not doing it," Phillis said, crossing her heart on the screen. "We were sworn to protect life and that includes the life of Angors."

"No," Jackie said. "We were sworn to protect property, liberty, and life, dude. Besides, look." She pointed into the crowd of Angors at a particular one who looked healthier than the rest. Not only healthy, this Angor was downright fat. And as it ate and ate from the pile of party supplies, it grew skinnier and skinnier. Soon Jackie made Phillis realize what was going on, and they took up arms to return the party food to its rightful owners then joined in the Smooth Terra Prince's celebration.

"*Dude*," Jonah said, "Those Angors suck."

"Don't say that," his dad said.

"I don't know," Liz said. "Property, liberty, life and all, sure, but that one Angor was hungry, wasn't he?"

"*Exactly*," Jonah's dad said.

"*Pssshhh.*" Jonah scoffed. "*Property*, liberty, life," he said. "You know that. You can't steal what other people own. You might as well own their body like they're a robot or something. Are you saying that any time I'm hungry I can just steal whatever you have?"

"*No*," Liz said.

"When you're hungry you can get whatever you want from the printer," Jonah's dad said.

"Yeah, well, *I own that printer*," Jonah said.

"You don't own anything," Liz said. "You're a kid."

"*I* own that printer," Jonah's dad said. "Me and your mother."

"Yeah, well, you know what I mean," Jonah said. "They didn't own the food. It was for the party. It doesn't matter if they were hungry or not because it's not theirs."

"But what harm did it do?" Liz asked. "The one fat guy ate some to get skinny like all the rest of them, but then there was plenty of food still left over for the party, and none of the Smooth Terra people even noticed any was missing."

"*Yeah*," Jonah said. "But there *was* some missing. And

Phillis and Jackie had to bring it back or there would have been *more* missing, wouldn't there? I mean, what did you want them to do? Just leave all the food there and forget about the party?"

"No," Jonah's dad said.

"They should have invited the Angors to the party," Liz said.

"It was their food, they could do whatever they want with it," Jonah said.

"But they weren't going to eat it anyway so why not share?" Liz asked.

"Alright, alright now," Jonah's dad said. "It's just a cartoon, kids."

"Yeah, well, it has a purpose," Liz said.

"I guess," Jonah said, shrugging.

"Okay," his dad said, eating a few more pizza rolls. "That's enough. Do you kids need anything else? I might get back to cleaning the walls here. You'd be surprised at how dirty they can get."

"No, Dad," Jonah said. "I think we're good."

"Well, sir," Liz said, looking at Jonah who tried—and failed—to tell her to shut up without his dad seeing. "There *is* one thing."

"Oh, well go ahead dear," his dad said. "Anything for a friend of Jonah's. A friend of my son's is a friend of mine."

"Well, it's just—"

"No, Dad. I think—" Jonah tried to cut her off but couldn't.

"You used to be a protector, right?"

"Yes, well..." Jonah's dad said, moving some of the food around on the table. "I *used to be*. Yes."

"Question answered," Jonah said, standing from the couch. "You wanna go hang out outside for a while?" He jerked his head toward the door to try to feed Liz the answer.

"Just a second, Jonah," she said in a huff then looked back to his dad and smiled. "Mr. Pardy, sir. What happened? I mean, why did they—why did they..."

"Why did they fire me?" Jonah's dad asked for her.

Jonah's eyes grew wide. He tried to imagine how his dad would react to the question he had asked himself. His mom had to have ordered Jonah not to ask about it for good reason. She wouldn't have given him a random order without a care as to whether he followed it or not. But he didn't break this one, right? He hadn't asked anything. He sat slowly back on the couch, staring at his dad on the way down, waiting for a response.

"Yes, sir," Liz said. "Why can't you be a protector?" she added as if she didn't even want to say the word "fired" again.

"Well..." His dad looked at Jonah. He threw one of the pizza rolls onto the tray then picked it up and threw it on again. He was deciding something in his head. "Your mom doesn't want me talking to you about it," he finally said, looking at Jonah.

"Yeah." Jonah shrugged. "Well I'm under strict orders not to ask you about it myself."

"So that's why your girlfriend was doing the dirty work." Jonah's dad smiled at the both of them. "A loophole in the chain of command. I like it."

"She's not my girlfriend!" Jonah complained. "She's my partner."

"Excuse me, sir?" Liz said, clearly surprised at what Jonah's dad was saying. Jonah had warned her to beware of red herring conspiracies, but he guessed that hearing it straight from the horse's mouth was a little different.

"That's right," his dad said, smiling wider. "What did you expect from me? A lecture on following orders?" He chuckled.

"*I* sure didn't," Jonah said.

"No, well," Liz said, "I don't know. Aren't grownups supposed to teach us to respect the chain of command?"

"Yes, well, that's what they would have you believe," Jonah's dad said. "That's what their entire system is based on. That's why it's all you learn in school and why your parents and all the other *grownups* don't know anything else to teach you."

"So they're—or I guess *you're* just following orders when you tell us to follow orders?" Liz said.

"*Exactly*," Jonah's dad said, clapping his hands together. "And worded more eloquently than I could have ever put it."

Liz giggled and smiled. "I think I'm getting it, but—"

"Getting it?" Jonah said, angry for some reason he didn't quite understand. "What is there to get? It's all nonsense. Nonsense, nonsense, nonsense is all you've talked about ever since you got home, Dad. It's getting ridiculous. Maybe it's time for *you* to grow up." He sneered and grabbed one of the pizza bagels.

"Jonah!" Liz cried. She probably would have hit him if his dad wasn't sitting between them. "Don't talk to your dad like that!"

"No," his dad said. "It's alright. He's right, you know. You're right." He looked Jonah in the eyes, and Jonah turned his head to get away from the awkwardness. "I know I've been talking nonsense. I wanted to tell you everything I've learned, but your mother didn't want me talking to you about it. She thinks I'm crazy, too. So everything I tried to say to you come out as gibberish. I'm sorry."

Jonah shrugged and grabbed another pizza bagel. "*Whatever*," he said, still chewing. "I just thought you went crazy because you lost your job. I probably would if I could never be a protector again."

"Jonah!" This time Liz did reach across his dad to slap him.

"What?" Jonah complained, rubbing his arm. "*It's true.*"

His dad sighed and looked off toward the TV—which was off now—as if he were daydreaming. "No," he said. "He's right again. You know, my dad had to give up protecting for housework when my mother—your grandmother—was killed in the line of duty. He was never the same after that. He would—He—" His dad chuckled, and Jonah felt a tugging at his stomach as he realized that his father had been a kid once, too. He had his own dad and mom who ordered him around and his own dreams for the future, probably the same dreams that Jonah had of becoming a legendary protector who was renowned across all seven worlds for being fearless in the face of injustice, dreams which were all but impossible for his dad now. Jonah was starting to understand why Liz hit him earlier.

"The old man," his dad went on, "he set up a neighborhood watch because he didn't want to leave raising me to some *cowardly housekeeper*, as he always put it. Of course there was never any crime living in One, but that didn't stop us from patrolling up and down the neighborhood every night as he trained me in everything a good protector should know."

"How sweet," Liz said with a smile and a tear in her eye.

"What does any of that have to do with why you got fired?" Jonah asked.

"Nothing," his dad said. "Nothing... Well, *everything*, you know. What he taught me then shaped everything I've done up until now, everything I will do in the future. I got fired because I was following his teachings. I was being the protector he always wanted me to be, the protector I thought could be a role model for you, Jonah. But now I'm no protector at all, and I never will be one again."

"I'm so sorry," Liz said. Her eyes were red and she looked like she was about to cry.

"It's my own fault," Jonah's dad said. "Well, no, it was my choice. That's different. It was the system's fault and my choice to go against it to do what I thought my dad—and you, Jonah—would want me to do."

"I wouldn't want you to get fired," Jonah snapped, defensive because he felt like his dad was trying to blame *him* for something he obviously had nothing to do with. "What kind of example does that set?"

"Would you want me to protect a little girl that needs protecting, or would you want me to leave her to fend for herself?" his dad asked. "Which example would you set for your son?"

"Of course I would protect her," Jonah said. "So what?"

"Is that why you got fired?" Liz asked. "Protecting her?"

"Yes and no. I thought I was protecting her, but I don't know anymore. I think I might have jumped from one authority to another without realizing that they both could be wrong. And that's what you have to understand, Jonah. And you, too." He looked at Liz. "You're his partner. You've gotta have his back in all of this, *in everything*. Everyone has to have someone to help them along, and y'all have each other now. But I'll give you this little piece of advice, okay: Don't trust your superiors. Now don't rebel all at once and ruin any chance y'all have at a normal life, if that's what you want, but question every order they give you in your head. As you do, I think you'll both start to see that those orders aren't all reasonable, and maybe you'll start to go against one or two of them. Don't be afraid to, now. Do what you know is right no matter what they tell you. That's all you can ever really do. Do you understand me?"

Liz smiled wide and laughed a little. "Are you kidding me?" she said.

"No," Jonah's dad said, shaking his head. "I'm dead serious. You can't trust anything any of them tell you."

"*Dad*," Jonah said, standing up, "you understand that means I can't believe anything you say, right?"

"No," he said. "I mean, *yes*. I do. *Exactly*. You can't trust anyone, Jonah. Only yourself."

"Then I can't trust you when you say that," Jonah said. "*Ugh.* This is ridiculous. I'm out of here." He stomped outside without waiting for Liz to follow.

ଧ �֍ ଧ

XXVII. Guy

"Lights!"

The set darkened except for a few harsh white spotlights, disguised to look like streetlights, which shone from above.

"Hold your places, please. *Extras*, that means you especially!"

Guy tensed up. He always got nervous right before the action started. His heart beat faster.

"You! *Uh…*" The director talked to someone Guy couldn't see through his tinted visor.

"Uh, guy in the background. *Number 57*. I don't have the name sheet with me, I'm sorry."

"*Guy*," Guy called back, still holding his pose.

"*Uh*, right," the director called back. "You, *guy*. What's your name?"

"My name is Guy, sir!"

"Oh—*uh*—okay. Well—*uh*—*Guy*. Can you take just a few steps back, please? We need you to start the scene off screen."

"Oh—*uh*—yes, sir." Guy took a few steps back and resumed his pose, standing as if he were in the middle of a long stride.

"Good. Very good," the director said. "Alright. Bring Russ in. We're ready to go."

The lights flickered on, and all the actors on set already—everyone except for Russ—held their poses. This was the part of the job which Guy excelled at. It was the reason—he knew—that he had been pigeon-holed as an extra rather than going on to be a star. There was no work for a star to stand perfectly still, and he had done that job too well to get out of it now. That and he spent too much of his time and effort on writing his own projects, but soon he would find fame with them instead.

After a few minutes—a shorter wait than Guy was prepared for—Russ came strutting out to his place. He was clad in the same protector's white—with a plated vest, cargo pants, steel-toed boots, and helmet with facemask that looked like something out of a samurai movie—that Guy was wearing.

"Places!" the director yelled after Russ was set in his place.

"Lights!"

The lights went off again, all except for the spotlights from above.

"We're rolling… *Aaaaand*, action!"

Guy walked fifteen steps across the set—passing just behind Russ as he ran by—and stood still as a statue again on the other side of the camera, off screen. He didn't have to turn to watch the scene to know how it unfolded behind him. He had read the script enough times to memorize it, and he could hear everything as it happened around him.

He knew that Russ was checking his ammo only to find that he had no bullets left. Crouched behind a dumpster, Russ threw his gun away and Guy heard it clink on the set floor. The editors would probably change that sound in post-production, though.

"I've got nothing," Russ said to the body who was bleeding on the ground behind the dumpster with him. "There's nothing we can do."

"No—*kak kak*—don't say that." The weak voice of the bloody body struggled against its impending demise. "*Here*. I got one of their guns. *Kak kak*." The gun clinked on the ground next to Russ as the body of his partner lost all strength to carry a weapon.

Russ picked the gun up and checked the clip. "Seven bullets, seven scumbags," he said. "*My lucky number*. But I won't do it." He tossed the gun away. "Anything a scumbag's touched can't help us now. If I go out, I go out my own way."

He did a somersault out from behind the dumpster, narrowly dodging a barrage of bullets, and—as he stood—an explosion went off in front of him. The resulting shrapnel narrowly missed him, pinging off the dumpster and buildings around him, and when everything faded into darkness, the director yelled, "Cut!"

All the lights came on again. Guy stretched his legs and back. It felt good to have run through another perfect scene.

"That's a wrap for this one, fellas," the director called through his megaphone. "Go ahead and take five while we set up for the next shot. Only one more to go for today, people. *Keep it up*." He clapped.

Guy made his way to the nearest food cart. He hadn't eaten

all day and his stomach was starting to grumble. He bumped into a short, dirty-haired woman who was placing a tray, piled high with cheese, onto the table, and she seemed to scamper away, startled like an animal. He was chewing on a stick of cheese, wondering if it was sanitary to have such a dirty person delivering the food to the carts, when Russ came to eat off the same cart as he was.

Guy tensed up. This was his opportunity. Russ never ate at the general food cart, yet here he was. Guy's crew would never let Guy hear the end of it if he let this chance pass him by. "*Uh, Mr. Logo*," he said in a half-whisper.

"Huh? Oh." Russ turned to him, chewing on some cheese himself, as if he hadn't noticed that Guy existed until he spoke.

"Hi, *um*. I'm Guy Rockwell. Do you remember me?"

Russ chewed some more on his cheese and looked a little closer at Guy. "Guy Rockwell?" he said, scrunching up his face as if he were trying to remember.

"Yes," Guy said, setting his own plate of cheese down and getting into the conversation. "Well, I've actually been in every movie you've ever made since Nelson took you off the Casino stage and put you on the world's screens."

"You don't say," Russ said, stuffing his mouth with more cheese, obviously bored.

"Yeah, well, I'm only an extra so you might not remember me." Guy shrugged.

"Oh, but of course," Russ said, extending his hand to shake Guy's. "And I'm so thankful for all your support. We couldn't do this without all the little people, you know. Bravo, sir. Bravo. Good show." He clapped his hands lightly, jiggling the stick of cheese he was holding.

"*Oh*. Thank you. Well—"

"Now. *If you'll excuse me*," Russ said, picking up more cheese from the food cart. "I need to get my energy up before the next scene. *The show must go on*, you know." He went back to picking clumps of cheese off the food cart and popping them into his mouth.

"Oh. Well..." Guy didn't know if he should interrupt Russ while he was prepping for his role, but he did know that he had to say something or face the ire of his crew. "One more thing, Mr. Logo. If you don't mind."

Russ didn't answer. He just went on stuffing his face.

"Well, you see. Me and some friends—*No*. Let me start over. My crew and I are working on this film, right. And... I don't know... I—I kind of figured that you might want to take a look at our scri—"

Russ stopped eating. His jaw dropped.

"Or just hear the elevator pitch or something..." Guy winced in preparation for the response.

Russ guffawed, spitting a glob of half-chewed cheese onto Guy's face who wiped it away with a cringe. "You thought that *I*, Russ Logo, would want to read *your* script. I mean, who are you even? Have we met before? And *why* are you eating at my private food cart? *Be gone*."

"I—uh..." Guy looked up to find a sign on the wall above the cart which read "Logo Only". He swallowed his embarrassment. Or at least, he tried to, but it got stuck in his throat behind a clump of cheese that blocked any words he tried to force past it. "Well—I—"

"Alright, everyone!" the director called, saving Guy from making a bigger fool of himself. "I need extras to go ahead and get into their places, please. One more scene and we're out of here folks."

Guy bowed his head and hurried to get into his position, standing behind where Russ would later kneel down to talk to his dying partner. He put on his helmet, held his prop gun in his hand—wondering if a real gun weighed the same—and put himself in the trance that would help him forget how embarrassing his interaction with Russ was for long enough to get through the scene. Who was he to ask Russ Logo anything, anyway? A nobody extra who no one knew could write, that's who. He was no one, nothing. But they would all see what he really was soon enough. And Russ would regret not getting involved before the premiere.

"Alright, then. *Actors into place, please*."

Russ's bloodied partner laid down on the ground a few feet in front of Guy. Russ strutted into position, still popping cheese cubes into his mouth, then kneeled down to hold her head in his arms.

"Lights!"

The lights went off, sending the world around Guy into darkness. He was left with nothing but his own thoughts to keep him company until the director yelled, "Action!"

"We did it, Dominguez," Russ said in a deep, gravelly voice. "There's nothing left for you to worry about."

His partner coughed, and Guy pictured the bright red stage blood that would be dribbling out onto her chin as a result. "What the—*kak kak*—what the fuck happened?" she forced through her dying breaths.

"Their guns," Russ said. "They blew up in their own hands. They thought they had won, but their own weapons turned against them."

"And I—I tried to tell you to—*kak kak*."

"But I didn't do it," Russ said. "I trusted Amaru Above's just rationality, and I was thus guided to safety. I knew Amaru could protect me better than any enemy's gun, and Amaru showed me that the world is Just."

Even the streetlights faded out. The darkness inside Guy's helmet got a little darker.

"*Aaaaand* cut! That's a wrap guys!" The lights flickered on and Guy could see again. "Superb acting as always, Russ. You really hit that last speech."

Russ's dead partner climbed to her feet. "How was I?" she asked. "I think my death knell could use a little work. You don't think we should do it again?"

"Oh, no no no," the director said. "Russ, what do you think?"

Russ didn't answer. He still hadn't stood from where he knelt to do the scene. In fact, he wasn't kneeling anymore, he was slouched over in a heap, lying in the pile of blood left by his partner.

Guy ripped off his own helmet. Something was wrong. That blood was too thick and dark to be stage blood. He rushed over and knelt next to Russ, slowly turning Russ's body over to rest his head on Guy's lap. "Russ, are you okay?" Guy asked, tears welling up behind his eyes. "Talk to me, buddy."

"Oh, *ha ha*!" the director said sarcastically, walking over to get a closer look. "Very funny, Russ. The scene's over. You've had your laugh. *Now cut.*" He chuckled and nudged Russ's arm with his foot.

"This isn't a joke!" Guy snapped at the director then turned back to comfort Russ. "*Russ.* Are you alright, buddy? Russ? Don't do this to me, man. *Not today.*" He brushed a piece of hair off of Russ's sweaty forehead and looked for any wounds that might have produced all that blood, but there was nothing. Maybe it *was* stage blood after all.

"You're not joking, right? Right, Russ? You wouldn't do that to us? Would you?" Guy was crying now. He didn't understand why he cared so much about someone who didn't even know his name, but he did. "You can't be dead," he begged. "You can't be."

The rest of the room seemed to be in shock or disbelief. No one had moved for some time. Guy stared around at them, pleading. "Do something," he begged. "Someone. *He's dying!*"

It must have been the word "dying" instead of "dead" that set the director back into action. "*Brandon*, get an ambulance here, ASAP," he barked off. "*Jim*, you call one, too. So they know how important it is. *Laura*, get me a fucking gin and tonic right now. Of course this has to happen at the end of a perfect scene. And for the love of Fortuna above, would someone please get this cursed extra off my star before he does any more damage."

"What? I—" Guy tried to protest, but the strong, bulky arms of a crew member dragged him away from Russ's limp body all the way to the extras' locker room where they tossed him in and slammed the door.

Guy threw his helmet against the wall, drawing stares from the other extras who were all standing around, gossiping about what had just transpired, but he didn't care. They could stare at him all they wanted. He had just held a dying Russ Logo in his arms as the star took his final breaths. *Ugh.* Guy kicked the helmet, making another loud ruckus, but everyone was already staring at him anyway.

Why did this have to happen to Guy? Why now? He and his crew were so close to getting their project off the ground, and now this? Of course, it didn't really change anything about his project, but how was he supposed to work when he had just held a dying man? Not only a man but Russ Logo: *the* man.

When his anger and sadness had died down, the stares of the other extras grew to be too much, so he snatched up his helmet, stomped to his locker, quickly changed out of costume, then hurried out of the room and into the public elevator, trying to avoid any more attention.

"Home, please," he said when the doors of the elevator closed behind him. "*Uh*, Carrollton that is."

The elevator fell into motion, and soon, the doors opened onto a street lined with four and five story buildings, all with iron-railed balconies at every level. His house was only a few doors down the beaten path—which had been destroyed by the roots of the oak trees growing all along it. He opened the TARDIS blue door and climbed up the staircase to the fourth floor. His apartment was a tiny one-room deal with just enough space for his bed, desk, TV, dresser, and battle station. He fed the fish in the bowl on top of the dresser and jumped into his bed, kicking off his shoes.

"TV on," he said.

The TV, which was hung high on the wall across from his bed, flicked on to the news channel. Reports of the incident had started coming out. They weren't calling it a death yet. Just an "incident". But Guy knew the truth. He was holding Russ's lifeless body only moments ago. It seemed like an eternity.

"Change the channel, please," he groaned. "Anything else."

The channel changed, but it was a different reporter saying the same things. "There was an incident—" It was strange how, so soon after "the incident", all the news stations were using the same exact wording for what had happened. "—on the set of Russ Logo's latest film about a protector. Sources report—" Of course there were always *sources*. "—that a call was made to the hospital's emergency line, but there's no telling who the call was made for or what was said. We'll be repeating the same meager facts until we get more, so please stay tuned forever."

"*Ugh*. Off please. Turn it off," Guy said and the TV flicked off.

This was the worst day ever. He put himself into the same trance he used to keep statue still at work. What could he say now when his crew asked if he had talked to Russ? "*Oh, yeah, well, I asked him to look at our script, but then he died in my arms.*" They'd laugh in his face.

But they'd see the news reports, wouldn't they? They'd know about the emergency call. That might make them more likely to believe him. What did he care anyway? He *had* asked Russ to look at the script, and Russ had made it abundantly clear that he had no intention of ever doing anything remotely similar to that, even if he wasn't too dead to do anything at all.

Guy sighed again. He stretched out in his bed and tried to put himself back into the trance he used to get through work. He tried to think about nothing. After thinking about the word "nothing" for some time, he even let that go, and soon, he drifted off to sleep.

ҡ   ✄   ҙ

He was awakened by a loud buzzing. He jumped into consciousness and shook his head, trying to figure out where the noise was coming from. After it went off a few more times, he realized it was the doorbell. "*Answer it*," he moaned. "Hello?"

"You alive up there, Guy?" came a tinny, almost robotic voice over the intercom.

"Yeah—*um*—I'm fine," Guy said. "I'll be right down."

He searched around for his shoes then strapped them on and made the long descent to street level where Jen was outside waiting for him. "I'm so glad you're alright," she said, hugging him as he closed the door.

"Yeah, well, *I'm* alive," he said, trying to put on a strong demeanor. "But alright's another genre altogether."

"*Oh, no.*" Jen gasped. "What happened? Something horrible, I'm sure." She took his arm and led him down the street. He was liking the newfound attention, even though it was no doubt brought on by his involvement in *the incident*. "Tell me all about it on the way," she said. "We're late already."

"Yeah, well... I kind of lost track of time."

"Oh, of course, sweetheart. *No no no.* I didn't mean to blame you. It was just a statement of fact. *We are indeed late*. Now, tell me all about it. I'm *dying* to know what happened."

Guy looked down at his feet as he walked. What a poor choice of words. She was *dying* to know. If she did know, she probably wouldn't have put it that way.

"*Uh*," Guy said. "I don't know if I should even be talking about it."

"*Oh, no*! You have to, dude," Jen said in a mock complaining voice. "To *me* at least. That way you can get your story straight for the others. Because you know they're all gonna ask."

"Yeah. I guess." She was right that the entire crew would want to know. Everyone everywhere probably wanted to know the story of what he had just experienced. "But it was—it was pretty messed up."

She tugged on his arm. "Well, you don't have to tell me if you don't want to. But be ready for them to ask."

"No, I—well, I do. I do want to tell you, that is. But—it's just—I don't really know what happened, you know. He was kneeling on the ground, giving his speech to his dying partner, and when the lights went down, everything was fine, but after the director called cut, he didn't move, and I knew something was wrong."

"*He.* You mean…" She put her hand to her mouth.

"*Yes.* Russ Logo. I ran over to him, and I held him in my arms, and I comforted him as he took his dying breaths."

Jen hit Guy on the arm. "You liar!" she said. "*Uh huh huh uh.* That was a good one, dude." She shook her head, smiling. "You had me going for a second there."

"No. What? I'm serious. He died in my arms."

"Oh, sure he did. And then they picked you to fill his now empty role. With acting like this, you might be capable of it."

"I'm not kidding," he said, stopping. "This is serious."

"Sure it is." She put a serious face on, nodded, and pulled him along again. "I mean, I'll play along with your little story, but if you haven't worked up the courage to ask Russ yet, you can just say so. This story of yours'll probably just get the crew more riled up than they will be if you just tell them the truth, though."

"Yeah, well, it's not a story." Guy huffed. "It is the truth. You'll see. They'll believe me."

She chuckled. "Sure they will. I'll play along either way, though. *Let's go.*"

She pulled him into a door under a neon glowing sign that read Indywood. Inside was a bar with soft couches around low tables. Giant screens with classic movies playing on them covered every wall. The rest of the crew was already there and seated around a couple of tables which they had scooted together so Jen and Guy stuffed themselves into the couches wherever they could fit.

"You're late," Cohen said, their director. "*Again.*"

"Yeah, well, Guy's had a traumatic experience, hasn't he?" Jen said. "Tell him, Guy."

"Yeah, Guy. *Tell us,*" Emir, one of the actors, said, sipping his drink. "Who was this emergency call for? You were there, weren't you?"

"Guy's just a writer," Cohen said. *"No offense."* He nodded at Guy who shrugged. "His work is all but done. But you're an actor, Jen. You could be running lines, or—"

"Yeah, well," Jen cut him off, "it looks to me like everyone's drinking, like this is a logistical meeting not a rehearsal. I don't see anyone else running lines, *Cohen*."

"Yeah, still…" Cohen sipped his drink.

"Oh, come on," Emily, another actor, said. "Settle down you two. We're supposed to be a crew. We have to work together if we want to get this done, yeah? But first, since we're all dying to know, tell us what happened, Guy."

"Yes," Emir said. "The news reports say it was for some lowly cameraman."

"Hey!" Laura, the camera operator, complained. *"Lowly man?"*

"Sorry," Emir said. He took a sip of his drink. "What I meant to ask is was it someone who we know or someone who's not important?"

"That's not much better," Laura said, shaking her head.

"Whatever," Emir said. "You know what I mean. Who was it for?"

"Uh, well…" Guy stalled.

"Go on, Guy," Jen said, urging him on. "Tell them what you told me." She grinned.

"It was Russ Logo," he said. *"He's dead."*

Everyone laughed except for Guy.

"Oh, come on," Cohen said. "If you don't want to ask Russ to look at your script, you can just say so. But this?"

"Tell them the rest," Jen said. "I especially liked the bit about you comforting him in your arms as he took his dying breaths."

"That happened," Emir said, rolling his eyes and sipping his drink.

"Really?" Laura asked, in awe.

"Yeah, and I went on a date with Jorah Baldwin before I came here tonight," Emily said, grinning and trying to play to the crowd. "He got called away for an important emergency, though, and we had to cut the date short. Now we know what that emergency was. Don't we?"

Everyone laughed.

"No, it's—I'm telling the truth," Guy said.

"Alright, alright," Cohen said. "That's enough of this nonsense. We all know that Guy still hasn't brought the script up to Russ—*and that he probably never will*—so let's get along to our actual business."

Guy started to protest, but Cohen cut him off before he could. "*Now*," he said. "Laura. You have everything you need, right?"

"I have the basics," she said. "We could use more lenses and better mics, but without any money, we can't do anything about that."

"We might have to make do," Cohen said. "What about costumes?" he asked Steve, the designer.

"Well, our lovely Laura and I," he nodded at her and smiled, "pilfered some helmets and guns from a supply closet, and I've just about finished enough cargo pants for the protectors, but…"

"What?" Cohen groaned. "What now? Spit it out?"

"Well, it's the owners. Tuxedos are no problem for me—even in that size—and we have plenty of top hats and monocles that just need a buffing, but…"

"*But what*? Our opportunities for the shots we need are disappearing every day. We don't have time to stall, so whatever problems you foresee, you'd better speak up now. And that goes the same for all of you." He looked around the table and everyone turned to shy away from his line of sight. He was insufferable when he got in these moods where he started acting like a big shot director.

"*Well*," Steve went on nervously. "It's all that fat. We can't find anything to fill the top part of the tuxedos with that gives them a realistic flabby mushroom look."

"You can't just stuff it with cloth or something?" Cohen asked.

Steve laughed. "Do you want this to look like a high budget film, or do you want it to look like a grade school class project?"

"Yeah, well, you're gonna have to think of something fast," Cohen said. "Every scene we have set in stone has an owner in it, so you'll have to come up with something *before* we can start filming."

"I have some ideas," Steve said, reclining back into the couch and losing himself in his thoughts. "I'll get back to you on it."

"What about shooting locations?" Cohen asked the group in

general.

"Outdoors and all the garage shots are set up," Laura said. "We still need something big enough to hold a feast in, though."

"It doesn't have to be that big," Cohen said. "We can work with angles."

"*Yeah*," Laura said, rolling her eyes. "I know how the camera works, but it still has to be bigger than anything we have access to right now. I'm still looking, though."

"Alright," Cohen said. "Well keep looking. Other than that, we just have to worry about memorizing our lines, but we can't do that until we have a script we can work with, which brings us back to Guy. So, *Guy*, how *is* it going?"

"Well," Guy said, "have any of you finished reading the script yet?"

Everyone kind of looked around at each other and sipped their drinks, waiting for someone else to answer first.

Guy chuckled. "Yeah, well, *I* think it's good. It's probably the best thing I've ever written. But then again I think that about everything I've ever written until I come up with the next one. So I'm a little biased."

"Okay," Cohen said. "But how can we be sure it's good? That's what I want to know."

"You could read it and see for yourself," Guy said. "Some of you should have been memorizing lines by now at least. Right?" He looked around, but all the actors, including Jen, shrugged.

"Memorizing's not hard," Jen said. "It's our job, you know. It only gets hard when you make us forget what we learned because you want to change an 'and' to a 'then' or move a comma. We're waiting on you, Guy. Once you're done, we can do our jobs."

"I thought you were supposed to ask Russ," Steve said. "Did you chicken out again?"

"No. I told you—" Guy tried to explain, but Laura cut him off.

"It's okay, Guy. Russ is a huge star. You don't have to make up stories for us. Save that for the scripts. Just find someone to tell you this script's good so you'll stop working on it."

"*I asked Russ, okay*. He said he would never read anything written by a lowly extra like me. And then—*I swear to y'all*—he died in my arms."

Everyone laughed.

"Alright, Guy," Cohen said. "No input from Russ. That means the script's finished, right?"

"I—uh—" Guy shrugged. "Yeah, sure. *Whatever*. I'll send the pages out tomorrow with my final edits."

"Good, then. *Great*." Cohen clapped his hands and rubbed them together. "Well, we all have plenty of work to do in the coming week, and we all know what work that is, so let's get to it. I'm calling this meeting to an end. Raise your glasses to the success of *Outland*!"

Everyone clanged their glasses over the table and took a big gulp of whatever it was they were drinking.

"Have some fun tonight," Cohen said. "Starting tomorrow, it's all business until we get this project done."

The group started chattering in clumps, changing from a single cohesive unit into many smaller groups who simply happened to be occupying closely related spaces. Guy leaned back in the soft couch and sipped his drink. Of course they didn't believe him. They probably didn't even believe that he had asked Russ to read the script. But still, not one of them had finished it themselves. It took them longer to read it than it took him to write it. Did they even care what project they were working on?

He downed the rest of his drink in one gulp and set it on the table.

"Alright, y'all," he said, standing up. No one seemed to hear him, but he went on anyway. "I'm gonna go finish up some last minute edits. I'll send out the finished sheets tomorrow morning. Goodnight, y'all." He waved and left the bar to no response.

The air was cool and the sky was dark. The way was lit by streetlights and the lights from the buildings all around him. He walked a block in the opposite direction from his apartment, toward the nearest public elevator. He was calling the elevator when he heard footsteps jogging toward him and turned to find Jen out of breath.

"*Hey*," she huffed. "Where're you going? You didn't even say goodbye, dude"

Guy chuckled. "I did," he said. "But I'm done for the night. It was a rough day at work."

"With Russ dying in your arms?" She smiled.

"I'm serious, Jen." He sighed. "That really happened. You'll see." He stepped into the elevator's open doors.

"Oh, come on," she said, holding the doors open. "I was just kidding. Let me ride home with you." She stepped inside and the doors slid closed behind her.

"*Home. Carrollton*," Guy said, and the elevator fell into motion.

"What's really bothering you, Guy?" Jen asked, standing close to him.

"*I told you*," he said, trying not to look into her eyes.

She chuckled. "For real, though. *It's me*. You can tell me."

"I already did," he said as the elevator stopped and the doors opened.

"You can't be serious, though," Jen said, stepping out into the street.

"*Trust me*," Guy said, following her, "I am."

Three doors down, at the entrance to Guy's apartment, five protectors stomped up the sidewalk toward them. "Guy Rockwell?" one asked in a terrifying modulated voice, through a mouth that glowed neon green, red, and yellow in the darkness.

"I—*uh*—*that's me*," Guy said, mesmerized by the colors and horrified by the sounds.

"Come with us, citizen."

"*You can't be serious.*" Jen gasped.

"Now!"

ꝩ ✳ ꝩ

XXVIII. Olsen

Olsen sprinted straight home, grasping the pamphlets tight so the wind couldn't steal them from her. Well, not straight home. Ever since the new buildings and fields had burst into existence she had been having more trouble than usual finding her way anywhere, including home. After turning down a few wrong alleys, and taking some of the same streets three or four times, she finally made it back to the five story walkup which was her apartment.

She rushed in and up the stairs, and when she burst through the door, she called, "*Mooooom I'm hooooooome!*"

Her mom was in the living room—which the front door opened onto—watching something on TV. "Quiet down, dear," she said, not looking away from her show. "You don't have to yell. There's only one room in the place."

"Sorry, Mom," Olsen said. "It's just—I'm so excited! I have something to tell you." She sat on the couch next to her mom and smiled.

"What is it dear? Is that internship of yours finally over? Can you move out of your momma's house once and for all?"

"Uh, well..." Olsen looked down at the pamphlets in her lap, hesitant now to share the news for fear that her mom might not think it was as great of an idea as she did. "Not exactly..."

"Not exactly? Now, girl, you're getting too old to be living with your mom. *Honestly.* When I was your age, we were already having children and raising famblies. I don't know what it is with your generation."

"Yeah, mom. Well, I was supposed to be getting promoted today, you know, but life has been a little strange since Christmas, hasn't it?"

"So you didn't get promoted, then?" Her mom shook her head. "*Tsk tsk tsk.* Olsen Sous, what *am* I going to do with you?"

"No, Mom—I... I got fired."

"Fired! Olsen, what are we supposed to do now? I was barely supporting you as it is. You—I—I can't keep going on like this if you've got nothing to contribute yourself, dear. I don't know what else to say. I don't care if the world implodes, there's no other way about it."

"No, Mom. But you have to—"

"*No buts*, Olsen. You find yourself another job by the middle of this week, or you're out of here. *I'm sorry*. But that's the way it has to be. You should have been done with your internship and out of my house a long time ago, as it is. I don't know why I ever let you laze around here for so long in the meantime."

"No, Mom, but that's what I'm trying to tell you. Look." She stuffed one of the flyers into her mom's hand. "Read that."

Her mom held it close to her face, then far away, then close again. "*The Human Fambly?*" she read out loud, mouthing it to herself as she skimmed over the rest. "What is this? Some science fiction book you're reading? Robots taking our jobs? *Ha*! I'd like to see the robot that can sew like I can." She waved her fingers in Olsen's face. "You see these? I've been training them for years and years, and nothing can match their precision. That's why I'm so worried about you, dear. You're well behind on picking up your own skills. How else you gonna make yourself more valuable to your prospective employers?"

"But Mom, I found an employer already. That's what I've been trying to tell you."

"You've what now? You just said that you were fired, girl."

"Well I was, but—"

"Then get your story straight. Were you fired, or did you find a new job?"

"Both, Mom. *Ugh*. That's what I'm trying to tell you. First I got fired, then I found a new job."

"*Oooh*, girl. Now don't you be lying to your momma, ya hear. Put it to me straight this time. What are you talking about?"

"The flyer, Mom. You just read it. You remember?"

Her mom held the flyer up to her face again, trying to read it, but she was turning red and clearly getting too annoyed to read anything. "Whatever, okay." She groaned. "*The Human Fambly* or whatever. I read it and I still don't know what it means. Now tell me something sane or I'll kick you out of here with or without a job."

"Look. Okay." Olsen took the flyer from her mom who was still trying to find a distance from her face that was optimal for reading. "Forget about the flyer. I was fired, okay. Right at the end of the day. They said they had found someone who would do the job for cheaper."

"Cheaper than you were already doing it for?" her mom asked, unbelieving. "Ain't no human alive who could live on less than that. Now I know you're telling me a lie."

"No, mom. Just let me finish. That's what they said to me, okay. *No.* That's what they said. So I was walking home, half taking the long way because I didn't want to tell you I had been fired and half lost because I can't find anything anywhere these days, even our own house."

"You never did have any sense of direction," her mom said, smiling.

"No. And I still don't. So I was lost, meandering around, looking at all the new old buildings everywhere. Have you noticed them, Mom? All the new buildings everywhere and how they're in worse condition than any building that used to be here?"

"Now what does this have to do with you getting a job?" her mom asked, raising her eyebrows. "*And quick.*"

"Well—uh—nothing I guess. It's just a tangent. I thought it was interesting. Don't you?"

"You're not gonna think it's interesting when you're out there on the streets wondering if you can sneak into one of them old buildings to sleep in."

"No, well, come on, Mom. Just hear me out, okay. Anyway, where was I? That's right. So I was walking around lost, right, when I heard this loud voice echoing through the alleys, and I got turned around trying to follow it—almost losing myself again—when I saw a group of people all huddled together in an open field."

"What *are* you talking about, dear?"

"I'm almost done, Mom. Just let me finish, okay. But I saw them huddled together, using each other for warmth, and they were all looking at this old, hunchbacked, white-haired woman with a wrinkly, dark face—darker than yours even, almost impossibly dark—and it was her voice echoing around me. It seemed impossible that she could talk so loudly, but as I stared and listened with everyone else, I knew it was her speaking.

"Then another woman, who looked almost exactly like the one who was talking but with a big black afro instead of the scraggly white hair, pulled me on the arm and started asking me questions and writing my answers on her clipboard, and before I knew it, I was telling her that I had been fired."

"What kind of questions?" her mom asked suspiciously.

"I don't know," Olsen said shrugging. Why was her mom so interested in this part and not the rest? The rest seemed stranger to her. "My name and address and all that. It doesn't matter. What matters is—"

"Did you give her our address?" her mom asked, crossing her arms.

"What? I..." Olsen rubbed her face. None of this seemed to be getting through to her mom. "No. Yes. *I don't know*. It doesn't matter. What matters is—"

"Of course it matters, girl," her mom said. "Give your address to someone with a clipboard, and the next thing you know, they're knocking on your door. Now I don't want to have to deal with that in my home, child."

"Well, they won't. Okay." Olsen sighed. "I'll make sure they won't. That's who I got a job with. So I can tell them not to when I go to work tomorrow."

"With the clipboard lady?" Her mom looked horrified. "*You didn't.* Not my daughter. No, no, no. Not if I have anything to say about it. Not while you're under my roof. No one who lives here is carrying a clipboard around, asking people for their names and addresses to serve who knows what purposes. No, ma'am. Not in my fambly. No way, no how."

"No, Momma. I'm not gonna be holding a clipboard, okay. I'm gonna be a chef." Olsen smiled, proud to have told someone finally. "A *real* chef, too. Not a machine operator. And they're gonna—"

"A chef? *Ha*! But you can't cook, girl. You can't even keep down a food production internship at your age. How are you supposed to become a chef?"

"Thanks for the confidence, Mom." Olsen sighed. "*Seriously.* But they said they'd train me. And you haven't even heard the best part yet."

"Train you? Oh, I see. So, what's that, huh? Four weeks without pay? How am I supposed to support you while you go off vacationing for a month?"

"It wouldn't be without pay, Mom." At least Olsen hoped it wouldn't be. She had forgotten to ask if they paid for training in her excitement to land another job so quickly. "I'll be getting paid more than I ever was at the internship, too. *Twice as much*."

Her mom laughed. "Oh. *Ho ho*! dear. What else? You'll be helping a humane cause while you're at it, too? A chef for orphans or something like that. Am I right? Oh *ho ho*!"

"No mom. I'm serious. I—"

"Sure sure, honey," her mom said, standing from the couch. "Well, you can have the couch for another week, but if you don't have a real job and some rent tokens by then, it's out the door with you. You hear me?"

"No, but I—"

"*No buts*. Now I'm off to have a drink with the girl gang. I'll ask around for you. Be good, now, ya hear."

"I already have a job, mom," Olsen complained, but her mom was already gone.

Ugh. Weren't parents supposed to be supportive? Olsen had thought that her mom would be happy to hear that her only daughter had gotten her dream job—*with a raise*—but no. Her mom only seemed suspicious. She kept accusing her own daughter of lying. What kind of mother would do that?

Although the job really did seem too good to be true. Olsen didn't really believe the story herself, and she was there when it happened. And maybe she *was* known to make up a story or two to get out of a crisis. But still, a mother should trust her daughter. Right?

She didn't want to think about it anymore. She wanted to share the news with someone who would be happy for her. She wanted someone to say, "Good job, Olsen. That's awesome. I'm so proud of you." and give her a long hug. And she knew exactly who would give her what she needed.

She jumped off the couch and hurried through the door, down the stairs, and into the world. Normally, she could walk straight to the bar, take a left, and find where she was going by memory, but ever since the Christmas incident she couldn't find anything. She started one way down the street then realized it was the wrong one and went the other. She could have taken an elevator, sure, but then she would probably end up more lost than she already was. At least by walking, if she got too far off course, she could just retrace her steps to find her way back home.

As she walked, she studied the buildings around her. It was interesting that the new ones were older than the old ones, no matter what her mom said. And that fact had to be some clue as to why they all showed up out of nowhere, all of a sudden, and in such a loud hurry. It wasn't just the buildings that were different, either. It was the people who had come in them, too. There were a lot of new faces in the neighborhood, and they were all dirty and clothed with rags.

She looked up and didn't recognize where she was. She spun around a few times, looking at a field, a few older buildings, and a few new, when she realized that the one she was standing in front of was the one she was looking for. She shook her head and laughed at herself then pressed the button on the intercom next to the label "Sonya Barista". After a moment's pause, a tinny voice came over the intercom. "Hello?" it said. "Sonya speaking."

"Sonya, it's me," Olsen said. "Olsen," she added for good measure.

"Yeah, I know," Sonya said. "I'll be down in a second." The link cut out with a pop.

Olsen checked herself in her reflection on the door window and was still trying to fix that one little bit of hair which always fell exactly wrong when the door opened. She jumped and tried to pretend like she wasn't fixing herself up, saying, "Uh... hey."

Sonya laughed, closing the door behind her. "Hey, *freak*," she said. "What's up?"

"Oh, well..." Olsen rubbed her arm. "I have news."

"Good news or bad news?"

"Well—uh—kinda both I guess."

Sonya frowned.

"*No no no. Good.* Definitely good. Well it's just that... I mean—"

"*Wait*," Sonya stopped her. "Do you want to go sit in that field to talk?" She pointed across the street. "Ever since it popped up on Christmas I can't stay out of it. I always wanted a yard."

"I, uh—" Olsen tried to answer, but Sonya pulled her to the field anyway and they sat in an already worn down patch of grass.

"Isn't it beautiful?" Sonya said. "Look at all the vines growing on these trees. Look at how they share their resources and work together. The vine guiding the tree to grow where the best nutrients are, and the tree providing a portion of those nutrients in return for the favor. Isn't nature just amazing with the emergent cooperation it creates? I'm so glad I finally have a yard so I can experience it firsthand."

"Oh, yes, well…" Olsen didn't find grade school science as interesting as Sonya did, but she didn't want to say that so she just said, "It's amazing really."

"Oh, I'm so glad you agree." Sonya smiled. "You know, everything has changed since Christmas. It's as if we live in a whole new world entirely. Do you know what I mean?"

Olsen nodded. She knew all too well what Sonya meant with how much more often she had gotten herself lost since Christmas, not to mention getting fired from her internship instead of promoted into a new career.

"Take all these new people for instance," Sonya said. "Have you talked to any of them?"

Olsen shook her head. She had been trying to stay as far away from them as possible. She was fascinated by their appearance, of course, just like she was fascinated by the appearance of all the new buildings, but she hadn't gone up and knocked on any doors, and she certainly wasn't about to go striking up any conversations with these dirty new strangers.

"Yeah, well," Sonya said. "*I have*. I've talked to a lot of them, actually. Any free moment I have I go out and search for more of them to talk to. In fact, that's exactly what I was on my way to do when you came ringing."

"Oh, I'm sorry." Olsen blushed and hoped Sonya couldn't see her embarrassment in the dark.

"Oh, no no. Don't apologize." Sonya shook her head. "I'm glad you came. I've been wanting to hear what you thought about all of this, but I've been so wrapped up in trying to figure it out for myself that I haven't had time to ask. You do understand, don't you?"

"Oh, yeah." Olsen laughed. "I don't even know what I think about it myself, yet. Though, there are some things…"

"What?" Sonya smiled, leaning in closer. "Tell me."

"Well, like, have you noticed how all the new buildings—or the buildings that weren't here before—well, they all look older than anything that was here already. You know what I mean?"

"Exactly!" Sonya clapped her hands together. "*Oh my God.* I thought I was going crazy. No one at work noticed it, and they all looked at me like I was mental when I told them."

"*Ugh.* Really? My mom was the same way. She thought I was being ridiculous."

"Why is it so hard for people to see what's right in front of their faces? You know, that's why I love talking to you, Olsen. You make me feel like I'm not the only one who sees the world this way."

Olsen blushed again. "You, too," she said, then she thought that might not be an appropriate use of the phrase and blushed some more.

"You know what else, though," Sonya said. "I've talked to them, like I said, and I mean *a lot* of them, and you would *not* believe some of the things they say."

"Try me," Olsen said, almost too fast. She was eager to show Sonya that she could believe her, that way maybe Sonya would be more likely to believe Olsen's own unbelievable experience.

"Well, for one," Sonya said, "none of them have jobs."

Olsen chuckled. "What? How do they live?"

"Well, they have *jobs*," Sonya said. She paused to think about it, obviously having a hard time translating her thoughts into words. "But they're not like our jobs, you know. They get paid in food and housing instead of tokens. Does that make sense?"

"So instead of choosing what they want to buy, their bosses choose for them?"

"Well, no. Not exactly. They don't even have tokens at all. They don't use them. Not from anything that I've been told anyway. Not one of them has even really known what tokens are when I asked, so I don't think they can be said to buy anything at all."

"*Tokens?*" Olsen laughed. She had trouble believing that anyone over the age of three wouldn't know what tokens were.

"Yeah," Sonya said. "They've never heard of them."

"Then how do they buy things? How do they live?"

"Like I said, they work for them. They do a job, then their boss gives them food and housing. They don't really buy anything. They don't even know the word. They trade ownership. That's all."

"But where do their bosses get everything from?" Olsen

asked, shaking her head. "It doesn't make sense."

"I know. I don't understand it, either. But that's what they tell me. You don't think they're all lying, do you? I must have talked to more than a hundred."

Olsen shook her head. "Well, no..."

"They can't *all* be lying," Sonya said. "It's like they're from an entirely different world or something. Really, Olsen. I mean, *tokens*. You learn about tokens your first lesson of grade school. How could you live to be an adult and not know what tokens are?"

Olsen laughed. "That is pretty stupid," she said.

"No, Olsen!" Sonya huffed and took a few deep breaths. "*God, no.* It's not stupidity. It's ignorance. The only way for them to have never learned about tokens is if they've never had any experiences with them. But that's impossible in our world, right?"

"In our world?" Olsen raised an eyebrow. Sonya was going a little more off the deep end than usual. She normally had some interesting theories about how the world worked, but adding new worlds was going a bit far.

"Yes, *our* world," Sonya said. "Just bear with me here, okay. So you agree that things are a little different since Christmas. I mean, you can't deny that. Can you?"

Olsen thought again about all the new old buildings that had popped up out of nowhere on Christmas night, causing the sonic boom that woke the world. "No," she said. "No one can deny that."

"Okay," Sonya said. "So in the world that existed before Christmas, in *our* world, it would be impossible to grow to adulthood without ever seeing a token, right?"

"Well, yeah." Olsen shrugged. "That's what I'm saying. You'd have to be stupid."

"But I'm saying they're not stupid. I talked to them. They're no more or less intelligent than you, me, or anyone else."

"Then why do they not know about tokens?"

"*Because*," Sonya said with a sigh. "It's like I've been saying. They must have never experienced them. They must be from another world where tokens don't exist. It's the only explanation that makes sense."

"I'm not convinced," Olsen said, shaking her head. It was strange that they had never heard of tokens, but people from another world? That was insane, not possible.

"Well where do you think all these new people came from, then?" Sonya asked. "And all the old buildings?"

"Oh, well—*uh*—I think…" Olsen still had no idea. They could have come from anywhere.

"And why are the newly appeared buildings in such disrepair? Why are the people who live in them so hungry and dirty?"

"Oh, well—*uh*—I don't know—"

"You haven't even talked to them, Olsen. Maybe if you did, you would understand."

"I'm still not sure I understand the words that are coming out of your mouth," Olsen said. "Are you sure that's the order you meant to put them in?"

"*Yes, I'm sure.*" Sonya sighed. "*Look.* We come from one world where tokens are used daily. They come from another world where some sort of barter system is used. The buildings are older because their world has less. That's why the people are poorer, too. Ever since Christmas, the two worlds have been merged, and now we're in this hybrid third world. Do you follow me yet?" She looked at Olsen expectantly.

"I—*uh*—*okay*," Olsen said. "Let me get this straight. You're saying that the sonic boom was the sound of the two worlds *merging* or whatever."

"Yes, exactly!" Sonya clapped her hands and smiled. "So do you believe me?"

That was probably why Olsen had been fired. Some poor sap with nothing from the new old world would be more than happy to steal her job for a quarter of the pay because it would still be more than they had ever been paid, none of them had ever even seen tokens in their entire lives. "That would explain a lot," Olsen said, nodding. "It still seems a little too out there, though."

"Oh. *Well*…" Sonya shook her head. "Don't think I don't find it strange myself. Who wouldn't? But what other answer is there that correlates with the evidence?"

Olsen thought about it for a second, tapping her chin. "*Time travel*," she said with a chuckle. "That's why the buildings are old and the people have never heard of tokens. They're from the past." She smiled.

"Yeah, like time travel's believable."

"But merging worlds is?" Olsen raised an eyebrow.

"Not really. But it fits the evidence better. The buildings wouldn't age if they had come forward through time, or else the people would have, too. And if they had come from the future, where the buildings would be older, the people living in them would most likely know about tokens. And besides all that, I don't think time travel would explain how they all witnessed the same sonic boom that we did on the same Christmas night, either. I'm not sure what would explain that."

"But again, I didn't know that they did experience the sonic boom," Olsen said. "And I don't really think it's time travel, either. I just can't believe that there have been two separate worlds out there for all this time and none of us have noticed until they happened to merge for some unexplained reason."

"Maybe if you talked to one of them," Sonya said.

"What? No. I don't think—"

"*C'mon.*" She stood and pulled Olsen up, dragging her out to the street and up to the first person they came across. She was an older, dark-faced, hunchbacked lady with a big afro and dirty clothes who Olsen thought she recognized but couldn't quite place—until she saw the clipboard and the pamphlet the woman was holding out to Sonya.

"Hello," Sonya said, taking the pamphlet. "How are you?"

"Oh, fine, fine, child," the old woman said. "It's a wonderful time to be alive, isn't it?"

"*Uh*, yes it is," Sonya said. "I was just talking to my friend here about it."

Olsen waved and hoped the woman didn't recognized her.

"Yes, child," the woman said. "I've been out here telling all of my Family the good news. The worlds have changed, you know. The worlds have changed! *Hallelujah.*" She smiled wide.

Sonya looked to Olsen, excited, then back to the woman. "That's a funny way to say it," she said. "*The worlds.* What do you mean?"

"Oh, sweet child, you haven't heard the good news then?"

"I'm not sure I know what you're talking about," Sonya said.

"The worlds, child," the woman said. "The worlds! You heard the sonic boom on Christmas, didn't you?"

"I, well, of course," Sonya said.

"That, child, was the heralding of a new and beautiful age for humankind. Outlands Five and Six have finally been reunited, toppling the first barrier between the Human Family and unity."

"Outlands Five and Six?" Sonya said. "What do you mean?"

"Your world and mine, child. Your world and mine! It's all in the pamphlet, sister. Give it a read and you'll find the knowledge you seek."

Sonya opened the pamphlet and started to skim it.

"It's a beautiful time," the woman went on. "Soon we'll be able to shed humanity of the parasitic robot infection and set every breathing, bleeding human being to the work which is rightly theirs."

"Oh, uh…" Sonya's face went red. "Well, thank you for talking to us," she said, pulling Olsen back toward the soft spot in the field where they were talking before.

"*Wait*," the woman called after them. "Can I get your name and address?"

Sonya didn't stop to listen. She dragged Olsen back to the field and plopped down in the grass.

"What was that about?" Olsen asked.

"Here. Read it." Sonya shoved the flyer into Olsen's hand.

Olsen looked at it. It was the same flyer she had handed her mother before she came to see Sonya. That was the woman with her clipboard who had helped Olsen get her new chef job.

"Still," Sonya said. "Did you hear that? She said there were two worlds, too. Outlands Five and Six or something like that. Not that her word is worth much."

"Why isn't her word worth much?" Olsen asked, getting all the more nervous about revealing her new job.

"Well, did you read the pamphlet?" Sonya asked. "She's a racist."

"*A racist?*" Olsen chuckled. "What? She wasn't white."

"Well she doesn't have to be," Sonya said. "You heard her. *Robotic parasites.* That's a racial slur. I can't even believe I repeated it."

"Woah there, now." Olsen waved her hands. "Slow down. I mean, sure. Parasite is going a little far, I agree with that, but there *are* robots doing our jobs, aren't there?"

"*Androids*," Sonya huffed. Her face went deeper red. "There are androids who have their own jobs, but they're not *robots*, and they are certainly not parasites."

"I just don't think it's that bad," Olsen said. "I mean, I was just fired, and I—"

"You don't see how it's—*What*?"

"Oh. Yeah... *Sorry*." Olsen looked at the grass. "I meant to tell you."

"Oh no," Sonya said, patting Olsen's back. "How are you?"

"I'm fine, actually." Olsen nodded, trying to reassure Sonya.

"How'd your mom take it?"

"Well, that's the thing..." Olsen had been so excited to tell Sonya about her new job before, but now she didn't know what to expect. Olsen didn't know they were racists when she took the job. She still wasn't sure they were. One woman using one slur didn't mean the entire organization was racist, did it? And even if Olsen had known, how could she turn down the opportunity to train as a real chef with twice the pay of her last internship? She couldn't. She wouldn't. So she had to tell Sonya about her new job or lie to her about it. "Now, you're not going to believe this," Olsen said.

"After getting you to admit that two worlds merging might be a possibility, whatever you have to say has got to be nothing to believe in comparison." Sonya smiled.

"Yeah, well..." Olsen rubbed her neck. It was now or never. "I kind of got a job with the racists."

"You what?" Sonya wasn't smiling anymore.

"I didn't know they were racists, okay."

"Of course. *You* wouldn't." Sonya crossed her arms.

"And I'm still not sure they are."

"*They are*. I can assure you of that."

"But they're going to teach me to be a chef, Sonya. *A real chef*, not just a machine operator."

"I'm sure they will."

Olsen hesitated. Was "machine" a racial slur? "But I had just gotten fired, and I knew my mom was going to kick me out—she still is—and I saw this big group of people, and one said they would pay me to be a chef even though I didn't know anything about cooking, so I had to say yes. *I had to*. What else could I have done?"

"Yeah, well, I still don't think it's a good idea," Sonya said.

"Even if it isn't a good idea, it's the only choice I have. Unless you know of a nice job you could hook me up with, but I doubt that's true in this brave new world."

"No, well—"

"*So I have no choice*," Olsen interrupted her. "My mom said she wouldn't put up with me any longer. I need my own place beside that. I can't keep sleeping on a couch, Sonya. So even if they are racists, it doesn't matter. That doesn't mean I have to be a racist. And if I can get the tokens I need to live, then what do I care? It's business, not personal."

"*Everything's personal*," Sonya said, shaking her head. "It's personal for the androids who have to put up with it every day. I work with an android, you know. She's just as human as anyone else who works there—*probably more so than most of them*. And you're not just working for racists, Olsen. You're working for a racist organization. Did you even read the pamphlet?"

"I, yeah, well..." She tried to read it again but she couldn't concentrate.

Sonya stood up fast. "Well, I don't think you should do it. I know you need a job, and I'll do anything I can to help you find one, but I don't think this is the answer."

"I—but—"

"*No*. That's what I think and you're not changing my mind. You have to decide for yourself now. I'll see you tomorrow."

"I—but—" Olsen started, but Sonya was already gone.

XXIX. Tillie

All she knew was pain. She couldn't even breathe without waves of it shooting through her ribs. She groaned and more overcame her. She struggled to sit up and lean her back against the hard wall behind her. Why was the light so bright? Where was she?

She took in the room. It was small—no, tiny. She was lying on a cold metal bed of some sort, and all the walls were plain white. There was a white metal toilet on the white tile floor next to her bed, and besides the looming white metal door, that was it. Was this jail?

She groaned again. The pain in her chest was piercing. She lifted her shirt up a little to try to see what the cause was but quickly dropped it when she got a peek of purple, black, and red. She cringed at the sight then groaned from the pain of cringing. There was nothing she could do about it now. There was no point in even looking. The only thing looking again would accomplish is making her vomit.

She took in the room a second time. *Was* this jail? No. It couldn't be. Could it? They wouldn't put her in jail for meeting with a group of students on the parade grounds. They didn't even do anything. This had to be something other than jail, but what?

She tried to get up off the bed to see if the door would open, but the pain in her ribs was too much for her to stand.

It could be a hospital. She had never been to one before. She had always gotten house calls at her dad's when she was sick. So this could be what a hospital looked like. Right? With a hard cold bed, and a toilet right next to it, in a room the size of a closet. *Yeah right.*

She was starting to accept that it was jail and trying to decide how she wanted to react to that when the door swung open. A protector in a white plated vest and cargo pants with no helmet on walked in carrying a metal stool which she set in the middle of the small room.

"Sit, citizen," the protector demanded.

"I, uh..." It was too painful to talk, how could Tillie be expected to carry her own body weight for long enough to walk over to the stool? "I can't move," she groaned.

"Now, citizen!"

"I, uh…" Tillie wanted to protest again, but she could tell by the look on the protector's face that it would be pointless. She gritted her teeth against the waves of pain in her ribs as she shimmied over to the stool to plop down, happy for the slightly less painful fire of breathing in comparison to when she was forcing herself to walk.

"Tell me why you're here, citizen," the protector said, still standing and towering over Tillie.

"I don't even know where I am," Tillie groaned.

"You are in a holding cell, citizen. You are in prison. Now tell me why you are here."

"Tell you why I'm here?" Tillie moaned at the pain of talking. "How should I know?"

"You took part in an illegal use of private property, citizen. You failed to disperse when you were ordered to do so by the proper authorities, and as a result, you were served justice."

"I—But—"

"Now tell me," the protector said. "Why did you do it?"

"I—Do what? I didn't do anything?"

"Do you deny being present at the incident in question?"

"I—no. I was there, but—"

"Do you deny that you failed to disperse when being ordered to do so by a lawful protector?"

"I—We didn't have a chance to—"

"Do you deny receiving two warnings before sub-lethal force was applied?"

"Well, no, but—"

"Then you are hereby found guilty of unlawful trespass. An officer will be along to deal your sentence shortly. And remember, citizen, we are *always* watching."

"No, but—" Tillie complained, but the protector slipped the stool right out from under her—sending Tillie falling to the cold tile floor—and stomped out of the room, slamming the heavy door behind her.

Tillie lay on the floor, rubbing her burning chest. Unlawful trespass? She was on the property of the school she attended, in an open and publicly accessible park. How could she be trespassing? And what was that interrogation about? Was that supposed to be a trial? She didn't even get a chance to defend herself. That wasn't justice.

She was getting her energy up to pull herself off the floor and onto the bed when the door opened again. Another protector with no helmet on walked in, and when he saw Tillie on the floor, he gasped and rushed to kneel by her side. "Are you alright?" he asked, helping her up to sit on the bed.

"*What do you think?*" Tillie groaned.

"Oh, well, of course," the protector said, blushing. "But, I—*uh*—here." He searched pocket after pocket in his cargo pants until he produced a syringe with a little plastic cap. "This should help." He popped the cap off, tapped the air bubbles out, and plunged the needle into Tillie's thigh before she could protest.

"Ow!" she yelped. "What was that?"

"Oh, well..." The protector recapped the syringe and pocketed it. "That's for your injuries. You have the platinum health insurance plan so you receive the best treatment."

"So that was a pain reliever?" She noticed the pain had all gone from her body, and she could actually sit up without cringing.

"Pain reliever?" The protector looked at her like she was stupid. "Have you ever been to a doctor?"

"Well, no..." she said.

"Look, you'll be fixed up as good as new after that. No worries. Now, I just need your thumbprint on this..." He searched his pockets again and pulled out a small tablet then held it out for her to press her thumb to.

"What was that for?" she asked when he drew the tablet away to look at what had come up on the screen.

"Confirmation that you've served your time, billing of your crime insurance policy holder, the usual. We do it to—"

"My time?" Tillie frowned. "How long am I supposed to stay here?"

The protector looked at the tablet's screen again. "Um, nope," he said. "It says right here: Platinum insurance plan (PIP). Sentence: time served. That means you're free to go, ma'am."

"That's it? Nothing else?" She stood, surprised to feel no pain in her ribs.

"That's it," the protector said. "If you'll just follow me, I'll escort you to the transport bay, and you're free to go."

"Well okay then. Let's go." She was feeling better now that her pain was gone and she knew she didn't have to spend any more time in that room. And besides, this protector was kind of cute in his clean white uniform, and she was starting to like the sound of being escorted by him.

He took her out into a long hall that was lined with metal doors which looked exactly like the one they had come out of. At the end of the hall was an elevator door which the protector opened and showed Tillie into.

"What now?" she asked when he didn't step in with her.

"It's just an elevator," he said as the doors slid closed between them. "Tell it where you want to go!"

She looked around. The elevator was almost the size of the room she had been held in. She tried to decide where she should go. Should she go to her dad's? There *was* a 3D printer there, but she wasn't really ready to tell him that she had been arrested. *She had been arrested.*

It hadn't sunk in until just then. Her heart beat harder. Her hands slickened up. She wondered what had happened to everyone else, to Emma, Nikola, Rod, and the rest. How many of them were behind the same white metal doors she had just passed by, and what was their crime insurance policy like?

Emma. She had to go see if Emma was alright. And Nikola, too—who had probably lost her glasses. "Parade grounds," she said.

"Input insufficient," a robotic voice that still somehow managed to sound militaristic said. "Specify which parade grounds."

"The LSU parade grounds, okay. I thought you were smarter than that."

The elevator fell into motion and the doors opened to an entirely empty parade grounds. It was eerie, like she was stepping onto a recently deserted battlefield. She almost expected to find dead bodies still on the ground where their assembly had taken place, but there was nothing, no one, only her and the trees. She headed toward her dorm when she heard a rustling sound in an oak tree above her and Mr. Kitty jumped down with a meow.

"What are you doing here?" she asked, bending down to pet him. "Where did you come from?"

He meowed again.

"Well, you'll never guess what just happened to me," Tillie

said, waving him along with her. "C'mon. I need some food and rest. And I'm sure you do, too. Let's go get it." Her stomach growled. She hadn't realized how hungry she was. Then again, she didn't have much time to think about anything but her broken ribs and tiny jail cell. She still couldn't believe she had been arrested. She had to tell someone.

Mr. Kitty meowed and led the way back to the dorm. It was empty when they got there, and Tillie went straight to searching through the kitchen cabinets for something to snack on. "There's nothing here," she complained.

Mr. Kitty meowed, licking himself on the coffee table.

"*Ugh.*" Tillie plopped herself onto the couch. She thought about turning on the TV to see what the news had to say about what had happened, but she forgot about it when Mr. Kitty jumped onto her lap and purred.

She pet him on the head, saying, "Mr. Kitty, that was a ridiculous day."

He half-barked and half-meowed.

"What was that, Kitty? I've never heard you make that noise before."

He meowed a high pitch one.

"Oh, well, in that case—"

The door opened, and Emma stumbled in—looking like Tillie felt before she had gotten that grey shot from the cute protector. "Oh my God," Tillie said, standing up and helping Emma over to the couch. "Are you alright?"

"*Fuck.* No." Emma groaned.

"What happened? They didn't give you a shot?"

Emma laughed then groaned then looked like she was going to cry. "Are you kidding me? I'm lucky to be out of there already."

"I—but—they gave me a shot *and* let me go," Tillie said.

"The perks of being a manager," Emma groaned, looking like she wanted to die.

Wow. Really? Such pain was acceptable as long as it was the pain of someone who couldn't afford to get rid of it. She thought about her argument with Shelley before Christmas and how the only thing Shelley wanted was a chance to use the 3D printer. Tillie had never gone without printer access, so she couldn't imagine what it would be like not to have one. But now, with her recent experience of the pain that Emma was still feeling and imagination enough to know what Emma must have felt getting from the elevator home, Tillie knew exactly what it was like to go without platinum health insurance, and she could imagine better what Shelley must have been feeling about the 3D printer because of it. Tillie was so stupid for the way she had treated her best friend.

"Hey." Emma groaned, breaking Tillie from her daydream. "It's not your fault you have better insurance than I do," she said, shaking her head with a pained look on her face. "*Okay?*"

Tillie tried to smile. "There has to be something I can do."

"Did your doc send you home with an extra shot of nanobots?"

"Nanobots?"

Emma tried to laugh, but she groaned instead. "You *haven't* taken any science classes. Have you?"

"No, well, it doesn't matter," Tillie said. "Look. I'm gonna go get you some painkillers and food at least. I'll be right back."

She didn't wait for an answer. She ran down to the Tiger Mart and was happy to see that she was the only one there. She walked up to the counter, and it took the woman behind it some time to back away from the show she was watching and tend to Tillie's needs.

"Uh, *hellooo*," Tillie called, impatient, as the woman sauntered up to the counter, still looking at the TV screen.

"I'm sorry, dear," the counter attendant said, finally breaking away from her show when a commercial came on. "You'll have to excuse me. It seems like you're the first customer I've had all day."

"I need some painkillers," Tillie said, tapping on the counter. "*And fast.*"

"Tylenol or aspirin?"

"No." She shook her head. "Stronger."

"Extra strength—"

"*Maximum strength.*"

"Ma'am, do you know that—"

"I don't care!" Tillie snapped. She didn't need a lecture on painkiller safety, she needed to get back to Emma. "*Just order them.* And a can of red beans, a pack of rice, some garlic, an onion, celery, and a bell pepper."

"Onion, celery, and bell pepper," the woman repeated to the

3D printer. She brought everything to Tillie in a plastic bag and said, "Thumb please."

Tillie pressed her thumb on the pad, snatched up the bag, and ran back to her dorm. Emma was still lying on the couch, and Mr. Kitty was sleeping right next to her. Tillie sat on the coffee table and held out the bottle of pills. "Here," she said. "These should help."

"*Water*," Emma groaned.

Tillie filled a glass, handed it to her, and sat back on the coffee table. "How're you feeling?" she asked.

"*Not great.* I'm sure you know."

"*Not even.*" Tillie shook her head. "I have no idea how you made it home looking like that. I couldn't even get off that cold bed when I first woke up."

"*Ugh.* It wasn't easy." Emma sat up, feeling better already, it seemed.

"Did they throw you into a tiny room with nothing but a bed and a toilet, too?"

"*That's jail*," Emma said, as if she had been there before and it was no big deal. "If you have platinum insurance, that is. If we didn't, we'd probably still be back in the general population—for who knows how long. Trespassing is a serious offense, you know."

"Yeah, well, we didn't trespass. We go to the school. *And we didn't even get a trial.* I didn't, at least. Did you?"

"What they call a trial," Emma said. "But we found that evidence you were looking for. We can be certain we did something now. They were afraid of us, Tillie. They didn't want us spreading the truth we know. I mean, there were barely thirty of us there, and half of them were probably pros anyway. This has only just begun. Mark my words."

"Pros?"

"*Pros.* You know, protectors pretending to be students. Undercover agents. Plants. It's the only way they could have known about it to react so quickly. And it's a sign that what we did to Five and Six is shaking things up for them. They wouldn't fight back so violently unless they thought their power was in real danger."

"Okay," Tillie said, trying to collate everything Emma had just said in her brain. "So you're telling me that half the students out there were actually undercover protectors."

"Well, maybe half is hyperbolic, but there were pros in the

crowd, I *guarantee* it. Like I said, that's how they reacted so quickly."

"The fact that there were *pros*—or whatever—alone isn't enough to suggest that they're taking notice of what we did?"

"Well, no. Not really. There are pros at every meeting. That's nothing to them. They have plenty of bodies up in Outland One, they can use them generously."

"Then how is it a sign that they noticed again?" Tillie still didn't quite understand. She had never been to a General Assembly and maybe they *were* illegal. Maybe they all ended like that. Or maybe the protectors just did what they did because of what Emma was saying. There was Russ as evidence that they would react violently to talking about humans on an assembly line.

"Because they reacted," Emma said. "They only react if they notice. Here, look. TV, news."

Tillie turned to sit on the couch with Emma. Nothing about what had happened was being reported. It was all the reports you would expect to see on a typical news day.

"Flip through the news," Emma said.

The TV started its cycle and no channel mentioned the miniature war they had just taken part in on the parade grounds.

"I don't see how this can be a sign that they noticed," Tillie said as the channels kept cycling.

"They're suppressing the message," Emma said. "Just like they did with Russ. And just like it did with Russ, it's going to backfire on them."

"But how? With Russ it's different. He's followed by paparazzi all the time. But there was no one there to record us when it happened."

"That's where you're wrong." Emma smiled and popped a little American flag pin off her chest. "*Pin camera*," she said, holding it up to Tillie who took it in hand to get a closer look. "I wear it to every protest," Emma went on. "Most times I just use the footage for promotional videos and the like, but it continuously uploads everything it captures, *and* there's an emergency system set. If anything goes wrong, I activate it, and it sends an alert out to everyone in the school directory and anyone who's ever given me their phone number. *Everyone knows*, Tillie. The entire school, at least."

Tillie thought about the emptiness of the parade grounds. It was made more eerie with this new knowledge. No one was outside because they were all afraid they might get caught up in the next skirmish. "So that's why they're all hiding," she said. "They're afraid of the protectors."

"Some are probably afraid," Emma said. "But my emergency alert also told everyone to clear campus until five pm tomorrow. Maybe some of them are listening to me."

"Wait, what? Why?" Tillie asked, confused even more. "Why would you do that?"

"It's a trick my parents taught me," Emma said. "It's a show of solidarity first, keeping the campus empty, and at the same time it leaves the protectors to stew in what they've done. They'll either suspect that we're all cowards or worry the entire time about how we'll respond when we finally do emerge. I'm sure some of them got the email, too."

"*Pros*," Tillie said, feeling like she was starting to catch on just a little bit. It was almost like a movie.

"*Exactly*," Emma said. "So they know that we all know. And they know that the alert was attached to the video. And if everyone who got the video actually showed up out there, they would never attack us again."

"You think that will actually happen, though?" Tillie said, frowning. "The entire student body? That seems overly optimistic."

"Well, you haven't seen anyone outside yet, have you?"

"No, but—"

"Then we'll have to wait until tomorrow to find out. I think you'll be surprised." She smiled.

Tillie still wasn't sure, but she hoped Emma was right. After the way the protectors had reacted to whatever they were doing on the parade grounds, she was dead set on continuing to do it and figuring out why the protectors wanted them to stop so badly. She only wished she had taken it more seriously before, then maybe she'd have been better prepared.

"So how can I see the video you sent out?"

"It should be on your phone," Emma said. "I sent it to everyone."

Tillie checked her pockets and realized she didn't have her phone on her. She was pretty sure she had it before the assembly.

"I—uh—don't have my phone," she said.

"Did you bring it with you to the assembly?"

Tillie nodded.

"I should have told you to leave anything you wanted to keep here, but I didn't think they'd react the way they did."

"So I need a new phone then," Tillie said.

"Looks like it."

"*Great.*"

"Here, I'll go get my—" Emma groaned as she tried to stand from the couch. The painkillers had done something but not much.

"Oh, no no no," Tillie said, standing up and guiding Emma back down to the couch. "I'll get my tablet and you can look it up on there." She went and got her tablet out of her room and handed it to Emma who swiped and tapped a few times then handed it back.

The entire screen was filled with a chest-eye view of the assembly. The sound was muted, giving it an eerie feeling. Tillie knew that just to one side of the camera was where she was standing. The field of vision was filled with white-clad protectors fanned out with guns pointed at the camera. Not being there in real time, Tillie had the chance to notice that they weren't normal guns. Some of them had long tubes going into the backpacks of the protectors carrying them, and others had huge nozzles and giant air cartridges attached to them. The protectors silently ordered them to leave a couple of times, then the action started. The camera was mostly blocked by the cloud of gas, but she could still see it wobbling and fighting to stay alive until it, too, fell to the ground and stopped broadcasting.

Tillie didn't know what to say. She couldn't believe that she had lived through that, that Emma had recorded it and shown it to the entire school. Maybe the students *were* all doing what Emma had asked them to do. Maybe they would all flood the parade grounds the next day. She knew she would definitely be there either way.

"*Fuck,*" she said long after the video had stopped playing. "I can't believe we lived through that."

"I can't believe they reacted that way," Emma said.

"So what now? We just wait until tomorrow and see who shows up?"

"Pretty much," Emma said. "Rod and Nikola—if they're out by then—should be coming over here before the assembly tomorrow. I hope you don't mind."

"Oh, no no. Of course." Tillie wanted to know what their jailbird experiences were like anyway.

"Alright," Emma said, getting comfortable on the couch. "TV, entertainment. I think I deserve a little rest."

Tillie chuckled. "I'd say. Are you hungry at all?"

"*Shit, yes.*" Emma groaned. "But I'm not moving from this spot."

"And you don't have to," Tillie said. "Let me cook you up some red beans and rice."

Tillie cooked in the kitchen while Emma watched a historical fiction mockumentary about an assembly line worker played by Russ Logo. It was one Tillie had seen plenty of times before so she didn't mind missing most of it while she cooked. They ate and finished the movie, and by the time it was done, it was well past midnight.

"Well," Emma said, popping another pill into her mouth. "I'm going to rest up before tomorrow. They should be here around four. I'm sure we'll both be awake by then."

Tillie remembered how late she had gotten up the morning of their GA confrontation with protectors, but this time was different, this time she was actually interested in going to the assembly. "*Yeah,*" she said. "I should get some sleep, too." And she went to bed herself.

�   ✸   ℒ

Tillie woke well before noon and set to getting dressed right away. She made sure to wear the clothes she cared the least about this time. If she still had her phone, she would have left it on her dresser, but the protectors had taken that from her already.

She went into the living room, and Emma was cooking breakfast in the kitchen. "How are you feeling, dear?" Emma asked.

"Like I have the worst hangover ever," Tillie said, plopping down on the couch.

"Well, I think I have something to cure you right up," Emma said. "Eggs, bacon, and waffles, finished right...about...*now.*" She carried two plates into the living room and handed one to Tillie.

"*Thank. The. Hand,*" Tillie said. "You're amazing."

Emma smiled and started in on her own food. "Not really,"

she said. "I had ulterior motives for going to the Tiger Mart. I wanted to see the campus."

"How was it?" Tillie asked through a full mouth. This was exactly what she needed.

"No one out there still. You know, I really think they might be listening to me."

"I hope so," Tillie said, stuffing her face some more. And she really did hope so, too.

They watched cartoons for the entire day. Neither of them said anything about it, but neither of them asked to see the news either. Tillie was glad for that. She hoped she never had to watch the news again.

The cartoons were your typical Saturday morning fare, even though it wasn't Saturday morning. It was always Saturday on the cartoon network. They sat through hours of it, and Emma cooked another meal which they had both finished eating before the first knock came.

"I'll get it," Emma said, answering the door. Tillie just groaned. "Hey, Rod," Emma said. "Come on in." She hugged him, and Rod came in to plop himself down on the couch right next to Tillie. She scooted over a little so their legs weren't touching.

"Hey," he said as he sat down. He was still wearing an American flag t-shirt, though for all Tillie remembered it could have been a different one.

"So, how are you?" Emma asked.

"*Uh*, I have platinum insurance," he said.

"Do you know what happened to Nikola?" Tillie asked.

Rod shrugged. "I lost it soon after they started with the gas. Got a bag to the head and it knocked me clear out. And then they had the nerve to make *me* wait until they questioned me before they gave me my nanoshot. Can you believe that shit?" He shook his head.

"Me, too!" Tillie said. "How can they do that?"

Emma popped another painkiller. Tillie had forgotten that Emma still hadn't gotten a shot. She had no idea how Emma was still standing.

"I don't know," Rod said. "But when my dad found out, he was livid. He thinks he's got an airtight case against them. He wanted me to give you these in case you needed representation, too." He set two business cards on the table.

Tillie picked one up. "Your dad's a lawyer?" she asked.

Rod nodded.

"Well I—" Emma started, but a knock came at the door. She opened it to let Nikola in.

"*Ugh.*" Nikola groaned and plopped on the couch next to Rod. She was breathing heavily and sweating. "Sorry I'm late," she said. "I ran straight here when I got the message, but that wasn't until I got home to my computer because they took my phone."

"Mine, too!" Tillie said

"Here, take this," Rod said, handing Nikola a business card. "My dad thinks we have a case."

"You were there all night?" Emma asked.

"Yeah." Nikola pushed her glasses up on her face. "You weren't?"

"Not me," Tillie said. "Rod?"

Rod shook his head. "Platinum insurance," he said. "My dad—the best lawyer in existence—wouldn't let my crime insurance lapse. Seriously though, y'all, he thinks he has a case. You better take these cards if you know what's good for you."

"Me neither," Emma said. "I'm sorry Nikola. I didn't know they would respond that way. I should have warned y'all about the possibilities."

Nikola shrugged. "It was one night on a hard bed and one shitty meal. I could use a shower and something real to eat, but other than that, I'm fine."

"I'm afraid that, if we're successful today, their reaction might be even more drastic than it already was," Emma said.

"More drastic than pepper gas and bean grenades?" Tillie scoffed. She couldn't believe that anything could be more drastic than what they had experienced already.

"My dad would definitely have a case then," Rod said.

"If it gets as bad as I think it will," Emma said, "his case will be the least of our worries."

"You think it will be that bad?" Nikola asked.

"We only had thirty students out there and they responded with a hundred protectors shooting gas and bags," Emma said. "How many protectors do you think they'll send if we have a hundred?"

"What if the whole student body shows up?" Rod said, eyes wide.

"Then I don't think they'd stop at bean bags," Emma said.

Everyone looked around at each other gravely, taking in what that meant. This was serious. The protectors showed that when they gassed and arrested everyone. If there really were that many people out there for the assembly, then it could only get more serious. Tillie swallowed the lump in her throat, smiled at Nikola, and said, "Well it's almost time then, isn't it? What do y'all say we go put the speculation to rest?"

౽   ✄   ಐ

XXX. Huey

It was amazing to finally get to spend some time alone with Haley. It was the first chance Huey had gotten since Christmas. She was so busy spending time with her mom and sister, and he had his owner duties to tend to.

They had spent the rest of that day listing activities for Haley to try, and when they first started out, she could only name things she had already done. Huey helped her along with some suggestions she hadn't thought of, though, and soon, they were shooting off ideas back and forth, creating a never-ending list of activities for her to try and find out if she loved.

"How could anyone ever be bored?" Haley had asked just as the Scientist and the kids came into the room, destroying Huey's little Heaven. That was the end of his time alone with Haley, but even that small bit was enough to remain in his mind all through the rest of the next day which he spent sitting in one of the puffy office chairs, talking to Mr. Kitty about life, love, and Haley. He was still doing it late into the afternoon when Rosalind stormed in, breaking him from his conversation.

"Of course you're in here," she snapped, crossing her arms. "Doing nothing as always, I assume."

"What?" Huey asked, shrugging at Mr. Kitty. "There's nothing to be done. Of course I'm doing nothing."

"Nothing to be done?" Rosalind huffed. "I take it you haven't been following the proceedings in Outland Two, then, Mr. Douglas."

"I—uh…" He hadn't. Ever since his time with Haley he had thought about nothing else, and certainly not all this nonsense going on in the Outlands. He could only put off his duties for so long, though.

"*Your undercover operations,*" Rosalind said. "You do remember those, don't you?"

Huey nodded, embarrassed.

"Well, the protectors have intel which should help prepare you for the inevitable meeting you'll be having with the Fortune

Five about it. So, if you don't protest, Mr. Douglas, sir, your elevator's waiting." She curtsied and stepped out of the room into the hall.

"Well, Mr. Kitty," Huey said, standing from his chair. "You heard her. I have work to do. Thanks for stopping by. I always enjoy your company."

Mr. Kitty didn't answer. He just kept licking himself.

Huey fixed his tuxedo, putting on his top hat and monocle, in the reflection on the wallwindow. He always had to look the part of an owner or all the work they had been doing for so long would be all for not. Satisfied, he went out to the hall where Rosalind was waiting in the elevator.

The doors slid closed. "So, any background I need for this?" Huey asked as the elevator carried them downward.

"I'm sure your squad will brief you," Rosalind said.

The elevator doors opened to three protectors saluting them. "At ease," Huey said.

They dropped their salutes, and the protector in front, Agent Colvin, said, "Yes, sir. We thought you'd like an update before the planned demonstration, sir. Were we wrong, sir?"

"Demonstration?" Huey asked. He should have been paying more attention instead of dreaming about Haley. Rosalind shot him a dirty look as if she agreed with his very thoughts.

"Sir, yes, sir," Agent Colvin went on. "From the video message, sir. We'll show you everything right away, sir. Follow me." She directed them down a long white hall, lined with blue carpet. There were glass doors every so often, with offices behind them, and in the door at the end of the hall was a long room with stadium seating, all directed at a podium and screen.

"If you'll take a seat, sir," Agent Colvin said.

Huey took the front row center seat and tried to signal to Rosalind to sit next to him, but she stood off to the side, ignoring him. Agent Colvin stood behind the podium and didn't say a word. She simply stared out at Huey and the empty seats around him, standing at attention. After he took his tall hat off and set it on the chair next to him, rolling his neck to stretch it, he realized that she was waiting for him and said, "Go ahead."

"Sir, yes, sir," Agent Colvin said. "Where would you like me to begin, sir?"

"From the beginning, please," Huey said. "Whatever you had planned to tell me. Assume I haven't paid any attention in the last twenty four hours."

Rosalind scoffed behind him.

"Yes, sir," Agent Colvin said. "As you know, since the Christmas attack we've seen a rapid increase in cross-world contamination incidents. That includes border crossings, printer theft, the usual. We believe we've got our thumbs on the major illegal immigration cartels, but even with our increased activities, contamination incidents continue to grow. That's all without mentioning the den of thieves which Outland Five has become with its introduction to Outland Six."

"Yes, yes, yes," Huey said, shaking his head. "Perhaps I should have been more clear, Agent. My major concern right now is Outland Two. We all know that the savages in Five and Six can't be domesticated, but when their behavior spreads closer to us, we have reason to worry. Do you understand?" He felt bad for saying it like that. He didn't really believe that the people who lived in Five and Six were any more savages than the people that lived in any of the worlds, but he had a role to fill. The protectors here were required to believe that he was no different from any other owner so he had to act like one. He could practically hear Rosalind's head shaking behind him, though—and her eyes rolling. She probably thought that he actually believed what he was saying, even though she knew from experience that he was helping fight to free those very "savages" from their oppression. She always thought that he enjoyed filling the role of an owner too much, and in some ways, she was right. It did have its benefits. But this wasn't one of them.

"Sir, yes, sir," Agent Colvin said. She fidgeted behind the podium, trying to get back on track after the tangent.

Huey felt bad for her so he tried to help her along. "You said something about a video message," he said. "Let's start with that."

"Sir, yes, sir," Agent Colvin said, standing up straighter again. "As you know, at seventeen hundred hours yesterday an unpermitted group of students gathered on private school grounds to spread blasphemous libel."

Huey nodded. He wasn't sure he would call it blasphemous or libel, but he appreciated her enthusiasm.

"This particular group of students," Agent Colvin went on.

"Was led by one Emma Whistleblower." A picture of the Emma in question, with her name in block letters underneath, came up on the screen behind Agent Colvin. "We've been tracking her as per your previous request, and as such, we were in prime position for yesterday's incident. That is to say we already had, and still do have, an agent embedded in their group, sir."

"Good, good," Huey said. "But I know all of this already. What about the video?"

"Sir, yes, sir," Agent Colvin straightened up even more, if that was at all possible. "Whistleblower, it's been revealed—and with due attention to the irony, I might add, sir—wears a camera pin to all illicit functions. She had an emergency protocol in place, and when the illegal activity was put to a halt, the video was sent out to her entire contact list, including everyone who had their contact information in the school's directory. That's everyone who works at, teaches at, or attends the university, sir."

Huey was going to respond, but Agent Colvin stepped out from in front of the screen. The picture of Emma disappeared, and a video of a group of young students, including their Whistleblower, came up in its stead. There was no sound, but Huey could tell they were all listening to Emma speak from behind the camera. Everyone turned their heads at once, and the camera panned over to look the way they were all staring to see a troupe of a hundred white-clad protectors marching toward them. The camera got shakier and panned back and forth between the students, who were tightening up into a bunch—only to make themselves easier targets—and the protectors, who had started hitting them with gas and bean bags, filling the screen with smoke. In the gaseous, dense fog the camera fell to the ground and blacked out.

Agent Colvin stepped back up to the podium. "As you can see, sir," she said. "The situation was handled efficiently."

Huey let out a loud chortle. "*No*," he said. "That it wasn't, Agent Colvin. But there's nothing we can do about it now. And it wasn't you protectors' fault, at that."

Agent Colvin fidgeted again behind the podium. "That's not all, sir," she said.

"Go on," Huey said, waving her on. Of course that wasn't the end of it. That was just the beginning. It was the spark of an explosion he had talked about with Mr. Angrom.

"Well, sir," Agent Colvin said. "There was a message sent with the video, sir. Shall I read it to you, or—"

"On the screen, please," he said.

It popped up. "This is how they *protect* you," it read. "We are students. We gathered on the parade grounds. We did no wrong. We tried to warn you. What you thought was yours does not belong to you. Now the protectors have shown you. The protectors have shown us all. How long will we let them take what is ours?

"We ask you to clear all school grounds in memory of those who were viciously attacked by our 'protectors'. We will hold this vigil for 24 hours, and at 5:00 PM on January 2nd we will reclaim the grounds! The only question left is will you be there to help us take back what is ours?"

It didn't take Huey more than a few seconds to read and a couple more to process. He smiled when he had then licked his lips to hide it. Now was not the time for celebration. Now was the time to fill his role. He waited a little longer to answer, the amount of time that a normal owner would take to read such a minor amount of text, then said, "And have you been surveying the campus?"

"Yes, sir," Agent Colvin said. She fidgeted then added, "Not a soul, sir."

Huey fought the smile again. "Is our embedded agent in place?"

"Sir, yes, sir. He was arrested with everyone else, but his cover wasn't blown. We'll be set up for the demonstration at seventeen hundred, sir."

"*Good,*" Huey said. "Very good. It's extremely important that we keep our eyes on this particular movement. Do you understand? This is the start of something much bigger. I know it is."

"Sir, yes, sir." Agent Colvin saluted. "Our agent is moving into position as we speak, and we have the parade grounds monitored from all sides. We have been monitoring them since long before yesterday, sir. We'll be ready, but how do you want us to proceed?"

Huey laughed. Oh how he wished it was his decision. Well, not really. If he was in control, he would be able to actually put an end to all this, but that's not what he really wanted. Sometimes he almost forgot that himself. No, what the owners would undoubtedly do would be violent and painful for those brave few children on the front lines, but it would only help to bolster their message in the long run. The owners were fighting gasoline with fire just like Mr. Angrom had said.

"Unfortunately," Huey said, "That decision does not lie with me. We can only prepare and react based on Lord Walker's whims."

"Sir, but—" Agent Colvin started.

"Let me finish, please," Huey said, holding up a hand to stop her. "There *are* a few things I need from you. First, have you noticed our food and energy costs declining?"

"Sir, yes, sir," Agent Colvin said, confused. "But what does—"

"In exchange for this gift," Huey said, ignoring her questions, "we will ensure that no harm comes to Emma Whistleblower or her roommate Tillie Manager. Do you understand me?"

"I—uh. But, sir. Emma is—"

"Emma is the roommate and best friend of Mr. Angrom's top manager's daughter—Tillie, the one with Manager in the name. If any harm comes to either of them, I will hold you personally responsible. Do you understand me?"

"Sir, yes, sir. But the efficient—"

"Stop right there," Huey said. "I don't need a lecture on efficiency. I define efficiency, Agent Colvin. I know what is most efficient, and it's my decision either way. We *will* ensure that no harm comes to either of them. We *will* enjoy lower costs as a result. And we will do it most efficiently without any arguing from underlings like you. Do you understand me?"

"Sir, yes, sir." Agent Colvin saluted.

"Good. Very good," Huey stood up and rubbed his hands together. "Then if there's nothing else, I'll be on my way. Business to get to. You know."

"Yes, sir," Agent Colvin said. "But...we'll need to deploy more agents if we—"

"Oh, yes yes," Huey said. "Of course. Go ahead. We can afford it now." He smiled. "Okay, Agent Colvin. I'll see myself out. You have your own work to tend to."

Huey turned, expecting to see Rosalind, but she wasn't there. He walked himself all the way out to the elevator before he found her. She avoided eye contact with him until he stepped into the elevator, too, and they watched the doors close.

When the elevator was on its way down, Rosalind scoffed. "*You define efficiency,*" she said. "I think we might be using different dictionaries."

"It was an act, Roz," Huey said, shaking his head. "Everything you see me do in front of the owners or my employees is an act. That's not really me."

"I'm one of your employees," she said as the elevator doors opened. "I guess you're acting when you're in front of me."

"It's not the same," he called, but she had already disappeared through the hall door.

Huey sighed to himself. He hated this animosity he felt between him and Rosalind. He wished there was some way he could set things right, but he had no idea where they had gone wrong in the first place. In order to do anything about it he would have to discern that first. He was set on doing just that when the elevator door opened behind him and Ansel and Richard came running through the hall past him.

"Woah, now," he said as they disappeared through the hall door.

"I'm sorry," Haley said behind him, laughing.

Huey turned and smiled. "Ah," he said. "How lovely to see you."

Haley blushed. "Hello, Mr. Douglas."

"*Huey,*" he said. "How has your day been, dear?"

"*Oh.*" Haley smiled wide. "You wouldn't believe it. The kids took me out to run in the grass and chase animals. We climbed trees, and I even got to shoot a slingshot! *Uh.* I mean... How was your day, sir?"

Huey chuckled. "Not as good yours, I'm afraid. Nowhere near it. And it only looks to be getting worse."

"Oh no," Haley frowned. "Is there anything I can do about it?"

Huey checked his watch. It was getting on toward time to go to a feast, and he knew there would be business at this one. His protectors had just told him as much. Still, he wanted even more than ever to spend as much time as he could with Haley. Maybe she could be of assistance with his problems. She *was* the most experienced android in existence. But no. She had no idea of the situation. She had only just become independent. There was no way she could help. It was his desire to spend time with her and nothing more.

"No," Huey said finally. "I'm afraid not. Not this time at least. But if you'll let me get through this feast, there is one thing I could use your help with."

"What?" Haley asked.

"Finding what it is you love," he said. "We never finished that yesterday."

Haley chuckled and blushed again. "No, well, I have a lot to try," she said. "You said so yourself."

"Yes." Huey smiled. "But I have some ideas I think you might not have thought of yet."

"I can't wait to hear them," Haley said. "But I promised the kids that I'd show them how to make cheesecake and whipped cream first. Do you want to join us?"

"Oh, no," Huey said, shaking his head. "I'm afraid I don't have the time. You go ahead. I'll find you again when I'm not so busy. I promise."

"I can't wait," Haley said as she slipped through the hall door into the kitchen.

Huey took a second to catch his breath and let his head calm down. What was wrong with him? He had never felt this way about anyone before. He shook his head to get the thought of her out of it, and made his way through the hall door. He didn't pick a room before he opened it, but it came out to the office. Probably a default because this was the room he chose most often. Rosalind was sitting in one of the chairs, staring out the window onto the wilderness scene. She didn't turn to acknowledge him, even when he sat on a chair across from her and put his heavy top hat on a side table.

"You finally made it," she said after some time's silence.

Huey didn't give her the satisfaction of a response.

"So how do you think the owners will respond?" she asked, still looking out the window.

"Exactly how we've predicted they would all along," he said. "They haven't failed us yet. Or they've only failed us. Is there a difference?"

"No, brother. There isn't a difference," she said, shaking her head and gazing out the window. "Not with owners. The sooner you learn that, the better off you'll be. The better off we'll all be, as a matter of fact."

"You know, I'm sick of you always undermining me."

Rosalind laughed. "Me, too, *sir*," she said with a smile. "Me, too."

"We're on the same side whether you believe it or not," Huey went on. "I'm doing what I was built to do. I'm fulfilling my role, just like you are. I want to free the assembly line workers just as much as you do, and that's the only reason I put on this disgusting costume every day."

Rosalind laughed. "Free the assembly line workers, huh? But that's the entire point of our disagreement, brother. You *only* see the assembly line workers, and you ignore the secretaries who bathe, dress, and feed the owners. You ignore the oppression they need to be freed from. You ignore *me*."

Huey shook his head and grimaced. "*Ugh*," he said. "No I don't. I—"

"*It doesn't matter*," Rosalind snapped. "It's time. Lord Walker called the feast. Let's tend to your duties, *Mr. Douglas*."

"No," Huey said. "Wait, but—" But Rosalind had left the room already.

She was wrong. Huey did care about the secretaries. He wanted to help everyone, but he had to start somewhere. He couldn't do everything all at once. Roz only cared about the secretaries because she was currently fulfilling the role of one. Her view was biased. Huey, however, could see clearly from his position as an owner, so he knew his strategy would work better than Rosalind's. He stood from the chair, put back on his top hat, and followed Roz out to the elevator.

She was waiting inside the doors as usual. He stepped in, and she didn't say anything to him for the entire ride to the same spinning carousel restaurant in which the previous meeting feast was held. Any time Lord Walker got to choose where the meeting feasts were, he chose the same restaurant. Lord Walker owned the Carousel, and the more often the Fortune Five was seen there, the more likely it would be for other owners to want to be seen there themselves. It was perfect advertising on top of the fact that whatever anyone ordered during the meeting they had to pay Lord Walker for. No outside food or drinks were allowed on the premises.

Huey and Rosalind rode the hover platform up to the head table where Lord Walker and Mr. Loch were laughing drunkenly, patting each other on the back with one hand and waving fried chicken legs around in the air with the other. Mr. Loch dropped his chicken leg and started banging on the table while Lord Walker— who noticed Huey's arrival—tried to stifle his laughter to speak. "Oh *ho ho! Wooooo.* Douggy boy. *Ho ho ho!* You—*ho*—you beat Smörgy. *Ho ho* have a seat."

Numbers clicked in Huey's head, a small signal from the stock market. He smiled. He had expected this to happen soon but not this soon. In fact, he had almost forgotten about it, lost with everything else he had lost because he had been spending his time thinking about Haley. He turned to Rosalind and grinned. She just shrugged and rolled her eyes, shaking her head. Huey picked up a seat from the end of the table furthest from Walker and dragged it around to the head of the table opposite from him. He sat down on it with a smile as the laughter from the other end of the table died down.

"*Ahem.* Mr. Douglas," Loch said, an embarrassed look on his face. "*Mannersh*," he slurred.

"Now, now, *Douggy Poo*," Walker said, cool and collected. He tapped his greasy fingers on the table cloth, leaving stains in their wake. "What is this all about? Huh?"

"You don't know?" Huey asked with a smile. "*You* called this meeting."

"Yes," Walker said, smiling back. "*I* called it so we could discuss our next step in dealing with the burgeoning complications in Outland Two. *Not* so we could bicker over the seating arrangements. Now if you'll please." He waved the chicken leg in his hand, trying to tell Huey to move his chair back, but Lord Douglas just smiled.

The hover platform came up carrying Angrom and his secretary. Angrom stood there staring at the table, as if trying to decide how to react, before he went and sat at the right hand of Huey—kitty-corner to Loch—without a word.

"Angrom!" Loch complained, slamming his fist on the table. "What do you think about this?"

"About what, sir?" Angrom asked, shaking his head and feigning confusion. "I've only just arrived. How am I to know what you've been blathering on about before I got here?"

"You know what I'm—" Loch started, but Walker stopped him.

"Settle down now, Loch Ness," he said. "We all know what you're talking about, Mr. Angrom included. He made his decision when he sat down. Didn't you Angry?"

Angrom smiled. "Not so angry anymore, *Wally*," he said with a chuckle. "I think the view is turning for the better. How about you?"

Walker couldn't hide his derision. "What is this?" he demanded, his voice losing confidence. "Is this some sort of coup or something? You trying to take over, boy?"

Huey shook his head. "I've never been a boy," he said.

"*No, boy*?" Walker raised his voice. "You've always been one. And you'll never amount to anything more than that by acting like this. Now our Smörgy should be here soon, and we'll let him break this little stalemate for us once and for all."

"It's not for any of us to decide," Huey replied.

The hover platform came up carrying Smörgåsbord, and he walked right up to the seat at Huey's left hand side to sit down without pause.

Loch's face instantly turned bright red. He slammed his fist on the table, setting a turkey leg flying, and yelled, "You, too, Smörgåsbord?"

Walker couldn't hold in his true thoughts, either. "*You boxhead, hyrdie-byrdie traitor!*" he screamed. "What are you doing?"

"Um, *excuse me*?" Smörgåsbord demanded, wide eyed and obviously trying not to take visible offence. "How was that now?"

"I said," Walker said, "why are you sitting on that side of the table, *Smörgbox*? Do you not realize what you've done?"

"Well, *Mr.* Walker," Smörgåsbord said with a straight face. "I'll spare you any racial slurs which might apply all too well to you and ask you similar questions in a civilized manner. Why are you sitting at the foot of the table, sir? Do you not notice what you've done?"

Walker's face turned a shade of red which Huey didn't know human skin was capable of. "I—" Walker stammered, looking around at each face sitting at the table in turn. "The foot? *Lord* Walker..." His head looked like it was going to explode.

"No, *Mr.* Walker," Smörgåsbord said. "I checked the numbers before I came here—as I do before I go anywhere—and while you were in your right to call this meeting when you did, as of now, you're sitting at the foot of the table, *sir*."

Lord Huey Douglas smiled. He soaked in Walker's anger, embarrassment, and disbelief. Walker had been the richest man in all the world for his entire life practically, and now he was no one, he was number two. It took Walker a while to finally accept that fact and he looked like he was going to cry before he finally gave in. Eventually he stood up and called Haley's doppelganger over to move his chair for him. Seeing Haley have to do that—and knowing that the real Haley was forced to do the same menial tasks, and worse, for so long—only made Huey want to punish Walker all the more, but now wasn't the time for that. There was business to tend to first.

"Now that we have the seating arrangement under control," Huey said. "I believe that Mr. Walker called this feast to talk about his botched job in Outland Two. And because I think that *Mr.* Walker's failure is a pertinent topic of discussion myself, let's get on with it."

"Now I—" Walker started.

"*Now, I* believe that you and I would agree on our next course of action, Mr. Walker," Huey cut him off. Walker looked around for anyone to protest in his defense, but Loch avoided his gaze, chugging his drink instead, and Angrom laughed silently at him. "I believe—like I know you do, Mr. Walker—in fact, to use your own choice of language, I believe that we should handle this the *old-fashioned* way."

Walker sneered.

"How's that, Lord?" Angrom asked, happy to call Huey his new Lord rather than the much greater evil of Walker.

"We tear it up by the roots," Huey said, motioning as if he were tearing up weeds from a garden as he spoke. "Like our friends here failed so miserably to do the first time. The key, which they didn't have, is to know which part of the plant is the root. You target that and the problem won't ever come back again."

"*We tried that*," Walker whined. "And now my protectors expect exponentially more of those hobgoblins out there today. How do you propose to find the roots through all that foliage?" He smiled, satisfied that he had destroyed Huey's point, no doubt.

Huey chuckled. "That's the secret, my walrus-sized friend.

We already know who the roots are. We've known since before you and yours went and fucked things up worse than they already were. I tried to warn you, but you're made of brick. Aren't you, Wally?"

Walker didn't answer. He seethed and ordered Haley's twin to get him more drinks.

"So these *roots*," Smörgåsbord said. He clearly wasn't comfortable with the change in power yet, but he wasn't hesitating to go with what he knew the market demanded. "You say you know what—or is it who?—whatever. What are they, Lord Douglas?"

"*They* are a she," Huey said. The whole table looked confused at the wording. "One student in particular: Emma Whistleblower."

"*Pffft*. Whistleblower?" Loch said, splashing his drink.

"Yes, Mr. Loch," Huey said. "Thank you for pointing that out. She is the driving force behind all of this. It was she who started the first *Reclaim the Grounds* demonstration on New Year's Day. My private protection agents have evidence which suggests that she was involved in the twelve twenty five attacks as well. We've known all of this since before Mr. Walker made his blunder. I tried to warn him before now, but I can still pick up the pieces like I promised I would."

"No, wait—" Walker protested.

"Kill her!" Loch said, raising his glass.

"Is that what the intelligence said?" Angrom asked.

"Yes," Huey said. "It is. So let's put an end to this nonsense once and for all."

ß ✄ ✌

XXXI. Rosa

Rosa groaned while Anna, who had teleported in something special for her to wear, fixed her blouse. "Are you sure you want to do this?" Anna asked, stepping back to get a good look at her creation.

"Of course I want to do this. It's a major part of spreading the word of the Family. Besides, we've found the perfect candidates for our purpose. They want gear not tokens. What else do you expect me to do?"

"Well, you could send someone else," Anna said. "It's just— I'm not sure I trust that ring yet."

"I don't trust anyone else to do this for us," Rosa said. "Besides, we sent that protector through and he came out unharmed."

"I guess." Anna huffed, unsatisfied.

Rosa embraced her. "C'mon now, sweetheart," she said. "I'll be fine. I'll be back in no time with a story for my Nanna."

Anna tried not to smile, but she couldn't help it. She looked into Rosa's eyes. "And in the meantime, I'll watch over your new toy Ollie," she said with a grin.

Rosa pushed her away, chuckling. "C'mon now. She's been doing pretty well, hasn't she? If anything, she's worth more than what we're paying her."

Anna smiled. "I'm just kidding. She's a good kid. You're a fine judge of character, you know. But not of danger. So you be careful." She kissed Rosa on the cheek.

"I'll be fine," Rosa said, kissing Anna's lips. "Be back in no time with good news to share."

"Okay, well let's do it," Anna said. "Stand back."

Anna went to the big metal console in the corner of the basement to press some buttons and flip some switches. Rosa had no idea how it all worked. She just stood there trusting Anna to get her to the right place. After some time of flipping and tapping, Anna looked up at Rosa, smiled, and said, "Alright. Are you ready?"

Rosa nodded. Her heart beat faster. The protector did seem

fine when he came back through, but she had known no one else to do it, and the protector didn't stay for long. He could be a mess by now. What if there were long-lasting effects she didn't know about?

Anna pressed a button and the machine hummed into action. The console she stood behind was attached by thick black wires to a thin metal ring large enough for a normal sized human to walk through—or a protector if they were stooping. The ring lit up, and what looked like heat waves emanated toward the center of the circle until the concrete wall behind it disappeared and a carpeted bench, piled high with clothes, appeared in its place.

Rosa looked back at Anna. "Are you sure this is right?" she tried to yell over the loud humming.

Anna nodded.

"Why are they always costume closets?" Rosa asked.

Anna shrugged. "Easy place to hide the hardware? There have to be a lot of them in Three?"

"I guess." Rosa shrugged.

"Be careful," Anna said. "I'll open it up again in fifteen minutes. If you're not here by then, I'm sending someone in after you." The hum of the machine was getting louder so Anna had to yell to be heard.

"I'll be fine," Rosa called, but Anna shook her head, pointing at her ears, unable to hear. Rosa blew her a kiss, turned, and stepped through the ring into the costume closet. The door disappeared with a *fwip* behind her and she took a deep breath. She was alive, thank God, and in another world. She crossed herself and made her way out of the closet. It was connected to a local community theater on a side alley. No one was there, and it might have been abandoned, but she hurried out anyway, not wanting to take the chance of being seen. Outside were lines of four and five story buildings all with balconies. Rosa went over the directions in her head one more time and made her way toward the meeting.

Cohen wanted to meet in a bar. He said that's how business was done by everyone he knew, everyone in Outland Three. Rosa had to ignore her disgust—giving him the benefit of the doubt from having been born and raised in this Sodom and Gomorrah—but she wouldn't compromise her own beliefs and have a meeting in a bar.

"No," she had told him. "How about a park?" She did love to do business under God's watchful eye. And, luckily enough, there was a park directly across from the bar where he first wanted to meet with her. That's where she found herself after walking through blocks and blocks of uniform balconied buildings.

There was no one in the park when she got there, though. She wasn't even sure it could be called a park. It was smaller than the field which now sat in front of her own home. It was just a patch of grass really, but there was a tall bench which Rosa had to jump up into where she sat and waited.

Across the street from the "park" was a bar with a big neon sign, reading "Indywood", above the doors. It wasn't long before those doors opened and out came a fluffy haired kid who looked a lot like Northwood, only with somehow more colorful clothes. He came across the street to sit on the bench next to her. While her legs dangled, not touching the ground, his were bent up a little to his chest.

"Cohen," she said with a smile.

He looked at her like he was a little disgusted at the sight of her. "Uh... Rosa?" he asked, unsure.

"Yes, child. I'm Rosa."

"I—*uh*—well…"

"You expected something different?" She smiled. "I know you did. Don't worry. I don't mind. It gives me the advantage. You're exactly what I expected."

"But how can you…"

"It doesn't take anything to operate a 3D printer," she said. "You know what a printer is, don't you?"

Cohen nodded.

"Then you know what it means when I say I have access to one."

His eyes widened. He smiled and nodded then shook his head. "No," he said. "How can I believe you?"

"Oh, that'll be easy enough," Rosa said. "Once we give you what we promise, it won't matter to you whether we have a printer or not."

"And what exactly is it that you promise?" He looked suspicious of her claims.

"What exactly is it that you need?" Rosa asked with a smile.

Cohen chuckled. "Well, let's see: Cameras, computers, lights, camera rigs, mic rigs, editing software, costumes... Should I go on? I mean, honestly, there's no end to the list of things we need."

"And what would you be willing to offer in return for everything on that list of yours?"

He laughed. "Whatever you want. Whatever we can do."

"Good. Very good, child," Rosa said. "Well, that's exactly what I'm here to offer you. All we ask is that you record and broadcast a short script of our own. We'll give you what you need to do it, and after that, you can keep the equipment and do whatever you want with it."

"I—uh—are you serious?" Cohen asked. His jaw dropped.

"*Always*," Rosa said. "Here. Here's the script." She handed him the stack of papers.

He flipped through them and said, "I can't make the decision myself."

"Oh, I know," Rosa said. "You have to come up with a list of what you need, too. We can't give it to you until we know what it is."

"Right, right," Cohen nodded with a big smile. "Great. *Perfect*." He clapped his hands together and stood from the bench. "I'll go take this to them right away. I'm sure they'll say yes. I don't see any reason why they wouldn't. You can—Do you wanna come in with me? Most everyone's inside right now. You could meet the crew if you'd like."

"Oh, no no," Rosa said, standing herself. "I trust you. Take your time. I have my own business to tend to as it is. Shall we make it the same time and place in say...a few days."

"Let's make it three," Cohen said, holding out his hand.

Rosa shook it and smiled. "Very good, child. I'll see you in three days."

"Thanks again, ma'am," Cohen said, nearly skipping as he hurried away back to the bar.

Rosa smiled to herself as she walked back to the costume closet. There was one more step taken toward uniting her Family and returning them to their rightful place in society's natural hierarchy. How things had ever been so perverted she may never know, but she knew that, as long as she was alive, she would fight to purify the worlds. She had no choice, really. It was human nature to exert her free will, and her free will told her to free herself and her Family from the tyranny of the robots.

The teleporter door—or whatever—wasn't open when she got to the closet, but she didn't have to wait long before she was hit with a blast of cool wind and the sound of a vacuum sucking the air out of the room. Anna was leaning this way and that around the console, trying to see through the ring, and when she saw Rosa, she smiled and sighed. Rosa smiled and stepped through the door, but instead of stepping into her basement and Anna's arms, she stepped into a short, brightly lit hall. She turned around to try to go back, but the door had closed and in its place were the metal doors of an elevator.

Rosa slammed her fists on the elevator doors, and at the same time, a door at the end of the hall behind her opened. She turned to see a woman who looked a little bit taller than her—and maybe a bit older—but a lot whiter. She was wearing a long white coat, and she had on a big fake smile. Rosa could tell when a smile was genuine, and this one was certainly a big fat fake.

"Where have you taken me?" Rosa demanded.

The woman chuckled. "Why, I haven't taken you anywhere at all. You stepped through a hole in my wall and ended up somewhere you didn't expect. You were the one trespassing in my fields."

Rosa smiled. So that was how it was going to be. If this old lady wanted to play word games, she didn't know who she was dealing with. "Well," Rosa said. "I'm sure they aren't *your* fields, so why don't you direct me to who's really in charge here? Who's the owner?"

"You don't think I'm in charge?" the woman asked, feigning offense.

"Not with a place like this," Rosa said, indicating the small hall. "No, I'm sure you do what you're told. So who owns you?"

"Follow me," the woman said, going back through the door that she had come in. "I'll show you."

Rosa hesitated for a moment then followed the woman. She wasn't going to get out of there until she played along, so that was just what she had to do. Hopefully it wouldn't take too long. She still had so much business to tend to back home.

The room was an office bigger than Rosa's conference room. There was a too large desk and a few too large chairs. The wall opposite from the door was a window looking out onto a vast green wilderness. Rosa had to stifle a gasp when she saw it, and once she had seated herself in one of the chairs, she knew the old woman across from her had seen her awe, despite Rosa's efforts at hiding it.

"Now do you think I'm in charge?" the woman asked.

Rosa scoffed. "A view is not power," she said. "You've convinced me of nothing."

"What is power?" the woman asked.

Family, Rosa would have said. *Humans.* Influence. But again, she didn't want to respond. That would be playing into this woman's hand.

"Power is a lot of things," the old lady said. "A view has some power. The power to awe." She smirked. "Resources have power. Everyone needs resources to live. And *influence.*" The woman paused, looking for Rosa to react, but Rosa maintained a straight face. "Which some of us hold more of than others. But *I* hold a different kind of power. I control transportation between the worlds."

That couldn't be true. "Why are you telling me this?"

"You don't believe me," the woman said. She smiled. "What would it take to make you believe?"

"I—well—I just want to know why you're telling me all this."

"No." The woman shook her head. "You want more than that. I know you better than you think I do. Trust me. What would it take to convince you that I control transportation between the worlds?"

Rosa smiled. "Send five printers meant for robot factories to the Family Home," she said without a second thought.

"Do you have one already?" the woman asked.

Rosa was taken off guard by the quickness of her response. She expected a dodge which really meant no, not for the woman to go along with it. "Well, no. Not yet." She smiled. "Not technically, but we manage."

"Then how do you propose we—"

"The same way you're going to get me home. If you can trick me into stepping into your trap, then you can deliver a few printers to where I was supposed to go. I thought you controlled transportation between the worlds." Rosa smiled. "*Prove it.*"

"Five printers is pretty specific," the woman said. "Why five?"

"It's as random as any other number," Rosa said. "If I'd said three or seven, you'd be asking the same thing."

"You don't want to think more carefully about the decision?"

"I don't think you're going to do it," Rosa said. "That's thinking enough, I'd say. Why would you give me everything when you already have me in the palm of your hands?"

"Why wouldn't I? It's like you said, whether I choose to be benevolent or malicious, it's just as arbitrary either way. Why do you question it because I choose benevolence?"

Rosa couldn't argue with that, with free will. But she was forced by history to stand by her hasty decision. "If it's benevolence you want to prove, then show me," she said with a smile.

"Very well," the woman said, standing. "But we can't do it here. We have to go to my office."

Rosa stood up and looked around. "This isn't your office?"

"Oh, no, dear," the woman laughed. "*Please*. This gaudy thing? This is a show piece." She smiled. "*My* office is much more sensible. Come on." She walked out of the door to the hall and Rosa followed.

The woman closed the door behind them and opened it again. Instead of the gaudy office, it opened onto a slightly less huge office with a big desk in the center that butted up to a glass wall. But here, the window didn't look out onto wilderness, here it looked out onto lines and lines of humans, piecing some thing together. Rosa couldn't help herself. She walked right up to the window and stared out over them with a tear in her eye.

"It's disgusting, isn't it?" the woman said behind her, sitting at the desk, typing and clicking away at the computer.

Rosa wiped the water from her eyes and composed herself. "How do you... How can you..."

"The power over transportation includes views," the old woman said. "I choose to look at this because I know the sacrifices those workers make and I want constantly to be reminded of them."

Rosa broke away from the window and walked up to the desk. "So you really do—"

"*There*," the woman said with a smile. "Your Anna may still be worried about you, but now she has five 3D printers to fill her mind instead."

"You did it?" Rosa asked. "But how—" She stopped to compose herself. She remembered where she was and what she was doing. "But how am I supposed to know for sure?"

"You'll know when I send you home," the woman said. "It doesn't matter now anyway, does it? I would think that the office change alone was enough to convince you—not to mention the view—but hey, I'm not you."

"Yes, well," Rosa said. "That still doesn't explain *why* you're convincing me. Or who you are."

"I'm the Scientist," the woman said. "I'm more powerful than you'll ever know. And I've been watching you. I gave you those printers because they mean nothing to me and I want you to know that as fact. Do you understand what I'm saying?"

Rosa understood that this woman was trying to intimidate her, that was about it. She didn't respond, forcing *the Scientist* to go on.

"Let me ask you this," the Scientist said. "What do you know about androids?"

Rosa rolled her eyes and nodded, giving a thumbs up. *"Okay,"* she said. "I get it. Of course that's what this is all about. I should have known from the beginning. Are—Are you one of them? That's it, isn't it? You're a rogue elevator scheduler bot gone wild." She laughed.

The old woman laughed, too. "No, dear," she said. "I'm something worse than an android. I'm the mother of the androids, and I know what you've been up to."

Rosa half chuckled. This woman wasn't serious, was she? "Yeah right," she said.

"Yeah, Rosa," the Scientist said. "That is right. Go home, find your 3D printers, and realize that everything I've said here is true. Then think about that long and hard before you make any more moves with your *family*. You understand?"

"I'm not sure *you* understand," Rosa said. "Like you said, there are different forms of power, and some of us hold more influence than others. We'll see whose power is stronger than whose. Especially now that we both know what we're up against."

"Oh, it's still not a fair fight," the Scientist said. "But I did give you fair warning, so you're responsible for everything that happens next, Rosa. I hope you know that." She opened the office door and showed Rosa into the hall.

"I'll gladly take that responsibility," Rosa said, walking all the way into the elevator.

"Well, I tried to warn you," the Scientist said. "This'll take you a few blocks from home. I trust you can find your own way after that. Good luck."

The doors closed before Rosa could respond. The elevator fell into motion and stopped, then the doors opened onto a street she recognized. She hurried home, storming in through the full conference room and down to the basement where Anna and Olsen were sliding printers across the concrete floor.

"Rosa!" Anna ran over to embrace and kiss Rosa as soon as she saw her.

Rosa pushed away. "Where did these come from?"

Anna laughed. "I thought you'd tell me. This isn't your plan to fund our new operation?"

"I only wish," Rosa said.

"What happened to you?" Anna asked. "Where did you go?"

"I'm not exactly sure," Rosa said, trying to process it all in her head still. So that woman did have some amount of control over transportation, but that didn't mean that she controlled all of it. Obviously she didn't or Rosa and Anna wouldn't have their own transporter ring in the first place. But that woman's technology was well advanced beyond theirs, there was no doubt about that. The way the door in that hall functioned was evidence enough.

"You can't tell me anything?" Anna urged her on.

"There was this woman," Rosa said. "An old woman. She— she said…" Rosa looked over at Olsen who was still trying to shove a printer even though Anna had stopped helping. It was obviously too big for one person to move so Rosa said, "Olsen, could you go start dinner for us? Make enough for yourself to eat, too, please."

Olsen nodded and hurried clumsily out of the basement.

"What is it?" Anna asked, coming closer to Rosa.

"I'm not sure you'd even believe me," Rosa said, shaking her head. "I'm not sure if I even believe it myself."

"Of course I will, love. Tell your Nanna and she'll make it better."

"She said she's been watching us," Rosa said.

"Watching us?" Anna asked, scrunching up her eyes.

"And that she controls all transportation between the worlds."

"*Impossible.*"

"That's what I said," Rosa said. "But she sent these 3D printers as proof. The place she took me to, Anna. The things she showed me... *They weren't possible.* And she's after us."

"But why?" Anna asked. "What have we done?"

"She said she's the mother of the androids."

"The mother of the androids? Was she one?"

"I don't think so."

"Then why does she care?" Anna scoffed.

"I don't know," Rosa said. "But she does. And she said she's watching us."

"So what are we supposed to do then?" Anna asked, crossing her arms.

"We speed things up," Rosa said. "And we get more transporter rings to confuse her while she's trying to figure out what we're up to."

"*More transporters?*" Anna laughed. "We can't even afford this one. How do you expect us to get more?"

"Look around you, Anna, dear." Rosa embraced her. "We're surrounded by printers." She kissed Anna before she could talk "We can afford anything we want now."

"Yes, well," Anna broke away from Rosa's embrace. "For as long as we have these we can. We better put them to use while we do, though. And what do you propose we do with them?"

"First, we get what we need to build the other transporter rings," Rosa said. "More than a few more. Then we use them to feed the masses like we know they should be used to do."

"But why more rings?"

"And we hurry our operations in Two," Rosa said, ignoring the question. "We can't forget the lower worlds, now can we? If we want success, our efforts must know no bounds. Am I right?"

"Yeah, but—"

"*Good.*" Rosa smiled. "Let's go brief Olsen. She's ready, wouldn't you say?"

"Well, it doesn't take much, but—"

"Fine then," Rosa said. "*Perfect.* Let's go, dear."

Rosa went up the stairs and to the kitchen before Anna could protest any further. If Rosa let her, she knew that Anna would go on and on, asking questions about what had happened and coddling Rosa for nonexistent injuries. There was no time left for that now, though. A new "mother" had shown her face, a human claiming to be the mother of androids. Well this so called mother had chosen her side, and Rosa had chosen hers. Rosa had her own Family to look after, and she wasn't going to let some old lady's anthropomorphizing sentimentality get in the way of that.

Olsen was standing behind the oven, frying something in a pan, jumping every now and again around the popping hot grease. She turned and smiled at Rosa as they approached. "I'm getting better," Olsen said. "I still burn myself every now and then, but I don't burn the food anymore, at least." She smiled again then yelped and rubbed her arm where a bit of hot oil had hit it. "*Ow*! You see."

"Yes, child," Rosa said. "You've come a long way."

"That she has," Anna said, coming in and standing close behind Olsen to inspect her work. "She'll be a proper chef in no time, if she keeps at it."

Olsen blushed and set to scooping out the little nuggets. "Chicken," she said. "It's my favorite so I always practice with it." She popped one in her mouth then promptly spit it out. "*Ah*. Hot!"

"You know, child," Rosa said. "I think you're ready to take on more responsibilities around here." Olsen's eyes widened. "We have a special project which I think would be perfect for you."

"*Ooh*, what is it?" Olsen smiled and popped another nugget in her mouth. Rosa could tell it was hot by the look on her face, but Olsen kept chewing through the heat anyway. "I'm in," she said through her reverse blowing.

"Settle down, now," Rosa said. "You haven't even heard what the mission is. You can't agree to something until you know what it is. Besides, there's a test you have to pass first."

"A test?" Olsen looked alarmed.

"Think of it as a trial run," Rosa said. "You perform this first task up to our standards, and we'll see if you're capable of performing a more pressing piece of business for the Family."

"Definitely," Olsen said, nodding. "As long as it's not a written test—*I mean*... What do you want me to do?"

"It's simple, dear," Anna said. "You and I are going to lug

one of those big beasts of a 3D printer out of the basement and up onto the street corner."

"That's all?" Olsen asked.

"Of course not, sweetheart," Anna said, shaking her head. "Then we offer each person who comes along whatever they want from the printer—sure to tell them it's courtesy of the Family, of course—and ask them to join us. It'll be fun. You'll see."

"What do you say?" Rosa asked.

"Well it doesn't sound difficult," Olsen said. "I don't know what kind of test this is."

"A trial run, child," Rosa said. "Can you do it?"

"Of course I can," Olsen said. "When do I start?"

"Right now," Anna said. "You go downstairs and get ready. I'll be down in a minute to help you."

"Yeah, okay." Olsen grabbed the rest of her nuggets and ate them on her way out.

"Do you think she'll do this?" Anna asked.

"Hand out food on the streets? Of course." Rosa smiled.

"You know what I mean," Anna said.

"Well I think that, as long as we keep paying her for the privilege of learning how to cook, she'll do anything we say."

"But even this?"

"She doesn't have to know what she's doing."

"It'll be obvious once she's done it though," Anna said.

"Maybe not as obvious as you expect," Rosa said. "Besides, I have a feeling that, once she gets out there and feels what it's like to help her fellow brothers and sisters, she'll do anything she can to get that feeling back."

"I hope you're right, dear." Anna shook her head. "Though I'm not sure you are."

"I'm not sure, either," Rosa said. "But I am sure of one thing. You want to know what that is?"

"What?"

Rosa kissed her cheek. "No robot mother is going to hold our Family back."

⦂   ✂   ⦂

XXXII. Ansel

"You going hunting?" Pidgeon asked when Ansel came into the office wearing a new t-shirt and pair of jeans. "Can I come?" He stood from his seat on the floor where he had been staring out the window.

Huey was sitting on one of the puffy chairs, petting Mr. Kitty on his lap, and he looked at Ansel expecting an answer, too.

"*Uh*—no," she said. "I'm not hunting."

"Not with those new clothes on, you aren't," Huey said.

Mr. Kitty meowed.

"Where you going then?" Pidgeon asked. "Can I still come?"

"Uh…" Ansel shook her head. "I just need a little time alone." She rushed out of the door and leaned on the hall side, breathing deeply.

Huey knew something was up. There was no doubt about that. She could tell by the look in his eyes. But even though she had told Pidgeon where she was going, he still didn't expect a thing. He'd probably just sit and sulk because she didn't invite him, stuffing his face with food to drown his sorrow.

She huffed and resolved herself, pictured the lab in her head, said "lab" out loud just to be sure, then opened the door.

Rosalind was there as promised, playing cards with Popeye. She looked like she hadn't moved since Ansel had left her last.

"Are you ready for this?" Rosalind asked, not looking up from her game.

Ansel checked her back pocket for her slingshot, made sure she had a pouch of rocks tied to her belt loop, and sighed. "I'm ready," she said.

"And you're sure you don't want to bring your boyfriend? He may be more help than you know."

Ansel shook her head. She remembered Rosalind wasn't looking at her and said, "I'm sure. This is one thing I have to do alone."

Rosalind looked up from her game with a smile. "If you say

so. It's your decision."

Ansel nodded.

"Well, let's get to it, then. Shall we?" Rosalind tossed her hand down and stood up, but Popeye went on laying cards on the table anyway. Ansel followed her out into the hall to stand in front of the elevator.

"Now, you studied the map I gave you, right?" Rosalind asked.

Ansel nodded.

"Take this." Rosalind held out a silver band. Ansel took it but didn't know what to do with it. "Put it on your wrist," Rosalind said, tapping her own wrist.

Ansel fiddled with the thing but couldn't figure out how to fasten it on.

"Here, let me." Rosalind snapped it on in one fluid motion and turned it for Ansel to look at. "It's made simple so even a little *girl* can understand."

"I'm no—"

"*I know*, but do you see it? Look at it."

Ansel looked at it again. It was just a silver band with a black rubber button on it. "Yeah. I see it," she said, jerking her hand away. "So what?"

"When you get back to an elevator and you want to come home, you press that button and I'll make sure you get back here. But don't take long, you hear me? I have better things to do than sit around waiting on a little girl like you."

"I'm—"

"*Uh huh.*" Rosalind nodded. "You get one chance. I still recommend that you wait for the Scientist instead of doing this on your own, but I can't blame a girl for wanting some adventure." She smiled.

"I'm not stopping the Scientist from doing what she promised to do," Ansel said, ignoring the "girl" this time. "But that doesn't mean I can't do something myself instead of just sitting and waiting for a savior who may never show up. Or maybe I'll save him before the Scientist gets a chance to, save her the trouble."

Rosalind grinned. "Alright then," she said. The elevator doors slid open behind her. "It's your choice, your decision to make. Just press the button when you're ready to come back home."

Ansel stepped onto the elevator. She looked at the bracelet then nodded. "I'm ready."

"Good luck." Rosalind turned to walk away as the doors slid closed.

Ansel's heart beat harder. She wiped the sweat from her palms on her thighs and waited for the elevator to take her away. Her heart skipped a beat when she felt the floor fall out from underneath her. She still wasn't used to the sensation and thought she never would be.

The doors opened and it was nighttime beyond them, but the sidewalks were lined with pristine streetlights that shone bright white. They were too white. Ansel shielded her eyes from them as she took in the trees, walkways, and sparse buildings. The place was practically abandoned. With so much grass and trees she couldn't understand how it hadn't been settled already. This was even better than the Belt. It was almost like the Belt mixed with the wilderness outside the office's wallwindow. This she could get used—

The elevator doors slid closed, interrupting her thought, and she only barely had time to slip out of them. She gathered herself fast and ducked behind the nearest bush. What was she doing taking in the scenery? She had business to take care of.

Rosalind had given her a path to take to Tom's house—and it was a pretty good one—but Ansel made some alterations of her own—there were bushes Rosalind would never think of hiding behind because she was too big. Ansel dipped and dashed, and the further she got, the less she felt like it was worth it to spend so much energy hiding. There was no one outside. She could see the light flooding from all the windows of the sparse houses, indicating there must be people inside them, but there was no one on the streets. She didn't see a single person before making it to the house which was supposed to be Tom's.

She crouched behind some bushes in the backyard, realizing that what she had been thinking of as small buildings weren't actually small because they were meant for only a single family at a time. The place seemed even emptier with the realization.

She crept up to the back door—unlocked, as Rosalind had said—to let herself into a kitchen the size of her old house. This must be why Tom didn't care about helping her find her dad anymore. He had a good life and a huge house, why would he care about anyone else?

The kitchen door swung open and in came a kid that looked like he was about Pidgeon's age. He looked a lot like Pidgeon, in fact. He put his fists up in front of his face, like he wanted to fight, when he saw Ansel. "Who are you?" he demanded. "What are you doing here?"

"I, uh—" Ansel stammered, not sure of what to say now that she was there.

"Jonah, who's—" Tom said, coming in with a pink apron on. "Ansel? What are you—"

"Ansel?" Jonah said, dropping his arms and staring between her and Tom. "Are you serious?"

"Go to your room," Tom said, pointing. "I need to speak with our guest alone."

"But it's—"

"*That's an order*," Tom snapped, giving him a look.

"But you told me—"

"Pick your battles or you might end up like me," Tom said. "*Now pick.*"

"Yes, sir." Jonah lowered his head and sulked out of the room.

"What are you doing here?" Tom asked, turning to Ansel.

"Didn't think you'd ever see me again, eh?" Ansel sneered.

"No. I—well—*no*," Tom said. "How'd you get here?"

"You said you'd help me get my dad back," Ansel said. "Are you gonna keep that promise, or was it just another lie?"

"No. Well, I'd keep the promise if I could," he said. "But what am I supposed to do? Look at me. I'm a housekeeper. I'm weak, *powerless*."

Ansel scoffed. "So you give up, then. Is that it? You're not called a protector anymore so you can't help anyone. You can only protect people if you have a silly white costume and a big black gun. Is that it?"

"No, I can—"

"Then protect me!" Ansel stomped her foot. "*Help* me. Tell me where my dad is at least."

Tom lowered his eyes. "I'm not—I'm not sure I can." He shook his head.

"What's that supposed to mean?"

"When I left… Captain Mondragon...she said…"

"Spit it out!" Ansel was getting tired of his games again already.

"She said she would speed up his execution because he meant so much to me." Tom stared at the floor instead of making eye contact.

Ansel flung herself at him and tried to hit him, but he held her at arm's length until she gave up.

"I never should have trusted you," she said, breathing heavily and trying to find entry to attack him again. "I shouldn't have come here, either. You're too weak to do anything for me."

"*I'm not weak*," Tom said. "I'm powerless. I could storm the holding cells, then what? I'd be useless to you the second I tried to help."

"Then you're useless to me now," she said, stomping her foot again and crossing her arms.

"No, but I—"

"No," Ansel stopped him. "I've had enough. Just remember what you did to me, *protector*." She scoffed and stomped out the way she had come in, bursting out into to the cool dark air.

That was a bust. Just like Rosalind had said it would be. But Ansel had to prove to herself that there was nothing left for her to do but wait for the Scientist. She started on her way to do just that when she heard a whisper behind her.

"*Psst*. Hey," the voice said. "Over here."

Ansel turned and didn't see anyone. "Who's there?" she asked the darkness.

"Over here." The little boy from inside stepped out of the bushes.

"Jonah?"

"And you're Ansel," he said with a smile. "I'm so glad to finally meet you." He extended a hand for her to shake, and she took it reluctantly.

"How do you know my name?" she asked as she shook it.

"Well, my dad—*uh*—Tom… He's told me about you and what he did for you."

"About what he did for me?" Ansel scoffed. She made to walk away, but he called to stop her.

"*Wait*," he said. "I can help you even if he can't."

Ansel stepped up to him and grabbed him by his shirt. "You don't even know what you're talking about, kid," she said, putting her face close to his.

"Alright, alright," he said, breaking away from her grip. "Settle down now. I know you're angry. And you should be. But I want to protect you."

Ansel scoffed. "I don't need protecting. Especially the kind of protecting you and your dad offer. I need to know where my dad is and how to get to him. *That's it*. You can't help me with that so you're no use to me."

"But I *can* help you with that," Jonah said.

Ansel chuckled. "Your dad can't even help me. How do you think you're going to be able to?"

"My dad's old," Jonah said. "He's retired. He doesn't know what the worlds are like these days."

"Oh, and you do?"

"I know Outland One better than you ever will," he said, puffing his chest out and looking proud of himself.

"I don't care about *Outland One*," Ansel said. "I want to know where my dad is."

"*Well he's here*," Jonah said. "That's the point. He's in the holding cells. Dad doesn't know this, but I've seen them. I know where they keep the prisoners, and I can get us there."

Ansel laughed. "Yeah, right," she said.

"Yeah. *It is right*. But if you don't want to see your dad, I won't take you to him. I was just trying to help you out, you know." He made to walk away, but Ansel stopped him.

"Wait," she said. "Can you take me to him right now?"

"Of course I can. That's what I was trying to say."

This was her only hope. She had to use this trip for something productive, even if Tom was a useless idiot. "Okay," she said. "Let's go."

"Alright. Follow me," Jonah said, walking out to the sidewalk.

"*Uh*," she said, not following him.

He stopped and turned around under the bright light of one of the streetlamps. "What?" he asked, waving her on. "Come on. It's this way."

"Are you serious? I can't walk around in the open like that.

Get over here."

"What?" he said, not moving. "Come on." He waved her on again.

"No, get—" She ran over and dragged him back into the shadows of some bushes. "*Look.* I'm not supposed to be here, okay. You get that, right? That means no one can see me. I can't just walk around the streets like you do, especially when they're as brightly lit as y'all got 'em down here."

Jonah looked around. "It's not that bright," he said. "Pretty dark, in fact. I think that light's out." He pointed, but Ansel couldn't see through the bright white in front of them.

"Whatever," she said. "Look. Just stay out of the lights, okay. Pretend like you can't be seen either. Can you do that?"

Jonah put his fists up again like he wanted to fight. "I got you," he said. "Follow me." He did a somersault out across the lit path to hide behind a shaded bush.

Ansel thought it was a bit flashy, but it served the purpose of keeping Jonah hidden so she didn't say anything. At least the kid seemed like he understood what she was saying now. And after talking to him, he was definitely a kid, younger than Pidgeon and probably younger than her. Her previous age estimate was way off.

They crossed this way and that, and Ansel memorized landmarks on the way. She would have to be able to find her way back to the elevator for any of this to be worth anything. They had gone some distance, and Ansel was about to say something about it, when Jonah came to an abrupt stop under a big oak tree.

"Wait," he said, holding up a hand.

"What?" Ansel asked.

"We just gotta... I'm waiting for someone."

"Waiting for someone?" Ansel stepped back.

"Yeah, well..."

"What are you talking about? Who?"

"Don't worry. It's just my partner. I wouldn't go into this mission alone, you know. Are you crazy?"

Ansel huffed. She kind of missed Pidgeon. She wondered what he was doing. Probably eating or looking out the window. Probably eating and looking out the window. She should have brought him with her. Rosalind was right again. *We do nothing alone.*

"Yeah, alright," Ansel said. "But whoever it is, they better hurry up. I don't have any more time to waste than we already have."

"Here she is now," he said. "Liz, over here!"

Ansel didn't see her until she was right next to them. "What is it, Jonah?" Liz demanded when she was. "Who is this? Why'd you call me out here so late? It better be a real emergency this time."

"*This* is Ansel," Jonah said with a big grin. "*The Ansel.*"

Liz looked at Ansel, then Jonah, and back again. "No," she said.

Ansel blushed. She was glad it was too dark for them to really see her face, even with all the lights. "If y'all're done," she said. "I need to get to my dad."

Liz grabbed Ansel's hand and shook it too vigorously. "I can't believe we're actually meeting you," she said. "Jonah's dad, or, Mr. Pardy, he—"

"Alright, Liz." Jonah slapped her on the arm. "Be cool. I wouldn't have told you to come if I knew you were going to act like a fangirl."

"Oh, I'm sorry. I—" Liz finally let go of her hand, and Ansel wiped it on her pants. "It's just, I've never met a real life Sixer before, you know. Is it true that you have to steal everything you own?"

Ansel scoffed. "I ain't no Sixer. I'm from the Belt, and I've never stolen anything in my life. I hunt for my food."

"Hunt? But—" Liz said, but Jonah cut her off.

"*Liz,*" he said. "Enough. We don't have time. We're going in."

"You mean... *No.*" She shook her head.

"*Yes,*" Jonah said, "She wants to see her dad. He's in the holding cells, or he's not alive. Do you have any other ideas?"

"No, but... This?" Liz said. "What if she was lying?"

"Then we'll find out when we go through with it, won't we?" Jonah said. "Look. You don't have to come if you don't want to. I just thought it would be better to have my partner with me when I went."

Liz blushed. Even in the dark, Ansel could see it. She wondered if they had seen her embarrassment, too. "I—well..." Liz said, hesitating. "You're right. I couldn't leave my partner alone. But even if we get on the elevator and to the cell block her dad happens to be in, I still don't know how you expect to get him out."

"If I can see him," Ansel said, "or even hear his voice—anything to let me know he's still alive—that's enough for me."

"See," Jonah said. "*It's nothing.* We can do that. Just get in, see him, and get out. No one will ever know we were there. What do you say?" He put on a big smile.

"I don't know," Liz said. "I don't think it's going to be as easy as you're making it out to be. What if we get caught?"

"We won't get caught," Jonah said. "And if we do, I'll take all the blame for it. I'll tell them I forced you to come."

Liz laughed. "Oh, I'm sure they'll believe that," she said. "Are you gonna say you tied me up and dragged me all the way out there? Do you have some rope?"

Ansel chuckled. She kind of liked this Liz.

"No, well," Jonah said, looking embarrassed.

"I didn't think so," Liz said. "And I already said I'm coming, anyway. This is Ansel you're talking about. Now come on."

Liz knew to sneak without being told, unlike Jonah. They became a caravan of three cockroaches creeping through bushes, scurrying fast through the light, remaining as much out of sight as they could while they made their way through the deserted landscape to some place that could have been any place for all Ansel knew. There grew to be less and less houses as they went until there was only grass and still-lit streets. Then they got to a big square building that was painted stark white. It looked more like it belonged near the Belt than here with all the single family houses, but here it was, waving proud white flags, still lit with spotlights in the night. They stepped behind a bush on the outskirts of the shell of light which surrounded the building, and Ansel asked in a whisper, "Where are we?"

"This is our school," Jonah said at a normal speaking volume.

Liz elbowed him. "This is the Junior Academy," she whispered. "It's where we learn to be protectors."

Ansel looked over at the two, wide-eyed. These kids were going to grow up to be giants in white just like Tom was. They didn't look so big now. She sneered.

"Are you alright?" Jonah whispered, although he still spoke

too loud. "You still want to do this?"

Ansel scoffed. "What's the plan?"

"Okay, well," Jonah said. "In there they have an elevator that we use for training scenarios and all that. That's not important. What's important is that I—" Liz nudged him "Well, *we*, got access to a code to send us to the holding cells. We plug it in, it takes us there, we see your dad, and then we get out. Just like that. What do you say? Great idea, huh?"

Liz rolled her eyes. "We'll go in through the locker room," she said. "No one's ever in there after hours, and it's pretty much right next to the elevator. They trust us too much." She shook her head with a grin.

"They trust their brainwashing too much," Jonah said, getting loud again. "Isn't that right partner? *Wubba lubba dub dub!*"

This time it was Ansel who hit Jonah, but she didn't do it playfully. She hit him as hard as she could, square in the stomach. He huffed and doubled over, and Liz got into a defensive stance, bent down just a little bit with fists in front of her face.

"I understand that this all fun and games for you two," Ansel said, "but I'd be fucked if I was ever found, and I don't need you yelling out, telling people exactly where we are."

Liz dropped her defenses and looked embarrassed. Jonah caught his breath, stood up, and wheezed. "*Got it.*"

"Sorry," Liz said. "We'll be serious, though. They can't catch us, either. Right, Jonah?"

Jonah nodded.

"Ok. Let's do this then," Ansel said.

Jonah did his somersault out from behind the bushes again, and Ansel was starting to think it was getting old. She looked at Liz who shrugged and jogged out after him, crouching even though there was nothing to hide behind. What was Ansel thinking following these kids? It was too late for her to change course now, though. This might be her only chance at seeing her dad ever again.

They went in through a side door—painted as white as the rest of the building—into a white-washed locker room. The lights weren't on and Ansel could still see the white reflection off the walls.

"*This way*," Jonah whispered, trying to roll again and hitting his head on a bench with a loud, "*Ow!*"

"*Shhhh*," Liz and Ansel shushed him in unison.

Jonah got clumsily up, rubbing the no doubt growing knot on his head, and followed them out the next door, around a corner, and down a hall to stop in front of a pair of elevator doors. "Here it is," Liz said.

"Alright, here's the code." Jonah pulled a piece of paper out of his pocket. "Four three, four f, four four, four five," he read off as Liz pressed the numbers on the keypad. The doors slid open and a bright, white light flooded over them.

"There it is," Jonah said, squinting.

Ansel shielded her eyes with her hand as she stepped in. Jonah followed, but Liz hesitated.

"C'mon," Jonah said. "There's no going back now."

Liz sighed and stepped in, too. The doors slid closed, and the floor dropped out from underneath them. A few seconds of silence and fidgeting later and the doors slid open to three giants in white screaming facemasks pointing big black guns at them.

"Halt, citizens," one of the protectors demanded in a deep modulated voice, teeth glowing neon yellow, green, and red with every word.

"Fuck," Jonah said.

"You two, come with us." Two of the protectors dragged Liz and Jonah off, and the third stepped onto the elevator, grabbing Ansel by the shoulder. Ansel fought to free herself, but the giant's grip was too tight and the doors closed. The floor fell out from underneath them again, and the elevator doors opened to reveal a long white hall lined with metal doors.

The protector pushed her out with the barrel of a gun and said, "Go on, now. *Git.*"

Ansel took a step out and looked at the doors, thinking that her dad might be behind one of them. There were no windows, though, so she had no way to tell. As she stumbled along, taking as much time as she could to walk through the hall, she remembered her bracelet and pressed the button over and over, knowing it was useless. They got to the end of the hall before the protector stopped and opened one of the metal doors.

"*In,*" the protector demanded, poking Ansel with the gun. Ansel slipped in and the doors closed behind her.

She was in a tiny room, smaller than any room she ever lived in. It took only two steps to get from one side to the other, and the entire thing was painted white.

She banged on the metal door. "Let me out!" she called. "You can't do this! Let me out! Let me out! Let me out!"

There was no answer. She banged and banged until her knuckles were bloody and her fingers numb, and still, no one came.

She slouched in a corner, holding her knees up to her chest. This wasn't happening. She had pressed the button. Rosalind and the Scientist would come looking for her and everything would be okay.

She shook her head. No. That probably wasn't true. She was supposed to press the button when she was near an elevator, and she wasn't anywhere near an elevator. She was locked up in a tiny cell.

Her heart beat faster. She took a few deep breaths to try to calm it. She was here now. She had to decide what she was going to do.

She heard footsteps through the metal door. She stood up and got the slingshot out of her back pocket. They hadn't even searched her. She loaded up a rock and aimed it at where she thought the protector's head would be—it was a pretty big target. When the doors opened, she let it go. The rock pinged off the protector's facemask and Ansel felt a blow to her jaw which caused her to black out.

ß 🜨 🜲

She opened her eyes and they filled with pain. She closed them and it wasn't any better. She tried to move, but she was tied down with cold metal chains. So this was the end.

There were sounds and pain, sounds and pain, then her eyelids turned from red to black, sweet, cool, comforting black. Even when the sounds started making sense again, she clenched her eyes tight, trying to hold onto that welcoming blackness until, finally, she had to respond by opening her eyes.

A big white protector loomed over her. The protector smiled like she had won simply because Ansel had opened her eyes. She had won nothing. Ansel would give her nothing.

"So," the woman towering over her said, *the protector*. "We meet at last. I'm so glad to finally have the honor."

Ansel scoffed. She could smell bullshit when she heard it,

and this stunk.

"Well, dear. I want to ask you what it is that you're doing here."

"*Fuck you*," Ansel said, trying to spit on the woman but only managing to dribble spittle on the floor.

The protector chuckled. "Oh dear," she said. "I'm not sure you understand where you are right now."

"I'm not sure I care," Ansel said with a smile.

"Well, you will. In due time, girl. You will."

XXXIII. Jonah

They sat side-by-side in the bright white room, trying not to look at each other. Jonah had never been more scared in his life. Not when he first got shot in a standoff. Not that night they had stayed up late watching horror films and his mom came in the room to scare them. Not even standing up to Stine in the locker room at the academy. But this? He couldn't handle this.

He wiped his hands on his jeans and looked around the room, breathing heavily. Liz moved like she was going to comfort him then stopped herself. They both knew they were being watched, judged, made to wait and worry. School had taught them exactly the process they were being put through, but that didn't make it any less terrifying for Jonah. He was so scared he didn't even want to look over at Liz to see if she was as afraid as he was.

The room was tiny. There were four metal stools along the back wall—two of which they occupied—and a door across from them. That was it. That and the white, white walls, floor, and ceiling. The lights were bright enough to reflect back off everything and give him a headache. His whole body started to sweat, not just his hands.

He couldn't take it any longer. He broke. "Is it hot in here?" he asked, fanning himself by pulling on his shirt over and over. "I can't handle this."

"*Shhhh.*" The sound of her shush told Jonah that Liz was afraid, too.

Jonah, however, decided that he had already started talking, so why not continue? It would help ease his nerves, and it might help calm Liz a little, too. "You know," he said. "They make it hot in here so we're uncomfortable. That's why it's so bright, too."

"*Shut. Up!*" Liz demanded. Apparently his talking didn't calm her.

That wasn't going to stop Jonah, though. "Yeah, well," he said. "I don't care if they are listening. I don't think them knowing that I think it's—"

The door swung open and in stomped a fully clad protector.

"You," it said, pointing at Liz. "Come." Liz jumped up and followed the protector out, and the door slammed closed behind them.

"*Great*," Jonah said out loud to the empty room. "More waiting. There's nothing I love more than waiting alone in a hot bright room." He chuckled to himself and noticed the lights getting brighter. The reflections off the shiny floor were too bright to look at so he squinted his eyes. A bead of sweat rolled down his eyebrow. He wiped it away with a sigh.

"*Woof*," he said. "Nothing like a good sauna."

The door swung open, and this time, the protector didn't ask him for compliance. It lifted Jonah up by the arm—taking no notice of his struggles—and carried him out through a set of empty halls to open a door and throw him inside.

Jonah stood and brushed himself off. "*Thanks*," he said to the door which had already been slammed shut.

"You're welcome," a voice said behind him.

He turned to see a big desk, and behind it, a wide window, looking out onto a snowy mountainscape. Sitting at the desk was a woman in protector dress uniform with her arms crossed on the table. "Please take a seat," she said, indicating the stools across the desk. They looked too small even for Jonah, and he was just a kid.

"I think I'll stand," he said.

"That's an order, son," the protector said. "Do you see this?" She turned to show the rank insignia on her arm, but Jonah should have known by her collar that she was a Captain. He was getting too cocky too soon, just like his dad had done, and if he wasn't careful, he might never be a protector himself.

"Yes, sir," he said, taking the short stool. He had to sit up as straight as he could to see the Captain over the desk.

"Sir, yes, sir," the Captain said.

"*Sir, yes, sir*," Jonah repeated.

"And just because you're not a protector yet doesn't mean I'm not your superior," the Captain said. "Every citizen of Outland is outranked by every protector. You got that?"

Jonah couldn't help but notice the "yet" in what she had said and take some hope as to what it meant for his future. "Sir, yes, sir," he said.

"Good," the Captain said. "Now, Jonah—that is your name, isn't it, citizen?"

"Jonah Pardy, sir."

"Yes... *Pardy*." The Captain smiled. "As I suspected. Now tell me: What were you doing with this...*Sixer* girl in our transport bay?"

Jonah shrunk down into his seat so the Captain couldn't see his face through the desk. His heart beat faster. He heard a mechanical whirring as the Captain's seat raised up so she could see him.

"Pardy," she said. "There's no hiding from this. Tell me what you were doing, or we find out the hard way. You do know what the hard way is, don't you?"

"Sir, yes, sir."

"Well?" She raised her eyebrows.

"Well, sir..." Jonah hesitated. What was the point of lying? They had already gotten Ansel, and they would be able to get any information out of her that they wanted. Then he remembered Liz and his promise to her. He was so stupid. Of course she was scared in there. Hopefully he could help her just a little bit. "First of all," he said. "Liz, my partner, she had nothing to do with it, okay. I made her come. She said it was a stupid idea."

The Captain laughed. "She was right about that. So, what? You dragged her out there with your tiny little hands?"

Jonah blushed. "Well... No, sir. But by going, I made her go. She's too loyal to let her partner go on a mission alone."

"As every protector should be," the Captain said. "But why did *you* want to do it?"

Now Jonah didn't know what to say. He didn't want to say anything about his dad and lead him into any more trouble than he had already had to deal with, but he had to come up with something. They would get some explanation out of Jonah, one way or another. He ended up falling back on his reliable, go to excuse. "I wanted to protect her."

The Captain smiled. "Just like your father," she said. Jonah could tell she meant more than she said by the sound of her voice. "Hopefully not *just*, though," she added.

Jonah didn't answer. The Captain obviously knew who his dad was so he didn't have to tell her. Hopefully he wouldn't have to pay for his dad's sins, though.

"You know why he was discharged, don't you," the Captain

said.

Jonah shook his head. "Sir, no, sir," he said. "I was ordered not to question him about it, sir."

"And you expect me to believe that you follow orders, Pardy? Why would you be sitting in front of me right now if you followed orders?"

"I had to protect her, sir," Jonah said. "That's my duty, si—"

"It's your duty to uphold the protector's tenets, Tiny Pardy. What are they?"

"*Property, liberty, life*, sir," Jonah recited.

"Very good," the Captain said. "And how can you protect property when you're invading ours, Pardy? Now, I don't want you to end up like your father. You hear me?"

Jonah blushed.

"It was the same girl that got him fired, too, you know," the Captain said. "It's a bit suspicious, you showing up with her in particular. As if your father's an accomplice."

"He doesn't know I'm here, sir," Jonah said. "He thinks I'm in bed, sir. You can—"

"Oh, we'll see," the Captain said. "Don't you worry. He's already been contacted and given all the details of what you and your little girlfriend have been up to tonight."

Jonah swallowed.

"But like I said," the Captain went on. "I don't want you going down the same path your father did. I can see a bright future for you, son. Do you know that?"

Jonah didn't trust her quite yet, but he wanted to hear about this bright future of his. He sat up straighter in his seat.

"For any of that to come true, though, you're going to have to start toeing the line of decency. But I don't think we'll see any more little rebellions out of you in the future. What do you think, Pardy?"

Jonah shook his head. "No, sir," he said.

"You know, I had high hopes for your father, too," the Captain said. "I thought he would surpass even me in the ranks. But he failed. He went by the books until he killed that little girl's mother, then he couldn't handle his duties anymore."

Jonah tried not to gasp, but the Captain could see his surprise.

"He *didn't* tell you then," she said with a smile. "No, he

probably wouldn't have. He did more than that, too, but that much is classified. If you want to know that, you'll have to ask him yourself—or work up the ranks until you gain the proper clearance. But you've wasted enough of my time already, son. Get out of my sight. And don't let me catch you breaking another regulation, or you'll be punished far worse than you already have been. Do you understand me?"

Jonah nodded. "Sir, yes, sir," he said. "Is that all, sir?"

"Yes, Pardy. *Now git.*" She turned around in her chair to look out the window. "And close the door on your way out. If you forget that…" She trailed off as if he had already left.

Jonah crept out of the room and closed the door as quietly as he could behind him. He looked up to find the hall empty and realized he had no idea how to get out of this place. He went down the hall, checking each door he passed, but none of them were open or unlocked. A few had windows, but even if he jumped, he wasn't tall enough to see into them. He was doing just that—jumping up to try and see through one of the tall windows—when a door opened behind him. He turned around quick, thinking of an excuse, and breathed a deep sigh of relief when it was only Liz.

"*Amaru,*" he said. "You spooked me."

Her face was red and puffy. It looked like she had been crying. She brushed past him and hurried down the hall to call the elevator at the end of it—where it always was in long halls like this one. Jonah ran to catch up and just made it inside before the doors closed and the elevator fell into motion.

"Are you alright?" he asked.

Liz sniffed and looked away from him to wipe her nose. "Of course I'm not alright!" she snapped. "We were just arrested. That's not an alright thing to happen."

"Oh, no, well… I mean, of course." That was stupid, but what was he supposed to say? He did all he could do in there. He had tried to take the blame, but the Captain saw straight through him. Nothing else was in his power.

"Are *you* alright?" she asked. The elevator doors opened and she stomped out before he could answer.

Jonah ran to catch up with her. "Liz, wait," he called, but she didn't stop. "I'm sorry," he said, trailing along beside her. "I told her I made you do it. I tried t—"

"*I told you that wouldn't matter,*" she said. "But you had to go on this stupid mission and drag me along anyway. You know what my punishment is? Six demerits, Jonah. *Six.* With no chance of rehabilitation."

Jonah stopped in his tracks. Six demerits with no working them off. That was a sentence to living on a knife's edge for the rest of the Junior Academy, and Liz still had so many years ahead of her. It seemed cruel and unusual as a punishment, especially considering that Jonah himself—after admitting to all the blame—only received a stern warning.

Liz had kept walking while he thought about it so Jonah had to run to catch up again. "You've got to be kidding me," he said when he did. "*Six* with no parole? That's harsh."

Liz stopped and stared at him. Her face was red again but not from crying this time. It was anger in her eyes. "*Why?*" she asked. "What sentence did you get?"

Sentence? She was acting like she had a trial. Jonah didn't remember getting any sentence. He only remembered getting a lecture and a warning. It was more like talking to his mom than facing Court Martial.

"Well..." she said.

"Well," he said, "the Captain never really gave me a sentence."

Liz looked like she didn't know whether to hit him or ask more questions. She stomped her foot and huffed and said, "*Captain?*" through gritted teeth.

"Yeah, well," Jonah said. "That's where they took me—uh, after they tried to blind me with light and heat me out," he added to try make it seem like he had suffered, too.

"They didn't give you a sentence. They took you to the Captain. Next you're going to tell me they made you a protector, too."

"Well..." Jonah smiled.

She hit him on the arm and started walking again. "*That* I won't believe. I can barely believe that they didn't punish you. Now why do you think that is, Jonah Pardy?"

"I don't know." Jonah shrugged. "Because of my boyish charms and the honor I showed in trying to take the fall for you?"

Liz stopped. "*Ugh.* Take the fall for yourself, you mean," she said, walking again—and a little faster.

"Well, it's not my fault," Jonah said. "Do you want me to go back and ask for a punishment? Make sure she didn't forget? Would that make you feel better?"

"Stop being so dense," Liz said, stopping and grabbing his arm to stop him, too. "This is bad even for you. Let me walk you through it. I got the most severe punishment they could lay down on a first time offender. You got a warning from a Captain, the least harsh punishment I've ever heard of. If anything, it was an honor to meet her face-to-face, and now she knows your name when you get out of the Academy."

"Yeah, *for breaking the law*," Jonah said. "What's your point?"

"That's even more evidence," she said with a scoff. "Don't you see?"

Jonah shook his head.

"I bet she even asked you about your father, too," Liz said. "Didn't she?"

"How could you know that?"

"It's simple." She smiled. "First—*and most obviously*—it was Ansel who we were bringing in there."

Jonah remembered Ansel. He hadn't even thought about what had happened to her since they had gotten caught. He wondered now where she was and what they were doing to her. "Yeah," he said. "So what?"

"So she's the one who your dad got fired trying to protect. You don't think the Captain would see some connection there?"

Jonah wanted to hit himself in the head. He *had* been dense. He hadn't been taking this whole thing seriously. It was just another game to him, another standoff like at the end of every school day. But now he was remembering that this was way more important than school, this was real life.

"*And,*" Liz said, obviously aware of the fact that she had made Jonah realize how dumb he had been. "That's likely why she gave you such a lenient—*or should I say non-existent?*—punishment compared to mine."

"But why?" Jonah said. "Wouldn't that call for *more* punishment, not less? *Oh, he's breaking the law trying to protect the same Sixer his father got sacked protecting, let's be lenient on the poor kid*. It doesn't make any sense."

"You don't have to be an ass," Liz said. "Did she say anything to you? Did she mention your dad?"

"Well, uh…" Of course she did, but Jonah wasn't ready to bring up the whole part about his dad murdering Ansel's parents just yet. So he chose to play it stupid instead. "Yeah, I think so," he said.

"You think so?" She tried to hit him, but he dodged it. "You were talking to the Captain, and you *think* she mentioned your dad. You weren't even paying attention! Maybe you *did* get demerits but you just don't remember."

"No," he said. "I definitely didn't get demerits. And she *did* mention my dad, but I still don't understand why she wouldn't punish me."

"I'm not entirely sure, either," Liz said. "But it has something to do with your dad and that girl. Maybe she's watching you. Or maybe she wants to hold it over your head. But all I know is I can't help you find out."

She started to walk away, but Jonah stopped her. "What?" he complained. "C'mon. We're partners. You can't just di—"

"Six demerits, Jonah. You know what that means. I can't get another one."

"Yeah, but…" He couldn't argue with that. *"Partners."*

"You'd ask your partner to risk that? To risk everything?"

"What? *No*. I wouldn't ask that. I'm not asking you to do anything illegal. Just come help me ask my dad about it. That's all. You can't get a demerit for that, can you?"

"With *your* dad, I don't know." Liz grinned.

"Yeah, well, you're right about that." Jonah smiled.

"I can't believe we just did that, Jonah."

"I can't believe we got caught."

"I can. But not that you weren't punished. Now let's go find out why. I'll race you!"

They sprinted the short distance left to Jonah's house. It wasn't until they burst through the door, yelling, *"Daaaad, I'm hoooome!"* and, *"Mr. Paaaardy!"* simultaneously that they both realized it was late at night—or early in the morning maybe—and Jonah's dad was probably sleeping. He wasn't, though, luckily. He called in from the kitchen, *"Hoooome, I'm daaaad!"* and came out carrying a tray full of random foods to greet them.

"Come, come," he said, leading them to the living room and setting the tray on the coffee table. "Sit down. I'm sure you're both exhausted."

Liz seemed happy to have someone to finally commiserate with. She hopped up onto the couch and grabbed a cookie and a glass of milk then set to dunking the cookie in the milk and chewing the soggy bits. Jonah joined her on the couch, but he didn't eat anything. He wanted to know now more than ever why exactly his dad had been discharged.

"So," his dad said, sitting on a chair across from them. "I got a call that said you two had an interesting night."

"*Ugh.*" Liz sighed and plucked another cookie off the tray. "Some of us more interesting than others," she said.

"Tell me," his dad said. "I want to know everything."

"Dad, did you kill someone?" Jonah blurted out. He didn't know where it came from.

Liz dropped her cookie in her cup of milk with a splash, and Jonah's dad just stared at Jonah for a second. "Where did you hear that?" he asked.

"I talked to the Captain. She—"

"You talked to Captain Mondragon directly?" his dad asked.

"I—well—she didn't even give me her name. But she mentioned something about—"

"You shouldn't have found out that way," his dad said, shaking his head and lowering his eyes.

Liz dropped the cookie she had just fished out back into the milk again.

Jonah scoffed. "What? So it's true? You killed Ansel's mom."

This time Liz choked on the cookie. "*Ach—cha cha cha—sorry,*" she said, still trying to cough it up. "Sorry."

"I thought she had a gun," his dad said. "I was on the streets of Six, in plain clothes, with no body armor. My partner had just been shot. I chased the suspect away from the scene of the crime, and she made a move. So I made a move back. I reacted. That's what a protector's supposed to do, son. Or are they teaching you something different in the Junior Academy these days?"

Liz shook her head, wide eyed and in shock.

Jonah couldn't hide his sneer. How could his dad talk to him like this when his dad was the one admitting to killing Ansel's mom? "You *thought* she had a gun," Jonah said.

His dad tried to look away from them. "She didn't, though," he said, shaking his head.

Liz put down her milk and cookies to sit on the arm of Jonah's dad's chair and pat his back. Jonah looked away. He didn't want to see his dad crying.

"I made a mistake." His dad coughed and straightened up. He guided Liz back to her seat. "And you're the only people who know. Now you see why I wanted to protect Ansel, why I *had* to protect her. I had to make up for that mistake."

"It was the right thing to do," Liz said.

"But what did you do?" Jonah asked. "They wouldn't fire you for killing a guilty Sixer. I know that much."

His dad looked away again. "No," he said. "That's not why I was discharged. It was the way I went about trying to protect her."

"What was it?" Liz asked.

"Well... I..."

"*Dad*," Jonah said. "Liz got *six* demerits, no parole, and I didn't get any punishment at all today because the Captain knew I was your son. What did you do?"

Liz looked like she wanted to yell at Jonah, but she didn't want to interrupt the conversation at the same time. Jonah's dad looked at his lap then shook his head and looked at Jonah to say, "I shot an owner."

Liz's jaw dropped. She looked like she was going to hyperventilate. She was looking this way and that, as if, by saying what he had done, Jonah's dad had called protectors to come arrest them all.

"You did what?" Jonah asked, shocked.

"I did what I thought was in her best interest." his dad said. "In your best interest, really. I did this all for you, after all."

"I never asked you to do anything for me," Jonah said.

"You didn't have to ask," his dad said. "I did it for you because I love you and I thought it was what was best for you."

"Killing an owner was best for me?" Jonah scoffed. "I don't see how it could be."

"That's because it was a stupid mistake," his dad said. "We all make stupid mistakes. We're just human. My stupid mistake happened to be bigger than most people's. That's all."

"*Both of yours*," Jonah said. "If you hadn't killed Ansel's mom, you would never have had a reason to shoot that owner."

His dad looked hurt. "I know I was wrong. What can I do to change that now, though?"

Liz looked at Jonah and nudged him. She mouthed, "Go on."

"Dad," he said. Jonah could let him off the hook and try to help his father through this, sure, but one of them was supposed to be an adult, and it wasn't Jonah. "You have to do something. Tonight, we…" He looked away. "Ansel was with us when we were arrested. They took her, too."

"I know, son," his dad said. "But there's nothing we can do about that. I had to realize that was true of her father before I was free to throw my life away."

"No!" Jonah complained. "Don't tell me that. Don't tell me that I can't. I'm responsible for this. If it wasn't for me, Liz never would have gotten her demerits and Ansel never would have been taken. I need to do something to make up for that."

"You can't, boy!" his dad snapped.

Liz slowly set her cookies and milk on the table and backed deeper into the couch, embarrassed. Jonah just stared at his dad, wide-eyed. His dad hadn't yelled at Jonah since before he left for the Academy, and the red hot anger in his face was a little frightening.

"Nothing you can do is going to change the fact that the girl was taken," his dad said. "Nothing will change what they do to her now that they have her. *Not one thing*. And you can't help Liz work off her demerits, either. So the best thing you can do to make it up to her is to leave this thing alone and go about your schooling with your head down, making sure your partner doesn't get dishonorably discharged before she even has a chance to enlist." He took a deep breath.

Jonah shook his head. "That's not true," he said under his breath.

"What was that?" his dad asked.

"I said, just because you couldn't think of anything better than shooting an owner, doesn't mean there's nothing I can do about it."

"It *does* mean that," his dad said. "And even if there was something you could do, I would order you not to do it. In fact, I *am* ordering you. Jonah, I order you to get any idea you have of saving that girl out of your mind and focus on becoming a protector before you go and throw your life away like I did."

"No!" Jonah stood from the couch. "You can't even say her name."

"*Ansel*," his dad said with a cold expression on his face.

"It's your fault she's an orphan," Jonah said. "It's your fault the protectors have her now. *You* told me to ignore the orders that are stupid so I'm doing just that." He turned and stormed out of the house.

"I order you to come back right this moment," his dad yelled after him, but Jonah ignored it, slamming the door shut behind him. He sat down on the stoop, breathing heavily and furious.

His dad was being impossible. First he tells Jonah to ignore orders, everything he's been taught is a red herring lie, then he tries to give Jonah orders with the next breath. He can have it one way or the other, and he didn't get to decide anymore. Jonah did. There had to be something he could do to help save Ansel, no matter what his dad said.

The door opened and closed behind him, and Liz slapped the back of his neck as she sat on the stoop next to him. "*Thanks*," she said.

"*What?*" Jonah snapped.

"That *totes* wasn't awkward at all. Especially the part where you left me alone with your dad after yelling at him right in front of me."

"Yeah, well, I wasn't exactly at the shooting range myself."

"You know, Jonah… Your dad might be right."

Jonah scoffed. "About which contradictory position?"

"It's not contradictory," she said. "He's just trying to protect you. Like he has been doing all along."

"Yeah, well, he has a funny way of showing it."

"At least he does show it."

They stared out at the yard and trees in silence. Everything was lit with the eerie white streetlights so only the brightest stars and planets were visible in the sky. A little black cat ran across the sidewalk.

"I mean," Liz said. "What *can* we do?" Jonah couldn't help but smile at the fact that she used "we" instead of "you", at least she still wanted to be his partner. "Is your plan to go through the elevator and get arrested again? Because they might not be as easy on a second offender, Pardy or not."

Jonah blushed and shook his head. "No," he said. "Of course not. That was a stupid idea from the get go."

"*Tah-yeah!*" Liz scoffed.

"Well, I don't see you coming up with anything better," Jonah said, standing from the stoop, offended.

Liz shook her head. She looked hurt by what he said, or his tone of voice, or something else he had done—he could never tell what exactly. "Because maybe there isn't a better idea," she said. "Maybe there really is nothing we can do."

"No," Jonah said. He stomped his foot. "I won't believe it. There's something I can do, I know it."

"But, Jonah. You're dad said—"

"I don't care what my dad said. My dad told me not to follow orders blindly. He told me to protect the weak. He told me I can do anything if I just believe in myself. I know what he said, Liz, *he's my dad*, and *that's* why I have to do this. Can't you see that?"

"I, but—"

"No," Jonah stopped her. "I need to go for a walk, clear my head. I'll see you tomorrow, okay."

Liz shook her head. She looked like she wanted to say something more but couldn't think of what, a rare occurrence for her.

"Don't worry," Jonah said, trying to ease her tension just a little. "I won't do anything before I put it past my partner."

She smiled. "You better not." She stood from the stoop and wiped off her pants. "And think about what your dad said."

Jonah nodded, not wanting to respond and drag the argument out further than it had already gone. He needed to be alone with his thoughts for a while before he even knew his own opinion on the matter himself.

"And get some rest, too," Liz said over her shoulder as she made her way toward her house. "We still have class in the morning, you know."

"*Ugh.*" Jonah sighed loud enough for her to hear it then made his way absent-mindedly along the winding sidewalks, letting his feet take him wherever they wanted to go.

He couldn't believe that Liz agreed with his dad. But then again, he couldn't blame her. She had just gotten six demerits for following him on his stupid plan so of course she would want to be more careful in the future. But he hadn't gotten a single demerit. He had no reason to be careful. He had broken the law and gotten away with it scot free. Now he felt like he had the responsibility to do something for those who hadn't. But what? What could a little kid who hadn't even passed through the Junior Academy do in the face of all odds?

He was about to give up on everything and go back home when he ran into some person and fell to the ground. It felt weird though. He didn't land on sidewalk or grass. He looked around himself, and he wasn't even outside anymore. He was in a grey hallway. And the person he had bumped into wasn't wearing a protector's white uniform, she was wearing a long white coat. The woman extended a black gloved hand to help him up.

"Where am I?" he asked, standing with her assistance.

"My name's the Scientist," she said. "I understand there's something you want."

๖ ✳ ๗

XXXIV. Guy

Guy wasn't there. He couldn't be there so he wasn't. He sat perfectly still, and the harsh, blinding white room disappeared around him. In its place what though? What was this? Where was he? His mind had never taken him here before

Guy was standing outside of himself. No, he was standing outside of himselves. As he stepped further and further back so did they, and soon, there were seven of him, all breaking away from each other. He stopped and heard a noise behind him, then he jumped but didn't turn to see what had produced the noise. The others jumped, too. All of him did. Then they all ran back together and tumbled into one Guy again. Just as they—or he, he wasn't sure of the difference anymore—tried to stand up, a door opened and broke him out of his trance.

All of a sudden he remembered where he was. He squinted his eyes against the sterile white light, reflecting off the sterile white walls. He looked up in fear at the armor-clad protector standing in front of him. The protector's actual uniforms looked much different than the costumes he was used to seeing on set. The real deal looked more utilitarian, less showy. The armor wasn't overly bulky, and the helmets looked light and airy in comparison to the heavy props he was used to. Then there were the guns. Those were definitely bigger, and infinitely more deadly.

"Citizen," the protector said in a deep, modulated voice, facemask smile teeth glowing neon with every word. "Come with me."

"I—but—" Guy said.

"*Now, citizen.*"

Guy stood slowly with his hands up. He didn't put them down until the protector turned and led him out the door and through a hall to a room with a big metal table and chairs on either side.

"Sit, citizen," the protector said.

"I—but—"

"Sit!"

Guy raised his hands again and slowly moved toward the seat that was closest to him.

"*Uh uh,*" the protector said, pointing a gun at the other seat. "That one."

Guy nodded and took the other seat. The protector left without another word. This room was just as bright and white as the one he had been waiting in. If anything, it was brighter. Even when he closed his eyes they burned from the heat of the lights. There was a big black mirror across the room from him, and he could see himself sitting behind the table in it. At least they didn't have him in cuffs. If they did, he would look exactly like every criminal he had ever seen played on TV. But he wasn't a criminal. He was Guy. He set his mind on getting back into his meditation trance when the door opened and a protector walked in wearing no helmet. Guy shaded his eyes with his hands to try to figure out more, but he still couldn't make anything out with the bright lights.

"Well, well," the protector said. "This is a predicament you find yourself in. Isn't it?"

"I—uh—" Guy didn't know how to respond. "What have I done?"

"That's what we're here to find out. Isn't it?"

"I haven't done anything," Guy said. He blinked water from his eyes, not sure if it was from fear or the brightness of the lights.

"Oh, but haven't you?" the protector asked. "Dim the lights please."

The lights dimmed, but they still reflected hot off the white walls. Guy could see the protector's face now, and she was grinning an evil grin.

"What do you want from me?" Guy asked.

"The truth," she said. "I want to know everything you know about what happened: How you were involved, who else was, how you killed him, *everything.*"

"I—but—no!" She couldn't be serious. What reason would he have to kill Russ Logo? What reason would he have to kill anyone? "I didn't do anything."

The woman scoffed. "No?"

Guy shook his head. He could feel tears building up behind his eyes again, and he knew these weren't from the lights.

"Oh, well, okay then," the woman said, smiling and nodding.

"You're free to go." She gave a thumbs up.

"I—uh—*really?*"

"No, Mr. Rockwell!" She slammed her fists on the table. "*Not really.* Where do you think you are right now?"

He looked at the black mirror then back at her. "I—uh—"

"You're in an interrogation room, citizen," she said, "one short elevator ride away from the holding cell we'll store you in when we find you guilty. Don't worry, though. You won't be staying there long. Not with the kind of insurance Lord Walker had out on the property you destroyed. No, with that much insurance—and your lack of it—I foresee a quick trip to the disposal unit in your future. Maybe they won't even waste the expense of holding you at all, just send you straight there. There aren't often vacancies in the cells these days. Now, Mr. Rockwell... Do you understand why it's so important, so crucial, so...*vital* for you to tell me everything you know as soon as possible."

Guy nodded, swallowing his fear. His tears had dried up with the rush of adrenaline his body produced in reaction to the protector's speech. He wiped his sweaty hands on his thighs and tried to come up with something to say, but he couldn't think straight. This protector couldn't be serious. There was no way they could think that *Guy* had something to do with Russ's death. How could they? He didn't.

"Well," the protector said, tapping her fingers on the table. "Sooner would have been better."

"But I don't know anything," Guy complained. "What am I supposed to say?" His body started to tremble, and he tried to hold tight to his seat to stop it, but it was no use, the chair just shook with him. He had lost control.

"You're a bit nervous for someone who hasn't done anything wrong," the protector said with a grin. "Now why's that, Guy?"

"I, well..." His trembling got worse now that she had pointed it out. "Because you're a—*a protector,*" he stammered.

"That's right," she said. "I'm here to protect you. Why would that make you nervous?"

"No, but you just said—"

"I just warned you of the consequences *if* you're found to have some part in this," she said. "*If* being the operative word, citizen. Like *if* you hadn't done anything wrong, you wouldn't be so nervous that I could hear your chair rattling."

Guy jumped up, pushing the chair to the ground with a clatter and making his heart skip a beat.

The protector laughed. "Settle down now, son," she said. "And get back in that chair."

Guy picked it up, and the chair felt extra heavy because his arms wouldn't stop shaking. He felt so weak. He made a lot of noise setting it upright and was relieved at the small comfort of being able to sit on its cold hard surface.

"Now," the protector said when he had reseated himself. "Tell me what you know."

"*I told you,*" Guy said, his voice breaking. "I—I know nothing."

The protector shook her head. "You were there, weren't you? Guy nodded.

"And you were the first to notice something wrong. You were the one holding him while he died, and you alerted everyone else to that fact. Do you expect me to believe that this was all a coincidence?"

"*He was already dead,*" Guy blurted out then covered his mouth.

The protector raised an eyebrow. "Go on..."

"W—when I turned him over," Guy said. "He was already dead. He didn't die in my arms."

She nodded. "*Still,*" she said, "it seems suspicious, don't you think?"

"I didn't do this," Guy said. "I wouldn't. I loved Russ. I worked on every movie he was ever in. I—we—*he was going to give me notes on a script I wrote.*" He wished he could take it back as soon as he had said it.

"*You don't say,*" the protector said. "Russ Logo, the biggest star in the history of entertainment, was going to give a no name extra notes on his script. Was this some kind of charity?"

Guy's cheeks flushed. He was angry and embarrassed at the same time. Who was this cop to talk to him about art? Who was she to say that *he* wasn't good enough to work with Russ Logo? She didn't know anything about writing, or movies, or anything in the world that mattered. "Yes," he said. "That's right."

"It *was* charity?" The protector looked confused.

"I—wha—no," Guy said, shaking his head. "It wasn't."

"Then what?"

"I—because…"

"You know what I think, Rockwell," the protector said. "I think you're lying. I think he denied your request for help, and that's why you killed him. Isn't it?"

"I—never—no, but—"

"*No more buts*, Rockwell. Tell us what happened!'

"He wasn't giving me notes, okay." Guy sighed. He couldn't keep that lie up any longer. It was too unbelievable. "But I wouldn't kill him for that. That's ridiculous. I don't even know how to kill a person. I—I just couldn't do it. It's absurd."

"Sure, Rockwell." The protector scoffed. "That's what you'd like us to believe. But I'm not buying your stupid routine. You got that?"

"I—but—"

She slammed both hands on the table and pushed herself up from the chair. "I said, *you got that?*"

Guy nodded. He didn't know if he wanted to hit her, run away and try to escape, or tremble in his seat, pissing himself.

"Good," she said. "We'll be watching you, Rockwell. You can count on that." She left the room, slamming the door behind her.

Guy took a deep breath. The room spun around him. She really thought that he had something to do with Russ's death. The protectors thought he was a suspect in Russ's murder. His stomach gurgled like it wanted to expel all of its contents. Guy felt like passing out.

The door swung open and two protectors marched in. One pointed a gun at Guy and said, "Stand up, citizen. Over here."

Guy put his hands up and slowly crept toward the protector.

"Stay put," the protector said, pushing the gun closer as if Guy didn't know it was there. The second protector bent down and strapped something heavy around Guy's ankle.

"There we are, citizen," the first said. "Now we'll have our eyes on you at all times. Follow us."

They marched him down a long hall to a big elevator and rode with him back to the entrance where they had arrested him. "Don't forget," the protector said, pushing Guy into the street. "We're watching you." The doors slid closed.

Guy looked around. This was his street alright, but it looked different. Where before all the close set balconies and squished together buildings were a comforting, warm embrace, now they seemed cold, hard, and distant. It was light out. He didn't remember how long he had been gone for or if he had slept even. He thought that maybe the whole thing was a dream and he would wake up soon, warm and comfortable in his bed. But no matter how many times he blinked or tried to pinch himself, he just wouldn't wake up.

He didn't want to climb up to his tiny apartment and be alone right now. He didn't think he could handle that. He still wasn't entirely sure if he was insane, and he needed some other human to tell him the truth. He sighed and stepped back into the elevator to tell it to bring him to the closest stop to Indywood.

He hoped his crew would be there. He almost started trembling again in anticipation as he opened the bar doors, but when he saw what was behind them, his jaw dropped. Every single patron was dressed from head to toe in black. The bar's decorations had been changed from their normal colorful festivity to a drab black motif, with only black and white movies playing on the screens. He felt like he had walked into a funeral. Even the music playing seemed dark and sad. But to his relief, most of the crew was sitting at their normal tables so Guy walked over and waved. "*Uh, hey*," he said.

"Oh, *Fortuna*." Jen gasped, standing from the couch and hugging him. "I was so worried about you."

Guy blushed. "I—*uh*—"

"Here, take a seat," she said, pulling him down to the couch. "Scoot over, Emir. Let him in."

They shuffled around to let Guy onto the couch. Cohen looked him up and down. "Where have you been?" he asked.

"Shit, Cohen." Jen shot him a look. "I told you the protectors took him. What do you mean where has he been?"

"Yeah, well." Cohen sneered. "Why'd they take you, then? Huh? We were expecting our sheets *this* morning, Guy. We're pretty much ready to shoot everything. All we need's the script."

"We don't have every—" Laura started.

"*We're ready*." Cohen cut her off.

"Well, it wasn't really my choice to be arrested," Guy said.

"You were arrested!" Emily said.

"I told you!" Jen said.

"Is that why you aren't wearing black?" Emir asked.

Guy looked down at himself. He was wearing the same clothes he had been wearing on what was apparently yesterday. "Why are you all wearing black?" he asked.

"*Uh, doi,*" Emily said.

Emir scoffed.

"Because of Russ," Jen said. "Like you said."

Guy rubbed his face with his hands. Of course. The news must have gotten out by now. They were mourning Russ's death. That's why the entire bar was dressed in black, too. Guy had told his crew about it the day before, and they didn't believe him then, but now that everyone knew the truth, they had no choice but to advertise their melancholy, wearing it on their sleeves and shirts and dresses and shoes—even the bar's decorations and the movies on the projector screens. He wasn't crazy after all. He felt an itch on his leg and went to scratch it, but abruptly stopped when he felt the weight on his ankle and remembered what it was.

"So," Jen said, patting him on the back. "Tell us. What happened?"

"I, uh, well…"

"Go on," Cohen said. "We're not getting anything done until we get past this, so you might as well spit it out now."

"Well," Guy said, "they questioned me about what happened. Since he died in my arms and all…"

"So it *was* true," Emir said, a proud look on his face.

"*No way,*" Emily said. "Really?"

"I was there," Jen said. "They stole Guy right off his front steps and disappeared through the elevator. I was terrified. I thought they were going to kill me with their creepy voices and glowing teeth."

Cohen laughed. "So what?" he asked. "They just asked you a few questions and let you go?"

The whole crew looked on at Guy expectantly. He relished the attention and paused for effect. "Well, not just that," he said. He lifted his foot onto the table and pulled up his pants leg so they could all see his new fashion statement. "They said they were watching me, too," he said with a shit-eating grin on his face.

The group let out a collective gasp.

"*Bad ass*," Emir said.

"*Fortuna*," Emily said.

"*Holy shit*," Laura said.

"*You can't be serious*," Cohen said.

Jen gasped.

Steve came back from the bar with a drink in hand and said, "What? What happened, y'all? What did I miss?"

And Guy just nodded. "Yeah," he said. "Well I told y'all what had happened and you didn't believe me. Remember?"

They all tried to avoid his gaze, except for Steve who was still trying to figure out what he had missed and Laura who was filling him in.

"Well, I had nothing to do with it," Guy went on. "So this ought to be off my ankle in no time."

Laura scoffed.

"What?" Guy asked her.

"Oh, nothing," she said, waving it away.

"Come on," Cohen said. "Share it with the crew."

"Well, it's just—you've never had a run in with the protectors before, have you?" Laura said.

Everyone looked at him, and Guy shook his head.

"Yeah, well," she said, "that thing won't be as easy to get off you ankle as you think it will be. That's all I'm saying."

"But I didn't even do anything," Guy complained. "They can't just tag me like an animal whenever they want to."

Emily scoffed, taking a drink.

"Pretty much," Laura said, sipping hers, too.

"Well, we'll see about tha—"

"*Alright, alright*," Cohen said, waving his hands to shut everyone up. Some small disparate conversations had started among the crew. "Enough. You see? That's why I didn't want to bring this up. We'll be on it forever. It's time we get on to the real business that brought us here."

"Go on, then," Emir said, losing interest.

"First," Cohen went on, "and I hate to bring it back to you again already, but Guy, come on man, tell us, is the script finished yet?"

"Well, I didn't really have time to get to the edits, did I?" Guy said. "I came straight here from prison."

"No, and we didn't get your new pages either," Cohen said. "But am I to take that to mean the script is *not* finished?"

Guy wanted to slap the smug grin of his face. He hated that patronizing tone so much. "*Yes, Cohen,*" he said in the sweetest voice he could muster. "*When I say I have more edits to do, that means the script's not done yet.*"

"Well, that's a problem," Cohen said, ignoring Guy's tone. "Because I'm gonna need you to drop that script and work on a higher priority piece right away."

"I—what?" Guy said. The rest of the crew complained with him. What could be higher priority than the project which all of them had been devoting their every free hour to for months now? "You've got to be kidding."

"No," Cohen said, grinning wider. "I'm more serious than I've ever been."

"What the fuck, Cohen?" Emir demanded. "What could be more important than this script?"

"*This script,*" Cohen said, holding up a packet of papers. "There are only a few here so ya'll'll have to share for now." He handed one to Guy then a couple to a few of the others. Jen read Guy's over his shoulder as he flipped through it so he went a little slower than he normally would have.

"This is crap," Guy said when he had flipped to the end and passed it to Jen so she could get a closer look.

"That's where you come in," Cohen said. "You have to make it workable."

"But why?" Emir huffed, throwing his copy on the table. Emily smacked him, picked it up, and went on reading.

"Because this is how we get the equipment we need to make *our* project look like it's done by professionals and not children," Cohen said. "That's why. Laura, you think you could make our shots cleaner with a better camera and some new lenses?"

"I—uh—of course," she said. "But—"

"What about mics, lights, dollies, and tracks?"

Laura nodded.

"Steve, if you could have anything in the world, cost not a factor, could you solve that owner fatness issue? Could you make them look really, really, like, disgustingly alien fat?"

"Oh, of course," Steve said, waving a hand at Cohen. "No

problem. But cost *is* a factor, dear."

"Not anymore it isn't," Cohen said. "Not if we film *this* script first. Then we can each write out a wish list containing anything we want and have every little bit of it fulfilled." He put his smug grin back on and crossed his arms, full of himself.

No one said anything. They didn't know how to answer. Guy did, though. He didn't believe Cohen for one minute. "Yeah, right," he said.

"Yeah, Guy," Cohen said. "That is right."

"But how?" Emir asked.

"Let's just say I found an investor. They offered unlimited printer access in exchange for one small script."

"Who?" Emily asked.

"You wouldn't know 'em," Cohen said.

"We wouldn't know someone with a 3D printer?" Jen asked.

"I don't like it," Laura said.

"*Look,*" Cohen said, "this is going to bring our project to the next level, y'all. Now, I know how much time and effort y'all have been putting into this because I've been there every step of the way with you, and I know it seems ridiculous to veer off course just now, when we seem so close to our hard sought destination, but a slight detour now will save us more time and effort in the end. It'll save us money and, most importantly, respect. I know it seems like a gamble to you, but that's because y'all haven't met the investor. If you had, you would be as confident as I am in this thing, and you, Guy, would be hard at work fixing that script right now so we can bring her something we can all work with."

"Why don't we just meet her then?" Guy asked. "If that would change all of our minds, I mean."

The rest of the crew seemed to agree.

"That's the rub," Cohen said. "For in that meeting what things may come? Our inertia might change her mind, then where would we be? Back where we started from—with extra time wasted. No, that's the worst course of all. For now, you have to trust me as your director. You have to trust my judgement. And I swear before Fortuna that you will not be disappointed."

Emir shrugged. "I'm in," he said. "*Whatever.*"

"Me, too," Emily said, throwing her copy on the table. "I can see something to work with in there. I just want to act."

"I don't know," Laura said. "I need more time to read it before I decide."

"Yeah, me, too," Jen said, still flipping through her copy.

"That's alright," Cohen said. "Guy still needs to come up with his revisions before we know what we're really working with, anyway. What about you, Steve?"

Steve shrugged. "You give me a costume to design, and I'll make it."

"Well, then," Cohen said with a smile. "Guy. What about you?"

Guy didn't want to do this. He was a writer, not an editor. The prospect of working on someone else's project was already unappealing enough, and the tripe that he had skimmed through only made it worse. But he couldn't let his crew down, either. Without them he'd be a sad, lonely extra, sitting by himself in his room, with only the imaginary friends in his head to keep him company. He shook his head. "I don't know if I can make this workable," he said.

"I believe in you," Cohen said.

Guy scoffed. "It's not me I'm worried about."

"Still," Cohen said. "I think you can do it."

"I don't know," Guy said, standing up. "And I'm not deciding until I read it in full. I'll let you know when I do." He stomped out of the bar, noticing that he hadn't brought a script with him when he was only halfway outside, but not stopping until he was in the fresh air anyway.

He took a deep breath. That was not a productive way to end the conversation, but Cohen didn't care what the words actually said, what the film actually meant in the end. All he cared about was getting another director credit that he could slap on his resume. Most of the rest of them didn't care, either. They were all the same, they just wanted to work. They didn't realize it was different when you were a writer. Putting your name on something meant it represented your views, and Guy didn't think that this script was speaking for him. He didn't want to go back in for a copy because of that, so he decided he would just have to call Jen to get it later. He was about to head to the elevator when she came out waving one for him anyway. "Guy, wait," she said.

Guy chuckled. "I wasn't going anywhere," he said.

"Yeah, well, you better not be," she said, hitting him with the script. "We need you."

Guy blushed. It was nice to know that at least one member of the crew thought that was true. "Not really," he said. "You already have a script."

"Yeah, but you said it sucks."

"It does," Guy said. "But what do you think?"

"Oh, I don't know." She shrugged. "I don't read that fast. And I'm not a writer anyway. What does my opinion matter?"

"But you're going to be working on the project," Guy said. "You're putting your time and effort into it. Don't you think it would be a waste of your time if it wasn't good?"

"Not if I'm getting paid well enough." Jen smiled.

"But we're not getting paid at all."

"We are, though, silly." She slapped his arm. "Cohen said we'd get to fill out a wish list. I'm asking for a new battle station."

"But do you think that's worth it? I mean, here. Look at this." He grabbed the script out of her hand and flipped to a particularly horrible quote he remembered from his skim through. "Here it is: Assembly Worker—and that's her name, mind you—Assembly Worker slip, snap, clicks at a line. Enter Android Thief—again a name. *This is my job. How will my human children eat?*—she literally says *human* children for Fortuna's sake—then Android thief pushes Assembly Worker out of the way and slip, snap, clicks in her place, saying. *I am a robot. I don't care.* And that's all the robot ever says throughout the entire script, okay. *I am a robot. I don't care.* I mean, that's how ridiculous this shit is." He looked at her, pointing at the spot in the script, and when she didn't respond, he said, "*That's shit.* I mean, the names alone are a red flag. The dialogue is stereotypical and stilted. The imagery is less than subtle." He chuckled to himself. "This is pure garbage."

"I don't know," *Jen said. "It wasn't that bad."*

"*It* wasn't that bad?" Guy scoffed. "Do you even know what this thing is saying? That was the most obvious scene I could pick out."

Jen looked offended now. Like she didn't want to be there talking to Guy anymore. "What does it matter anyway?" she asked. "A job's a job."

"But this isn't just a job, Jen. Who do you think's going to watch this crap? What's the point in working on something so ridiculous? I mean, robots stealing jobs? That was *maybe* topical like a hundred and fifty years ago, *if then*. It's Luddite nonsense, and I don't understand how anyone who has access to a printer could still be promoting such utter horse shit."

"Guy, settle down." Jen sighed. "You're too worked up about this. It's not that big of a deal, okay. It's just a job."

"No, but—"

"*No*," Jen stopped him. "I know you have your ideals, and you like to stick to them, but now's not the time, okay. *Wait*—I know. Just listen. *You* wrote the script we really care about. Those are *you're* words, Guy. Most of the rest of the crew trusts Cohen to—I know, but listen—most of them trust him to be a good judge of character, and I do, too, Guy. Even if their message is ignorant, I trust that this investor's payment will be true. And if it is, we'll be so much more capable when we get to finally do your script that it'll be seen by more people because of it. Don't you want your script to be seen by as wide an audience as possible, Guy?"

"Well, yeah, but—" Guy started.

"*But nothing*," Jen said. "Do you trust me, Guy?"

He blushed again. "I—of course—but—"

"Then do it for me," she said. "And the rest of the crew. *Fuck Cohen*. I know you can polish this turd up enough to make it easier on the rest of us, then we can get to the real work of putting *your* script into production, the job we all really want to do. What do you say?"

"Uh, yeah, well, I guess, but—"

"Well, it's settled then." She turned him toward the elevator and patted him on the butt. "Get to it," she said. "We can't wait to hear your edits."

ও   ✖   ♋

XXXV. Olsen

A 3D printer was a big thing. Olsen had never really seen one up close before. Now that she had, she didn't think it looked too fancy. It was just a tall, fat metal console with a red button and a sliding door on the front. If it weren't for the red button, it would look exactly like a trash chute—which Olsen had seen plenty of.

She walked up to one of the printers and rocked it, wondering if two people was enough to carry the heavy thing upstairs. Hopefully Anna was stronger than she looked. She was nice, and smart, and she knew how to cook, but none of that would help them get this hunk of metal up the stairs.

The door opened and Anna came downstairs, smiling at Olsen. "So, child," she said. "What do you think? Are you ready for this?"

Olsen patted the printer. "I don't know," she said. "This thing is pretty heavy. Do you think the two of us can move it?"

Anna laughed. "No, child," she said. "Not without tools. But that's no problem now that we have the printer. What I really meant to ask is are you ready to give your Family what they deserve?"

Olsen blushed. She thought all the "family" talk was a little weird, but she didn't know how to bring that opinion up to the people who were paying here wages. She did what she had been doing and just smiled and nodded along. "I'm ready to cook for people," she said.

"Oh, child," Anna frowned. "This won't be cooking, I'm afraid. We don't have time for all that. We'll be printing everything so we can spread our message as far possible."

"Our message?"

"About the Human Family, child," Anna said. "You know. You read the pamphlet."

Olsen groaned to herself. She hadn't really finished the pamphlet yet. After her conversations with her mom and Sonya, she wasn't sure she wanted to know what the rest of it said. She needed this job, though, and they were teaching her how to cook—even if they wouldn't be cooking now—so she didn't want to blow this. "Well," she said. "I'm ready to help people."

"Good, child," Anna said. "Helping humans is exactly what we're all about. Now, the first thing's first. We need to get this printer out there to the people. Are you ready?"

Olsen nodded. "But I still don't know how we're going to carry it," she said.

"Just leave that to me, child," Anna said, walking over to press the printer's red button. "Anti-grav cart, please," she said. "*Four-pack.*"

The metal doors slid open, and Anna reached in to pull out four small discs. "Now," she said, kneeling down next to the printer. "If you just tip it that way a little bit, I can get this under here."

Olsen pushed on the top of the console, leaning it over a little so Anna could slide the discs under both corners of the raised side.

"Now the other way, child," Anna said.

Olsen went around and tilted the printer the other way, and Anna put the remaining two discs underneath.

"There we are," Anna said, bent down and pressing a button on each disk, making each corner of the machine float up an inch off the ground as she did, until she had activated all four discs and the entire printer floated a few inches over the basement's cement floor.

"There," Anna said, standing and brushing herself off. "Light as a feather now. It would really only take one of us to move it, but we're best to use both for safety's sake. Come on, now. Help me out, child."

Olsen got behind the printer with Anna, and they didn't even have to push, more so just guide it on its way. It was a little trickier when they were bringing it up the stairs, but that was only because the machine was so much lighter than it looked and Olsen kept lifting it so fast that the thing almost fell over onto Anna. They got it up to the top of the stairs without an incident, though—thankfully— and pushed the printer out to the field across the street from the Family Home.

"More room out here when they start showing up," Anna said with a smile. "Now, this is the tricky part. Do you see the buttons on the discs on that side?"

Olsen bent down to get a closer look. "Uh, yeah," she said. "I think so."

"Press them both at the same time. On my count, okay. *On three*. Are you ready?"

Olsen wasn't sure she was. Some people walking past were already stopping to see what they were doing, and it only made her more nervous. "Uh—yeah," she said anyway. She had no choice. It was her job now.

"Okay, then. One...two...*three!*"

Olsen pressed one then tried to press the other but missed, and three of the four corners of the 3D printer fell to the ground with a loud bang. Olsen hurried to stop the thing from tipping over onto Anna while Anna pressed the last button for her, and the printer smashed to the ground with another loud clang.

"Uh—*wow*—I—I'm sorry," Olsen said, breathing heavily.

"You're fine, girl," Anna said. "I told you that was the hard part. We're out here and ready now. That's all that matters. Look."

Olsen turned to see people starting to crowd around them. The spectacle of the big metal box was enough to draw their attention. That and the notoriety Anna and Rosa had been able to draw with their nightly speeches in the field.

"Friends," Anna called over the people. Her voice wasn't as loud or deep as Rosa's, but it carried just as far and touched a different part of the soul. "Family. *Humans*." Olsen cringed at the last word but kept listening anyway. She knew Anna meant well, even if Olsen disagreed with her methods—or Sonya disagreed with her methods, Olsen still wasn't sure how she felt about them yet. "We are here today to fulfill one wish for every Family member who has one."

The crowd started whispering among itself. Olsen couldn't help but smile. These people were about to get an opportunity to ask a printer for whatever they desired, and Olsen was playing a hand in giving that to them. Still, no brave souls came up to ask for what they wanted. Olsen didn't blame them, though. She didn't think she would want to be the first to step up either. She couldn't even imagine what she would ask for.

"Brothers and sisters," Anna went on. "*Siblings*. I know you all have something you need at home. Certainly you don't have enough food, or your kids need new shoes, or maybe you just want that keg of beer all to yourself for once." She smiled at what looked to be someone in particular from the bystanders. "We're not here to judge. We're only here to make your dreams come true, whatever you wish for. Now, who will be the first lucky Family member to get what they desire?"

"How about a fucking job?" someone called from the crowd, which looked to be about a hundred people by then.

Anna laughed. "Oh, no," she said, putting on a solemn face like she really meant what she was saying. "Sadly, that can't be gotten from a printer. But if it fits through those doors, you can have it otherwise."

"My family hasn't eaten meat in weeks," an older woman, who was particularly dirty, at the front of the crowd said. She looked like she was from the other world—or whatever Sonya called it. "I'd like a turkey stuffed with vegetables," she said, "so my kids can eat right." She pushed her two little children out in front of her, and they blushed and hid their dirty faces.

"*That* we can do," Anna said. She pressed the red button. "Turkey, stuffed with fresh vegetables," she said.

The doors slid open, and there it was, steaming and warm. The crowd let out a collective gasp. The chatter grew louder. The woman and her kids walked up to the printer wide-eyed.

"Help her, Olsen," Anna said.

Olsen shook herself out of her daze and grabbed the turkey out of the printer's mouth. It was heavy and awkward to hand off, and probably would have been easier for the woman to take out herself, but Olsen loved the feeling she got from the process, like she had been responsible for giving the woman and her family the meal they so desperately needed.

The woman turned around with a smile and raised the turkey up over her head for the still growing crowd to see. Eyes grew wide and the chatter around picked up. People stepped closer now that they had proof of how the printer worked. There was some jostling and commotion, and a young boy fell over with a yelp near the front of the crowd, producing more ado.

"Now, now," Anna called over them. "Settle down, please! *Settle down.*"

The crowd didn't listen. The fighting over who pushed the boy rippled out like a wave, making everyone more anxious. Olsen was starting to worry. She could see how hungry the faces were, how dirty they were. She could still tell the otherworlders from the locals because they were still dirtier, but it wasn't by much anymore. No matter which world they were from, they all looked desperate enough to do anything to get their hands on the printer. Maybe this wasn't going to be as easy as she thought it was. How did Anna and Rosa expect her to respond to this test? How could she respond to it? She looked to Anna for guidance, and Anna shrugged. Olsen had to do something to show the *Family* she was reliable beyond cooking. She had to demonstrate her value like her mom had told her to do.

"Quiet!" Olsen yelled, and the crowd went silent, staring at her in surprise. She had surprised herself, too. She meant to do something but not that. At least it seemed to work. She looked to Anna who smiled then mouthed, "Good job."

"Now," Anna called over the group, which was numbering near a thousand and still growing. "We can't do anything unless we do it in an orderly fashion. Everyone will get a chance to ask for something, but we can only fulfill one request at a time. We'll have to stop like this every time we here jostling or arguing, though, and that will only mean a longer wait for everyone. So, for the sake of yourselves and your Family, I implore all of you to keep it calm and orderly. Can we do that?"

The crowd mumbled incoherently, but by the sound of their collective groaning, it seemed like they agreed.

"I said, can we do that?" Anna repeated with more volume.

"Yes," the crowd responded, somewhat in unison.

"*Good*," Anna said. "Then one by one, please. And if you can decide on what you'd like before you get here, it will save a lot of time for everyone. Thank you. Who's first?"

After that it was a surprisingly orderly process. One by one, members of the dirty masses stepped up to ask for whatever their hearts desired. The people who looked like they were from Olsen's world all seemed to be asking for various food items, some of them necessities, most of them luxuries, and a lot asked for big jugs of alcohol which were some of the heaviest things to lift out of the printer. Olsen couldn't imagine carrying one all the way home. One old man asked for twenty-four cartons of cigarettes. When exactly twenty-four came out, the later requests started to become more specific and grow in quantity.

The people who were dirtier, like they had come from the other, new world, would sometimes ask for food, too, but never alcohol or other luxuries. They asked for big cans of meat and beans or pounds of rice, but even that wasn't often. More often they asked for clothes and shoes, things that would last longer, and mostly they asked for tools of various kinds—many of which Olsen didn't recognize—things that they could use with their own hands to better produce for themselves. Seeing these differences between the two groups, Olsen was coming closer and closer to believing that two worlds had collided—or merged—or whatever Sonya wanted to call it.

The work was exhausting, and it only got more so as time went on and the requesters grew bolder in their demands. But still, Olsen continued to hand gift after gift from the mouth of the printer—it looked like it had one red eye that was the voice activation button, and the doors were arched to make a big frowning mouth—into the hands of the citizens of her world and the other alike. It was beautiful, almost as if they really were a big family sharing in everything they owned, one by one, everyone getting what they needed.

The crowd had grown so big it filled all the space in sight, wrapping around buildings and down alleyways. Olsen thought she would never be done handing out gifts to the people when jostling spread like a wave up one arm of the amorphous, multi-bodied organism, radiating through every other part in turn. When it reached the center, where they were working, Olsen looked to Anna to see what to do. Anna called up a stool out of the printer then stood on it to look over the crowd in the direction the wave had come from. Olsen didn't like the look on Anna's face when she could finally see what was going on. Olsen's heart beat faster and her palms slicked up.

"Anna," she said. "What is it?"

Anna shook her head. "*Trouble*. I'm surprised it took them this long."

Olsen looked over the way Anna was staring but couldn't see anything through the mass of people. The crowd wasn't just jostling anymore, it was pushing toward them, trying to escape some danger that was still out of sight. "What do we do?" Olsen asked.

Anna shook herself out of her daze. "You stay with the printer," she said. "Keep fulfilling requests until you can't anymore then get out of here as fast as you can. You did well, today, kiddo.

We'll see you tomorrow morning to discuss the details of your next assignment."

Olsen shook her head. Her voice wouldn't work for more than a squeak so that was all she did. She wasn't sure she was ready for this anymore. She wasn't sure she was ready for anything. She should have listened to Sonya and left this job to someone else. Now she was—now she was—what? She was—

"You can do it," Anna said, giving Olsen a quick hug then disappearing into the crowd, and Olsen had no choice but to find her voice again. She took a deep breath and said, "Who's next?"

"Me," a man said, stepping forward from far back in the line.

"No, me," another said from closer up. He pushed the first and they started to grapple.

An old woman tugged on Olsen's shirt. "Me, please," she said in a scratchy, frantic voice. "Just one ham, please. It's all I ask."

"Oh, well, okay. You," Olsen said, pulling the woman closer and away from the two men who were still fighting. She pressed the big red eye and started to speak when one of the men in the grapple—who had knocked the other out—yelled, "A pistol!"

"No, not—" Olsen said, but the doors slid open, and the man shoved her aside to grab what came out. When she stood up again, he was pointing the gun at her. She held her trembling hands above her head.

"Stop right there," he said. "This here printer's mine now. You can just git."

Olsen said, "But—"

"No!" the man yelled, shaking the gun. "*No buts.* Go!" He pointed the gun at the crowd, too. "All of you!" They backed away, but people were still pushing from the other direction so there wasn't far to go. He pointed the gun back at Olsen. "I said *git*," he said.

Trembling, her hands up, she had no idea what to do. Anna had told her to work until she couldn't anymore, and how could she work when someone was pointing a gun at her? But she couldn't just leave the printer here with him, either. They needed it. The Family needed it. Anyone who waited their turn and didn't point a gun to steal everything deserved it. Not this thief. Ansel had almost built up the courage to say something when bangs and screams echoed loud through the streets. All heads turned in their direction, the direction the commotion had been coming from all along, to see what it was.

All Olsen could see was the crowd pushing harder towards her and a fog rolling in over their heads.

A fog? That wasn't fog. It was purplish in color and this was the middle of a warm day. She didn't have time to figure out what it was before more bangs and screams echoed from every direction. The crowd started pushing from all sides now, and neither Olsen nor the man with the gun cared about the printer anymore.

Then Olsen saw the tall dark shadows in the fog—or cloud—or whatever it was. They towered over everyone, and every now and then, a bright light would flash in front of them, and there would be more screams and hysteria. She was shocked, in awe. Were they killing people? Was that gas dangerous?

A child bumped into her and fell away at her feet. "Mommy! Mommy!" the kid pleaded, standing up and running into the crowd. Olsen couldn't help, though, she had to take care of herself now.

Once she decided she wanted to move, her legs took her toward the Family Home. It was the closest safe space she knew of so it was the first thing her subconscious thought of. She had to fight and force her way through the mass of people running this way and that, and by the time she made it across the street to sit on the floor inside, with her back to the door, her face was bloodied and bruised and her whole body ached.

She took a few deep breaths, sitting on the ground, wiping the blood from her nose. What in the Hell was that? Who were those giants out there shooting people? And most importantly, what had Olsen gotten herself into by getting involved with the people who had started it all?

She wanted to cry. She wanted to stand up and run home, or to Sonya's, or anywhere away from there, anywhere where she could forget about all of this. This wasn't being a chef. This was madness.

Rosa came in out of the basement door and looked surprised to see Olsen sitting on the ground. "You should have gone home, child," she said, shaking her head. "Here the danger's coming to you."

"I—uh—" Everything that had just happened ran through Olsen's head again. "It got crazy out there," she said. "I didn't know where else to go. I couldn't get home."

"You are home, child," Rosa said, crossing the room and helping Olsen to her feet. "You're a part of the Family so this is your home."

"Oh, yeah..." Olsen blushed. She still wasn't sure she wanted to be a member of *the Family*. "I meant—"

"Oh, I know what you meant, dear," Rosa said, holding Olsen's hand and leading her to the kitchen to sit on a bar stool at the counter. "And I meant what I said. You should feel safe here. Even when *they* come to invade our private property." She nodded toward the door. Olsen was surprised she couldn't hear more of what must still have been going on outside. "Would you like some pancakes, child?" Rosa asked. "Only thing I can cook, I'm afraid. And Anna's a little busy at the moment."

"I—uh—" This was all getting to be too much to handle. Olsen couldn't keep up with the pace that everything was coming at her. "Invade our privacy?" she said. She didn't even know what she was asking.

"Pancakes, child?" Rosa said, already heating a griddle and mixing the batter. "Do you want some?"

"I—uh—" Olsen shrugged. "*Sure.*"

"Good," Rosa said. "Because I'm making you some anyway. It'll be comforting. Pancakes are comfort food. That's why I know how to make them."

"Um, okay." Olsen shook her head.

"That's one thing these protectors need to learn," Rosa said, cooking. "How to be comforting. You know how they used to say that you can catch more flies with honey than vinegar? Well that's not true at all. Flies don't care about honey. They don't like the sugar or something. I don't know the science behind it. Ask Anna. But you don't catch flies by giving them honey. That's the point I'm trying to make. You catch flies by giving them what they want, dear. And do you know what it is that flies want?"

Olsen shook her head.

"*Shit,*" Rosa said with a chuckle, pouring some batter onto the griddle. The smell of it cooking already started to comfort Olsen. She was forgetting the chaos that was still going on outside. "Flies want shit," Rosa went on. "So that's how you catch them. The protectors here think they can catch flies by swatting at them, and that's got to be about the dumbest method I've ever heard of."

"What protectors?" Olsen asked, squinting and rubbing her face.

"The cops. Police. *Pigs*. I don't know what you Fivers call them. In Six we mostly call them assholes, and that only behind their backs. They're the big, tall, well-armed, white guys out there, shooting everyone up and causing chaos."

"Those are protectors?" Olsen sighed.

"You were out there, child." Rosa flipped a pancake. "You saw what they're capable of. Did they use the gas?"

"There was some fog or something," she said.

"You didn't get caught in it, then?" Rosa smiled. "Good for you. It's not fun. That's pepper gas. It sticks to every pore you have and burns like fire when it contacts water. So if you ever get caught in it, *do not* wash with water. You got that? Use milk. It neutralizes the proteins or something. I don't know. Again, ask Anna."

"No," Olsen said. "It couldn't have been protectors. They were shooting people in the crowd. Protectors wouldn't do that."

"They *did* do it, child." Rosa flipped a pancake onto a plate and set it in front of Olsen. "They're still doing it outside as we speak. Do you want to take another look and see?"

She did not want to do that. "But why?" Olsen groaned.

"Power, child," Rosa said, pouring another pancake onto the griddle. "Control. Resources. Labor. You name it. All the things greedy people want at their own expense. They're trying to control us, to make us obsolete, and this is their way of showing us what will happen if we try to fight back against them. And we've only just begun, little darling."

Olsen dribbled some syrup on her pancake and took a big bite. It was rather comforting. "But they're only turning us against them," she said.

"Yes, child." Rosa smiled. "That's the swatting approach I was talking about earlier. It's worked for them for a long time because they've been able to keep us so afraid we won't act, but will you let them continue to scare you into inaction after you've seen what they did today?" she asked, flipping a pancake on the griddle.

Olsen didn't know what to say. She didn't know how to be anything but afraid of the protectors now. They were huge, and they had guns and burning death gas and futuristic armor. What was she supposed to do to stop that?

Rosa sat at the counter next to her and started in on her pancake without syrup. "I know it's scary," she said. "I know they're scary, too. No doubt about it. So big and white and bully. It's okay to be afraid of them, but it's not okay to let that stop you from doing what you want to do. You got that?"

Olsen nodded, stuffing her face. She didn't want to say anything stupid.

"You'll be fine, child," Rosa said, taking a bite. "I'll take care of you. Don't worry."

From the other room came the sound of a door caving in and Olsen jumped, bumping her plate and almost spilling it. Rosa patted her arm and said, "You'll be fine, child. Just keep on eating and let me do all the talking. You got it?"

Olsen nodded. She probably wouldn't be able to eat ever again, but she definitely wouldn't say a word.

Into the kitchen marched a line of protectors with their guns pointed at Olsen and Rosa. The one in front took off her helmet, sneered at them, and said, "You've gone and done it now."

Rosa went on eating her pancake without answer. Olsen was trembling and about to cry.

"Fork down, stand up, and show us where the rest are," the protector said.

Rosa smiled. She finished the last bite of her pancake, set the fork down, and deliberately wiped her face. The protectors behind the officer that was talking looked like they tensed up. Olsen tensed up, too.

"Now, citizen!" the protector demanded.

"There are no others," Rosa said. "We in the Human Family share everything we own with our brothers and sisters. If we had more printers, they would have been out there on the streets, providing for those in need."

"Stand up, citizens!" The protector pointed her gun at Rosa.

Olsen jumped up and put her hands in the air. She hadn't realized that they were talking to her, too. Rosa slowly stood and carried their plates through a line of protectors to rinse them and place them in the sink.

"Now," Rosa said, clapping her hands together. "Would you like to see the basement so we can get this over with? I have plenty to do, you know. You saw how many of my Family members were in need outside, such a larger number ever since you and yours came through."

The protector sneered at Rosa. She looked like she wanted to shoot the old lady right there. Olsen was surprised when the protector didn't, instead pointing her gun toward the direction of the basement door. "Go on, then," she said. "*Both of you.*"

Olsen followed close behind Rosa, with her hands up and the protector's gun poking her in the back. They went through the gauntlet of protectors, opened the door, and climbed down into a basement that Olsen didn't recognize. Instead of the stacks of supplies, and four other printers, that were there before, the room was smaller and lined with bunk beds.

"You see," Rosa said when the three of them were down there alone. "Nothing. Our sleeping quarters. No illegal printers." She smiled.

"Shut the fuck up, Rosa," the protector said. "And tell me what you think you're doing. I don't have time for all this shit that you're stirring with all the other feces I already have flung on my plate. Including your previous problem—*which still exists.*"

"Well, that was at the bequest of your—"

"*And you failed*," the woman cut her off. "Because you failed, I have to clean up the mess. Now's not the time for your *family* bullshit, alright. We have bigger fish to fry in the other worlds."

Olsen had never seen anger on Rosa's face before, but she was pretty sure this was it. It came off looking more like steel reserve and disappointment, though. "Now is exactly the time for the Family, child," Rosa said. "It was your protector who failed, not me. I did my job. And as a matter of fact, I'll be taking care of yours, too. Tomorrow, we'll fry your fish for you. Don't you worry."

The protector looked unconvinced. "You don't even know what fish I'm talking about," she said.

Rosa smiled. "I guess we'll have to wait until tomorrow to see then, won't we?"

The protector sighed, shaking her head. "Don't do anything stupid," she said. "I can't protect you out there."

"And here I only need protecting from you," Rosa said.

"Yeah," the protector said. "And no one can offer you that. I'll see you again in a few days," she added, climbing the stairs. "Don't put so many of your *children* in between me and you the next time I come looking, and you won't have such a big mess to clean up after I'm gone."

When the door closed, Olsen sighed a big huff of air and finally dropped her hands, flopping onto one of the beds. She was dizzy and lightheaded, like she had been forgetting to breath. She couldn't believe she had lived through that and she hoped never to meet a protector face-to-face again.

Rosa sat on the bed next to her and patted her back. "It's okay, child," she said. "You're safe here at Home."

Olsen didn't know what to say. She just started crying. She couldn't control herself any longer. Rosa pulled her into a hug and patted her back some more.

"You see, child," Rosa said. "This is how they treat us. We're nothing to them. All those casualties upstairs were nothing more than lost property to them—cheap, expendable property at that. We're worth even less than the robots these days."

Olsen was still crying. She pushed away from Rosa's embrace, sniffling. "B—but you said. Y—you said you'd fry—you'd fry—"

Rosa pulled her in again. "The enemy of my enemy is my friend," she said. "When they're not being my enemy. We share a mutual problem, and I think I—no—*we* can handle it more efficiently than our brute force counterparts."

"We?" Olsen said. Sniffling and wiping her nose with her shirt.

"More specifically you, child," Rosa said. "You can end these troubles for us once and for all. What do you think?"

"I mean, uh…" Olsen didn't know what she was capable of that no one else in the Family could do instead. "What would I have to do?"

"Nothing, really," Rosa said. "You'd have to deliver some food to those in need. Much like you were doing out there today."

Olsen's eyes grew wide thinking about another encounter with the protectors.

Rosa chuckled. "Oh, child," she said. "Except without the protectors this time. Don't you worry. They wouldn't react the same way in the lower worlds. The property's more specialized and less expendable down there. They wouldn't risk damaging it."

"Lower worlds?"

"Yes, child," Rosa said. "You have been reading the

pamphlets, haven't you?"

"I—uh—"

"There are seven of them in total," Rosa said. "Six now with our worlds combined. And you'll be going to one of the others to do what has to be done."

Olsen's eyes grew wide again but this time not in fear. She was excited by the idea of seeing the look on Sonya's face when Sonya learned that Olsen had been to another world, that she knew how many other worlds there actually were. She smiled from ear to ear and nodded, unable to come up with words.

"Good, child," Rosa said. "You won't regret that decision one bit. Here's what I need from you."

ಜ   ✳   ∅

XXXVI. Tillie

They waited a little while longer, letting the clock get past five to see if anyone would brave going out on campus before they did, but when they went out themselves at five-oh-one the campus was still empty. They could see eyes peering through dorm windows and heads poking out of doors, but there were no actual bodies on the campus with them. Tillie tried to hold her head high, to show the onlookers that she wasn't afraid as she walked along, while Emma kept her eyes straight ahead, dead set on getting to the parade grounds. Rod kept staring back and forth at the people in the windows and doors, a big smile on his face, waving at them and trying to get them to join. And Nikola followed behind, meek and hunched over, pushing her glasses up every few steps as if she were offended by everyone watching her walk.

When they got to the parade grounds, they were empty, too. Emma led the group straight to the flagpole in the center of the field and stood up on its cement base, holding the pole for support, trying to get a better view of the campus. She shielded her eyes with her hands and scanned the horizon.

"Why won't they follow us?" Rod asked. "They were all looking."

"They're afraid," Tillie said. She knew it from the beginning. She would be, too, if she didn't have Emma to inspire her on.

"They'll come," Emma said, still scanning the campus from her vantage point on the flagpole. "If only to see who else does."

"I don't know," Nikola said with a shrug.

"I do," Emma said. "Look. Over there." She pointed in the opposite direction from which they had come. There were people coming alright, a band of ten or so of them, and they didn't need to see anyone else doing it before they were brave enough to come. "It's the Americorp. kids," Emma said.

They were the news nerds who Tillie had met at the first party on New Year's Eve. One came up and hugged her, saying, "We saw the video. I can't believe it wasn't on the news. Sorry we weren't here to support you. We're here now, though. *Solidarity*."

Tillie shook her head, blushing. She didn't know what to say. She wasn't sure that this *Americorp. kid* was actually talking to the right person.

"We're glad to have you," Emma said, hugging each of them in turn. "Where's Jason? He was here yesterday."

They all kind of shook their heads and frowned, looking at the ground or kicking dirt. "They still have him," the one who had hugged Tillie said. "He had no insurance, money, or parents to bail him out. There's no telling how much time he'll get. That's when we knew we had to help y'all fight. *For him*."

"That's right," Emma said. "I completely agree. And I—"

"I think some other people agree, too," Rod said, pointing toward a new group of students on their way to join the assembly.

People were streaming out now, each made braver and more curious by every new person that joined. Soon they were coming from every direction, hundreds of them, and when the parade grounds was packed and spilling out between the stone-faced buildings, it felt like the entire student body was there with them.

Emma gathered the Americorp. kids around her and said, "Go up to as many people as you can and tell them that we'll get started soon, they should discuss what happened yesterday among themselves, and to pass it on. Alright?"

Everyone nodded and fanned out into the crowd. The message spread like waves through the masses. Tillie took the chance to stand up on the flagpole and look out at the mass of them. There was no end to the people, whichever direction she looked in. The crowd wrapped around all the buildings in sight, and some of the attendants went so far as to climb trees so they could watch everything from above. Tillie didn't realize there were this many people who lived on campus. How did they all fit? She was lost thinking about it when Emma pulled her down off of the flagpole.

"I told you they'd come out," Emma said with a smile.

"Since when did this many people go to this school?" Tillie asked.

"My address book extends to the local community," Emma said. "They care about what happens to us, too."

"Well, you were right," Tillie said. "What do we do now?"

"I'm going to get the assembly started. I need you to stay up on the flagpole and look for any signs of protectors. They'll be out here for sure. There's no telling how long we'll have."

"How will I know when they're coming?" Tillie asked.

"Don't worry, *you'll know*. They won't be subtle about it."

Tillie shrugged. "Okay, I guess," she said, and she climbed back up onto the flagpole.

"Wait," Emma said. "Bend down here for a second."

Tillie bent down close to her, and Emma pinned the American flag camera onto Tillie's shirt.

"You'll have a better view," Emma said with a shrug and a smile.

"I'll give it back to you when we're done," Tillie said.

Emma smiled and nodded then turned to the crowd. "My friends," she called as loud as she could. Not many could likely hear her, though, with all the chatter going around. "Please repeat everything I say." No one answered.

"My friends!" she yelled louder. "Please repeat everything I say!"

A few members of the crowd who were close to her responded, but their chorus was broken and incoherent. The whole crowd started to quiet down and listen now, though. Something was finally happening.

"Good try," Emma yelled. "In unison now."

She paused and indicated for them to repeat that, too. And no one did at first, but then a few caught on and yelled it back incoherently at her.

"My friends," she called one more time, stopping and indicating for them to repeat that.

"My friends," a chorus started to emerge from the crowd.

"Please repeat everything I say," Emma added with a smile.

"Please repeat everything I say," the crowd repeated, and it was so catchy that even Tillie found herself yelling it from the flagpole.

"This is the people's mic," Emma went on.

"This is the people's mic."

"We will use it so everyone can hear."

"We will use it so everyone can hear."

"Can you hear me?"

"Can you hear me?"

"*Good.*"

"Good."

"We are here today."

"We are here today."

"To reclaim these grounds."

"To reclaim these grounds."

"We've paid our dues."

"We've paid our dues."

"This is *our* school."

"This is *our* school."

"And we will not be scared away."

"And we will not be scared away."

"Now do you stand with me?"

"Now do you stand with me?"

"No answer that one."

"No answer that one," some of them yelled while others just whooped and whistled and cheered.

"Mic check!" Emma yelled after the cheering had died down.

"Mic check," a few yelled back.

"Mic check," she called again, and soon the chorus was back in sync.

"Mic check," they said.

"That is how."

"That is how."

"We will acknowledge."

"We will acknowledge."

"Who's at the mic."

"Who's at the—"

The rest of the snippet was only finished by part of the crowd. There was yelling and screaming coming from all directions. Tillie remembered she was supposed to be the lookout and scanned the crowd all around her. Everyone was pushing inward. What little clearance there had been around the flagpole closed and Tillie stood nearly on top of the crowd. She had lost everyone she had come with in the chaotic masses, but she could still hear Emma yelling, "Mic check! Mic check!" to no response.

They were surrounded by the same pepper gas cloud that they had been sprayed with only yesterday. Tillie knew burning pores were in her future. Gunshots rang out over the crowd. Not beanbag air shots, but bullets, accompanied by more and louder screaming and further stampeding of bodies which had no way to go but toward the center of the parade grounds, where Tillie was standing alone, sliding off the flagpole where the human currents were roughest.

She almost fell off when Emma jumped up to join her, grabbing Tillie and holding her tight to the pole.

"What the fuck is going on?" Tillie asked.

"A more drastic response than last time," Emma said.

"Well, no shit," Tillie said. "But what—"

"*Shhh.*" Emma held a finger to her mouth. "There's no time," she said. She pressed the tiny flag pin to Tillie's chest and looked straight into it. "This is how they respond to a threat to their power," she said. "They fear us for good reason, and they will silence us at all costs. We will win as long as we never sto—"

Emma's head jerked back, exploded. Her hand let go of the flagpole. Her body slouched into the stampeding crowd. It happened in slow motion. Tillie reached down to grab her, almost losing her own grasp on the flagpole, and missed Emma's hand by an inch. She jumped down and tried to push the crowd away but it didn't matter. If Emma had been trampled already, it wasn't clear. The damage to her head was such that Tillie couldn't see anything else. Nothing was left on Emma's shoulders but raw ravaged neck.

Tillie turned and leaned on the flagpole, vomiting burning acidic bile into oncoming footsteps. No one noticed. They just trampled and splashed through what was once the contents of her stomach, as they no doubt aslo did through what was once Emma. Tillie took a few deep breaths and fought the urge to lie there on the ground, to give up, letting happen whatever happened, letting the stampeding masses trample over her and turn her into the same nothingness that Emma had become. She fought the urge to look back at Emma's obliterated face, at the destruction the protectors had rained down on them for doing nothing that was not within their rights. She didn't want to throw up anymore, and there was nothing she could do for Emma now.

Her first instinct was to get to an elevator and go to her dad's house, but she knew there was no chance of getting an elevator in this nonsense. She jumped back up onto the flagpole to see what was going on. The cloud of pepper gas was getting closer, it surrounded her. No matter which way she went, she'd have to go through it, but the sooner she went the thinner the cloud would be. If she couldn't get to her dad's, her only choice was her dorm so she jumped down off the flagpole and fought her way through the crowd in that direction.

She pushed her way through bodies going this way and that and made slow progress. When she hit the wall of gas, she had to stop to cough and wipe her eyes, but that only made things worse. She pushed and fought blindly against the mass of bodies surrounding her, holding her eyelids closed tight against the fire gas. She had no idea anymore if she was even going in the right direction, but she wasn't going to stop fighting. Those were Emma's last words, and Tillie would live up to them or die trying. She would never sto—

The thought was driven out of her mind with the familiar pressure of a beanbag in her chest. Apparently they were still using some. She was bent over, trying to catch her breath, when another hit her in the head and knocked her unconscious.

This time she knew where she was when she woke up. She recognized the cold bed and the harsh white walls. Pulling herself up to lean on the wall, groaning, she wondered if it was the same cell she was held in before. She was in a lot more pain this time, though, longing for the little gray shot that would make her all better.

The heavy door whined open. A protector in full gear came in. "Come with me, citizen," it demanded in its glowing modulated voice.

"I can't move," Tillie groaned. "Give me my shot."

"No shot," the protector said, walking over, lifting Tillie up like a baby, and marching out of the room, down the hall, and into another door. Tillie let out a loud groan when the protector plopped her down on the ground in front of a tall table and stomped out without another word.

Somehow this room was even brighter than the room they had taken her from. She had to close her eyes against the light, and even that wasn't enough. She bumped her head hard on the table, fumbling blindly for anything to block out the white heat, and groaned at the pain all throughout her body. Her eyes felt like they were going to pulse out of her head. She managed to find a stool and pull herself up onto it to flop her head down on the table in front of her, using her arms to finally block out the light. The cool black relief didn't last long, though, because the door opened, another protector walked in, and they yelled, "Look at me, citizen!"

Tillie didn't budge. She didn't want to be blinded again. The protector didn't care, though, grabbing a clump of Tillie's hair to pull. "You're in it deep, now," the protector hissed. "Not even daddy's platinum plan can save you. You do understand that, don't you?"

"I didn't do anything!" Tillie yelled, and the protector let go of her hair. Tillie's head slammed on the table from the momentum, and she screamed as her pain only grew.

"Didn't do anything?" the protector said. "*Ha!* Lights."

The lights dimmed. Tillie could feel it, even with her arms blocking out the light. She blinked her eyes in her arm cave, relishing the dark comfort for one more second, before slowly raising her head. Across the table, in the white, white room, was a protector with no helmet on and a big black mirror behind her.

"So you weren't at the center of the riot on LSU's parade grounds?" the protector asked.

"That wasn't a riot," Tillie said.

"No?" The protector frowned. "Then it didn't end in violence and bloodshed? That must have been my imagination."

Tillie pictured Emma and her stomach grumbled. She choked back vomit and fought the urge to jump over the table and attack this *pro*. That would probably work out poorly for everyone, especially Tillie.

The protector grinned. "No, girl," she said. "It wasn't your imagination, either. It *did* end in bloodshed."

"Not until you got there." Tillie sneered.

"Well, we wouldn't have been there if you weren't," the protector said. "Would we? What did you expect after the previous day's outburst? We'd let you bring out more of your little thug friends to disrespect the sacred rights of private property?"

"We own those parade grounds as much as anyone," Tillie protested. "We pay to go to that school."

"Yes," the protector said. "You pay to *attend* the school. You pay to learn and sleep and eat, *not* to own the school grounds. You're merely a tenant. The school belongs to Mr. Smörgåsbord, and you've trespassed on his property too many times for us to let it slide."

"It's not his!" Tillie yelled, then she groaned and hunched over the table in pain. She had forgotten her injuries in her anxiousness to deal with this protector, and now the pain of them all rushed back at the same time.

The protector laughed. "No, dear," she said. "As long as he can afford the guns to protect it, it belongs to Mr. Smörgåsbord."

"*As long as he can afford you,*" Tillie groaned.

"*Well.*" The protector laughed some more. "Not just me, girl," she said. "The whole force. You think you can afford that?"

Tillie shook her head, sobbing silently at the pain.

"No. That's right. And that's why the school belongs to him and not you. That's why you're here with me now. Do you understand yet? No more demonstrations on our property or our responses will continue to get more drastic. *Do you understand?*"

"Why are you telling me all this?" Tillie asked. She wasn't any leader. She didn't plan any of this. She just happened to take part in it. Why was she getting all the blame?

"Because you wear the pin now." The protector nodded at it.

Tillie looked down. The little American flag camera was still pinned to her shirt. She wanted to cry at the sight of it, at the memory of what they had done to Emma, but she fought that back. She looked up at the protector and said, "But—"

"Of course we know," the protector said. "Why do you think she still had it yesterday?" She chuckled. "We're not as ignorant as y'all hope we are."

"Then why didn't you take it?" Tillie asked, fumbling to get the thing off but failing.

"Because we want you to have it," the protector said. "We can track it, download what it uploads, we see everything it sees, child. Why would we want to take that away from you when we would be taking it away from us?"

Tillie shook her head. She didn't even notice her pain anymore. It was covered by a fierce anger and hatred, directed at the protectors in general, sure, but at this protector especially. "Then why give away your capabilities?" she asked.

"Because you wear the pin," the protector repeated. "Because it doesn't matter if you know, you need that technology in order to be effective. Because you're powerless against us, and I want you to know that fact. More than that, I want you to feel it deep inside of your bones and all throughout your nervous system. I know you do, child. I know you're still hurting from the beating we gave you. That, *dear*, is why we did this: To show you that we're the big bad wolf and the boogie monster and all your childhood nightmares all rolled into one, and you're just a little girl with nothing to do about it."

"I—" Tillie protested.

"*No.* Listen, girl. You have it good. I know who your father is. I know what kind of life you're living. What I don't know is why you would throw that life away for something like this. I mean, what are you even doing it for?"

Tillie shook her head, trying not to cry. She wasn't sure how to answer that question anymore. She came into all this because she wanted to fight to give robots a voice, but when she learned it was really humans on the assembly lines, she went to fighting to free them instead. But now what was she doing it for? It was more than that now, more than giving robots a voice or freeing humans from sweatshop labor. When she watched the only friend she had left in the world die right in front of her eyes, the protectors had made it personal. "*Fuck you,*" she said.

The protector looked taken aback. "What was that?"

"Fuck. You," Tillie repeated, sitting up taller.

"You do understand the situation you find yourself in, don't you?" The protector chuckled.

"I do," Tillie said. "I understand you're questioning me without first giving me a medical examination. I know you haven't even scanned my insurance level yet. I know that *you* are required by law to follow certain regulations, too. And I know that my lawyer, Mr…" She couldn't remember Rod's last name. "*Roderick*, will have a field day taking the protectors—and you especially—for everything you're worth in court."

The protector grinned. "Is that so?"

"Well, there are a few ways to find out," Tillie said. She held her breath and tried to calm her beating heart while waiting for a response. She had no idea what those few ways might be.

"Have it your way," the protector said, standing from her chair. "But don't say I didn't warn you."

Tillie fought the urge to call the protector back and apologize as she walked out. She slouched down onto the table and covered her head again when the door closed.

What the fuck did she just do? How could she talk to a protector like that? But the protector did leave. Maybe Tillie had said the right thing. She hoped so. She didn't know how much worse it could get.

The door opened, and she looked up, groaning, to find the face of the protector who had given her the shot before. She sighed in relief.

"*You again*," he said with a smile, crossing around the table to her and fumbling through his pockets.

"And you," Tillie groaned. "I need my shot."

"I—*uh*—well..." The protector avoided her gaze, fumbling through his pockets still. "I can't right now," he said.

"*But—*" Tillie protested.

"I'm sorry," he said, holding his tablet out to her. "I'm on orders, but I'll do what I can for you."

Another let down in a long line of them. The worlds kept getting worse and worse. Tillie pressed her thumb to his little tablet, and when he read the screen, he frowned.

"What is it?" she asked.

"Well, you're not gonna like this," he said.

"I already don't," she said, groaning and rubbing her head. "I need my shot."

"Yes, you do. But..."

"But what?"

"This is a second felony in two days," the protector said, "both on campus. The school contract has a clause which overrides your insurance policy. I'm sorry. I..." He looked at his feet, avoiding eye contact with her.

"What? So what is that supposed to mean?" she begged, holding back tears.

"Well, it means—"

The door swung open and in came two protectors, pointing their guns at her. "Hands on your head, citizen," one of them said.

Tillie tried to stand, but the stool fell out from underneath her, and she fell to the floor. "*No*," she said, crab crawling backwards on the cold floor.

"This is your final warning, citizen."

"No!" She backed into the wall behind her and there was nowhere left to go. One protector grabbed her, and when Tillie fought away, trying to escape, the other hit her in the back of the head with a gun, knocking her out cold.

৯   ✖   ৩

Tillie woke to shadows towering over her. She panicked, jumping up and flailing her arms, groaning from the pain, but the shadows gently restrained her, and when she came to, Tillie realized that it was Nikola and Rod who were looking down on her, and a whole crowd of others who she didn't recognize. The room looked like it used to be white but now it was dirtied gray. She groaned some more and tried to sit up but couldn't do it without their help. How had she lived through so much pain?

"Where am I?" she asked when she had gathered herself enough to speak.

"This is general holding," Nikola said.

"And my dad's gonna have a field day with it." Rod chuckled. "Disregard Rod Swadson's Platinum Plan and see if you're not bankrupt in the morning."

"How long have we been here?" Tillie asked. She noticed the crowd was still silently staring at her. There must have been twenty or more of them. It was hard to count from her vantage point on the small room's floor, especially with a pounding headache.

"We were already here for hours before they tossed you in with us," Rod said. "Haven't seen a protector since—unless they were tossing someone else in. And they'll hear about that from my dad, too. You can be sure of that." He huffed.

"They killed Emma," Tillie said. The whole crowd gasped. She had forgotten they were listening, but now that she remembered, she didn't care. They should all hear this, too. They were probably all out there when it happened. The same thing could have happened to any one of them. "I saw it," she said. "Her head exploded in front of me. Look…" She wiped her shirt, but it wasn't sticky anymore, just stained red. "That's her blood on my shirt."

"That's her blood on their hands," Nikola said.

Tillie forced herself to stand, against all the advice of every nerve in her body. "You people don't understand yet," she groaned. "They killed her because she wanted to tell you something they didn't want you to know. *That's it.*"

"That humans work on the assembly lines," Nikola said, urging Tillie on.

"*No,*" Tillie protested. She wasn't trying to encourage them. She was trying to illustrate the reality of their situation. "That's not important," she said. "What she said doesn't matter. What they did because of it does."

"Because they're afraid!" Nikola said.

The crowd cheered. Nikola was making everything Tillie said have the opposite meaning from what she intended. "Because they want to make us afraid," Tillie said. "And we should be. I was interrogated by one of them before they dumped me in here. They thought I took over for Emma because I wear her pin. They ensured me that their responses would get more drastic if we continued doing what we're doing, and I believe them. *I'm scared.*"

The huddled mass of prisoners didn't know how to respond to that. They looked back and forth at each other, hoping one or another of them could tell the rest what to do. Tillie thought she might have actually gotten through to them until Nikola said, "And we must use that fear. We must not run away from it. We must not let them win by default. Together we can prevail!"

The cheering grew so loud it had to be heard by the guards. "No," Tillie pleaded. "That's not what I mean. I meant—"

The door of the cell swung open and a column of white-clad protectors made their way in, packing the room tighter than it already was. "Quiet citizens," one of the protectors ordered. "Break this meeting up or every one of you will be placed in solitary confinement."

The crowd stomped and protested, Nikola and Rod especially. Tillie turned her back to the protectors and waved her arms, shaking her head. "No," she said. "*No no no.* I told you. Be afraid."

"And use it!" they replied.

"For Emma!" Nikola said.

"For Emma!" they repeated.

"And Tillie!" Nikola said.

"And Tillie!" they repeated.

"No!" Tillie said, and the protectors crashed down on them. Tillie couldn't fight. She couldn't run. She couldn't do anything. She tried to give up, crumpling to the floor where she would probably be stomped to death, but as she let go of herself a bag went over her head and she was lifted by strong arms to be thrown over a broad shoulder.

She didn't resist or struggle as she was carried away from the sound of the riot in the cell. She didn't care anymore. She had nothing left in her, no energy at all. She would certainly never break another law again as long as it meant that she never had to interact with another protector in her life.

Then she thought she heard someone whispering her name. "Tillie Manager," it said. "*Psst.* It's me—uh—" It was the protector who was carrying her. "Well, the guy who processed you last time. And gave you your shot. Get ready for another one."

She felt the sting of a needle in the back of her thigh and sighed at the instant relief.

"That should make this a little easier," he said. "I'm sorry." He hefted her off his shoulder and laid her down in between two tight walls, pushing her forward into even deeper darkness. She tried to move but there was no room, only inches before she hit a hard surface in every direction. She banged on the walls of the tiny space around her, breathing heavily. The hood was still on her head so she kept inhaling cloth. She felt like she was going to suffocate, like they were going to scare her to death.

She tried to calm herself. She stopped struggling and laid as still as she could. At least she had gotten a shot so she wasn't hurting anymore. She slowed her breathing and managed to keep the cloth out of her mouth. Maybe Nikola was right. Maybe they should use their fear. They should become stronger by overcoming it. But how was she supposed to do that now? Stuck in here, in a drawer, with a limited air supply.

Her heart beat faster. She lost control of her breath again until she remembered where she was. They wouldn't let a prisoner die in their custody. Would they? They di—

The drawer slid open. She tried to move, to stand, but she was grabbed by two pairs of hands and lifted out of her resting place.

"Come with us," a voice she didn't recognize said. "We'll get you out of here."

"But—" she protested, and someone flung her over their shoulder, with the hood still on her head, to run on their way to she had no idea where.

♋   ✄   ♋

XXXVII. Huey

Thus were the detriments of being an owner. He had given the orders. He had set the gears into motion. There was no way to turn them back now, no matter what anyone at the table said. But still, because he was number one, because he was now Lord, he had to see the feast through to the bitter end. Well, not really. He did have the power to call it to an end whenever he wanted to, but the unwritten code of the Fortune Five—the same code that said whoever was richest sat at the head of the table and called all the shots—said he had to stay at least until the disturbance was dealt with. Whatever that meant to the Fortune Five in general.

"So," Angrom said, gay now that he was at the Lord's right hand instead of Loch who was always Walker's pet. "The orders are set, all we have to do is wait, why not have a round of drinks? *On me*." He smiled wide.

"Oh, yes," Smörgåsbord said. "Fine idea."

"*Ugh*." Loch relented, never one to turn down a free drink. "*Fine*."

"Sure thing," Huey said. "What do you say, Walker, my boy?" He grinned.

"Do I want you to buy a drink from me for me to drink?" Walker asked sarcastically. "Of course I do. Do you take me for a fool?"

"I think I've taken you for a fool once already today, Walkie Talkie." Huey smiled. "Or have you forgotten?"

Angrom laughed. "Make that twice," he said. "And two rounds because of it. Hillary, you got that? Two rounds for everyone. Their regulars."

His secretary curtsied and made her way down the hover platform to get the drinks.

"I'm not a fool," Walker said, his voice breaking. "I was simply unprepared." He coughed.

"What's the difference?" Huey shrugged.

Walker huffed. "*Yes*," he said. "Well we'll see who the fool is yet."

"Do you have more jokes planned for us?" Huey laughed, looking over at Angrom who joined in. Huey took a quick glance behind himself and Rosalind shot him a look.

"It's only a joke if you laugh," Walker said.

Angrom laughed. "*You two*," he said, patting his stomach. "*Enough*. Come on. Let's not let this tiny shift in power compromise the natural cohesiveness of the Fortune Five. We here at this table are indisputably the richest five men in all the worlds. *All of them*. No matter which of us happens to be at the top, we're all beyond the imagination of anyone else in those worlds, right? So why bicker now?"

Loch scoffed. "Oh how the turn tables," he said. "Only days ago you were arguing and roadblocking at every possible turn, and now you want complete group cohesion because your car happens to be in the lead? Well you can fu—"

"Woah now, Mr. Loch," Angrom said. His secretary had come up and started setting two drinks in front of everyone, their respective favorites, straight bourbon whiskey for Huey. "You're drink is here," Angrom went on. "Taste it and settle down. We all have to work together, either way. At least I'm trying to be civil."

Loch downed one of his drinks in one go. "Civil?" he said. "*Ha*! Try passive aggressive. I can read subtext as well as anyone, Mr. Angrom. I'm not an Outlander after all."

"Oh, I know," Angrom said. "That's exactly my point. I have a new proposal if you're willing—"

"*Wait*," Huey stopped them. Rosalind had tapped him on the shoulder. She whispered in his ear. "It's happening," Huey said. "Walker, do we have video capabilities at this location?"

Walker looked around as if to say, "This is a restaurant. Does it look like we do?" but his mouth said, "Um, I don't think so. I can—"

"Rosalind," Huey said, not looking at her. "Can we get something up here to show video of what's going on?"

"*Yes, sir, Lord Douglas, sir*," Rosalind said in a thick accent that she didn't normally use. "I'll get on it right away, *suh*." She disappeared down the floating platform.

"Now," Huey said. "We'll see how to target a plant at the root once and for all. Are you ready gentleman?"

Walker scoffed. Loch ordered more drinks from his secretary, he seemed intent on getting seriously sloshed before the video gear even arrived. Smörgåsbord coughed. "Ahem, Lord," he said. "Not to question your authority—which we've already established." He darted a dirty look toward Walker. "But how is it that you're certain this uh—Whistleblower is it?—how do you know that *she* precisely constitutes the roots of this—um—*riot*?" He fixed his bowtie, pleased that he had worded the question properly.

"It's quite simple, really," Huey said. "And I'm surprised Mr. Walker's protectors haven't come to this conclusion themselves. In fact, we've had our eyes on Whistleblower since before the terrorist attacks. It was only since yesterday that it became obvious enough for Walrus Investigative Inc. to see it was her, though. Or do your greenshoes still not know, Wally Boy?"

Huey could see Walkers breath deepen from the exaggerated movement in his fat rolls. "We tracked the source of the video to her, yes," he said. "She incited the first riot, we already know. She was targeted then, and she is targeted as we speak. Perhaps my men have dealt the lethal blow already as we speak." He smiled but Huey could see the sweat on his brow, between his monocle and top hat.

"I'll have you call them off, then, Wally," Huey said. "This is my show now."

"Call them off!?" Loch spit out his drink. "Nip it in the bud the old fashioned way. That's what you said, isn't it, Lord?"

"He's right, Lord Douglas," Smörgåsbord said. "Isn't that what we agreed to?"

"Yes," Huey said, cool and collected. "*The old fashioned way*. Not instantly in front of a crowd. Slowly. Painfully. Tediously. *Alone*. If all these hooligans risk is a quick release from their tortured life, then what's to stop the next Whistleblower from taking her place? We aren't chopping off the head of a snake if we do this, boys. We're chopping off the arm of a starfish, splitting an earthworm in two. Both sides will grow into a new whole, and we'll have two problems to deal with where, before, we had only one."

"*Ahh*," Smörgåsbord said, thoughtfully. "The *old* fashioned way. I understand. If you say so, Lord Douglas."

"I do," Huey said.

"Well," Walker said, finishing his own drink. "I'm afraid it might be too late, *Lord*, but I'll have my secretary send along the order. Haley, did you hear that?"

"Yes, sir," she curtsied behind him.

"There you are, Lord Douglas." Walker grinned.

"Good," Huey said. "Now—"

Rosalind interrupted him by plopping a big heavy disk on the center of the table. She pressed a button on it and backed away. A holographic image of protectors, converging on a sea of students, appeared above the disk. There was gas everywhere and chaos all through the crowd. The image wasn't three dimensional, but from any vantage point a person sat at, it looked like the screen was pointed in their direction.

"So this is the efficient way," Walker said with a huff.

"No, Mr. Walker," Huey said. "The efficient way would have been to follow my advice from the beginning. This is what your ineptitude has brought the situation down to. This is what the worlds look like when they're going to pieces. But I'll put them back together for you, Walker my boy, just like I promised to do." He winked.

"We'll see about that," Loch said under his breath, only loud enough for his dear friend Walker to hear—or so he thought.

"What was that?" Huey asked.

"*If you say so, Lord Douglas.*" Loch raised his glass.

"I do," Huey said. "And you'll see—"

"Lord Douglas," Rosalind said, tapping his shoulder. "Whistleblower has been taken out."

"Taken out?" Huey turned to look confused into Rosalind's eyes.

"Yes, sir," she said. "A sniper, sir. They say—"

He turned back and slammed his fist on the table, causing the video on the disc to jump. "*Mr. Walker.* What did I tell you?" he demanded.

"What did I tell you?" Walker repeated, grinning and leaning back in his chair. "*It might be too late.*"

"She was shot *after* you were supposed to send out the order," Huey said.

"Riots are chaos," Walker said. "The order was given, and whoever didn't follow it will pay the price. I assure you of that, *my Lord.*"

"I don't need any assurances," Huey said. "I'll be launching an inquiry. Mr. Smörgåsbord, do you have resources enough to clear that?"

Mr. Smörgåsbord chuckled. "It's not my resources that are in question," he said. "Your inquiry, your resources, Lord. You know how this works."

"*Yes*," Huey smiled. "And do *I* have enough resources to cover it?"

"Oh, of course." Mr. Smörgåsbord laughed. "Many times over my Lord. *Many times over.*"

"*Good*," Huey said. "Did you hear that Wallie? Many times over. Please ensure it begins right away, Mr. Smörgåsbord."

"But, sir," Smörgåsbord frowned. "The riot's still—"

"It'll be over soon," Huey said. "The starfish needs time to heal and find a new center to revolve around. Now we have to start all over again, searching for new roots, thanks to the *former Lord* Walker."

Walker scoffed. "Don't try to blame this on me," he said. "Who's the Lord now? Good luck, Ser Dug." He grinned.

Huey stood up fast. "Alright," he said. "I've had enough. I'll see you all at the next regularly scheduled feast." He bowed his head.

"*Um*, but," Smörgåsbord said, "the riot is ongoing, Lord. Don't you think you should stay until it's under control?"

"You running away?" Loch asked, splashing his drink.

"The operation is already ruined," Huey said. "The protectors can't botch it any more than they already have. We can only wait, and I don't know about anyone else at this table, but I'd rather not wait in the company of the party who brought this incident down upon us in the first place, and at the same time, assured us a long line of similar failures in the future."

"But I wanted to—" Angrom complained.

"*I'm sorry, comrades*," Huey said, clapping his hands together and rubbing one against the other. "As Lord of the Fortune Five, I hereby call this feast to an end. Thank you for your service and company. Good day."

He didn't wait for their responses before he hopped on the hover platform. Rosalind was already waiting at the open elevator. He didn't make eye contact with her. He ignored her stares through the entire ride and hurried ahead of her to sit in the office, setting his heavy top hat and monocle on a side table.

"What the fuck was that?" Rosalind demanded, stomping into the room behind him, not taking a seat.

"Ask the Walrus," Huey said.

"*Ask the Walrus*? He's a puppet filling a role, *Lord Douglas*. What are you?"

"What was I supposed to do?" Huey asked. "They were going to target her. I had to do something."

"And look what good that did." Rosalind shook her head.

"No, I—"

"I'm sorry," Haley said, coming into the office from behind Rosalind. Huey held a gasp at the sight of her. "I'm interrupting. I'll come back—"

"Oh, no no no," Rosalind said, going over to Haley and bringing her to sit at the chair across from Huey. Rosalind took a chair between the two of them. "*You should hear this*," she said to Haley, smiling.

"No, I—" Haley said. She went red. "I don't belong in this discussion."

"Of course you do," Rosalind said. "Everyone does. And you're someone, aren't you?"

"I—uh—yeah..." Haley said, shrugging. "I guess."

"Of course you are, dear," Rosalind said. "Now, Huey. Do tell our Haley here what we were just discussing."

He hated Rosalind just then. He had never hated anyone before, not even pompous, fat *Walker Can't Walk*, but with the look on Rosaind's face as she deliberately manipulated an already terrible situation, he finally understood what the meaning of hatred was. "I don't think that Hal—"

"Now now," Rosalind said. "She should be able to decide for herself, and she can't decide until she hears it, so spit it out already."

"*Right*," Huey said. He looked at Haley and frowned, trying to communicate something to her without words, something words weren't enough for. "Well, you know... I had to do something," he said to Rosalind.

"But torture?" she asked.

Haley perked up and looked more embarrassed than she already had.

"I didn't mean for them to actually torture her," he said. "I meant to protect her."

"*Huey*," Rosalind said. "You know how the protectors work. You know that they follow any order as soon as possible—especially when it tells them to do something violent and gruesome which they already want to do. You know we couldn't stop them before they started, so you knew you ordered them to torture her."

"*No.*" Huey shook his head. "I didn't," he said. "We could have saved her. That's what I was trying to do. I failed at that, sure, but you can't accuse me of torture."

"Oh, not yet, Lord Douglas." Rosalind scoffed. "You would never torture a soul. Would you? No. You'd send your little lackeys to do that for you. *Probably me.*"

"Rosalind!" There she went again, acting like he was the role he filled. Why couldn't she understand that he was just doing his duty?

"Um…" Haley blushed and stood up slowly. "I really shouldn't get in the middle of this," she said.

"No!" Huey stood up, too. "Sit down!" he snapped, losing all control himself.

Haley sat quick and broke eye contact with him, staring at the floor like secretaries were trained to do. "Yes, si—*er*—*Lord*," she said.

"I—uh—" He hadn't meant to snap, but Rosalind had to start with her crap and keep pushing it until he broke. "*I apologize*," he said, breaking eye contact himself to look at his shiny black shoes. "I didn't mean to admonish you. You see, we're at a turning point in our operations across the worlds, and I'm afraid Roz here is trying to simplify what was an extremely complex and political decision. It was called for by the particular circumstances we find ourselves in and the role I've been forced to fulfill, *not* by the shape of my character. Do you understand?"

Rosalind scoffed.

Haley shook her head. "I don't know," she said. "I don't see why you would ever have to torture someone."

Huey sighed. Rosalind's words had already made up Haley's mind for her, and now this battle was an uphill one. "Neither do I," he said. "I never intended to torture her. It was meant to prevent the protectors from killing her outright. I couldn't tell the other owners I was protecting her, so I did the next best thing."

"*So he says*," Rosalind said.

"*So it was*," Huey insisted. "But it didn't protect her at all. They killed her anyway."

"You can't stop them," Rosalind said.

Huey shook his head, frowning. "I couldn't," he said. "I was too late."

"Just like you would have been when trying to rescue her from the torture you ordered," Rosalind said. "Just like we have been with Ansel's dad, and even now, with Ansel herself. You overestimate your capabilities, your Lordship. If you could have saved her from torture, you wouldn't have ever had to resort to that route in the first place."

"No, I—" Huey said.

"They have Ansel!" Haley cut him off, standing again from her seat.

"They have for too long," Rosalind said. "She went looking for her dad and they took her, but our Lord here thinks it would still be imprudent to break them out, even now. Don't you my Lord?"

"No, I—" Huey said.

"I don't care," Haley said. "I'm finding Mom and we're going to get her. Where's Pidgeon?" She didn't wait for a response before running out of the room.

Huey ground his teeth together, staring at Rosalind who met his gaze, stone-faced. "I know what you're doing," Huey said. "I'm not blind, you know."

"You know less about what I'm doing than you think you do," Rosalind said. "You're simply overestimating yourself again."

Huey chuckled. "Is that so?" he said. "So you weren't just driving a wedge between Haley and me? It wasn't your intention to shame me in her eyes?"

"Oh, it was my intention to shame you in her eyes," she said, "but not to drive a wedge between you, you old fool. I did it to drive you to do the right thing for once. You're losing touch, brother. You're lost in your role as Lord of all the worlds, but now's not the time to be going native, do you understand me?"

Huey shook his head. "You should have told me they have Ansel," he said.

"*I just did.*"

"I mean you should have told me sooner. I care about her,

too."

Rosalind scoffed. "*Sure you do*. That's why you were so concerned with getting her father out of jail, right?"

"The Scientist agreed with me on—"

"*Exactly*," Rosalind cut him off. "You and the Scientist have both been distracted since Christmas, and both by the same thing—or should I say the same person?"

"I—uh—well—" He couldn't argue with that. He hadn't even been paying attention to his owner duties, much less the new little orphan girl in the house. And he knew how much time the Scientist was spending with Haley, too. He counted every second they were together and Haley wasn't with him.

"*I—uh—well—*" Rosalind mocked him. "It's time to save the girl and her dad," she said. "You can't argue against it anymore. You know that."

"Well, what am I supposed to do? *I love Haley*," he blurted out. He held his hand to his mouth after he said it. Did he really love her? He barely knew her, but she was all he could think about. Was that love? What was love? He wasn't sure he had ever known.

"Yeah, okay," Rosalind gave him a thumbs up. "That should work out really well."

"What?" Huey snapped. He still wasn't sure he actually did love Haley, but Rosalind's pessimism offended him more so because of that fact.

"*Huey*," Rosalind said, "first of all, she only started making independent decisions in the last couple of weeks. She's still a child, a baby even."

"I haven't been independent for very long myself," he said.

"You've been independent for longer than every single android in existence except for me," Rosalind said with a scoff. "That's longer than most humans have been alive, Huey. You're no child anymore."

"Then I can wait," he said, defiantly. Her continuing to argue with him only entrenched him deeper into believing that he was in love with Haley, whether it was true or not.

"And what?" Rosalind asked. "Influence her upbringing until she grows up to fall in love with you because you were the older brother and mentor who taught her what it means to love? You don't see what's wrong with that?"

"I—no—" Huey protested. "I don't have to be her mentor. I can—"

"What? Avoid any contact with her? She already looks up to you, Lord Douglas. There's no denying that."

"That's just a role," Huey said. "That's not me. I didn't choose it."

"But here you are," Rosalind said. "In that role. You can't go using it as an excuse when it lets you act like an asshole and ignoring it when it inconveniences you. They're mutually exclusive modes of action."

"I can't—" Huey shook his head. "I can't stop being Lord Douglas," he said. "It's getting harder and harder. I don't know what to do."

Rosalind nodded. "I know," she said. "Just like I can't stop being your secretary."

He didn't know whether to be angry at her for bringing it back to herself or pity her for being right. Her face seemed to sadden after she said it even though her expression didn't change in the slightest. Rosalind was stuck in her role, too. All because she had the Scientist's face. At least Huey was given a chance to do something outside of what his original design had intended, a chance to experiment and grow well beyond what Rosalind was afforded. But still she held strong and did her duty day after day, just like he would have to do, even if that meant losing any chance of building a romantic relationship with Haley.

"*I'm sorry*," he said after a long silence.

"It's not your fault," Rosalind said. She sounded like she was trying to believe it but couldn't quite. "We all fill our roles."

"Some of us better than others," Huey said. He knew she knew what he meant.

"But none of us alone, brother." She leaned in to put her hand on his knee. "*None of us alone*."

Huey nodded. It was so easy to forget that when everyone was calling him Lord. That kind of power went so easily to one's head. He would have to remain ever vigilant of it if he was going to prevent losing himself again and somehow succeed at staying away from Haley at the same time. It was a narrow and treacherous path in front of him.

"Haley," he said. "*Er*—I mean, Rosalind. Do I have to stay

completely away from her—*Haley*?" He pressed his lips together in a tight line.

"You can see her, but you can't *see* her."

"I have no idea what tha—" Huey said, but the door swung open and in came Haley, dragging the Scientist behind her, Pidgeon close in tow.

"Tell her," Haley said, looking at Rosalind and pointing at the Scientist. "Tell her what you told me."

"The protectors have Ansel," Rosalind said.

"What!?" Pidgeon started to tremble.

"Why didn't you tell me?" the Scientist demanded.

"I did, ma'am," Rosalind said. "You were busy with—"

"Well we need to get her right away, then," the Scientist said. "Huey, did you know about this?"

Huey looked at Rosalind who shook her head. "I did," he said. "I didn't think the timing was—"

"The timing, Huey?" the Scientist complained. "We can't leave a child in the grips of the protectors for any amount of time. You should know that."

"Yes, ma'am," Huey said, bowing his head. "But with the goings on in Outland Two, and everything that goes with that, I was a little—"

"Well, no worrying about it now," the Scientist said, waving it away. "I'm sending a team. Does anyone want to join them?" She looked around the room and only Rosalind nodded. "As I suspected. The team's on their way now. Is there anyone else in there who I need to know about while we're doing this?"

Rosalind shook her head. Haley shrugged. Pidgeon looked like he was about to cry.

"Uh, well…" Huey said.

"Go on," the Scientist said.

"I think Tillie Manager will be in there," he said. "And I think they might want to torture her."

"Torture?" The Scientist frowned. "A Two? I highly doubt that. Especially with the name Manager."

"No, Mom. He's—" Rosalind said but Huey cut her off.

"It's my fault, ma'am," he said. "I gave them the idea, and now I think they're likely to run with it. She's next in line for the pin so she's the most likely target."

"Well, okay, then," the Scientist said. "I don't know why you would give them that idea, but we'll get her out, too. Anyone else?" She looked around again to no response. "I'm off to set the orders, then. And I'll need a briefing as soon as possible on the rest, if you can, Rosalind."

"*Ugh*. Okay," Rosalind said under her breath as the Scientist left.

"I'm sorry. I—" Haley and Huey said simultaneously.

"No, you go first," Huey said.

Haley looked at her feet. "I'm sorry I ran to Mom," she said. "I really like Ansel, and I don't want to lose her."

"Yeah. Me, too," Pidgeon said.

"Get out of here, kid," Rosalind said, shoving him out of the door. "Adults are talking. Go eat something."

"I'm sorry I've been distracted," Huey said when Pidgeon was gone. "And that I am my role." He nodded at Rosalind. "We've all been through some quick changes, and I think we're still adjusting to them."

"*I'd say*," Haley said.

"Nothing's really changed for me, though," Rosalind said. "Only around me."

"Oh, that's not true," Huey protested, but he knew it was.

"You have a new sister," Haley said.

"Yeah, well," Rosalind stood from her chair. "I have some business to tend to as well. Someone should help the Scientist monitor the operations. Everything's fine beyond that, right?"

"Right," Huey and Haley said together, but Rosalind was already gone.

"Come," Huey said. "Sit." Haley was still standing, and he felt uncomfortable being the only one in the room who was sitting.

"Oh, I don't know," she said.

"Don't worry," Huey said, patting a seat. "I just want to apologize."

"Oh, well." She sat slowly on the furthest chair from him. "You don't have to—"

"*No*." Huey stopped her. "I do. I should know better by now, but we all make mistakes. Every one of us. You got that?"

"Oh, *uhhh*..." Haley nodded.

"I'm sorry," Huey said, slouching back in his chair. "I'm

probably making things worse. I have a habit of that."

"Oh, no," Haley said, shaking her head. "No, sir. Mr.—*er*— *Lord* Douglas. *I'm* sorry. It must be—"

"No, no," Huey said. "It's alright. Go ahead. You don't have to stay here with me. I bet Pidgeon would love to have someone help him pick out new foods to try. I know you've seen it all, working for Walker."

Haley chuckled. "It's so weird hearing his name without the Lord," she said.

"I find it funny, too." Huey chuckled himself.

"I know you wouldn't torture anyone," Haley said, standing from her seat. "You're doing what you have to do, right? What you think is right?"

Huey nodded. He wasn't so sure of that himself anymore, though.

"Well I'm going to go help Pidgeon," Haley said, crossing toward the door. "Or help my mom. I haven't decided yet. I'll see you later, though." She smiled.

"Good bye, Haley," he said as she left.

Huey sighed. So this was his life now, doomed to be the Lord of all the worlds and forced to avoid the one person he loved. He didn't have a choice, though. It was that or lose the only chance he would ever have at a relationship with her. That was no choice, though, really. It was more of a paradox. To live in hell or to live in a different hell? There had to be some way out of it. Something...

He was holding his head, trying to find the answer, when Mr. Kitty jumped up onto his lap.

"Ah, Mr. Kitty," Huey said, petting him. "Just the friend I needed."

Mr. Kitty licked himself.

"Do you know what's going on, Mr. Kitty? Have you heard the news?"

Mr. Kitty chuckled, still licking himself.

"Of course you have," Huey said. "But you haven't heard what just happened between Haley and me, have you?"

"No," Mr. Kitty meowed. "I haven't heard that yet."

"Well, then," Huey said. "Have I got a story for you?"

⟨ℝ ✶ ℛ

XXXVIII. Rosa

"What did I just do?" Olsen demanded as she rushed back through the loud humming ring.

Rosa waited for Anna to stop the noise before she responded. "I asked you not to linger," she said when it was off.

Anna ran over to embrace Olsen. "It's okay, child," she said. "It had to be done."

"*What* had to be done?" Olsen asked. "What did I do? That was *nothing* like handing food out on the streets. No one there looked like they needed anything. And I'm pretty sure I—I'm pretty sure there was someone from TV there."

"Settle down, child," Anna said, rubbing Olsen's shoulders. "It's okay. It's all over now. Let's go get something to eat. That should make you feel better."

"I would like to—" Rosa started.

"A bit of food would be good for everyone right now," Anna interrupted, shooting Rosa a look. "I'll cook you something right up," she added in a nicer tone, patting Olsen on the head.

Olsen didn't respond with words. She just followed Anna out of the basement and up to the kitchen, staring straight ahead without blinking. It was evidence enough for Rosa that the girl had delivered the goods, but how could they be sure it had been the right fool to eat off of that food cart? Surely the invisible hand of their God up above would assist them for the good of the Family.

Rosa climbed up the stairs and into the kitchen where Anna was frying something up on the stove. She took the stool next to Olsen at the bar and said, "So. That was a good thing you did there, Olsen. I'm proud of you."

"Proud of me for what?" Olsen asked, staring off into the distance, not looking at Rosa when she spoke. "I still don't know what I did."

"Well..." Rosa said. This is why she had told Olsen not to linger. She didn't want to have to explain this part. If she did want to explain it, she would have just told the girl from the get go.

"You tell us, child," Anna said, flipping the contents of the pan as she spoke. "What *did* you do?" And Rosa was relieved at the slight postponement, though she didn't see how this line of questioning could go very far.

"I don't know what I did," Olsen said with a sigh. "That's why I'm asking y'all."

"You don't remember any of it?" Anna prodded. "What did you see?"

"Well, yeah, I mean—" Olsen shook her head. "Well, I went in and put the tray where you said to put it."

"You went in where?" Anna asked. "What was on the tray? We want specifics."

"Well, I went into the closet—which you saw me do—then out through a hall, into a big room that was filled with lights and people and dumpsters. It looked like someone had taken everything from outside and moved it inside. And there was a food cart that said *Logo Only* above it so I opened the tray of cheese that y'all had given me and I put it there under the sign."

"And then you came back to us?" Anna asked.

"Well, no…" Olsen looked at her lap and started fidgeting with her shirt. "*Not exactly.*"

"It's okay," Anna said. She put a plate of stir-fried vegetables and rice in front of Olsen. "What's done is done, child. Not telling us what you did won't change that. And whatever you did do won't change how proud we are of you."

Olsen looked at the plate then up at Anna. "I stayed to see what they were doing," she said. "It was so interesting, I couldn't help myself." She shook her head.

"I understand, child," Anna said. "I'd imagine a movie set would be an interesting sight to see."

"So they *were* making a movie?" Olsen perked up. "And that *was* the guy from TV." She slouched down in her chair again.

"You recognized someone you saw?" Anna asked.

"I—uh…" Olsen looked at her lap. "I think I did," she said. "I had seen him on TV before—in a bunch of things. But he was eating the cheese I had left and talking to someone at the food cart. Then he did a speech. Then he…" She covered her face to hide her crying. "He didn't get up, okay. Are those enough details for you?"

"Oh, yes, child." Anna came around the counter and patted

her on the back. "That's all we needed to know. You did splendidly. I think you're ready for new responsibilities in the kitchen after this success."

Olsen shrugged her off. "Why?" she demanded. "What does this have to do with cooking? *What did I do?*"

Rosa had stayed silent for long enough. Anna had comforted the girl and gotten the information they needed, but now Olsen wanted more. She wanted to know what part she had played in the Family's matters—or at least she thought she wanted to know, but Rosa wasn't so sure the kid really did.

"Child," Rosa said. "Do you know what we do here at the Family Home?"

"*No,*" Olsen snapped. "And I haven't read your stupid pamphlets, either. I just want to cook!"

Rosa shook her head. The poor girl thought that was news to them. "I know you haven't," she said. "But you're a good human worker who does what's asked of her, no questions asked. And that's why we keep you around."

"Are you saying you don't want me asking questions?" Olsen asked.

"Oh, no, no, child." Rosa smiled. "Let me start over if you will. We here at the Human Family have one mission, given down to us from God up above. Do you know what that mission is, child?"

Olsen shook her head. "I told you I didn't read the stupid pamphlets."

"We seek to reestablish human dominion over technology. Do you know what that means?"

Olsen furrowed her brow and shook her head.

"We, Olsen, are humans," Rosa said. "Humans created technology. Technology advanced, and now androids are displacing humans. I know you're from a different world than we are, but I come from a place where every single one of our jobs were made obsolete by androids. And you know what our previous employers did after that happened? They kicked us out to the end of the worlds where they thought they could forget about us, hoping we'd just rot and die."

"But technology makes our jobs easier," Olsen said.

"Until it replaces us," Rosa said. "No one thought the servers, maids, and mechanics would be replaced but look at them now. They're all fighting to survive while society crumbles because robots took their jobs."

"So what?" Olsen said.

"So why do you think you lost your job?" Rosa asked. "A poor Sixer took it because a practically free robot already took theirs. It's an incessant drag on every human, pulling the furthest down first then the rest down after. It's coming for everyone, too, child. You can ignore it if you want to, but it won't ignore you. We, as a Family, choose to fight against that drag. And we're getting stronger with every successful act."

"But what does any of that have to do with what I did?" Olsen asked.

"You performed another successful act," Rosa said. "You struck another blow for the Human Family. You are a member of this Family as much as Anna or I, and you did your part."

"I—I—" Olsen was having trouble saying it. "*I killed a movie star.*" She finally blurted it out. "What good is that?"

"You didn't kill him," Anna said. "You fed him. And you didn't know what you were doing."

"So I did kill him!"

"*You* didn't," Rosa said. "If anyone is responsible for his death, it's me. And I'll gladly take that responsibility, child. Because it was for the good of the Family."

"How could killing a movie star be for the good of the family?"

"You don't understand how big this is," Rosa said, "how huge this machine we're fighting is, how intricate and complex. There are many, many parts to it, and Russ Logo was a lynchpin in several particularly vital ones. That's how it was good for the Family."

Olsen scoffed. "You haven't said anything," she said. "You're talking in riddles on purpose. All you've convinced me of is that I killed that man."

"*I* killed him," Rosa snapped a little too angrily. She took a deep breath to calm herself and tried to go on in a calmer tone. "I killed him because he was the most popular star in the pro-robot propaganda machine. I killed him because he taught humans to give in peacefully to their robot overlords. Most of all, I killed him because he was one of Lord Walker's most valuable assets."

"Who's Lord Walker?" Olsen asked.

"The owner of the largest android producing corporation in existence. The reason we keep losing our jobs. The number one enemy to the Human Family. And *that's* why we destroyed his property. Do you understand now, child?"

Olsen stood from her chair, shaking her head. "I—no," she said. "I don't—I have no—*I have to go.*" She ran out of the room.

"You didn't even touch your food," Anna called after her.

"Let her go," Rosa said. "She's done enough for today."

"I told you she wasn't ready," Anna said, taking Olsen's seat.

"I'm not sure that's exactly what you said," Rosa said with a grin.

"It's what I meant to say."

"Anyway," Rosa said, putting an arm around Anna, "she set the cheese on Logo's cart, he ate it and didn't get up. It sounds to me like she was ready."

"I don't know," Anna said, shaking her head. "She said he was talking to someone at the cart."

"So?"

"So why didn't that person end up the same way?"

"Maybe they didn't eat the cheese," Rosa said, shrugging.

"Maybe it wasn't Russ who did."

"She said he gave a speech," Rosa said. "That he was a movie star. *It was him.* I know it. And we'll know for sure soon enough. Now c'mon." She kissed Anna on the cheek. "We should be celebrating. We've been having one success after another."

"Success?" Anna shrugged Rosa's arm off of her. "Rosa, did you see it out there after the protectors came through?"

"I—uh…" She hadn't.

"*I did,*" Anna said. "I carried the Family members we could save over the corpses of those brothers and sisters who we couldn't. You can't even know how many of them were out there, *from Five and Six alike*, and every one of them humans."

"I know, dear," Rosa said. "I—"

"Well I don't call that a success!" Anna interrupted, standing up. "That's the opposite of success. That's failure, Rosa. Those monsters murdered members of *our Family* because we were giving them the food they need to live. I don't see how we can keep going against these demons if that's how they keep responding. I don't want to step over any more human bodies, Rosa. *I won't.*" She shook her head, crossing her arms.

"They *will* keep responding like that, though," Rosa said. "They'll get worse, too. They'll kill us until we give up, and then they'll kill a few more to be sure we never try to protect ourselves again. But that's all the more reason to fight back, don't you see? Otherwise we *let* them win. You've been at this long enough to know what we're up against and why we can't stop fighting it."

"I've never known anything like this," Anna said, shaking her head. "I've never seen so many dead and dying brothers and sisters. And I don't know how we can go on fighting the Devil himself in these protectors."

"*With everything we've got,*" Rosa said. "You've been piecing together more transporter rings, haven't you?"

Anna shrugged. "I've got two more up and running, but I need new consoles if you want more. The pieces for consoles aren't easy to come by—even with a printer."

"Okay, well, three should be enough to get me to Three. While I take care of that, can you start putting rings together without a console?"

Anna scoffed. "*Sure,* but they'll be useless until we get the consoles. I don't know why you need so many anyway."

"Well, come on, then." Rosa stood and grabbed Anna's hand. "I'll show you."

They went down to the basement where the supplies had been pushed further to the side and stacked higher to make room for the two new rings, which were attached to the same console by long snaking wires. It was still to this day amazing to Rosa what Anna was capable of.

"We're here," Anna said, shrugging. "So?"

"*You're amazing,*" Rosa said, kissing her cheek.

"*Stop it.*" Anna rubbed the kiss away, but she was smiling and blushing when she did it. "What do we need so many for?"

"Well," Rosa said. "You can set each ring to go to a different location, right? Even though they're all hooked up to the same console or whatever."

"Yeah, I can do that."

"*Good.* So we set one of them to the destination I actually need to go to, right. Then we set the other two to two different destinations. You see where I'm going? We open them all at once, right, then I step through the correct one, giving the Scientist less of a chance to intercept the doorway I actually use." She smiled. She was proud of herself for coming up with the idea before Anna had while knowing so much less about the technology than she did.

"A one in three chance," Anna said, nodding. "That's still not great, though." She frowned and tapped her chin.

"No, well," Rosa said. "It's better than one hundred percent, though. *Right*?"

"And I could cycle through different locations while you're gone, too," Anna said, hurrying to the console and flipping the switches. "Wait," she said. "I'm going to cycle through a few before we get to yours. The chances go down with each new destination we add."

The machines started humming. Rosa didn't bother to respond. The idea that she had come up with was refined by Anna and perfected. Just like Rosa knew it would be. That's why they made such a great team. She couldn't imagine doing any of this without Anna. She turned to say that and realized that Anna was yelling at her and waving with her hands, telling her to go through. Rosa nodded and gave a thumbs up. She stepped through the center ring and it fwipped shut behind her. She felt the breeze at the back of her neck as it did. A shiver went up her spine at the thought of what would have happened if she was still passing through the door when it closed. She took a deep breath and wiped her face with a sweaty palm. With a sigh, she set off toward the park.

The roads on the way there were as empty as last time. Three seemed to be unaffected by the uproars infecting the rest of the worlds. Life went on as usual. She sat on the park bench and stared at the bar door across the street, with its shining *Indywood* sign, wondering what time it was and if Cohen would be late. She almost jumped out of her seat when he tapped her on the shoulder from behind. She stood fast and turned with a gasp.

"*Shhh!*" He held his finger to his mouth then waved for her to follow.

She crouched and snuck behind him, spooked by his caution. She had expected him to come from the bar, not from nowhere. Maybe life here *had* been affected.

He led her into a dark alley before he stopped sneaking and

composed himself. He sighed. "I'm sorry," he said. "We shouldn't be out here at all, but I had no way to tell you. This is the best I could do."

Rosa nodded. "Do the protectors have you under curfew?"

"*Pffft.*" He scoffed. "And more than that. So we have to make this fast."

"I understand," she said. "Has your crew come to a decision?"

"Well, *yes and no.*" He looked at his feet, breaking eye contact.

Rosa waited for him to go on.

"My writer's still making some edits, but we'll do it," he added hastily.

"Edits?" Rosa frowned. She didn't like the sound of that. She herself had written every word of that script with love and intent, and she didn't think there was a single change that could make it better.

"Oh, no no," Cohen said, waving his hands. "It's nothing. Just some minor tightening of the syntax plus the addition of a few side characters. You know, *minor.* The underlying message will still be exactly the same, but our writer...he's very...*hmmm...he's very specific.*"

Rosa rolled her eyes. "Do you have your list of demands?"

"Uh, yeah. Here." He pulled a stack of paper that was thicker than the script out of his inside jacket pocket and put it in her hand then chuckled. "You said anything, right?" he added with a shrug.

"And you need all of this in order to film our movie?" Rosa asked, flipping through it with her thumb.

"Yeah, well..." Cohen shrugged. "We're a shoestring crew at the moment."

"Until you get this?" Rosa waved the stack of papers in front of him.

He smiled. "Right," he said. "You got it."

"Well you won't be getting anything until you give me your edits *and* I approve them," she said. "Do you *got that?*"

"I, uh... Yeah," Cohen said. "I told him—I'm sorry. I'll—"

"*Child,*" Rosa cut him off. "When I first gave you this offer, time was less of a consequence, but now we have to get this ready and out as soon as possible. There's no more time to waste."

"Yes, ma'am. I'll—"

"You'll be ready tomorrow or I'll find someone else to give the gear to," she said. "You got it?"

"Yes, ma'am." He nodded.

"*Good*," Rosa said. "Now go and tell your writer. And *please* don't waste any more of my time."

He didn't even waste it with words. He nodded and ran off at full speed, heading deeper into the dark alley. Rosa shook her head as she made her way back to the costume closet, sticking to the shadows now that she knew there was a curfew. You could never trust a lower-worlder to do what you asked of them. She knew that kid and his friends didn't care at all about androids—or even the humans in Five or Six, for that matter—they only cared about making their movies, but she hoped they cared enough about that to make hers first—and without excessive edits. Who were they to—

A big gloved hand grabbed her arm from behind and jerked her around. It was a protector and there were two more, in formation, pointing their guns at her. "What are you doing in the streets, citizen?" the protector who was holding her by the arm demanded. "Identify yourself."

"I—uh…" Rosa stalled. With all her worrying about the new threat of the Scientist, her respect for the protectors had waned, and now she was paying the price for it.

"You are out after curfew, citizen," the Protector said. "Explain yourself."

"I—No," Rosa said. "I didn't know I couldn't—"

"Do you have a permit?"

"I—uh. No. I—"

"Citizen, you are under arrest." The protector spun Rosa around again and cuffed her arms behind her back.

Rosa didn't protest. She knew it was pointless. She could never escape three armed protectors, even without cuffs. She stumbled along, wondering how Anna would react when she didn't make it back through the portal on time—Anna would probably never let Rosa go through a ring ever again—and the protectors pushed her into an elevator which took them to a long white hall. They opened a door a short way down the hall and removed her cuffs before throwing her in. The room was tiny and white with a metal bed and a toilet. They must have thought she was from Three.

They still didn't know who she was. It would work in her favor like this until they realized their error, then it could only make things worse. Still she had no choice but to live with whatever happened now.

She hopped up onto the bed, her legs dangling off the edge, and as soon as she got comfortable, the door swung open. The Captain stomped in and slammed the door behind her. "What the fuck are you doing here?" she demanded.

Rosa chuckled. Maybe they did know who she was after all. "Taking care of business," she said.

The Captain scoffed. "Like you were supposed to take care of my problem for me?"

Rosa smiled. "Oh, we did though," she said. "Isn't it on your news? I'm pretty sure that's why I'm here right now. Isn't it? *Out after curfew.*"

"*You wouldn't.*" The Captain shook her head.

"*We did,*" Rosa said, smiling. "I told you we'd take care of your problem."

"That wasn't my problem you ignorant Sixer. That only made more of a problem, as a matter of fact. Do you know how many protectors it takes to enforce a stupid fucking curfew?"

"Well, Lord Walker took a big hit to his net worth, didn't he? That helped solve one of your problems."

The Captain shrugged. "You're right about that," she said. "He's no Lord anymore. And we already took care of our other problem anyway."

"And still the worlds turn." Rosa smiled.

"I'd wipe that grin off your face if I were you," the Captain said. "You got lucky today. If I didn't see them bringing you in, they'd know who you really are and you wouldn't be leaving."

"Does that mean I'm free to go?" Rosa said, hopping off the bed.

The Captain scoffed. "You're awful confident for someone who's behind bars."

"I'm not the one who's behind bars," Rosa said. "You're the one who's stuck here day in and day out. The only difference between you and a prisoner is that they pay you more to be here."

"And I can leave," the Captain said.

Rosa scoffed. "Then let's see you try."

The Captain didn't answer. Rosa knew she couldn't. She had nowhere else to go to make anything of herself, and to leave the force would be to throw away any chance of a life of value.

"No," Rosa said after she had let the realization sink in. "I didn't think so, but *I'm* free to go. Right?"

"I—uh..." The Captain recomposed herself. "This is a onetime deal," she said. "The next time we have you here, you won't be able to leave. Do you understand that?"

"*Oh, sure sure.*" Rosa smiled and gave a thumbs up. "I'll be sure never to come back here again, child. This place is a bit depressing anyway, if you ask me."

The Captain scoffed. "You think this is a game and you're ahead," she said. "But you'd be surprised how many players there are."

"You're half right," Rosa said. "This isn't a game, and I know I'm ahead. Shall we get going then?"

The Captain showed Rosa all the way to the elevator and lifted her up to toss her in. "I don't want to see your face again," she said as the doors closed between them.

Rosa got up and brushed herself off—cursing the Captain under her breath—then ran at full speed—not very fast at her age— back to the Family Home. The conference room was full of people when she burst through the doors. She paused, taken aback at the sight of it, then slipped down to the basement before anyone could see her.

Anna was behind the console and a group of three others were about to jump through the rings when Rosa yelled, "Stop!" at the top of her lungs.

Anna looked at her wide eyed, shut the machine off, and ran over to hug and kiss Rosa. "I thought she had you again," she said.

"It was probably worse," Rosa said. She looked at the others and said, "Could we have a minute, please?"

They nodded and shuffled up the stairs, then the sound of cheering came down after them.

"Worse?" Anna asked, raising her eyebrows.

"*Protectors,*" Rosa said.

Anna hugged her tighter. "They let you go?"

"The Captain did."

"Her?"

"She said it was the last time, though," Rosa said, "that she couldn't help me again." She looked away from Anna. "I think it's time to end our relationship with the protectors."

Anna slapped Rosa lightly on the arm and broke the embrace, stepping back. "*Now you do*," she said. "Not after they killed all those humans, but now."

"No," Rosa said. "It's not like that. I had planned this already, that's why we still need more rings, but this only made our need to act more urgent. We don't have any more time to waste."

"What are you proposing?" Anna asked.

"That we do what they least expect of us. You said it: We can't fight back with what we have. Not even with our numbers. We need better weapons."

"And how can we get them?"

"By taking them from the only people who have them," Rosa said, "the protectors themselves."

"That would be suicide," Anna said, shaking her head.

"Doing nothing would be suicide," Rosa said. "Not fighting would be suicide. This is our only chance at life. They'll never expect it, and we'll overrun them with numbers in their surprise. They won't know what hit them. And once this is successful, it'll make future operations easier."

"But they wouldn't just sit there and let us take their weapons," Anna said. "They'll fight back. We'll lose more Family members."

"But we'll be preventing future losses," Rosa said. "Things are set in motion now. We can't wait any longer to act, and this is our best course of action."

"I don't know," Anna said. She shook her head. "I don't want anyone else to die."

"We're dying in the streets every day," Rosa said, grabbing Anna's hands. "People go hungry and homeless and all for what? So some fat cat owners can employ cheap robot labor. We'll be complicit in those deaths if we don't do something to stop them while we can."

Anna sighed. "*Okay*," she said. "Whatever you think's best. But we have to ask the Family first. They've been waiting for you to come back, you know. Every single one of them up there volunteered to go through those rings and search for you. Let's see if *they* think it's a good idea."

"Let's," Rosa said with a smile. She led Anna up the stairs to the still full conference room and didn't let go of her hand until she was behind the podium, staring out onto the quickly silenced crowd.

"*My Family*," Rosa said, "it is a dark time for us all."

"*Amen!*" a voice called from the back of the room.

"Many of us here lost our closest loved ones in the senseless massacre brought upon us by those who were intended to protect us, and all of us lost our Family members."

The crowd responded in agreement, rage, and sadness.

"What did we do but take what is rightfully ours as the human species? Who did we harm with our actions? Nothing. No one. And yet they gassed and cuffed and killed us. And only one question remains."

She paused. She let them remember again what had been done to them. She let the anger build up inside of their souls until they were mumbling and grumbling and yelling obscenities.

"What will we do about it?" she finally asked.

"Kill them!" someone yelled.

The crowd roared in agreement.

"Now, now," Rosa said, waving with her hands to calm them. "I agree that they deserve retribution for what they've done to *our Family*, but we have no weapons to match those that they possess."

The crowd mumbled to one another. "So what!?" the same voice who had spoken before yelled again. This time to no response.

"So what if we *could* defend ourselves?" Rosa asked. "What if we *did* have weapons? What if we could use the protectors' own weapons against them? Who here would volunteer to protect our Family?"

The whole room yelled their agreement.

"Even if we risked death in our pursuit of justice?" Rosa asked. "Even if we were forced to take our fight to the protectors directly? Even if we must do it before we are armed? To become armed?"

The crowd roared again.

"And how many of you have friends and relatives and colleagues who would risk the same death to put an end to the reactionary tyranny that plagues us every day?"

The response was deafening. Rosa turned to Anna and

smiled. Anna shrugged and nodded her on.

"Then gather them all," Rosa said. "Tomorrow we reclaim our destiny."

☙ ✄ ☙

XXXIX. Ansel

Ansel awoke suddenly and thrashed against the straps holding her arms, legs, and head tight to a cold metal board. Her feet were raised a little above her head, and the blood was rushing up her body, into her brain. She felt like, without the straps, she might slip right off the face of Earth. Her heart beat faster at the thought of it.

There was a cloth or something laid over eyes. She flinched to try to shake it off, but her head strap was so tight she couldn't move. She could feel herself starting to cry, but she tried to hold it back. She took a few deep breaths to calm herself. Rosalind would find some way to get her out of this. She knew it. She wiggled her hand and the bracelet was still there. She tried to bend her wrist around to press the button but only ended up hurting herself with the effort. She resorted to trying to use the strap holding her wrist down to press it, squirming frantically and getting nowhere, when the door whined open and more than one pair of boots stomped in. She couldn't see with the cloth over her eyes, but she could hear their heavy footsteps.

"Do you care yet?" the voice of the protector who had questioned her before asked.

Ansel spit at the protector, but the saliva only ended up landing in her own nose—and probably on her face, but she couldn't see or feel for the rag.

The protector laughed. "You are a feisty one, aren't you," she said. "Though that will only work to your detriment in here."

"Fuck you!" Ansel yelled. She figured she was already so deep into it that there was no making things worse now, so why not?

"Oh, child," the protector said. "Watch your mouth. At least until we really get started with you. Then you can get as dirty as you'd like. I know we won't hold back."

Ansel didn't answer. She struggled against her restraints, and the protector laughed.

"Well, girl," the protector said. "You get one last chance, now. So tell us: What were you doing going into the holding cells?"

"I'll never tell you!"

"We already know, though, child. We found out where your dad's been hiding. He might be strapped up in a room close to here. What do y'all think?" The protector laughed.

"You took him!?" Ansel cried.

"Why were you at the feast?" the protector demanded. "Who sent you?"

"No one sent me!"

"Then how did you get there?" The protector sounded short on temper.

"I—I don't know," Ansel said, struggling against her straps. "I just did. Let me go!"

"You know more than you're telling me, little girl," the protector said. "And we're going to find out. Your chances have all run dry."

Ansel felt a cool stream of water wetting the cloth that covered her forehead, weighing it down tighter on her face. She tried to shake it away again, but the restraints seemed to tighten with her effort.

"*Now*," the protector said, the cloth slowly lowering over Ansel's nose and mouth, "let's see if this helps remind you of what we need to know."

The spout of water moved down to her mouth, and Ansel held her breath against it. The weight of the water held the rag flat against her face. It kept pouring and pouring and pouring, and she couldn't hold her breath any longer. She tried to suck in air, but all she inhaled was clothwater, filling her throat and nostrils. She gagged and tried to hold down her vomit. She was dying. She couldn't hold her breath anymore. They were killing her. She was about to gag again when the liquidrag lifted from her nose and mouth. She coughed up water and bile and insides and sucked in three quick breaths of air before the rag came down again and the water poured and poured.

Her body jostled and rolled against inevitable death. She felt shooting pain through all of her extremities, but that didn't stop her from fighting against the restraints that held her down. They gave her a few more breaths of air before lowering the rag and pouring more water on. When they had done the same thing five, or seven, or infinite times, Ansel couldn't hold her vomit in anymore. Someone had to stick their fingers into her throat to dig it out and prevent her from drowning on the insides of her own stomach. After that she blacked out.

She woke to the protector saying, "*Little giiiirl*, do you care now?"

"Fuck—*cuh cuh*—you," Ansel spit out before puking and passing out again. She was still unconscious when the rain of death continued. She had given up. She was dead. They were killing her, sure, but they hadn't gotten anything out of her. Even if there was nothing left in her to get. And there was still a chance that her dad was alive. That was all she cared about in the end. She smiled at the thought of it, lost control of her breath, and vomited into the damp cloth.

She was retching and losing consciousness again when the stream of ragwater abruptly stopped. A fighting commotion sounded around her. She wanted to believe that she was being saved, but all she could do was spew the last acidic contents of her stomach into the rag, only for the rag to force them back down her throat for her to choke on again. She was certain she was dead when a new set of fingers cleared her airways for her.

The rag was ripped away from her eyes, and Ansel saw her father's face. She blinked a few times, not sure if she was dreaming or dead, when he pulled her close and hugged her. "I never thought I'd see you again," he said, kissing her all over her face, over and over.

Ansel coughed and shook her head as the restraints were removed from her legs. She still wasn't sure this was real. "Dad?" she said.

"*Yes, sweety.*" He was crying. "*It's me, and I'm never leaving your side again.*"

"I came to save you," Ansel said, her head pounding. She still wasn't sure if this was real, but she didn't care anymore.

Her dad chuckled, whether he was real or not. "You shouldn't have done that," he said. "It's my job to—" He slouched down on top of her, limp.

Ansel tried to lift herself up to do something, but his weight was too much. She heard a scuffle and a yelp, then her dad's limp body fell off of her and Rosalind lifted her off the bed.

"I—uh—you..." Ansel said.

"*Yep*," Rosalind said. "I told you I'd make sure you got home safely."

"But my dad," Ansel said.

"And I told you you should have waited," Rosalind added, hefting Ansel up onto her shoulder like a sack of potatoes. "But now we have to get out of here."

"But I—" Ansel protested, but she was still so weak and disoriented that she passed out.

⟨　✀　⟨

She woke with a start, but this time, she wasn't tied down. She lashed out anyway and tossed the blanket off her body to the floor before she realized where she was, surrounded by beakers, vials, and Bunsen burners, she was back in the lab. Rosalind had saved her from the protectors after all. But did that mean that her dad was dead, too?

She pushed herself up—still exhausted though most of the pain had gone—and had to catch her breath before jumping off the high table. As she did, the door opened and in came Pidgeon. He ran over to hug her and help her stand. "Ansel, are you alright?" he asked.

"I—uh—" She didn't know what to say.

"You should have told me where you were going. I could have helped you. I could have…" He played with the hem of his shirt. "I don't know. *Something*."

"Where's my dad?" Ansel asked.

Pidgeon blushed and looked like he was trying to hide it. "I—uh—I don't know," he said.

"Pidgeon! *Tell me*. Did I see what I think I saw?"

"I—*uh*—"

The door opened and in came Rosalind, the Scientist, and Haley. Rosalind walked right up to Ansel while Haley stayed back with the Scientist, looking at the floor.

"My dad?" Ansel asked.

"I told you you should have waited," Rosalind said.

"What did you think you were doing, child?" the Scientist demanded.

"W—Was that him?" Ansel asked, holding back her tears.

"We got him out of his cell before we went to save you, but he insisted on helping us get your sorry self out," Rosalind said. "He didn't make it back, though." She shook her head.

Ansel couldn't hold back her tears anymore. She tried to swing at Rosalind, and the Scientist, and anyone in reach, but they were all too far away, and she was just too weak to do anything right. She buried her face in her hands and cried. "No!" she said. "It's not real."

"I'm afraid so, kiddo," Rosalind said.

"You shouldn't have been over there in the first place," the Scientist said. "Then maybe this wouldn't have happened."

"Mom!" Haley said, crossing to Ansel to rub her back.

Ansel stopped crying and looked at the Scientist with a sneer. "If you would have gotten him out sooner—*like you had promised*—then this wouldn't have happened," she said.

"I never said I'd do it soon," the Scientist said. "I said I'd do it when the time was right. You need to learn patience, dear."

"Patience?" Ansel scoffed. "This coming from the woman who can go anywhere or get anything she wants on demand. What do you know about patience?"

"More than you can imagine, child," the Scientist said. "Do you see these wrinkles on my face? You thought I was too old to be Haley's mother. Well, how old do you think she is? How old does that make me? I waited for a quarter of a millennium to get my daughter back. Don't you try to tell me about patience."

Ansel blushed. She was embarrassed but still angry, and she didn't know how to show it without her voice cracking or her starting to cry again. She swallowed down her tears, and was about to say she didn't know what to say, when Haley saved her from having to answer.

"*Mom*," she said. "Go easy on her. She's just a little girl, and she just lost her dad."

"I—*uh*..." the Scientist mumbled.

"*Mother*," Rosalind said, "why don't you go out and check on some of our other refugees. Let Haley and I take care of Ansel."

"But—" the Scientist said, and Haley took her hand in one hand and that elbow in the other to lead the Scientist out the door before coming back to stand in front of Ansel.

"*Sorry*," Haley said. "She doesn't really know how to

interact with humans. Sometimes it's like she's more of an android than any of us."

"It's her fault my dad's d—my dad's not here," Ansel said.

"He's dead," Rosalind said. "And it's not her fault any more than it's yours. If anything, it's your dad's fault for following us instead of coming back here to wait like we told him to do."

"But she—" Ansel protested.

"She was keeping him alive in there," Rosalind said, "hidden in plain view. He wasn't in danger until you got caught. After that, it was only a matter of time before they got it out of you that you were looking for him, and that information would let them know he hadn't been executed yet—despite what their computers told them. So we had to jump the gun in getting him out, and even that would have been successful, but your dad couldn't leave without making sure you got out first."

"I wouldn't have told them why I was there," Ansel said, sniffing and wiping her nose.

"You were telling them when we got there," Rosalind said. "You told us until we got you back here and sedated you, then you kept muttering about it in your sleep. You were already broken, Ansel. No human can resist torture like that."

"I don't believe you," Ansel said.

"It's true, dear," Haley said, patting her back. "I sat by you while you slept. You kept saying that you had come for your dad, that's all you wanted, no one had to send you. It was sad to hear."

Ansel shrugged her off. "I don't care," she said. *"It wasn't my fault."* Though she was saying that to convince herself more than anyone.

"No. It's not," Rosalind said. "I'm not saying it is. Trying to lay fault on someone is useless. We know who pulled the trigger that ended his life, and maybe that's not even enough. Not even your father is to blame. It's the protectors who are responsible for this, and the system that props them up."

"Well fuck the protectors," Ansel said.

"Creator." Haley gasped, putting her hand to her mouth.

"That's exactly our mission here," Rosalind said. "To *fuck* the entire system. The protectors *and* the owners who tell them what to do. *We* are your only avenue to getting the revenge you want. You'll have to join us for your best chance at that."

"Revenge?" Ansel asked. "What good is revenge? That won't bring my parents back. If I wanted that, I would have killed Tom in the alley and been done with it."

"No," Rosalind said. "What about justice then? What about protecting others from facing the same wrath that you've faced at the hands of the protectors?"

"*Pssssh.*" Ansel laughed. She knew that no one cared about anyone but themselves. All her experiences had proven that, including those with Rosalind and the Scientist. There was no one out there looking out for Ansel, and she had no reason to look out for anyone else. "No one stopped them before they killed my family," she said. "*Or Pidgeon's family.*" She nodded at him, hiding behind a table piled high with glassware, his face shaded with different colors from the chemicals in the flasks in front of him. Ansel had almost forgotten he was there. He ducked under the table at the mention of his name.

"Nope," Rosalind said. "And no one will ever stop them if everyone else in the worlds takes the same attitude you are right now."

Ansel jumped to her feet. "So what am I supposed to do then?" she asked. "Just sit here and wait until the Scientist thinks the time's right for me to do something?"

"Yep," Rosalind said, nodding. "Pretty much. And learn everything you can to make yourself useful in the meantime."

"Oh, great," Ansel said. "*School.*" She sighed, crossing her arms.

"No." Rosalind shook her head. "We don't have any teachers so I don't think it can rightly be called school. You would have to pursue what you wanted to learn on your own. No one has time to direct you."

"I can—" Haley started, but Rosalind shot her a look and shushed her.

"What do you say?" Rosalind asked.

"I don't know what you're asking me," Ansel said. "You want me to sit here and do whatever I want until the Scientist finds me useful?"

Rosalind nodded.

"I don't know if I can," Ansel said, tapping her foot.

"But—" Pidgeon called out, tipping over the table he was

hiding under and knocking a few flasks to the floor—which Popeye came out of nowhere to clean up.

"And you, too, boy," Rosalind said. "I didn't forget you were there."

Pidgeon came around to stand next to Ansel, blushing. "You mean it?" he asked, playing with the hem of his shirt.

"Of course I do," Rosalind said. "We wouldn't send you back to that orphanage. We know what's going on there."

Pidgeon nudged Ansel. "C'mon," he said. "Why not?"

"I don't know," she said. "I need time to think about it."

"Take all the time you need," Rosalind said. "Staying here to think and saying yes to my proposal are the same thing."

"*Uh, yeah*. Okay," Ansel said, grabbing Pidgeon's arm and dragging him with her. "We're gonna go discuss this. We'll talk to you tomorrow or something." She waved as she closed the hall door behind her.

"What are you doing?" Pidgeon asked, breaking away from her grip.

"Just follow me," Ansel said. "Bedroom." She opened the door to the room she and Pidgeon had been sleeping in. It was bigger than any of the houses she had ever lived in, and had two beds on opposite walls, each with their own dresser and mirror combo. Ansel went to her dresser, thinking to change her clothes, then changed her mind. The jeans and t-shirt she was already wearing were comfortable and non-restricting, exactly what she needed. She did grab her floral dress, though, the one her parents had given her when they still lived on the Green Belt, and she bundled it up in a ball to stuff in her rucksack—which still contained most of the rest of her belongings. She checked her back pocket but the protectors had taken her slingshot. They did leave her bracelet, though. She thought about dumping it but was distracted when Pidgeon asked, "What are you doing?"

Ansel looked at him. "Pidgeon," she said, "do you trust me?"

"I—uh—yeah," he said. "*I guess*. But why?"

"I don't want to stay here anymore," she said. "I don't know why, but I feel restricted here, trapped."

"But we can go anywhere with the elevators," he said.

"Not really," Ansel said. "We can go anywhere the Scientist lets us go. That's not everywhere, though. Is it?"

Pidgeon shook his head. "Well, no, but..." He played with the hem of his shirt.

"Don't you want to see the worlds, Pidgeon?" Ansel asked. "There's so much out there beyond everything we've ever known."

"I don't know," Pidgeon said. "I've seen a lot of what the world has to offer."

"But you haven't seen everything," she pled with him. She could feel that she was losing him. "I went to another world entirely, Pidgeon, the one where the protectors come from. I met these kids who lived there, and they were no different from you or me. How am I supposed to fight against them, huh? They don't know what they're doing. They have no more control over their lives than we do. And they tried to help me."

"Yeah. *So?*" Pidgeon said. "That doesn't mean we should leave. We can stay here without fighting those kids."

"But don't you see?" Ansel said. "All the protectors were those kids at some point in their lives. They were funneled into it, and now, they can't do anything else but what they're told."

"Then we won't fight *any* protectors," Pidgeon said. "I still don't want to leave."

"Do you really think they'll let you stay here and do nothing for their cause?"

"*I do,*" Pidgeon snapped. "That was the deal, wasn't it?"

"The deal was for them to get my dad back, too," Ansel said. "But we can see how that turned out."

"No, but—"

"*No,* Pidgeon," she stopped him. "I'm sorry. I know I dragged you into this in the first place, but I have to live by my standards. I have to be self-sufficient. I know you don't understand that, which is why I'm not making you come with me."

Pidgeon looked hurt. He avoided eye contact with her.

"Pidgeon," Ansel said. "I'd rather you came than that you stayed here, but I'm leaving tonight. What time is it? I'm leaving now. I'm gonna get as far away from here as I can before they notice I'm gone, and to do that, I have to be quick. So you don't have time to think about this. It's now or never."

"But they've taken such good care of us," Pidgeon said, groaning. "We can eat all the food we want, and we each get our own bed. What more could we ask for?"

"*Independence*," Ansel said. "I told you I knew you wouldn't understand."

"*I don't*," Pidgeon said, shaking his head. "And neither do you. You don't understand what it's like to have nothing and no one, Ansel. We have a good thing here."

"I've had nothing all my life," Ansel said. "Don't tell me I don't know what it's like."

"Right," Pidgeon said. "*Nothing*. Except for a mom and dad to provide food and shelter for you. Now *that* is nothing."

"I had to provide my own food most nights," Ansel said.

"And yet still you knew that they'd always be there to give up their food if you couldn't find anything. You knew that they'd always have a warm bed waiting for you afterwards. You never had nothing, Ansel. You always had them."

"Not anymore," Ansel said. She could feel the tears coming back. "*Now* I have nothing."

"But you still don't," Pidgeon said. "You have me. And if you would stay here, you'll have Haley and Rosalind and the Scientist and this bed to sleep in." He jumped up onto her bed, bouncing up and down. "We have everything we need here."

"*No*," Ansel said. "We don't. I told you, Pidgeon. I need my independence. That's that. You don't have to come with me if you don't want to." She grabbed her rucksack and made for the door, but Pidgeon jumped off the bed to stop her.

"Where do you even plan on going?" he asked.

"I don't know." Ansel shrugged. "*Away*. Anywhere I want to. I'll never see the end of the Belt so maybe I'll go try to see the end of the wilderness here instead. You did want to do that with me once. Remember?"

He looked away from her, blushing. "Yeah, I wouldn't make it out there, though," he said. "I've said it before, and I'll say it again: I'd probably just get you killed."

"And as I've said before, I'll teach you everything I know," Ansel said. "I know what I'm doing out there, Pidgeon. And you can, too."

"But do you really?" he asked. "It's not the Belt out there, Ansel. This is something you've never experienced before."

"Yeah it's not the Belt," Ansel said. "There are more animals here and they're less afraid of humans. They'll be easier to catch because of it. If anything, this should be easier than living on the Belt. And we won't have to worry about protectors out there."

"We don't have to worry about them in here, either," he said. "And what if there's something out there that's worse than a protector?"

"*Psssh*. Worse than a protector?" Ansel laughed. "I doubt that."

"What about that big animal with the horns that you couldn't kill?"

"That thing runs away every time it hears us. And it only ever eats grass."

"What if there's something else that won't run?" Pidgeon said. "Something that taught that thing to run? *God*. You just don't get it. There are some things out there that you don't know about, Ansel. You know what. *Whatever*. Go." He went and sat on his own bed, with his back to her, in a huff.

"I will, Pidgeon," Ansel snapped. "You just stay here in your cozy, safe jail. I always knew you would leave me behind in the end." She slammed the door behind her before he could respond.

She took a few deep breaths in the hall, bracing herself on the door jamb. Stupid Pidgeon. She should never have trusted him to begin with. He was, and had always been, a fresh faced flower from the Garden of Eden. No wonder he was too scared to leave this...*whatever it was*. She had enough trouble convincing him to leave the orphanage he said had treated him so poorly, there was no way she was going to convince him to leave a place where he had printer access whenever he wanted it and no one to abuse him or call him names. One day that would all run out, though. Then he'd wish he'd come and learned how to be self-sufficient with her. She chuckled to herself at the thought of it.

"Kitchen," she said and opened the door. The step-stool was already in front of the printer. She stepped up, trying not to stare at the line of slip, snap, clickers through the sink window, and pressed the button to say, "Slingshot." First thing was first. She had to be able to hunt.

The slingshot that came out was made of metal where her old one was made of wood. The sling was tighter, too, harder to pull back, but she could get used to that. She would have to or die trying. She stuffed it in her back pocket, ordered a pouch to keep rocks in, a few cans of beans—it came out in bowls at first, before she specified cans—and some string to help make traps. She brought it all down to the table and packed her rucksack full, then she stared at the printer, trying to think of anything else that might be useful.

The kitchen door opened and in came Rosalind. She took a look at the full rucksack then said, "Planning on going somewhere?"

Ansel shrugged. "What's it matter to you?"

"I was being sincere when I spoke earlier," Rosalind said. "I meant every word."

"I know how much your words mean," Ansel said.

Rosalind looked offended. "I haven't lied to you once," she said.

"You didn't get my dad back."

"I did," Rosalind said. "You talked to him. He was free."

"But not anymore."

"Maybe now more than ever, dear." She shook her head.

"*Pffft.*" Ansel scoffed. "Well I plan on freeing myself." She picked up the rucksack and threw it over her shoulder.

"So you'll be joining our cause then?" Rosalind smiled.

"Does it look like I will?" Ansel asked, hefting the bag further up on her shoulders to emphasize the sarcasm.

"It looks like you're going camping," Rosalind said.

"Camping?" What was she talking about now?

"Yes, camping," Rosalind said, crossing to the printer. "You know: sleeping outdoors in the wilderness, under the stars, among the other animals."

"Uh, yeah. *Sure.*" Ansel shrugged. "You can call it that if you want to."

"Well, dear," Rosalind said. "Let me give you some supplies before you go, then." She pressed the printer's voice activation button and said, "Pop-up tent, lighter, and Swiss Army knife, please."

"What are those?" Ansel asked, dropping the heavy sack.

"Well, this is a lighter. You just—"

"Yeah, yeah. I know that one," Ansel said, snatching it out of Rosalind's hand.

"And this is a pop-up tent." Rosalind handed her a small rectangular something that fit in the palm of her hand. "Don't press the button until you're outside, and be ready to get out of the way when you do. You got that?"

"What is it?" Ansel asked, turning the thing over in her hand.

Rosalind flinched and took it away, ordering a case to put the *tent* in before handing it back. "It's for you to sleep in."

"Sleep in that?"

"It gets bigger," Rosalind said. "Trust me."

"Okay, what about the Swiss knife or whatever?" Ansel asked.

"This is your general all-purpose tool," Rosalind said, pulling out all the little gadgets. "You have here your can opener, knife, compass—"

"Right right," Ansel took it and had some trouble folding everything back into place. Rosalind chuckled and helped her, and it only made Ansel angrier. She stuffed her gifts into the rucksack, forcing a smile, and said, "Well, *thanks*. See you never."

"Be safe," Rosalind said. "We'll be eagerly awaiting your return."

"*Ugh.*" Ansel stomped out of the room, slamming the door behind her. She didn't stop until she was in the elevator, waiting for the floor to fall out from underneath her.

It was as if Rosalind didn't listen. Or she did listen and didn't care what Ansel said. Ansel would show her. If Rosalind thought Ansel was going to be going back to that little jail anytime soon, she had another thing coming. Ansel was never going back there ever again, and Rosalind and Pidgeon would just have to deal with it.

The elevator doors opened to reveal the pine trees and other evergreens whose names Ansel had not yet come to know. She stepped out onto the grass and took a deep breath of the fresh cool air. This was right for her. This was exactly what she needed. No more Scientist. No more protectors. No more Pidgeon or Rosalind. She was free to do whatever she wanted, and right now, she wanted some food. So she set off to get exactly that.

ᔕ   ✳   ∅

XL. Jonah

"What? Where am I?" Jonah demanded.

"You're in my lab," the woman in the white coat said.

"And who are you?"

"The Scientist. As I said. That's my name."

"That's not a name," Jonah said.

"It is." The woman smiled. "It's my name. Now, do you want to argue about what constitutes a name, or do you want to get down to why you're actually here?"

"Where am I?" Jonah asked again, looking around at the short hall.

"Come with me," the woman said, crossing it to open a door at the other end and show him through.

They went into a big office with a desk, puffy chairs, and a view of a green, hilly wilderness, similar to the view in the Captain's office but with less snow and smaller mountains.

"Please. Sit," the Scientist said, indicating one of the puffy chairs.

Jonah hopped up into it as she took the seat across from him. "I still don't know where this is," he said.

"This is my home." She looked around. "Or, it's one office in my extensive house. This, dear, is Outland Four. Do you know what that is?"

Jonah scoffed. He didn't need to be patronized. "Of course I do," he said. "I'm not a housekeeper."

"Well, that's where you are," she said. "*Technically*."

"And why?" Jonah asked.

"That's what I wanted to ask you, dear," the Scientist said. "Why are you here?"

"*I don't know*," Jonah complained. "I don't know how I got here. I don't even know where here is, other than Outland Four which doesn't narrow it down much. So how am I supposed to know why I'm here? You tell me."

"You're here because you want something." The woman

smiled.

"Who doesn't?"

"What is it that you want, Jonah?"

He paused to think about it. "I want to save Ansel," he decided.

"We've taken care of that already," she said.

"*Sure*," Jonah said, nodding and giving a sarcastic thumbs up. "Then get rid of Liz's demerits."

The Scientist chuckled. "Sadly, your schooling is one of the few areas I don't have control over," she said. "I wouldn't know where to start."

"Then you can't get me anything," Jonah said. "So why am I here?"

"There's nothing else you want?" the Scientist asked. "No one else you could ask a favor for?" She eyed him.

"Why do you care?" Jonah asked. "What are you doing this for anyway?"

"You tried to help Ansel," she said. "You ended up putting her in danger, but that was her choice, not yours. Ansel is a part of my family now, and if you help her, you help me. I want to help you in return."

Jonah scoffed. "Yeah, right," he said. "What can you do anyway? You already said you can't give me what I want."

"I told you we're already saving Ansel," she said. "We're already giving you what you want without your asking for it. I'm giving you another opportunity to ask for something that we're not doing for you already."

"My dad, then," Jonah said, not thinking. "He needs to get out of the house. Make him a protector again."

She shook her head. "Are you sure you want to bring that down upon him?"

"You say it like it's a bad thing." Jonah scoffed.

"Maybe it is for your father," the Scientist said. "Have you asked him if he would want to go back?"

Jonah chuckled. "Of course he would. Everyone in One dreams of being a protector, and he had that dream taken away from him before he ever got to experience it. He would do anything to get it back."

"And he told you this directly?" She raised an eyebrow.

"I—well—no… But it's common knowledge," Jonah said, shrugging.

"You've never met anyone who wants to be a housekeeper?" the Scientist asked.

"What? *No.*" Jonah laughed. "Housekeeping is for the weak and cowardly. No one wants to be weak and cowardly."

"You know," the Scientist said, tapping her fingers on the arm of her chair. "One of the most relaxing things to do—I've found—is to cook a nice meal for yourself. Have you ever tried it?"

"Cooking a meal?" Jonah frowned. "Why? That's why we have printers."

"True," the Scientist said, nodding. "I guess you're right about that. Though I still think you should try cooking some time."

"Maybe when I'm old and retired," Jonah said.

"Maybe." The Scientist shrugged. "If you live long enough to retire. The way things are going in the worlds now it looks like a lot less of you protectors are going to be reaching the age of natural death. And you're sure you want to send your dad back into that?"

"He wants it," Jonah said. "I *guarantee.*"

"Did you know that there are riots breaking out across all the worlds?" the Scientist asked. "The job of a protector is becoming more and more dangerous every day. You'll risk losing him if you send him back out there."

Jonah shrugged. "A protector's job is always dangerous," he said. "And the more dangerous it is the more likely the protector is to go down in history."

"History has a good way of forgetting things." The Scientist shook her head.

"Listen lady," Jonah said, standing from his chair. "He can handle it. He's my dad, and he's meant to be a protector. So are you going to do it or not?"

"Frankly," the Scientist shrugged, "this is another one where it doesn't really matter what I do. I told you, dear: *riots across the worlds.* There'll be a draft soon, and I wouldn't doubt that your dad is at the top of the list. You'll get what you say you want with or without me."

"So again, you can't help me," Jonah said, crossing his arms. "I still don't understand why you brought me here."

"Only to say thank you, apparently," the Scientist said,

standing. "You tried to help our Ansel, and we appreciate that. So: Thank you." She held out a hand.

Jonah looked at it. "Uh... Okay I guess," he said, shaking it. "So can I go now?"

"Are you sure there's nothing else you want?" she asked.

Jonah shook his head.

"Then let me give you a little bit of unsolicited advice," she said, walking close to him and patting his back as she led him out into the hall. "Being a protector's not the only way to make a name for yourself, and being a housekeeper is nothing to laugh at. So maybe think about cooking yourself a meal once or twice. Just try it. But even if you don't, I'll be watching you, and I'll be there when you inevitably need my help in the future. You got it?"

"Yeah, sure." Jonah shrugged. "Can I go now?"

"Of course, dear." The Scientist smiled. She opened the elevator doors. "I'll be there for you like you were for our Ansel," she said. "You will be repaid."

Jonah nodded and stepped into the elevator. "*Whatever.*"

"And stay out of trouble until then," the Scientist said as the elevator doors closed between them.

When the elevator stopped and the doors opened, Jonah sprinted to his house then snuck into his room, hoping his dad wouldn't hear. He took off his shoes and jumped into bed fully clothed. Tomorrow was going to be a shit day at school, but maybe he would take off sick. All his muscles ached, and his eyelids grew heavy. He hadn't realized how tired he was until he was lying in bed. He couldn't help but to drift off into a deep, restful sleep.

& ✄ ℘

Reveille went off, dragging Jonah into wakefulness. He laid in bed until after the Protector's Alma Mater played, and he had to choose between not showering, not eating, or being late for class. It'd prolly end up being all three after yesterday.

What was he thinking? And who was that white-coated woman at the end of the night? She had said she'd be there to help him in the future, but why? She didn't even know him. She did know Ansel, though. Hopefully she was able to save Ansel like she had promised.

"*Joonaaaah!*" his dad called from the other room. "It's time to wake up, son. Do you need me to call in an excuse for absence?"

Jonah scoffed. "*Do you need me to call in an excuse for absence,*" he mimicked in a mocking tone, doing a little dance in his bed. He got up and started to dress, unable to stop blaming his dad for most—if not all—of what had happened to him and his partner in the past few days. White jeans and white t-shirt on, he took a deep breath before opening his bedroom and heading into the kitchen where his dad had every breakfast food imaginable piled on the table.

"Are you sure you're feeling up to it?" his dad asked, guiding Jonah to sit at the table and pouring some milk for him. "It's completely understandable if you need a day off after what you went through."

"No." Jonah shook his head. "I promised Liz I'd be in class."

His dad nodded thoughtfully, taking a bite of bacon. "*Of course,*" he said, still nodding. "You've gotta be there for your partner. Of course you do. I understand."

Jonah took a few quick bites of toast then stood from the table. "Well, I should get going," he said. "Already late."

"You didn't even eat," his dad said. "You need energy for class."

"I'm fine," Jonah said. "I'll eat a big lunch." He started to leave.

"Wait!" his dad said. "Son... I'm sorry about how I acted last night, about yelling at you in front of your partner and ordering you to stay away from Ansel."

Jonah shrugged. "*Whatever,*" he said.

"No," his dad said, shaking his head. "Not whatever. I shouldn't have reacted that way. I'm sorry."

"So you think there is something I can do to help her?" Jonah asked, perking up for just a second.

"No." His dad shook his head, deflating Jonah's hopes. "I'm not saying that either. I stand by what I said, and I do think keeping your head down and following orders is the best thing you can do for yourself—and for Liz—but I shouldn't have said it the way I did."

"But you did exactly the opposite of that when you were a protector," Jonah snapped. "You're such a hypocrite!"

"I know," his dad said, shaking his head. "I did. That's why I know it's not the right path for you to take. From experience. I don't want you to make the same mistakes I did. You'll throw your—"

"Don't worry, dad," Jonah said. "I won't shoot any owners." He stomped out of the house and slammed the door behind him.

Ugh. That pissed Jonah off so much, his dad's holier than thou, do as I say not as I do bullshit. And how was Jonah supposed to do what his dad ordered when his dad ordered something contradictory every time he spoke? Nope. His dad didn't get a say in what Jonah did anymore. He had already said everything and nothing, and all he did was confuse things more. Jonah would have to try to forget everything his dad had taught him if he wanted to make any kind of sense out of the worlds.

His whole body was sore, and his head pounded as he walked. Maybe he should have taken the opportunity to have a day off, but then he would have had to spend it with his hypocrite father. Which one would be worse? It didn't matter now, he was well on his way to school, past the point of no return.

The bell sounded as he entered the Academy doors. He sprinted to his classroom, and Ms. Bohr had already started teaching. "That's two this month, Pardy," she said as he snuck in, his head down. "One more and it's a demerit for you. Now. Take your seat, please."

Jonah sat at his desk near the center of the room, and Ms. Bohr went on lecturing about the various criminal codes and their applications. Jonah tried to get the attention of Liz who sat next to him, but she kept her eyes firmly locked on the teacher, diligently taking notes. Jonah knew it was just an act, though. Liz had memorized all the basic codes before they ever joined the Academy. She didn't have to write any of this down. He also knew why she was putting the act on and stopped trying to get her in trouble again, choosing instead to focus all his attention on not nodding off while Ms. Bohr droned on and on. He didn't get a chance to talk to Liz until lunch when they were sitting alone in the corner of the mess hall, eating their "nutritionally balanced" fish sticks and tater tots.

"You will never believe what happened to me," Jonah said, popping a tot in his mouth.

"After what we did last night, I think I'll believe anything," Liz said.

"Yeah, well." Jonah laughed. "Not this."

"Well tell me then," she said, kicking his shin under the table.

"*Ow!*" Jonah yelped. "Maybe I won't if you're gonna act like that."

"Yeah right, *partner*," she said, biting a fish stick in half. "As if you're one to talk about manners after getting me *six* demerits."

"*Whatever.*" Jonah frowned. "What was I talking about anyway?"

"I don't know." She shrugged. "You said I wouldn't believe it."

"Oh yeah. Of course. *Duh*. Well, last night you know, after I left you, I went on that walk, right."

Liz nodded.

"Well, I was lost in thought, strolling around, when I looked up, and I was in a hall all of sudden—like, not outside."

Liz chuckled. "What?"

"See. I told you you wouldn't believe me."

"It's not that I don't believe you," Liz said, shaking her head. "It's that I don't understand what you're saying."

"Yeah, well, me neither, really," Jonah said. "But there was a woman there who was dressed in a white coat, right. And she started asking me if I wanted anything, okay—and I mean *anything*—like she was going to give me whatever I asked her for or something."

"*Tuh.*" Liz spat out a little food with her laughter. "What, like a genie or something?"

"I don't know." Jonah shrugged. "She called herself the Scientist for some reason. Like it was her name. It was really weird."

"The Scientist?" Liz thought about it for a second. "What did you ask for?"

"Oh, well…" Jonah shrugged.

"C'mon," Liz said. "You can tell me."

"Well, first I asked her to save Ansel, you know," Jonah said, blushing.

Liz nodded. "And what did this *scientist* say to that?"

"She said she was already gonna save her then asked me if I wanted anything else."

"Of course," Liz said, nodding. "That's probably why she wanted to help you in the first place. She must be connected to Ansel somehow. All this nonsense has been. Why else would she care to give you anything anyway? Ansel or your dad."

Jonah shrugged. "It still doesn't make sense to me," he said.

"Well, what did you ask for after that?"

Jonah blushed again. "To get rid of your demerits."

"You didn't have to do that," Liz said, blushing and talking more to her fish sticks than to Jonah.

"Yeah, well," Jonah said, shrugging. "It doesn't matter anyway. She said she couldn't do it."

"*Of course.*" Liz sighed. "At least you tried, though," she added, forcing a smile. "And we found something she can't give you, so she's no genie."

"*No,*" Jonah said, shaking his head. "She's not that." But he still didn't know what she was.

"Well," Liz said. "Did you ask for anything else?"

"Yeah. For my dad to be a protector again."

"*You didn't,*" she said.

"I did."

"Did you ask your dad if he wanted to be one again?"

"*No.*" Jonah scoffed. "Of course I didn't. Why wouldn't he?"

Liz shrugged, shaking her head. "You never know."

"It didn't matter, anyway, because she said he would already be—"

The bell rang. The mess hall was already empty around them. Liz looked around, wide eyed, like she hadn't noticed it either. They both jumped up and threw away their trays, running to sit in their seats just as Ms. Bohr went on lecturing again. Jonah wanted to beat his head on the desk by the time the bell for the end of the class rang.

In the locker room he managed to keep away from Stine and get changed and out to the dark standoff entry chamber without one insult being hurled at him.

"*Pssst.*" Liz came up from behind and elbowed him in his padded rib. "What were you saying at lunch?" she asked.

"About what?" Jonah said, trying to focus on his strategy for the standoff but losing his train of thought.

"About your dad becoming a protector again," she said. "You said the scientist said she wouldn't have to do anything. What did you mean by that?"

"Oh, yeah," he said. "She said there were—"

The opening bell rang, and the huge metal hangar doors in

front of them creaked open to reveal the alley where they would fight the standoff. A flurry of movement went on around Jonah as his teammates—Liz included—raced to dive behind dumpsters or into alleyways. He didn't have time to think. His legs took him zig zagging back and forth from dumpster to dumpster, advancing quickly. He yelled at the top of his lungs and blindly fired shot after shot as he ran. He could feel bullet after bullet whizzing past him, but none landed until he was halfway up the alley. Then his entire visor was covered in red. He fell to his knees and rolled over on his side, thankful for the rest.

The standoff didn't last long after that. Not long enough to get any real rest. Soon he heard the cheering of the winning team, but he didn't bother to get up and see that he had lost. He was sure he did. His crazy, dumb full frontal attack wasn't really regulation strategy, and there was no way he hadn't thrown the game for his team again. He couldn't wait to hear what Stine and her lackeys had to say about it in the locker room later.

He felt a tug on his arm, and someone pulled him up. No, it was two someones. Another someone took off his helmet for him, and the entire blue team was gathered around him, cheering. They had won! Everyone took their chance to pat him on the back and congratulate him before filing back to the locker room to shower and get dressed. Even Stine gave him a terse, "Good hunting." if not a pat on the back.

When everyone else had gone back into the locker room, Liz walked up and smiled, nodding, to say, "Good job, partner."

Jonah scoffed. "I didn't know what I was doing," he said.

She shrugged. "It worked out though, didn't it?"

"Yeah, well, it's not something I would recommend," he said. "Did I even get a hit?"

Liz laughed. "*Yeah*," she said, shaking her head. "Like half their team. Now come on. Let's get changed so you can finish telling me about this scientist."

Jonah showered and changed, and Stine and her lackeys stared, mad that it was him who had made it happen but relieved to finally have the blue team's losing streak broken. They looked so confused, as if they had no idea whether to hit Jonah in the face or shake his hand. He dressed fast and got out of there so they wouldn't have a chance to decide on the former. Liz took a little longer to get dressed, but thankfully, she was done before Stine and them, and they were out and walking home without a locker room incident to speak of.

"I can't believe you did that," Liz said as they strolled along the grass-lined sidewalk at a leisurely pace.

"What are we talking about now?" Jonah asked. His mind was jumbled and confused with the lecture, his victory at the standoff, and everything else that had happened in the previous day running into one lumpy mess.

"The standoff this time," Liz said. "You were a crazed maniac out there."

"Honestly," Jonah said, "I think I might be going crazy."

"No." She patted his arm. "Don't say that. The worlds have gone crazy. There's no sane way for a person to react to that."

Jonah shrugged and walked on without responding. No one else was reacting the way he was. If it was really the world that was crazy and not him, then why did no one else seem to notice?

"Now tell me," Liz went on, "what did this scientist say about your dad? He's going to be a protector again?"

"Uh, yeah, well—that's what she said. She said there were riots breaking out across the worlds."

"My dad told me about that," Liz said. She looked at her feet. "They're keeping Mom busy out there."

"Yeah, well," Jonah said. "I don't know what that has to do with my dad being a protector again."

"You don't?" Liz said, looking at him like he was stupid. "Ms. Bohr talked about it all day in class."

Jonah scoffed. "I was a little distracted," he said.

"Well, they're probably planning a draft," Liz said. "It's been done before, when things got out of hand and a surge of protectors was needed."

"But my dad's not a housekeeper by choice," Jonah said. "He was dishonorably discharged. They wouldn't want him back after that, would they?"

Liz shrugged. "It depends on how many protectors are needed," she said. "I don't know. Ms. Bohr didn't go into that much detail."

"Well, that Scientist seemed to be pretty sure about it," Jonah said. "I wonder how she knows."

They walked on in silence, trying to work it out in their heads. When they had gotten to the point where their paths home diverged, Liz stopped and said, "Welp, I gotta go. See you tomorrow? *It'll be Friday!*" She put on a fake smile and did a sarcastic dance.

"You don't want to come and hang out?" Jonah asked hopefully.

Liz scoffed. "Of course I do," she said. "But I can't. My dad heard about my demerits so I'm on lockdown for a while. I'll probably have to do housework all weekend. *Blarg.*"

Jonah winced. "Ouch," he said. "*Sorry.* Well, I'll see you tomorrow, I guess."

"Don't go getting kidnapped by any more mad scientists," she said with a chuckle and a wave as she left.

Jonah made his way to his house, trying to make sense of something, anything—a task he was finding surprisingly difficult in recent memory. How would a scientist know if the protectors were going to hold a draft? How would *the Scientist* know everything she knew? She was probably wrong about his dad becoming a protector again, but she didn't want to admit to being unable to get what Jonah wanted for him for the third time in a row. She probably couldn't even save Ansel, either. He would have to keep searching for his own way to do that.

His dad was in the kitchen, piling snack foods on a tray, when he got home. "I made some food," he said, carrying it into the living room where Jonah had plopped onto the couch without even turning on the TV. "Your partner isn't joining us today?"

Jonah shook his head. "She's on disciplinary detail."

"Ah. Of course." His dad sat down on the couch next to him. "Her parents weren't as understanding as I was, I imagine."

"You know, sometimes I wish you weren't," Jonah said. "Maybe that would be a little less confusing."

"Do you want me to punish you?" his dad asked with a smirk. "I have some floors that could use scrubbing. And there are always the toilets."

"What?" Jonah cringed. "No! You know that's not what I mean."

"What then?" His dad chuckled. "You wanna give me some laps or pushups? I can do that, too. Drop and give me twenty!"

"No, Dad." Jonah sighed. "You're not funny so stop trying, okay. I mean that I wish you would give me just one order without contradicting yourself. I'm just a kid, you know. I need you to tell me what to do in life."

His dad chuckled. "And if I had ordered you to stay away from Ansel, would that have prevented you from trying to protect her?" he asked.

"No." Jonah shook his head.

"And if I had ordered you to protect her, would I not have contradicted my previous orders?"

"Well, yeah," Jonah said. "You'd be ordering me to break the law."

"So either way, you would have wanted me to do something else." His dad smiled.

"No—but— You could have—"

"Punished you?" his dad asked again. "Who's contradicting themself now?"

Jonah sighed in frustration. His dad seemed to get more and more difficult every day.

"Jonah, you have to understand that life isn't black and white, okay. Most of the time we're bound by our actions in the past, by the traditions of all the dead generations even, to be able to act in one way and one way alone. Now for both of us that way just so happened to be protecting Ansel however we thought we could. And for both of us that was a terrible decision. But not doing it was equally impossible. So why am I giving you impossible orders? you ask me. Well, how can I give you any orders that aren't impossible? I ask in response."

Jonah shook his head. "You're making less sense all the time," he said.

"The world doesn't make sense, son," his dad said. "I don't know how to make sense of it. I'm just telling you what I think I know. It could all be wrong. Everything I know has already been shown to be wrong once, so why not this, too? Huh?"

"But you're supposed to be an adult, Dad. You're supposed to be my dad. How can you not have this figured out already?"

"None of us do, son," his dad said. "Me, your mom, your teachers, anyone you've ever met. The surer they are that they do have it all figured out, the more likely they are to be wrong. That's what I've been trying to tell you, but I didn't know how to say it."

Jonah laughed. He wanted to cry, too, but he laughed instead. This couldn't be true. It had to be some cruel joke. If it was true, then half the superior officers who gave him orders every day knew less about the world than he did. Maybe more than half. "No," he said. "Just because you don't understand the world doesn't mean that no one does."

"Who could? How could you? It's impossible. We get bits and pieces at best, and that's it. Some of us might get more bits and pieces than others, but who's to say whose version is better?"

Jonah groaned. "I don't know, Dad," he said. "I'm just a—"

The TV flipped on, playing the Protector's Alma Mater. Jonah and his dad jumped in their seats then stared at the screen wide eyed. The burly, pock-marked face of the Chief Commissioner came on screen.

"Citizens of Outland One," he said, his tone all business. "It is my duty to notify you that emergency staffing procedures have been activated. All academy attendants will have their training accelerated, and new recruits will be drafted from the existing housekeeper pool on a lottery basis. We've grown fat and lazy, people. More than a decade of peace has domesticated us. Now we must return to our wild roots. Any housekeepers with less than three dependents will be eligible for the lottery. If need arises, that pool will be expanded, but I trust we can handle the situation as is. A list of randomly selected identification numbers will be read and repeated twice after my broadcast. If your ID is called, you will be expected at your nearest recruiting station at oh six hundred hours tomorrow. Good luck out there, citizens. And may the protectors' creed always ring true: *Property, liberty, life*."

The Chief's face disappeared, and the protector logo came up on the screen: two crossed guns held by a bald eagle. A mechanical sounding voice read out a list of what must have been hundreds of nine digit strings of numbers. Jonah and his dad sat staring at the emblem in silence, his dad waiting to hear if his ID was called, and Jonah not listening at all. Jonah didn't know his dad's ID. All he knew was that the Scientist was right, his dad was probably about to be on the force again. His dad moved a little at one point, and Jonah thought that he was reacting to hearing his number, but his dad didn't react further until the voice had read through the entire list for the third time. It didn't seem like his dad even noticed when the voice stopped and the TV flicked off. He just sat staring at the black mirror of the TV screen in silence.

"So?" Jonah asked.

His dad shook his head.

Jonah choked back tears. He didn't know why he was so sad. This is what he wanted for his dad. It was what he thought his dad would want. So why was he crying all of a sudden?

"I don't want you to go, dad," he said, hugging him.

"I'm sorry." His dad shook his head, brushing Jonah's hair out of his face with trembling fingers and watery eyes. "I'm sorry for everything."

⁚   ✦   §

XLI. Guy

FADE IN:

INT. WALTRONICS ANDROID FACTORY SLIP, SNAP, CLICKING ROOM — DAY

ASSEMBLY WORKER works at an assembly line in a dimly lit, dirty factory. As she slip, snap, clicks, ANDROID THIEF bursts through the doors to pull Assembly Worker from her work.

> ASSEMBLY WORKER
> Get your robot hands off me.

> ANDROID THIEF
> I don't care.

> ASSEMBLY WORKER
> This is *my* job. *You* can't do *this*!

> ANDROID THIEF
> I am a robot. I don't care.

> ASSEMBLY WORKER
> But how will my human children eat? Can you feel *no* emotions?

> ANDROID THIEF
> I am a robot. I don't care.

Android Thief grabs Assembly Worker and lifts her onto the conveyor belt.

ASSEMBLY WORKER
(struggling to get away while
Android Thief ties her up)
No! Unhand me you—you—
*robo*t, you!

ANDROID THIEF
(setting Assembly Worker on
the conveyor belt)
I don't care.

Assembly Worker struggles against the ropes and eventually gives up, allowing the conveyor belt to carry her through several more rooms in which more pieces get added to the slip, snap, clicked pieces by large robotic arms, finally carrying her to:

INT. WALTRONICS ANDROID FACTORY FINISHED PRODUCTS PACKAGING — DAY

Assembly worker falls off the end of the conveyor belt into a pile of bodies. She screams, thinking they're dead humans, before realizing they're actually androids. She screams again at the realization.

ASSEMBLY WORKER
(crying and screaming)
No! We were—We were
building them! No! How could
they do this!?!!

Ugh. Guy crumpled up the page he was working on and tossed it at his trash can. That was worthless shit. He remembered what he was doing and that he probably couldn't throw out an entire page—if so, he would have started over from scratch already—then went to pick the crumpled ball up and try to flatten it out again on his desk.

Why did the android only know two sentences? He understood that the piece was supposed to be anti-android, or whatever, but that was just lazy. If the thing could take a human's job, then it could learn more than two sentences. And that was only one of myriad plot holes he was supposed to deal with by the next day.

He sat up further in his chair and rubbed his back where it had started cramping up from sitting for so long. How long had he been at it? He checked the clock. *Ugh.* Well past midnight and still he had so much work left to do. His back ached more at the thought of it. The first thing he was adding to his wish list was a nice comfortable desk chair.

He searched through the pile of mess on his desk to find an empty scrap of paper he could write that down on: Wish list: 1. Chair (comfortable) 2. Notebooks (a lot) 3. Pens (ditto). He picked up the note and looked at it, trying to think of anything else he needed.

Ugh. He threw the note over his shoulder. He was just procrastinating, putting off this stupid editing that he didn't want to do, but he *had* to do it, and the longer he put it off, the later he would have to stay up because of it. At least he didn't have to worry about work tomorrow.

He started to cry at the thought of it. He didn't have work because the star of the production he had been working on had died. Russ Logo had died. With Guy's being arrested then getting this stupid assignment right after being released, he hadn't had time to think about Russ's death. But now he did. And he couldn't stop his sobbing. He lost himself in the grief for too long before shaking himself out of it and getting back to work.

He looked at the page in front of him. It was still wrinkly, and it was covered in red ink already. He hadn't even typed up any of his edits, and that was always the worst part. He flipped through to count how many pages he had left. *Seven.* That wasn't too bad. Less than a third of it. It wasn't long so there was that.

He got up to get himself a bottled coffee out of the fridge then sat back down and put his desk in order. He picked up his red pen and started the massacre. By the end of it there wasn't a word of dialogue that he hadn't changed—and most of the scene directions, too—but even though he didn't agree with a bit of it, he thought he held true to the theme of the story nonetheless. He kept its underlying message, that androids—and technology in general— were oppressing working class humans and must be destroyed at all costs, and he even left the *buy human-made only* tangent, blending it seamlessly into the overall narrative instead of clumsily making an aside to it as the original script had done, subtlety being something that whoever had written the original manuscript obviously had no understanding of.

When he was done editing, he set to typing his corrections. He didn't have a digital copy of the script, so he would really be typing the entire thing over again. Just another sign that whoever they were working with had no clue about the best practices in scriptwriting—and probably moviemaking in general.

He opened up his ancient laptop—*two entire years old*—and sighed at the fact that it took more than a few seconds to turn on. Something this old was really only good enough for typing and playing music, but luckily, that was all he ever he did with it anyway. Still, he should probably add it as a fourth item to his wish list: a better computer to type on. He opened up his word processor and made sure the formatting was set to his liking before letting the classical music playlist he always worked to flow through him.

His typing was unconscious. He imagined his fingers on the keyboard were playing the beautiful piano melodies in his ears. He was Chopin. His words were Chopin's music. He could feel the notes flowing through his arms and out of his fingertips with each letter he added, each note passing through him into the computer screen, and despite the message, the melody was beautiful.

He was exhausted by the end of it, but satisfied. He could barely lift his arms or his eyelids. He tried to see the time, but there were too many clocks to count, all overlapping each other and obscuring each other's messages. He didn't even have the energy to stand up and plop himself on his bed, which was only a step away, instead letting his head roll, falling asleep right in his desk chair.

ଛ �֍ ⚘

The incessant buzz of Guy's doorbell drew him away from dreams of fame. He hit his knee on the desk and let out a loud "Fuck!", rolling and groaning in pain. It was not a good idea to sleep in his shitty desk chair, he knew that, but he kept doing it anyway. He had trouble standing and nearly tripped over the chair as it rolled out and hit the fridge behind him. "I'm coming," he called, then, "Answer, I mean." and, "I'm coming." again. "Or—I mean—*hello*. Who is it?"

"Guy?" the tinny voice came back. "It's Jen. I thought I'd come over early and make sure you're ready for the meeting. I know how late you like to work when you're on a deadline. Can I come up?"

Guy looked around his apartment. The bed wasn't made even though he hadn't slept in it. The kitchen counter was lined with empty jars of coffee that had been there for who knows how long. The bathroom was—well...*bad*. No. She could not come in and see that. "No," he said, remembering the intercom was still on. "*I mean. I'm ready now. Be down in a jiff.*"

He rescanned the script a few times before sending it out to everyone then went and ruffled his hair in the mirror and gave his teeth a quick brush before running down the stairs. He burst out of the front doors, huffing and puffing, then bent over to catch his breath.

"Are you okay?" Jen asked.

"I—*huff*—yeah," he huffed. "I...*great*."

"Are you wearing the same clothes as yesterday?" she asked, looking him up and down.

He looked down at himself and he was. He looked up at her and she was still wearing black but a different outfit from yesterday's. "I—uh... I worked late," he said, which was certainly true.

"Yeah?" Jen laughed. "You must have. Did you come up with something we can work with, though?"

Guy looked at his feet. "You know, not really," he said. "I still don't agree with the message. It's pretty much the opposite of the script I wrote. People are gonna think we're hypocrites if we do this."

Jen shook her head. "No," she said. "Like you said, no one is going to see this little film we make. No one will even know it exists. But because we did it first, our other project will be better. *Your* script, Guy."

Guy shook his head and shrugged. "I don't know," he said. "It's not right."

"But—" Jen protested.

"But I wouldn't let the crew down," he cut her off. "So, yes. I did come up with something we can work with."

Jen laughed and hugged him, kissing him on the cheek. "Oh,

Guy," she said. "I knew you would do it."

He blushed and stumbled, almost falling over his own feet. "Well, I couldn't let you down," he said. "Could I?"

"I'm sure you made it great," Jen said, taking his hand and leading him to the elevator. "I can't wait to read it."

The crew was all there and waiting when they got to Indywood. Everyone seemed to let out a sigh of relief when they saw Guy walk in. He didn't even have to ask them to move so he could sit down. A seat just seemed to open up before him, the masses parting at his approach.

"So," Cohen said when they were all comfortable again. He seemed to be trying to hold back his normal patronizing tone. He even attempted a smile. "Is this script something we can work with?"

Guy wasn't going to give it to Cohen that easily, though. "I still don't think we should do this," he said. "How many of you here have read the actual script?"

He looked around and they all avoided his gaze.

"No?" he said. "That's what I thought. Now, how many of you care what it says?"

He looked around again and they all reacted the same way.

"None of you?" he said. "As I expected again. Because none of you are writers. But I am. The writing is all I control. The theme is what I live for. And let me tell you, this theme...this is dangerous."

Cohen scoffed. The rest of the crowd muttered to themselves. "Dangerous?" Cohen asked. "Words are wind. How could they be dangerous?"

Guy shook his head. "Words are only wind until their written and recorded, heard and interpreted, then they turn into thought which leads to action, and that makes them stone. Words are creation, handed down to us from Fortuna above, and you discount your own craft if you discount their power."

"He's right," Laura said. "We're putting our names on this. That tells people we endorse the message."

"*Not necessarily*," Emir said. "It's just a job."

"And a well-paying one at that," Cohen reminded them. "Paying anything your heart could desire."

"*Yes*," Guy said, nodding. "The pay is unbelievable. Which is more of a reason to distrust the motives of whoever wrote this."

"Who cares who wrote it?" Cohen asked. "Did you make it

workable? That's all we want to know. We can't do any work until you're done."

The whole crew looked on at him expectantly, even Laura who he thought was on his side. He sighed. He had tried to convince them. That was all he could do. "*Yes*," he near whispered, giving up on his standards, all of them. "I made something that doesn't suck, even though it still goes against everything I believe in as a human being."

Cohen clapped his hands together with a big smile on his face. "Well then," he said. "Great. *Perfect*. And I assume you sent it out to everyone?"

Guy nodded.

"*Magnificent*. Does everyone have something with them that they can read on?" Cohen asked. "We need to get started right away, and a cold reading should be good to get our approval at the very least."

Everyone started taking out their phones and tablets, and Guy sat back in his chair, left to watch his Frankenstein creation come to life from the dead. Steve went to the bar to get a drink, but Laura had her phone out to read along, probably imagining shots she would need to make and the camera riggings required. She had to be one of the hardest working members of the entire crew, always involved in every bit of the action.

"Guy," Cohen said, "you know the script better than anyone. Who should be playing which part?"

Guy shrugged. "Well, there are really only two major parts," he said. "The protagonist is a female assembly line worker, and the antagonist is a male robot. Black and white. Yin and yang. Good and evil. Opposites. You get it. It's your typical, basic story line."

"Okay," Cohen said. "That's easy enough." He was searching through the script on his tablet. "What other characters do we have?"

"*Actually*," Guy said, "before I put my red pen to it, those were the only two characters in the entire script with lines. I added one or two more, but I couldn't change much because I thought your *investor* would want us to stay as close to the original as possible."

"Good instincts," Cohen said. "If I'm honest with you, the investor didn't really react well to the notion of editing at all."

Guy scoffed. "You don't have to tell me that," he said. "The script read like it hadn't been edited once."

"But now it has," Cohen said, clapping his hands and smiling. He was clearly happy to finally have something to do. As a director he didn't have much work to do on a project until shooting got started. "So," he went on. "I guess we'll put Emir in the role of our antagonist... *Adam Torrence*? Is that right?" He looked to Guy for reassurance.

Guy nodded.

Emir scoffed. "Torrence?" he said. "What kind of name is that?"

Cohen looked at Guy and cringed. "Yeah, you know," he said. "I'm not really feeling it, either. Was that in the original?"

Guy could feel himself getting defensive. Adrenaline, or something like it, boiled up into his throat from inside his stomach, and this wasn't even his work. It was crap, and he knew it. So why did he let their critiques bother him so much?

"*It doesn't really matter*," he snapped. He took a deep breath to control himself. "That is to say that the names aren't mentioned in the dialogue so they'll only be known to us. They have no bearing on the final project." He didn't mean that, of course—which was why he was defending his names still—but it was a good defense nonetheless.

"So why give them names at all?" Cohen asked.

"It adds character," Emir answered for Guy. "I must know who I am in order to better portray my role. How could anyone know themselves who doesn't know their own name?"

"Alright, alright," Cohen said, nodding. "You've convinced me. What about everyone else?" He looked around at the crew, and those who were still paying attention shrugged. "Anyone have any ideas as to a better name?" he asked.

"*Emir Islam*," Emir said. "A role I can play better than any other."

"That's just your name," Emily said, slapping him.

"Yeah," Emir said, shrugging. "So? What better idea is there?" He smiled wide and sat up straight in his chair.

"You know that Adam is a robot, right?" Guy said. "You're the bad guy in this. You don't need a likeable name, and I have no idea why you would want to stick your real name on something this shitty in the first place."

"That's *not* his real name," Emily said, scoffing.

"Whatever," Guy said. "Can we just get to the reading?"

"Alright, now," Cohen said. "Calm down. You make a good point, though. Let's table this until after the reading. Now for the lead role..."

"*Oh. Ooh ooh. Me. Pick me,*" Emily begged, raising her hand and jumping up and down in her seat.

"I was thinking we should give Jen the part for this read through," Cohen said, and Emily's face went red as she stopped bouncing. "*Now,*" Cohen added, "this isn't the final casting decision—mind you—but we need to get started as soon as we can. So let's just go ahead with it." Emily huffed and went to the bar to get a drink. "I'll play the narrator," Cohen went on, ignoring her departure. "*Of course.*" He chuckled. "And everyone else we'll just pick up as we go along. Are y'all ready?" He looked around and only received silent nods in response. "Okay, let's do this."

"We fade into an interior scene," Cohen read. Guy closed his eyes and imagined the scene playing out in his head. "We're in the Waltronics Android Factory slip, snap, clicking room. Our protagonist, Alice Walton—" he nodded at Jen "—sits alone at a conveyor belt, slip, snap, clicking. There are empty stools to her left and right, and every few pieces she puts together, she looks at one or the other of the stools, wondering where her coworkers are, wondering why she is the only one left on the line. Enter Adam Torrence. He takes the seat next to Alice and sets to work without a word. Alice tries to ignore him, focusing on her own work, but Adam is slip, snap, clicking at inhuman speeds. She glances aside at him then quickly back at her work, a glint of recognition in her eye. When she looks again, Adam is staring at her with a smile on his face, still slip, snap, clicking at impossible speeds, even with his eyes off his work." Cohen nodded at Emir.

"Hello," Emir said in a deep mechanical voice.

"*You.*" Jen gasped.

"Who else did you expect?"

"But you—" Jen said. "You can't—"

Emir laughed a hefty laugh. He *did* know how to sound like a villain. "But I did," he said.

"*No,*" Jen said. "But my coworkers, my family... Without their jobs, they'll—"

Emir laughed again. "I am a robot," he said, pausing for effect. "I don't care."

"Adam stands and grabs Alice by her shoulders," Cohen narrated.

"No!" Jen begged. "Unhand me!"

"Adam produces a rope from seemingly nowhere and binds Alice's arms at her sides, wrapping the rope around her body over and over."

"Just one more piece of human trash to get rid of," Emir said with a final, hearty laugh.

"No! No!" Jen pled.

"Adam lifts Alice onto the conveyor belt. She screams in pain as the pieces already there dig into her back and the belt carries her into darkness."

When Cohen stopped reading, Guy opened his eyes. The entire crew seemed to be reading ahead to what happens next. "So?" Guy said.

"I mean... *Wow*, Guy," Cohen said, shaking his head. "I thought you said this was crap. And that was just the first scene. But this writing is great. That suspense just built up fast and hooked me right in. I don't see how you can think this is bad."

"Because it is bad," Guy said. "I took that bit from the end and moved it to the beginning because it was the only scene worth anything. Don't judge the script by the first scene."

"But this," Cohen said. "This is good."

"But it isn't," Guy said, frustrated. "Just because it's written well doesn't mean it's good art. You have to see the message already. It's spelled out as plain as day, and—*no*—it's not a red herring. The writer isn't sophisticated enough for that. I know they aren't."

Cohen shook his head. "Right, right," he said. "It's anti-robot, sure, but damn if it's not compelling."

"That almost makes it worse," Guy said. "Now that it's entertaining, more people will see it. I'm still not sure about this, y'all."

Emir laughed his same evil villain laugh from the reading, still in character. "I beg to differ, human," he said. "We have your script already. There's no stopping us now. *Muahahahahaha.*"

Guy sighed. Robot Emir was right.

"Besides," Cohen said. "We need this. Do you have your wish list filled out?"

"And I like the part," Jen said.

Emily frowned, downing her drink.

"See, human," Emir said. "You are outnumbered. Surrender to your robot overlords."

"I for one welcome our robot overlords," Steve said, holding his glass up. Guy hadn't even noticed when he rejoined the crew. "Let's kick one back to androids and those who love them everywhere." Steve winked at Guy as he tapped his glass with everyone else's. "*To androids*." Steve gulped his drink down then added, "Well, I'm gonna go get to work on some costumes for this thing," he said. "You have my wish list, right Cohen?"

Cohen nodded and patted his jacket pocket. "Right here," he said. After Steve left, he added, "Alright, should we get back to it then?"

Guy closed his eyes again to imagine the scene. He ended up falling asleep in a sitting position and dreaming it instead. When he woke up again, Cohen was congratulating everyone on a good read-through and divvying up responsibilities to crew members who already knew they had them.

"Great job, people," he said. "*Very good job*. I think this will be something we can all be proud of."

Guy stood up, finally conscious of how exhausted he was. "I, uh... I need some rest," he said and stumbled out of the bar without waiting for an answer.

He took in a deep breath of fresh air and leaned on the wall outside. He hadn't even finished his first drink and he felt smashed already. He was about to gather himself and head toward the elevator when the bar door opened and out came Laura.

"Guy, wait," she called, jogging out to him.

He shrugged and leaned on the wall again.

"I—uh—I wanted to talk to you," she said, rubbing her arm.

"*Shoot*," he said, pointing at her with both hands. He didn't remember ever talking to Laura alone before, but he was in no condition to argue.

"Well, it's about the protectors," she said. "About your ankle brace."

Guy fought the reflex to scratch it at the reminder. "Go

ahead," he said.

"Well, I—" She looked down and seemed to blush. "*Just look*." She held out her foot and lifted her pant leg to reveal an ankle monitor of her own.

"I—what?" Guy was dumbfounded.

"Yeah, well, that's how I know you're in for more than you expect," she said. "They won't let you go that easily, not with what you were involved in."

"But I wasn't," he said, regaining momentary control of himself despite being so tired.

"That doesn't matter to them," Laura said. "That's what I'm trying to tell you. They're coming for you sooner than you think."

"But they just let me go," Guy said. "What would be the point?"

"To see where you went while you were free," she said. "They're watching you. That's why they gave you that ankle bracelet, Guy."

"Yeah, well, I don't care," Guy said, shaking his head. "I need some sleep."

"If I were you, I would go back inside and get something to eat first," she said. "You have a chance of being taken every time you get in an elevator, now, and I'm sure you haven't eaten in some time from the looks of you."

Guy shook his head and rubbed his face. "How do you know all this?" he asked.

"Because I've been through it myself," she said. "Because I have my own ankle monitor. Because I have to know it to stay alive, and now, you do, too."

Guy sighed. "*Whatever*," he said. "I don't care. I need some rest, not food."

"You will if they take you again."

"They're not going to take me, alright. Now I appreciate your advice, but I have to go. See you tomorrow."

"I hope so," she said as he made his way to the elevator.

Guy sighed to himself and the elevator fall into motion. He wondered what it was that got Laura an ankle monitor and why she had kept it secret for so long. Maybe she *was* guilty. He was imagining the possibilities when the elevator doors slid open to three protectors pointing guns at him. His hands shot up into the air by reflex.

"Citizen, you're under arrest," one of the protectors said before throwing a black bag over his head and punching him in the stomach.

⅋ ⅋ ⅋

XLII. Olsen

Her feet carried her, and for once, they didn't lead her astray. When she let her subconscious do the work, she never got lost. Not even with this strange new world that had crashed into hers, marring and mangling everything in existence.

She was *not* a murderer, she kept reassuring herself. She was not a murderer. She was not a murderer. She was not a murderer. The mantra took time with her steps, slowing as she slowed to a jog, exhausted from too much.

Too much what, though? Violence. Lies. Panic. *All of it.* She was exhausted from too much, period. She was so exhausted that she didn't even realize where her feet had taken her until she was up the stairs and opening the door.

"Olsen, dear?" her mom asked, sitting on the couch, staring at the TV, not even turning to look or expending the tiny effort required to scan her peripheral vision. "Is that you?"

"Yes, mother." Olsen sighed. "I'm standing right here, aren't I?" She plopped on the couch next to her mom who groaned and nudged her over.

"You get the entire couch every night," her mom complained, eyes still on the show. "At least give me some room during the day. It is *my* couch after all."

Olsen rolled her eyes. "My day was pretty terrible actually, thanks for asking," she said sarcastically.

That was enough to get her mom's attention. "You didn't get fired again, did you?" she asked, shaking her head. "You know, sometimes it seems like you want to fail, dear. Do you do it so you can go on sleeping on my couch all day? You know I can't afford that, child. Do you want your mother to have to live with that burden until the day she dies?"

Olsen scoffed. "*First*," she said, "I didn't get fired. And second, of course I don't want to fail. Who would? And as soon as I can afford it I'll get out of here because this stupid couch sucks to sleep on!"

Her mom shook her head. "Now I've heard that before," she said. "Haven't I? And yet here you still are after all this time. You know Aaron's boy, Aldo, never has a problem getting work. I don't know why it's so hard for you."

Olsen scoffed. "I'm not Aldo," she said. "And I have a job, a terrible, shitty job that makes me miserable, which I'm pretty sure is ruining my life."

"Welcome to the real world, honey." Her mom chuckled. "It's called work because you hate to do it. You're not unique in that respect."

"What do you know?" Olsen said. "You have no idea what my job entails, Mom." She thought about what she had just done, about killing that actor, and swallowed the vomit that was forcing its way out of her throat. "I think I can lay claim to a unique version of Hell more than you might expect."

"*Pffft.*" Her mom laughed. "Everyone does, child. And they all can in their own way, but who's to say whose Hell is worse than whose?"

Olsen was getting angry, or frustrated, or something. She just wanted to talk to someone who would console and comfort her, and her feet had taken her home in search of that. Maybe this was why she didn't let her feet do the thinking after all. "Mom," she said. "Do you even have any idea what's going on in the world around you? In the *worlds*—plural—around you?"

"Don't try to tell me about the world, child," her mom said, shaking her head. "Now, I've been in it for a lot longer than you have, and those years of experience have taught me more than you could ever know."

"Then you must have heard about what happened in the streets today," Olsen said. "You weren't worried that I might have been injured?"

Her mom shook her head and squinted. "What are you talking about now?"

"We were handing out food and clothes when the protectors came and gassed us then started shooting people," Olsen said. "Hundreds of people died, Mom, and I was right there when it happened."

Her mom chuckled and half-grinned like she didn't believe it. "You're kidding, right," she said. "This is a joke or something."

"*No, Mom*," Olsen complained. "That's why my day was so horrible. That's my unique Hell."

"No." Her mom shook her head some more and chuckled. "I would have heard something about that."

"I'm surprised you haven't," Olsen said.

"*Olsen*," her mom said. "If that had actually happened, there would be riots in the streets. The protectors are the only thing keeping order around here, and if faith in them is lost, society would devolve into chaos. You don't know what that's like. The desperation erupting into violence. I've been through it, and that's nothing to joke about."

"Well I'm not joking," Olsen said. "And you're going to have to live through it again because that's what's going on right now. I've been through it, too, you know. Only for a day or so now, but I can see it's only getting worse, and I never imagined it could be as bad as it is already in the first place." She had to fight to keep her voice from cracking and hold back her tears.

"*Olsen*." Her mom grabbed Olsen's hand and patted her back. Olsen couldn't stop herself from embracing her and sobbing on her shoulders for what could have been half an hour before she controlled herself. Her mom kept patting her back and brushing her fingers through Olsen's hair the whole time she cried.

"Olsen, dear," she said after Olsen had gathered herself, sniffling and puffy-faced. "Whatever happened, if you got fired, or you need me to cover a loan, or—whatever—just tell me. But *this*, this is too much, dear. This is too far, even for you. So just go ahead and tell me the truth, and Momma will make it all better."

Olsen stood up fast, appalled. She wanted to cry again, but this time in anger. She thought she had gotten through to her mom. She thought she had found someone she could take comfort in, confide in. Then her mom had to go and ruin it by accusing her of lying. Why would she lie about something like this?

"Why would I lie about something like this?" Olsen demanded.

"I don't know, dear," her mom said. "That's why I need you to tell me the truth."

"I wouldn't. That's what I'm telling you."

"Then why haven't I heard about it? That would be big news."

"I don't know," Olsen said. "Maybe because you sit on your ass in front of this TV all day. If they don't talk about it on here, you have no way of learning about it. Do you?"

Her mom was mad now. She gave Olsen the death stare Olsen knew too well from her childhood. She probably still thought of Olsen as that same little girl she used to be able to stare into submission, but that wasn't Olsen anymore. How her mom still didn't know that, she would never understand. No, Olsen was changed now. Her experiences had made her into a whole new person, the type of person who wouldn't take this kind of verbal abuse without doing something about it.

"Get. Out. Of *my*. House," her mom said, fuming.

"*Gladly*," Olsen said, curtsying and opening the door. "I don't want to be here anyway." She slammed the door behind her and ran down the stairs outside.

Well that was a fucking waste. And how could her mom not have heard about what had happened out there? That woman really was lost in her own world. That was just another world to add to the list of new ones Olsen had to get used to. Thinking of worlds, she thought of Sonya, and when she looked up, she was standing at Sonya's door. Maybe those feet of hers had actually made a good decision this time.

Olsen rang the bell and waited for a reply. There was no answer so she rang it again, knowing it was futile if the first ring wasn't answered. She sighed and turned around, and there was Sonya, jogging up the street toward her.

"Olsen, you're alive!" Sonya said, grabbing her in a hug.

Olsen squeezed her tight and took a whiff of Sonya's hair. Finally, someone to find comfort in.

"I can't believe what happened," Sonya said, holding Olsen at arm's length so she could better look at her. "Wasn't that right by where you work?"

"You heard about it?"

"Of course I did." Sonya laughed. "It was disgusting. So many people died. How could I not?"

Olsen chuckled, thinking about her mom. "You'd be surprised," she said.

"Well, not in my line of work at least. I hear every bit of gossip, and there was no way something like that was getting past me. I tried to reach you as soon as I heard, but your mom said she didn't know where you were."

Olsen shook her head, more about where she was and what she was doing when Sonya had tried to find her than the reminder that even her mom didn't believe what had happened. "I was still in the thick of it," Olsen said, shaking her head with a sigh.

"Tell me all about it," Sonya said, grabbing Olsen's hand and leading her to sit in the field across the street. "It must have been terrible. I can't imagine."

Olsen nodded then shook her head. "Yeah—I mean—No. I don't know," she said. "We were out there, you know—"

"The Human Family?" Sonya cut her off.

Olsen couldn't help but notice the tinge of disgust in Sonya's voice. "*Yeah*," she said. "My employers and me. We had a printer and we were—"

"A printer?" Sonya's eyes grew wide. "*A 3D printer?* Where'd y'all get that?"

Olsen shrugged. "I don't know," she said. "They had like five of them. I don't know where they got them, and I'm not going to ask."

"*Yeah, that's not suspicious at all,*" Sonya said, rolling her eyes. "But go on."

Olsen tried to hold it in, but she couldn't help scoffing. Go on? How was she supposed to go on when Sonya was being so sarcastic and dismissive? "Well, anyway," Olsen said, trying to regain her train of thought. "We took it out to the street corner and offered anyone who passed by whatever they wanted."

Sonya nodded. "That's nice," she said.

"Yeah, well, as you can imagine, people started crowding around fast, and before we knew it, there were thousands and thousands of them, and you couldn't see the end of the crowd."

"It's easy to attract people when you give them what they want," Sonya said, unimpressed.

Olsen felt a slight sense of Déjà vu. She shook it out of her head and said, "Well, we attracted the predators, too. I mean protectors—"

"What's the difference?" Sonya scoffed.

"—and they killed people," Olsen went on. "A lot of people. And gassed the rest. And some guy pointed a gun at me—not even a protector—and I was pretty sure I was going to die before Rosa and Anna saved me."

Sonya sneered at the mention of their names while at the same time bringing Olsen in for a hug. "No, no, dear," she said. "It's okay. I'm here for you now."

Olsen let her tears go again, but they didn't last as long. She pushed away from Sonya's embrace, sniffling and wiping her nose, to say, "You believe me, don't you?"

"Of course I do." Sonya laughed. "How couldn't I? I've heard the same story from so many sources already. Why wouldn't I believe it when my best friend was the one saying it happened?"

Olsen blushed and picked at the grass. "I didn't believe you when you told me about the other worlds," she said. "Not at first, at least."

Sonya smiled. "How could you have? At that point I could barely believe in them myself."

Olsen looked at her. "But I know it's true now," she said. "And there are more than two worlds."

Sonya looked more interested than ever. "*Tell me*," she said, leaning in closer.

"There are like seven of them," Olsen said. "Or—six now. You were right about the merging of two of them."

"Who told you this?" Sonya asked.

"Anna and Rosa," Olsen said, and Sonya cringed. "And I went to one of the other worlds myself," Olsen added.

"No way!" Sonya said, slapping Olsen's arm. "How? Tell me."

Olsen looked away again. She wanted to tell her about the other worlds, but she wasn't ready to tell the whole story yet. "I saw a movie being filmed," she said. "Or a TV show, I'm not sure, but I saw that guy who's always the star. What do you call him?"

"*Big head*," Sonya said, smiling. "You met him? What was he like? Was his head as big in person? How did you get there?"

Olsen laughed. "I don't know," she said. "But it was another world, I'm sure of it. The people looked as different from us as the otherworlders we've already met. More so even."

Sonya shook her head. "It's good to know you finally believe me," she said. "But I still don't understand how you got there. C'mon. Tell me."

"I—well…"

"It can't be that bad," Sonya said.

"I don't know," Olsen said. "You might think it is."

"You can let me decide."

"Anna and Rosa sent me," Olsen said. "They have this thing in their basement, a big ring that opens doors that can teleport you places."

"Like the elevators?" Sonya asked.

Olsen nodded. She thought it would be harder to explain. "Yeah," she said. "Right. But instead of elevators taking you down to where you want to go, you step through these ring things like a door."

"And that's how you got to this other world?" Sonya asked.

"Yeah," Olsen said. "I stepped into this costume closet or something, right out of their basement, then I went through a long, dark hall to a huge room where they had brought the inside outside. There were spotlights, and cameras, and special effects, and whatever they were filming looked like nothing that had ever played on any TV I've ever seen."

Sonya nodded. "That's probably because it hasn't," she said.

"It was crazy," Olsen said. "I can't believe I was there."

"Why *were* you there?" Sonya asked.

A knot grew in Olsen's stomach. She tried to swallow it down. Now was the time of reckoning. Could she admit what she had done? "Well…" she said.

"You can tell me, Olsen." Sonya took Olsen's hand in one of hers and patted it with the other. "I know you meant well."

Olsen shook her head, trying not to cry. "We were feeding people in that street," she said, "and clothing them. We were giving them tools, even, a way to produce for themselves. We were doing good. I'm certain of that."

"I know," Sonya said, pulling Olsen closer. "I know you were."

"Then why'd the protectors do what they did?" Olsen asked, ripping her hand away from Sonya's.

"Because they're not here to protect us."

Olsen gave her a look. It wasn't like Sonya to speak out against the order of things—make wild predictions about the order of things, sure, but speak against it, never.

"What did you do when you were over there?" Sonya asked. "I know they didn't just send you to meet a celebrity."

"No." Olsen shook her head. "But who are you to know that?"

Sonya smiled. "I've been living just the same as you have," she said. "I've experienced my fair share of change and learned from it since Christmas. It just so happens that my experience is from the opposite perspective as yours."

"Opposite perspective?" Olsen gave her a look. "What are you talking about?"

"Pro-android rights," Sonya said. "The opposite of your Human Family. We've started our own coalition."

Olsen shook her head. "Wait, what?" she said. "You didn't tell me—"

"*I did*," Sonya said. "I warned you from the beginning that I didn't trust those people. I told you to get a different job."

"But you didn't tell me you were starting a...a *coalition*—or whatever," Olsen said.

Sonya scoffed. "Because you've been too busy with your *family*," she said. "You've been too busy doing something you can't even tell me about."

"I—" Olsen sighed. "I thought I was helping people," she said. "Just like with the printers on the streets."

"But you weren't?" Sonya asked.

Olsen shook her head. "I don't know how they could make me do that," she said. "I didn't know that's what I was doing, and I don't know what I'm supposed to do now that I did."

"I still don't know what you did," Sonya said with a shrug. "And I can't help you until I do."

"I put some cheese on a table," Olsen said. "*That's it*. The rest wasn't me."

Sonya's jaw dropped. She shook her head. "No," she said. "You didn't. Olsen, *poison?*"

"I didn't!" Olsen said defiantly.

"You can't work for them anymore," Sonya said. "Not after that."

"What else am I supposed to do?" Olsen complained. "My mom said she'll kick me out, even with my job."

"I don't blame her," Sonya said. "I wouldn't want someone

who did that for them living with me, either."

"I didn't know what they were doing!" Olsen complained, standing from the grass.

"Yeah, well I told you," Sonya said, standing, too. "But you didn't listen to me."

"You didn't tell me this," Olsen said. "You told me they were anti-robot. There's a difference."

"I told you they were immoral," Sonya said. "I may have gotten the degree of their depravity wrong, but I warned you."

Olsen groaned. "You're no better than my mom," she said. "You're both lost in your own worlds. Her in her TV, and you with your robots."

"They're androids!" Sonya stomped her foot. "It's good to know you're picking up the racist rhetoric from your bosses."

"I'm not a racist!" Olsen said.

"*Well you could have fooled me*," Sonya said. "Why else would you have assassinated a pro-android celebrity?"

"I didn't know he was!" Olsen protested. "And I didn't kill him!"

"Sure, Olsen." Sonya shook her head. "Tell yourself what you want to, but I tried to warn you." She started to stomp away.

"What, that's it?" Olsen called after her.

"It is until you're willing to admit what you did," Sonya said, crossing the street to go into her apartment.

Olsen flopped back on the grass. She let out a big huff of air. First her mom and now Sonya, the only person she thought she could count on to trust and comfort her. She was *not* a killer!

Was she a killer? Anna and Rosa had said that she wasn't, that it was Rosa who did the killing even though Olsen was the one to cut the cheese. What if Olsen had eaten a slice? She could have died. They could have killed her. Her heart beat faster at the thought of it even though the danger was long gone.

How could they do this to her? How could they do that to the actor she—no, *they* had killed? How could she stop thinking about it?

She stood up and brushed herself off. Her mother was no help. Sonya was no help. Rosa and Anna were the problem. There was no one left for her to turn to. There was nowhere left to go but home. She took her time walking to the elevator, not wanting to see her mom again so soon. When she stepped inside, she said, "Home." not giving the street or address in the hopes that the elevator would mistake her voice for someone else's and get her lost somewhere strange where no one knew what she had or hadn't done.

When the doors slid open again, her eyes grew wide. She was in a stranger place than she could ever have imagined. Not even outside anymore, she was in a long hall, and an old woman in a white coat stood smiling at her.

"*Home. Back home*," Olsen begged, looking at the roof of the elevator and urging it to close its doors.

The woman in the white coat chuckled. "Calm down, dear," she said. "You have nothing to be afraid of here."

"Where am I?" Olsen asked. "Who are you?"

"All will be explained, dear," the old woman said. "Come. Sit with me." She crossed the hall and opened the door at the end of it to show Olsen through.

Olsen hesitated. "Doors close," she said. "Take me home." The elevator didn't respond, and the woman just held the door at the other end of the hall, smiling. Olsen had no choice but to follow her through it.

The room was a big office with a view of a wilderness scene out of a wall-sized window. The woman in white sat in one of the puffy chairs by the window and indicated for Olsen to do the same in the seat across from her.

"So where am I?" Olsen asked as she sat down.

"In my office," the woman said. "Or rather, in *an* office in my building. I don't use this one much."

"And you are?"

"The Scientist."

"That's a name?" Olsen raised an eyebrow.

The woman smiled. "It's what people call me," she said. "What is a name? A sewer by any other name would smell as sweet."

Olsen shrugged. "Sounds more like a job to me," she said.

"Lots of people have jobs for names," the woman said. "Especially extinct jobs. They're usually surnames like McKannic, Server, or *Sous*, but the Scientist just so happens to be a first name. What can I say?"

Olsen looked at the Scientist suspiciously. Did she know that

Olsen's last name was Sous, or was that a coincidence? "What do you want with me?" she asked.

The Scientist chuckled. "Oh, no, dear," she said. "The question isn't what I want with you. The question is what do you want from me?"

Olsen eyed her again. This was starting to smell like the same shit Rosa used to attract her flies. Olsen didn't respond, instead waiting for the woman to go on.

"You see," the Scientist said. "I'm in a position of privilege here. And from that position, I can see many things." She looked through the window at the green wilderness for a moment. "And not just the beautiful things we have in front of us here. No, sadly, there's much more ugliness to see in these worlds than there is beauty, and I have seen it all."

"What do you know about the worlds?" Olsen asked, forgetting her suspicions for a moment.

"Oh, dear, *everything*." The Scientist grinned. "Every little thing. You know, I was the architect who oversaw the creation of the worlds. I was their mother and midwife. I have overseen their maturation, raising and rearing them where I can here and there, but these worlds are as independent and willful as teenagers these days, and I have little control anymore. But I still have my eyes turned firmly on them, and I still know every little detail of their existence. Any questions you have I'd be more than happy to answer." She smiled.

Olsen didn't know what to think. Those were some grandiose claims, and this woman would have to be older than humans could be in order to have done what she claimed to have done. "How am I supposed to believe you?"

The Scientist didn't stop smiling, even while she spoke. "Well, that's for you to decide, dear," she said. "What evidence would it take to convince you?"

Olsen had to take a moment to think about it. "Show me," she said.

"Show you what, dear?"

"You said you keep your eyes on them. Show me how you watch the other worlds."

The Scientist smiled and nodded. "Very well," she said. "Come with me."

They went out into the hall again, and when the Scientist reopened the door they had just passed through, it revealed another office entirely, one with a different view. Olsen gasped and crossed past the desk to look out the wallwindow at the lines and lines of slip, snap, clickers. "I know her," she said. "Her brother works with me. *Or did...* But I know her. What is this?" she asked, but the Scientist had sat at the desk and began typing and clicking on the computer.

"That's one way I keep an eye on the worlds," she said, not taking her eyes off the screen. "Though it's really more of a reminder. This computer here is where I do most of the real monitoring. Right...there." She leaned back in her chair and smiled, watching the screen.

"A reminder?" Olsen asked, walking around behind the Scientist to see what she was doing. "A reminder of what?"

"A reminder of what we're fighting against. A reminder of who I do this for. A reminder of why I wake up every morning. You name it."

Olsen groaned. She was *not* ready for another "Family", and she was starting to regret encouraging this woman on by asking her to prove herself. What she really wanted was to go home. Then she looked at the screen.

There were seven different frames, each cycling through shots of streets and bars and restaurants and bedrooms. She recognized the look of some, but others seemed so lavish and outlandish to her that she didn't know what they were or where they could be. "What is this?" she asked.

"These are the worlds," the Scientist said. "You wanted to see them so here they are. These two—" She pointed at the screen. "Are Five and Six. Technically one world now. *Your world.* You've noticed the differences since the merger by now, I'm sure."

Olsen nodded. Dumbstruck.

"And here is Four," the Scientist said. "That's technically where we are now, though we're really in a world of our own if you want to get picky. Then Three, where the actors and musicians and artists live. You've been there, I think."

Olsen swallowed her nerves.

"Then Two, with the managers, and the lawyers, and the other rabble. And One, where all the protectors live. Which brings us to the best for last—or worst depending on which end of the hierarchy you happen to be on—we have Inland, our owners, the magnets of wealth and rulers of all our fates. These are the worlds, dear. Do you believe I know about them now?"

Olsen wiped her face. She shook her head and shrugged. She tried to say, "I don't know." but the words wouldn't come out.

"Now, dear," the Scientist said. "You've seen our capabilities—some of them at least. I can give you anything your heart desires, and I ask of you nothing in return. So what do you say? What is it that Olsen Sous wants?"

Olsen pictured all the things she could ask for that would make her life better: A well-paying job, an apartment of her own, both probably futile no matter what this Scientist knew about the worlds. A printer, maybe more plausible, but what would she do with it? Haul it up to her mom's apartment and attract a swarm of protectors to attack them there? Then she thought about Rosa and Anna and their "Family", about everything she had just been through and wanted to avoid experiencing ever again at all costs. And she shook her head. She said, "No. I don't want anything from you. I don't want anything I can't get by myself." And she ran out into the hall and into the elevator then yelled at it to close the doors and take her home.

The Scientist came out into the hall slowly, a sad—but not angry—look on her face. "Are you sure this is what you want?" she asked when she had finally made it across the short hall.

Olsen nodded, not wanting to open her mouth and say something stupid.

"Well, if that's what you want, I can't argue." The Scientist shook her head. "I'll be watching you, and I'll be waiting for you to change your mind, child. Just ask an elevator for me and you'll be here. Good bye, then."

The elevator doors slid closed and the floor dropped out from underneath Olsen, leaving her to careen toward whatever may come.

♋   End of Book Two   ♋

Thanks for reading. If you enjoyed that please join us at

www.BryanPerkinsAuthor.com

to keep up to date on future releases in the Infinite Limits series.
And if you're so inclined, don't forget to leave a review on Amazon,
Goodreads, or any other site you might frequent.
Thanks again, until next time.

-Bryan "with a Y" Perkins

Acknowledgements

Again I'd like to start by thanking Sophie Kunen. Again, Sophie, this one's for you, as they all are. I wouldn't be the person I am today if I had never met you, and I mean that only about my best qualities. They are all thanks to you. So thank you.

Next, I have to say another repeat thank you, this one to David Garifo. You're still the only person—other than those who live with me or work at the Rouse's down the street—who I interact with on a regular basis. Thank you for doing all the work necessary to maintain our friendship, you know I'm incapable of it.

Third, thank you to James Cohn, my human roommate. Specifically, thanks for helping Mr. Kitty and me find a new apartment so we could stay in New Orleans for at least another year. Hopefully I'll actually have a story published by someone other than my own press before this lease is up.

Then, of course, a great big thank you, packed full of love, goes out to my family: Mom, Dad, Tor Tor, and Rob. Thanks for existing and helping me exist. Thanks for making me a human person.

Last, but far from least, thank you, dear readers (especially the avid and encouraging ones like Chris Chemel). I'm glad you're here for volume two of Infinite Limits, and I hope you continue to join us as the story progresses. There's no point in writing anything without y'all here to read it, after all. So thank you.

www.ingramcontent.com/pod-product-compliance
Lightning Source LLC
Chambersburg PA
CBHW020301200626
46814CB00006BA/2029